Please return/renew this item by the last date shown.
Item may also be renewed by the internet*

https://library.eastriding.gov.uk

* Please note a PIN will be required to access this service
- this can be obtained from your library.

Every MOVE

ELLIE MARNEY

ALLEN&UNWIN
SYDNEY·MELBOURNE·AUCKLAND·LONDON

First published by Allen & Unwin in 2015

Allen & Unwin
83 Alexander Street
Crows Nest NSW 2065
Australia
Phone: (61 2) 8425 0100
Email: info@allenandunwin.com
Web: www.allenandunwin.com

Allen & Unwin – UK
c/o Murdoch Books, Erico House, 93–99 Upper Richmond Road,
London SW15 2TG, UK
Phone: (44 20) 8785 5995
Email: info@murdochbooks.co.uk
Web: www.allenandunwin.com
Murdoch Books is a wholly owned division of Allen & Unwin Pty Ltd

A Cataloguing-in-Publication entry is available from the
National Library of Australia
www.trove.nla.gov.au
A catalogue record for this book is available from the British Library

ISBN (AUS) 978 1 74331 853 9
ISBN (UK) 978 1 74336 719 3

Cover and text design by Lisa White
Cover photos by Getty Images/iStock: couple by Rubberball/Jason Todd; road by Swilmor
Set in 11pt Minion by Midland Typesetters, Australia
Printed and bound in Australia by Griffin Press

10 9 8 7 6 5 4 3 2

FOR MY MUM AND DAD

*Excellence at chess is one mark
of a scheming mind*

– SIR ARTHUR CONAN DOYLE

PROLOGUE

When you're trying to cut the lambs from the flock, you send in the dogs.

Tilly creeps in from the side, her body flattened, tail low. She sneaks among the throng of grazing sheep, looking for likely candidates. Once she's found them, she curls around, nipping, forcing them back.

Then Hoob comes in, barking like crazy, scattering the ewes, siphoning off their young. The ewes jump, nervy and anxious, knowing something's going on. By the time they figure it out, it's too late.

The lambs in the pen honk and bleat, but Tilly's got them cornered. She snarls and snaps at the desperate ones. Dad and Mike are inside the pen, gathering strays.

The smell of lanolin and dust is solid on my tongue. I stand over by the fence, stripped of one glove and worrying at a nail, worrying for the lambs. They're all sad-eyed, and their mothers are baaing for them.

I keep reminding myself why we're doing this. These lambs are old enough now to be separated. They're a drain on the ewes. This will be good for them – toughen them up.

Then I remember what we're toughening them up for. Because these lambs only have a few more months to put on weight before they're off to market.

These lambs are for the slaughter.

That's what it's like. You're cut off, cornered, backed to the wall. If you object, you get bitten, beaten, slapped back into line. Then while you're shivering, the knife comes out. Your blood's slicking the dust before you know it.

God, don't let it be like that for us. Don't make me watch Mycroft's eyes roll back as his red blood spills away. Don't let me feel the cold metal on my skin, or the shot piercing me, or the bolt from the blue. Don't force me to anticipate the wailing of my parents in that bare sterile room in the morgue.

Don't let me believe that every move I've made has come to this.

CHAPTER ONE

It's been nine months since I was in Five Mile. Nine months of longing.

For the first half of that, I wanted to be anywhere but the city. There were times I wanted out of Melbourne so bad I'd go up to Fawkner cemetery – the only isolated place nearby – and yell at the top of my lungs. Bawl into my fists. I wished for wings to carry me home. I wanted sky and open space and breathable air and pink dirt. The only place I had those things was in my memory, and it was my bread and water – never enough to fill me up.

Now I look out the window and see the land coming back to me – the vast stretches of paddock, the borders of scrub and saltbush, and the infrequent stands of gums. The way the sky seems to have opened up into one long horizon, galahs zooming around in married pairs, streaks of cloud streaming away towards the north.

For the first time in five weeks, something like happiness starts bubbling up in my chest.

'How's your face?' Mike asks.

'Fine.' I can't take my eyes off the view through the windscreen. When Mike touches the side of my cheek, I startle.

'It's not fine.' He presses his lips. 'You're gonna have a bruise.'

I push his hand away. 'It doesn't matter. We're so close now. Don't spoil it by talking about that.'

My brother sighs, turns Alicia's car off the highway from Five Mile and gives me a warning look. 'It'll be different.'

'I know.'

'No, Rache. You don't get it. *You'll* be different.'

I chew my thumbnail. 'What if I don't recognise it?'

Inside the warm car, my other fear, the more relevant one, fills up the pause: what if it doesn't recognise *me*?

But it's too late for fears. This is the approach. I know that tree, that fence. I peer out the window as Mike navigates around potholes and over the rail line.

'Jesus, the Monaghans have let their stock race go to shit.' I can't believe I'm almost home. I could walk from here. I could reach out and touch it with my hands.

'Yeah, dunno if they're still on the property,' Mike says quietly. 'We weren't the only ones the banks turfed.'

A few kays later I see the 'For Sale' sign, and then the driveway, the pitted track in the dust that snakes up to our place. My heart stutters in my chest.

'He's left the gate open,' Mike says approvingly.

I glance at him. 'Who's left the gate open?'

Mike grins. 'Nah, I want it to be a surprise.'

And then—

I mean, I know it's not Xanadu or Versailles or anything, but when the house comes into view, I catch my breath. This is the place I keep returning to – in my thoughts, in my dreams, sometimes even in my nightmares. This is it. And my god, it's hardly changed. I can see the header tank, and the verandah, and—

'Oh god,' I whisper.

'Yeah.' I hear the smile in Mike's voice.

'Wait . . . Is that smoke?' I scrabble at my seatbelt clip.

'Rachel—'

'It is. There's smoke. Mike, *stop*!'

I don't wait, because smoke means fire, and if there's a fire at our old house it can only mean disaster.

I thrust myself out of the car as Mike pulls into the front yard, and then I'm going as fast as I can with my knee brace on, pelting up the steps of the verandah, grabbing for the handle of the front door – the front door! Mike's yelling something in the background, but I don't really hear him.

I push into the house, into the hallway and then around to the right, practically falling into what was once our living room.

And there, stuffing a piece of knotted firewood into our old Coonara, is someone with hair so sun-bleached it's almost white on the ends, and he's wearing jeans and boots, and this enormous Driza-Bone . . .

The guy turns around and sees me, huge-eyed and panting. His gaze runs over me as he takes me in with a slowly widening grin.

'Rachel Watts. As I live and breathe.'

There's a clatter as Mike barrels in behind me, but I can only stare at what's in front, my heart sinking into my boots. I can't *believe* it. Of all the dickhead tearaways in the whole bloody district—

'Der-brain!' Mike laughs, shoulders past me with his hand stuck out. 'Jesus, mate, it's good to see you.'

'Likewise, Mikey, likewise.'

Harris Derwent – sun-bleached, Driza-Bone-wearing, dickhead tearaway – takes Mike's proffered hand and smiles from ear to ear as he pulls Mike into something that could be a hug but looks more like two bulls bumping chests. This is immediately followed by a short round of scuffling, chucking each other on the chin, slapping each other upside the head. I fight back tears. Because here's me and Mike on our special road trip, and here's the house that fills my memory, and here, right in front of me, is—

'Hey, Rache, whaddya reckon?' Mike says, grinning at me over his shoulder.

I stare at him. 'Please don't tell me this is the surprise you were talking about.'

Mike's face gets a goofy look. 'God, I've missed this bloke!'

He makes a bear-like roar and grabs Harris around the waist, hoists him off his feet. Harris starts swearing a blue streak, and I leave them like that, to walk out onto the verandah and look out over the place I used to call home.

———

CR-AACK!

'You got enough wood there?' Harris asks.

I pull the axe handle back. 'Not yet.'

'Cos you've already chopped enough for a family of four.'

'Maybe this is for next time.'

After the fight with Mum, last night's rest was like chicken sleep – dozing then jerking awake at intervals. Now, the long drive has left me feeling heavy in the head, and Harris's wriggling energy makes me want to snap at him.

I've spent a half-hour splitting old chunks of gum, grey left-overs from another age. Now I move on to the knotted bits. I need a challenge.

Harris grins. He's standing in front of me, a safe distance from the block, leaning against the corrugated iron tank that Dad up-ended years ago to serve as a wood store.

'Gonna be a next time, is there? You planning on moving back?'

'Anything's possible.' I swing. *CR-AACK!*

Harris curls his lip. 'Yeah, right. I can just see it. You and Mike buying the farm back from the bank, keeping the old place going . . .' He takes his hands out of his jeans pockets and picks grime out of a thumbnail. 'Sounds like bullshit to me.'

I shrug. 'Hasn't got anything to do with you.'

Wiping my hairline with the side of my glove, I wish Harris away. My splinted fingers are aching and my knee throbs. I've been off crutches for a week, but the knee brace has made it impossible to do anything strenuous, so no exercise, no roller derby, nothing. After five weeks in my room, I've coagulated. But it's more than that – I'm *soft* from so much time in the city. And I think I've overdone it with the woodchopping. If Harris wasn't standing there, I'd have taken a breather about five chunks of wood ago.

'Anyway,' Harris goes on, 'I like the new look. Longer hair. More upmarket clothes. Knee brace. You look like a townie.'

'No, I don't.'

'Yeah, you do.' Harris pauses for effect. 'You look like a Melbournite.'

I lift my head. 'You know I have an axe in my hands, right?'

'Got some panda-bear thing going on around your eyes. And the bruise – yeah, that's classy.'

I swing. *CR-AACK!!* He's persistent, I'll give him that.

'You're thin as a rail,' Harris continues blithely. 'Thought your mum was a good cook?'

'She is a good cook.' *It makes up for all the other crap she dishes out.* I don't say that. I don't want to talk about Mum.

My sore knee is really thundering now. If my physio saw me chopping wood, pulling the axe, he'd have a heart attack. I grimace, hiss air through my teeth.

Harris is smiling all over his face. 'Ahh, Rachel Watts . . . I've missed this, you know. Giving you heaps.'

I roll my eyes. 'Wow, Harris. The girls must go wild, that silver tongue of yours.'

'See what I'm talking about?'

Mike comes walking back from the windmill side of the house. 'Once you've finished hanging shit on each other, do you think you could come and help me fix the pump? Otherwise we'll be digging a hole out the back for a toilet.'

With the axe in my hand, I look out over the horizon. It's golden as a sponge cake on top, melding into blue, the cheap azure blacking up the trees for the approaching evening. Sundown has its own scent: the metallic smell of cold, the raw resin of mallee scrub, the dark mulchy waft of ancient sheep shit. I'm sweating now, but the air is freezing in my nostrils. I stand here, the tug on my heart like the ache of a bad filling, wondering where I fit into this picture. Maybe I don't anymore. Maybe as soon as I left for the city, I was already being forgotten.

———

The boys play a game of kick-to-kick under the big manna gum close to the driveway as the light fades. I take a walk. It's slow-going, my knee aching after the woodchopping marathon. Rosellas flash past like a flying tropical-fruit medley. The tang of scrub and the crunch of leaf litter under my boots is soothing. I try to block it all out of my mind: Mycroft, and Wild, and the nightmares, and Mum.

I walk for as long as my knee can handle, checking out old landmarks, the places the salt has taken over, stretching my arms to the sky as the cool dark descends. This is what I came for: a chance to reconnect with the place that made me, the place I've been missing. This trip might bring me right, away from the fallout, away from Mum—

'You were the one who threw yourself in, Rachel!'

Suddenly, it's Friday night and I'm back in the kitchen of our house in Melbourne, and Mum's voice is ringing like steel.

'You didn't have to go, but you—'

'I can bloody go where I want!' My mug slams onto the yellow laminex of the kitchen table, tea sloshing over the chipped rim. My voice is shaking. 'You're just pissed off that I didn't stay at home like a good little girl, that I—'

'You are a little girl!' Mum's cheeks flame pink. 'You take off with no thought in your head but your bloody boyfriend, then you come home in a mess and expect your father and me to—'

'So I shouldn't expect you to support me, is that it? Whenever I make a choice, or fuck up, you'll give me the cold shoulder and be a complete bitch—'

There's a cracking sound, and my head flings sideways. When I bring my face back around, it's to see Mum's frozen expression of shock at what I've said, at what she's done. It takes another second or two before the pain registers, hot and tingling. The pain is in my cheek, but somehow it's in my chest as well – glassy-sharp and shamefully bitter.

Back in the now, I grab for the fence post, close my eyes. I've had a few peaceful hours of not thinking about this, but the memory is still fresh. I run my thumb over my cheek: the place where Mum slapped me is tender, the cold air of Five Mile has done nothing to soothe it. But it's just skin. In a few days, it'll heal.

Wiping my eyes on my sleeve, I push hard to walk the remaining distance back to the house. Mike's with me – I try to keep that thought on repeat. We didn't talk much in the car on the way up, but maybe tonight he can help me work this mess out.

Instead, later that evening, there's Mike and Harris Der-brain Derwent roasting sausages for dinner over an outdoor fire. They sit next to each other, trading barbs and bullshit.

'Hey, Rachel.' Harris gives me a smirk. 'Mike said you've got some fella on a slow boil. Pommy bloke, works with the cops. Regular little Sherlock.'

I narrow my eyes at both of them, settle on Harris. 'Sherlock, yes. Little, not so much.' Mycroft would tower over Harris by half a head. But even thinking about Mycroft makes me wince.

I chew my lip and poke at the fire with a stick. Sparks wink and collide as I watch my brother and his best mate. Harris Derwent: I never understood what Mike saw in him. They're polar opposites. Actually, their builds are similar – tall, broad as doors, solid-muscled – but Harris is like the Anti-Mike. Where Mike is dark-haired, Harris is blond as a wheatfield. Where Mike's hair is short, Harris lets his grow wild. Mike's skin is fair, Harris is tanned. And while you can see genuine kindness and a hint of mischief in Mike's smile, Harris's is all smirk and snark.

I try to ignore the way Mike falls back so easily into the old blokey crap with Harris. We sit and watch the flames, hashing over Five Mile gossip – Harris is a treasure-trove of who's gone bust, who's broken up with who, which business has changed hands and what the prices of stock and feed are like. Mike talks about Melbourne, the change to city life.

Harris beams. 'Excellent,' he says, scratching his chest through his shirt like he's got fleas. 'Mate, I can't wait.'

I frown between him and my brother. 'What?'

'Gonna bust out of here with youse guys tomorrow, aren't I?' Harris says. 'Bags the front seat.'

I stare at Mike, who shrugs. He only looks a little bit guilty. 'I've offered Harris a ride. He wants to come to Melbourne for a while, so I said . . .'

'He could ride with *us*?'

Harris laughs at my expression. 'Big city lights, here I come. Melbourne won't know what's hit it.'

———

It's nearly ten-thirty, and Mike and Harris have relocated to the verandah. Rugged up in their windbreakers and sleeping bags, they're propped against the grey timbers of the outside wall, watching the stars. Joint thoroughly smoked, they're drinking beers from the pair of sixpacks Harris produced like magic. It must be about three degrees out here, this time of night, but they seem to be having a grand old time.

'I'm going to bed.' I lean against the frame of the double doors that open from the living room onto the verandah.

'Don't wanna have a drink with your brother and his best mate?' Harris winks, cracks the tab on another tinny with his free hand and offers it my way. His green eyes sparkle up at me, his breath coming out in a frosted cloud.

I clamp down on my comeback. 'Thanks, but I'm buggered.'

'Put another log on before you crash?' Mike's eyes are glazed. It's been a while since he's tried to keep up with Harris.

Limping back inside, I stuff another of the big splits into the Coonara and set the baffle to keep the fire banked through the night. I scratch open the velcro on my knee brace, slip the plastic splints off my fingers, set them all on the floor to one side. Then I crawl into my sleeping bag, feet towards the warm hearth. My knee aches, but I've taken plenty of ibuprofen, and I'm cosy in my sleeping bag. Now I just want to turn down the camp lantern and sleep without dreams.

It's Harris's lantern. The first thing I noticed this afternoon when we brought in our gear was Harris's stuff. His orange sleeping bag laid out near the fire, an open duffel bag of tumbled clothes sitting beside it. A primus stove on the countertop, with a baby gas bottle. A billy for tea, an old saucepan, plus cutlery, tin plate, toothbrush in a pannikin, oddsy-sodsy groceries.

I remember the bits of wood already stacked up in the store. Suddenly it all makes sense: Harris Derwent has been *squatting* at our old house, and god knows for how long. Shit. Bloody Harris.

I burrow my face into the pillow. I thought Mike was bringing me to Five Mile to give me an escape from Mum. I thought we could enjoy having the farm to ourselves, just for one night. If I'd known that Mike's real reason for this road trip was to answer the call of his old Five Mile mate, I wouldn't have come.

'. . . just wanna get away for a bit, is that it?' Mike's voice floats in through the walls.

'Nah, mate.' Harris, punctuated by the hiss of another ring-pull being opened. 'I'm over it. Dad wants me to take over the ropes on the property. Fuck that. I'll be twenty in a month, I can make my own way.'

'Don't wanna stay a country boy, then?'

'Go mad, I reckon. I need a bit of action.'

I hear Mike's chuckle. 'But you've seen a bit of action here, haven't you?'

Harris laughs. 'You remember Della Metcalfe? The one with the—'

I imagine his hands, making airy boulders at his chest. Harris's rep with the girls who hang at the Five Flags on a Saturday night is the stuff of legend.

'Shit.' Mike half-chokes on his beer. 'I remember her dad's ute.'

Mike and Harris laugh themselves stupid. This could go on for a while. Flame-shadows bob in the dark of the living room. On the lip of sleep, I go over the anatomical processes I've started learning from an old medical textbook I found in an op shop. I start from the back of my head.

Occipital bone – the unpaired bone constituting the base of the skull. *Atlas* – first cervical vertebra. *Axis* – second cervical vertebra. Remaining cervical vertebrae, then *thoracic* vertebrae, *lumbar* vertebrae, *sacrum*, *coccyx*.

I'm not sure why I find going over the names soothing. Anything to do with study has been a disaster lately, but this is the exception. Bones are concrete structures with a set order. They're solid, essential, contained. I like the latinate vowels of them. They have a nice flow – *scapula, clavicle, sternum, ribs* – and somehow reciting them helps me get to sleep. I can go over each part in the dark as I let my body settle.

I've reached my hips – *ilium, ischium, pubis* – and I'm almost completely unconscious when something snags my attention.

'. . . story with Rachel?'

Harris. I lie still, my ears pricking, remembering that no one ever hears nice things when they eavesdrop on conversations about themselves.

'Ah, fuck . . .' Mike seems to swear a lot more when he's with Harris. 'You wouldn't believe me.'

'Try me,' Harris says.

I can imagine his raised eyebrows, the half-smile on his lips. I try to recover my thread – I've finished the pelvis, now I go back for the arms. Arm bones are easy. *Humerus, radius, ulna . . .*

'First, there was this business at the zoo . . .' Mike backtracks blearily. 'Nah, first, she met that bloke. He's all right, I guess. Too smart for sense, if you know what I mean.'

I close my eyes, take a breath. Eight carpal bones. *Capitate, hamate, lunate . . .*

'Anyway,' Mike goes on, 'a coupla months ago he gets called away to England, and Rache races over there—'

'To *England*? Jesus. So it's serious, then?'

'Bloody serious. Rache got herself so wound up about him going to London – dealing with family shit alone – she ended up flying out the same day. You should've seen the olds. They went off like a bloody atomic bomb.'

I don't think about bombs. I think about wrist bones: *pisiform, scaphoid, trapezium, trapezoid . . .*

Harris laughs, throaty and warm. 'Shit, she's gutsy. So what'd she do to her knee?'

I press the back of my head into the brushed cotton of the pillow-case. How will Mike reply? Will he trot out the myth that we give to the neighbours and casual acquaintances, the same one that Mum believes, about how I was involved in an 'accident' over in England?

14

I hear someone slurp from his tinny, then belch.

'Mycroft – that's her fella – got himself involved in some heavy shit with the jacks over in London . . . Rachel got caught up in it, had a brush with this standover man, then they both came home looking like the walking wounded.'

Well, there you go – Mike's decided to give Harris the full story. I exhale, try to get back on track. Five metacarpals . . . Is it five? Yes. And the phalanges . . .

Harris's voice goes hard. 'Christ. They catch the guy?'

'Yeah. The cops've got him.' Mike's reply is clipped, sharp. 'Which is probably a good thing. Because if he'd gotten away, I'd have had to go over there and find him, and tear him limb from fucking limb.'

I swallow. There are fourteen phalanges. Fourteen phalanges, and they're classed as *proximal*, *intermediate*, and . . . and another one, which I can't . . .

Okay, stop. Nice deep breath. I'm in Five Mile, with Mike, miles and miles from anywhere, in the back of beyond. There's a clear line of sight all around this house, and the Colonel is behind bars and the phalanges are *proximal*, *intermediate* and *distal*.

My heart has almost stopped hammering, and now Mike's voice is superseded by Harris's.

'. . . pretty bloody full-on.'

'Yeah, she's had a rough trot,' Mike goes on. 'She and Mum have been at each other's throats. I'm standing in the kitchen last night, yeah? Like I'm trying to separate two blokes at the pub. And they're screaming at each other . . .'

'Sounds like me and my old man.' Harris snorts. 'Where's her bloke, then?'

Mike clears his throat, spits. 'Ah, I dunno. They haven't seen much of each other since they got back from the UK. Rachel's been moping around for the last five weeks like her budgie died.'

'Trouble in paradise, eh?'

Suddenly, all my bones are gone. The ache inside that's always there curdles into something tangible. I roll sideways, tuck my hands into my armpits and draw up my legs.

It's stupid – I know it's stupid. But suddenly I just *want* Mycroft. Just like that. There's nothing sensible about it. It's an automatic thing.

I dwell on the impossibility of this for a moment.

I roll over in my bag, rub my socked toes together. So far, this trip hasn't been what I'd expected. Somehow, coming back to Five Mile has made me feel particularly low. The Greeks said it right: nostalgia. From the words *algos*, pain, and *nostos*, coming home.

My mind drifts back to something else. An image, a name on a computer screen. It's red-lettered, bulging, worming its way into my head, the crisp font deforming as the letters take shape: *MORIARTY*.

MORIARTY, and the words nearby – *I know you . . .*

I close my eyes tight enough to make them water, force the image away. *I will not.* I'm exhausted from last night's drama, and the drive. I've got a bellyful of ibuprofen, and I have my processes.

Tonight, I will not think, will not dream.

———

It's evening. I'm sitting under a spotlight on a hard wooden chair in the big warehouse space, with Mycroft kneeling in front of me. We're kissing, caressing, letting our hands roam. My fingers reach into Mycroft's dark curls. They're silky soft and tumbling – Hair Chaos Theory. I lean forward to take his earlobe in my teeth.

'*Rachel.*' His lips are on my neck; he breathes softly onto my collarbone.

I clutch at Mycroft's shoulders, tugging the fabric of his shirt. He kisses across to the hollow at the base of my throat, then lower, between my breasts. My gasps echo in the quiet room, as the rain falls outside.

Then Mycroft stands, moves away from me, behind me. I can't see him anymore and this is where it all starts to change. My breathing tightens. Every nerve that's alive inside me suddenly stretches and pings with tension. The fear comes rushing back. I'm stuck to the chair, as the London cold seeps up through the floorboards. The hanging lamps sway, casting jerking shadows.

I smell blood and toothpaste. There's Paul – the side of his face slick with blood. He leers, broken teeth gnashing. He grabs me by the shoulders, holds me from behind, squeezing me tight, pressing me down. My diaphragm is compressed, my ribs creak in protest.

Then I smell leather and it's Tyson holding me. The hinge juts from his forehead, the burnt sections of his face raw and crisped black on the edges. His eyes goggle at me, grey and lifeless.

Then the person gripping me is Mike, or maybe it's Dad, or even Mum.

And then, worst of all: it's Mycroft.

I yell, kick, struggle. I fight and swear and weep; the iron bands around me hold firm. I can't squirm away. I can't *breathe.*

And then I hear the clunk and scrape of the tyre iron, and the Colonel is there. The panic I feel in this moment is overwhelming. In that slow-motion way of dreams, he puts my hand up on the table, spreads my fingers.

'*Now we see what the meat is like inside, yes?*' he says.

I groan, hoarse from screaming. Then the tyre iron is going up in the air, reaching critical altitude, then falling, whistling down . . .

I snap awake with a harsh gasp.

There's a scream built up inside my throat – I slap a hand over my mouth, operating on automatic. The dark and quiet throws me off for a second; I keen through my nose.

But after a moment's panic, my head rights itself. I'm in Five Mile, in the living room. The house is dark, but there's the glow from the Coonara. The boys are huddled in their sleeping-bag mounds to my right.

I take my hand away from my mouth, wipe my cheeks, draw a few deep breaths to stabilise myself. *Goddamnit.*

I reach a shaky hand for my sports bag – I'm so familiar with this routine after five weeks that I've prepared a spare change of clothes. Inside my sweaty sleeping bag I strip off my damp track-pants, pull on my jeans. I zip out of my bag, slip into my boots and hoodie, try not to rattle the glass when I crack the noisy double doors onto the verandah.

I need air.

The night is icy. I watch my breath turn to steam. Tuck my arms around myself. It's probably stupid to stand in the winter cold with no socks and a damp T-shirt under my hoodie, but there's no way I'll be able to get back to sleep. My body is shaking: my shoulders jerk, as though I'm still trying to wriggle away.

The sky is turning grey, the clouds scudding like black oil on water. I hobble down the verandah side-steps to drop my jeans and pee near the agapanthus. With my bad knee, it's awkward. By the time I button up, my fingers are frozen.

I climb back up the steps, lean on the rail. There's enough night left to see the stars, picked out in silver behind the clouds like a carelessly thrown handful of glitter. Somehow the complete absence of city sounds – the stillness of the dark – is comforting. Away to the right, there's the thump of a kangaroo passing.

Then someone puts a hand on my shoulder and I jump almost as high as the roo.

'*Jesus Christ!*'

'Sorry! Ah, shit, sorry—' Harris has one hand up, as though he's warding me off, when it should be the other way around. His other hand holds the bundle of his orange sleeping bag. He's dressed in jeans and an open flannie, his hair mussed and a windbreaker pulled on haphazardly. His voice is a husky hiss. 'I didn't mean to scare you.'

'*Well, what the bloody hell did you think was gonna happen?*' I'm doing that weird whispered screech. 'You creep up behind me, like a fucking—'

'*Rachel.*' Harris's voice drops into a lower register, goes quiet, calming. His eyes flare, like a fox's by torchlight. 'Mate, I didn't mean it. Are you all right? It's just . . . I heard you . . .'

He doesn't finish the sentence, and he doesn't need to. My night-time thrashing woke him up. I feel myself flush all the way up my neck to the roots of my hair. No one knows I've been having nightmares. Not Mum or Dad, not Mike or Mai – not even Mycroft. I feel exposed, like I've just been caught streaking or something.

'Sorry.' My mumble sounds rough, gravelly. 'Didn't mean to wake you.'

'Don't worry about it.' Harris lowers his hand and turns so I can see his profile. The predawn glow makes the light stubble on his jaw shine like frost. 'Makes you real tired.'

'What?'

He sighs and looks at me patiently as he buttons his flannie over his bare chest. 'The nightmare thing. It makes you tired. Shit, it's freezing out here.' He passes me his sleeping bag.

I gape at the orange fabric. 'What're you—'

'Go back inside, where it's warm,' Harris continues, matching the zipper's ends on his windbreaker. 'Or at least wrap that around you.' He nods to his sleeping bag. 'I'm goin' for a walk.'

I look at him, flabbergasted. 'Harris, it's barely dawn.'

He shrugs, zips his windbreaker to the collar. 'Gotta see a man about a dog.'

I pluck at the sleeve of his windbreaker, hesitant. 'You really want me to take your sleeping bag?'

'*Yes.*' Harris turns, looking exasperated. 'Jeez, are you deaf? Take my sleeping bag. I'm not in it, am I?' He grins. 'Unless you'd like me to be . . .'

'Rack off.' It pops out like my mouth's on autopilot.

'That's more like it.' He winks, then takes the stairs down and heads off.

I cloak myself in the sleeping bag, shaking my head. Maybe he's headed for his dad's place, but who knows what he's up to. Harris Derwent . . . bloody man of mystery.

Even with the puffy nylon around me, I can't stand on the verandah long. Back in the living room, I pick my way past my own damp sleeping bag on the edge of the hearth and over Mike's humpbacked shape. I lower myself to the floor, still cocooned in Harris's orange bag. There are a few ash burns on the nylon. It smells of stale beer, and boy sweat, and other unnameable things. But it's warm, and I'm so tired I hardly care. My eyes close involuntarily. I don't think about the Colonel, or Tyson, or Paul, or anything, as I give in to this exhaustion and float away.

———

At nine a.m. I'm standing by the Toyota, feeling hung-over. I somehow managed to get a bit more sleep after Harris left, but I woke up crick-necked, aching and still tired.

Harris lifts his chin at me. 'All ready for Melbourne then, are ya?'

'Not really.' I toss my sleeping bag into the boot of Alicia's car, heave Mike's bag in after it. 'But Mike's got work tomorrow. And I've got to face the music eventually.'

'Well, I'm ready. Can't wait to see the back of this place.' Harris looks very chipper in the morning sunlight, with his flannie sleeves rolled and his hands jammed in his pockets. He scans out past the paddock line, his expression smug.

'Did you get to say goodbye to your dad?'

'Sure.' Harris shrugs as he grabs his sleeping bag off the ground. 'But he'll only figure out I'm gone when he comes off his bender and sees the water's not pumped, and the wood's not in, and the place isn't running like normal.'

'Oh.' I'm not sure what to say. I didn't know it'd got so bad. Harris's dad has always been considered a bit of a local deadshit. His wife cut out for Adelaide, taking Harris's younger sister, a long time ago – no one could blame her, from all reports. Word around town, when we still lived here, was that Dennis Derwent spent more time down at the Five Flags pub than home on the farm. I never wondered before what that might mean for Harris.

Mike starts the engine, warming the car interior while we gather the rest of our belongings. Everything goes into the boot, and Harris hoys his extra luggage in with me in the back seat – he's bringing a *punching bag*, for god's sake. My sympathy for Harris doesn't extend to appreciating the fact that he's now riding shotgun.

I take my last, long look at the farm: the house, a dark-grey silhouette against the glaring expanse of sky, the century plants extending proud and brutish above the fence line. A flock of galahs swoops away to the east, and the air echoes with their sweet, mournful cries. At least, they sound mournful to me.

I've found this trip back to Five Mile a bit disillusioning, but I'm still sad to say goodbye. God knows what state the place will be in when I next make it back. Could be falling down, rotted and dry with salt, or someone might have bought it and fixed it up – *as if.* And Mike was right, I'll be different too. I'll never view the farm with these eyes again. In the same way I found my perspective had changed when we first drove up yesterday morning, the next time I come back I know I'll be a whole different person, my feelings and line of sight changed – maybe beyond recognition.

Even though my life's still a mess, the fresh air and space and exercise has made me feel better. I wonder if the feeling will last once we're back in Melbourne.

My contemplative mood is soured by Harris's whoop of triumph from the front seat as we pull out from the dirt-road driveway. He puts his hands on the window and yells through.

'You little *ripper!*'

He does the same thing when we drive through town. He sticks his head out the window – almost his whole torso, actually – and flings his hands wide, flipping off the entire town. *'SEE YOU, SUCKERS!'*

His hollers make everyone on the street – including old Mrs Delaney from the Post Office, god, is she still alive? – look up. I might be imagining the relief on their faces, but I'm pretty sure everyone in Five Mile is as glad to see Harris go as he is to be gone.

We're barely out of town when Harris taps Mike on the shoulder.

'Swing by the Falls for me? I wanna say cheerio to Westie, my old boss – he's fixing the gate.'

'Thought you said your goodbyes on Friday,' Mike grumbles, but he turns the wheel.

Another ten minutes and we're approaching the tall hurricane fence. The land has been mounded up gently on the right as a protective barrier; beyond the ridge it veers away downhill, into the cutting. Big signs are posted along the sides: *Ridgeback Falls. WestCo Quarries Ltd. No Entry Without Permission. Hard Hats Must Be Worn On-Site.* Mike pulls up near the security gate, and Harris jumps out to fistbump Mark West, a thirty-something guy with a beer gut and a fluoro-orange safety vest.

The car idles as Mike and I watch the two of them exchange pleasantries.

Mike slings himself around in his seat. 'You right in the back there?'

'I'd be righter if I was in the front.'

'Yeah, sorry about that.' Mike gives me an apologetic grin.

I don't grin back. 'So where's Harris gonna stay in Melbourne?'

Mike shrugs. 'Told him he could crash at ours for a week or two. He can sleep on the floor in my room.'

I groan. 'Alicia won't be happy.'

'Yeah, well, she's not getting back for a month.' Mike glances out the window. 'And if Harris's still there when she flies in, I'll chuck him out myself.'

I frown. 'Mike, is Harris really gonna be okay in the city? It's not that easy to get a job. And who's to say he's not gonna go out partying every night, pissing in alleyways and picking up chicks?'

'He's an all-right bloke.' Mike looks at Harris fondly through the windscreen. 'You just haven't seen his good side.'

'I didn't think he had a good side.' I sigh, then remember early this morning and realise that's not strictly true. I search for other options. 'God, Mike. Mum and Dad are gonna flip.'

'Like they flipped when you went overseas?' He gives me a firm look. 'Harris needs to get out. He's had a rough time with his old man lately.'

I can't help it; I smile at my brother, shake my head. 'Bloody good Samaritan, you are.'

Mike chucks me under the chin.

Harris *oofs* into his seat. 'Right. Good to go.'

'So what made you decide to pick up some quarry work?' Mike asks.

'Well, I couldn't live on what the old man was shelling out, could I? Westie's a good bloke. He gave me a trial, then put me on as a trainee shotfirer.'

Mike tries to back up the car and stare at Harris simultaneously. 'They put dynamite in your hands? That's just fucking frightening.'

'I like making things go *boom*.' Harris waggles his eyebrows at me.

Mike puffs air out his lips. 'I'll keep that under consideration when it's your turn to drive.'

———

The drive back seems to take less time. Harris and Mike gasbag the whole way, while I drift off, half-dozing. As soon as I see the dim grey skyline and stratified housing of Melbourne, the gnaw of tension in my gut starts up.

'Jeez, would you look at that. Kebabs!' Nothing seems to worry Harris. We're about to turn off Bell Street, and if Harris were a dog, he'd have his tongue hanging out the window.

I'm the tough girl; I should be able to handle this. But I'm not ready to face Mum yet. As the traffic around us becomes more constant, my anxiety grows sharper teeth, and I cave.

'Mike, can you drop me at Mai's?'

Outside Mai's apartment block, Mike cranes his head out the window to catch my eye. 'Make sure you get home for dinner, okay?'

'Yes, Dad.'

He doesn't seem to know what else to say. I refuse to feel bad about ditching. This is the end of the road trip. If it's an anti-climax, it wasn't me who made it that way.

Harris leers from Mike's other side. 'Hey, Rachel, maybe you could bring your girlfriend over later, and we could—'

I give him the finger to cut him off, walk away listening to his guffaws. Pray that Harris's visit will be a short one.

CHAPTER TWO

A rusted fence flaps near the apartment block, and the air feels like cold Clag paste. The wind sidles up to me and sticks its fingers down the back of my jumper as I head for the lift in the grungy foyer. I shiver, but this is the Melbourne I'm familiar with. I was sad when I felt like Five Mile had forgotten me. But Melbourne forgets everybody. At least here I know where I stand.

Mai welcomes me with a big smile at the door to her flat. 'Great timing. I just got off the phone from Gus.'

'Organising the next big date?'

It had been hard work, and involved barrels of angst, but Gus Deng has finally won Mai's mum over – which I'd considered a no-brainer, because who doesn't like Gus? Mrs Ng is now remarkably cool about Mai and Gus dating, although she'd been very concerned about Mai wearing a lurid *Robogeisha* T-shirt on the first official night out.

'Better than that.' Mai pushes up her black-framed glasses. 'We've been talking about a rental place, for when we go to uni.'

'That's great.' But my smile is a mask for my feelings. Mycroft and I talked about share-housing after school, in Baker Street in Richmond. We used to have that dream. 'Well, you need it. The rental, I mean. You can't keep shagging in his uncle's vacant flat forever.'

'We're not shagging. That sounds like something you do with a sheep and a vacuum cleaner. It's sex, Rachel. Actual, real life, honest-to-goodness, sweaty and embarrassing and amazing sex. With someone you care about, who cares about you—'

'*Mai.*' I blush, look elsewhere. 'Maybe you wanna keep your voice down, at least until you tell your mum the whole story?'

Mai steers me into her bedroom and tries to get details about the fight with Mum – I already texted her the flash version. I steer *Mai* back to her current preoccupation – the school dance.

I grab her laptop and bring up the relevant Facebook page. 'Have you had any more RSVPs? Gimme a look.'

'Not yet.' Mai sits on the end of her bed, scratching at the glittery jet varnish on her nails. The streak of hot pink in her hair has started to regrow black at the roots: she dyed a swatch of her fringe while I was overseas. 'I wish people would pull their collective fingers out and RSVP now. I'm trying to organise the catering, and Karo's supposed to be making the punch. He keeps texting me and asking how many bottles he should buy.'

'For god's sake.' I click through to the event page. 'Tell him to buy enough for a hundred and fifty. It's just juice and mineral water – it's not like he's buying bottles of vodka.' I frown at Mai. 'I mean, he's not, is he? Because if he tries to spike the punch with Principal Conroy standing in the corner, there'll be merry hell.'

'No, I was very emphatic.' Mai pauses. 'Be funny, though.'

We both crack grins. I try to restore my face to order. 'No, it wouldn't. It would be very, very bad. Anyway, look, we've got one more week of holidays. I'll call a few people and keep an eye on the RSVPs and you can sort out the rest of it, yeah?'

'Sure.' Mai's expression softens. 'Thanks for doing this.'

'Gotta be useful for something, right?' I massage the knuckles of my left hand; they're still aching from my woodchopping efforts. 'I might even be able to show up on the night. The physio said my leg is healing up okay.'

'It's awesome you got rid of the old cyborg brace!'

'Don't get too excited. The new brace is still clunky.' I grimace. 'And I won't be able to skate for ages.'

Mai flaps a hand, bangles tinkling. 'Hey, don't stress. Derby is the least of your problems.'

I shrug, because she's right. Roller derby is not even high on my list of priorities. It's just the promise of something physical, something *real*. 'God, I'm gonna be so flabby by the time I get back.'

'You're probably pretty out of shape, but . . .' She leans closer, squinting. 'What's that on your face?'

I shy away. After Harris noticed my panda look, I slapped on some makeup in the pub toilets in Nullawil. The girl who loaned me her compact seemed to think it was an improvement.

'It's just concealer. I've got a bruise from Mum's slap.'

'Around your *eyes*?' Mai frowns. 'Don't give me that.'

She grabs a tissue and starts attacking me. Once she's removed the concealer, the look on her face is enough to make me wish I'd stopped her.

'Oh, mate . . .' She plumps back down on the bed, smeary tissue in hand. 'What are you getting, a few hours a night?'

'Enough,' I say.

'Rachel, you're a crap liar. Why aren't you sleeping?'

'I don't know.' I feel naked without the concealer. 'It's fine, Mai. It'll pass.'

Mai throws up her hands. 'Rachel, come on. Is being this delusional some kind of disease? Is there a remedy? Because, no shit, I will donate for the cure.'

'*Mai*—'

She leans forward and grabs my hand, careful of my bad fingers. 'Rachel, you're my best mate. And I hate to be the one to point out the nose on your frickin' face, but you have PTSD. Jesus, you're as bad as Mycroft.'

I flinch a little when she says his name, then pull away to fiddle with her dock. Some Knife Party song is playing, the electronica effects groaning out like a continuous belch. 'How is he? Have you seen him over the holidays?'

'Not much. And you haven't either, I gather?'

I shake my head. When he's not researching, Mycroft's been pouring all his time into his job at the Forensics Unit. 'He's been . . . preoccupied.'

'With the search for this "Mr Wild". And you haven't been over to visit him.'

'You make it sound like that's easy.' I fiddle with my plastic splints, fold them and unfold them over my stiff fingers. 'I'm only just off crutches, and you know how paranoid my parents have been since I got back from England . . .'

'But Rachel, you live *two bloody doors away*—'

'Mai.' I close my eyes, open them. 'Last time I saw him, the research was all he could talk about. And I just . . .'

'You can't deal with it,' Mai says flatly. 'Fine. And I understand why he's stuck on it. It's Mycroft's family shit, I get that. If my mum or Aunty Lien got murdered, I'd want to find the bastard who did it too. But he's turned into a complete recluse!'

'I guess that's because he's got new information. He knows the carjacking was related to his dad working for British intelligence. He's emailed that guy who collected the Folio, Jonathan Cole, to see if he can help. He's just . . . trying to get all the puzzle pieces together.'

Mai adjusts her glasses. 'Rachel, I'll say it again – I don't think you were the only one affected by London. And I think Mycroft's become completely bloody-minded about it because he thinks you'll both feel better if he can find this "Mr Wild".'

The idea chills me. 'What I'd really like is for this whole thing to go away.'

'Sorry, darl, but it won't.' Mai wriggles on the bed until her back hits the wall. 'Anyway, all that aside, it's the "international conspiracy" thing that spins me out.'

'It's not an international conspiracy. It's just one crazy guy.'

'Sure, but come on – British intelligence? It's a helluva long way from investigating a homeless guy's murder at the local zoo.'

'I told Mycroft to try working backwards. Find out everything he can about his dad – his job, his friends, that kind of thing . . .' I rub my forehead. 'Look, could we maybe change the subject?'

'Does it freak you out?'

I don't meet her eyes. 'Have you got any idea how much I listened to Mycroft talk about what happened to us in London? That's one of the reasons I haven't been to see him.'

'Not because you're angry with him?'

'No.' I backpedal. 'I mean, yeah, but not because of that.'

'Because of the blog. Because he didn't tell the police that Wild made contact with him on *Diogenes*.'

'It's . . . complicated. The only reason Mycroft contacted Wild's men on *Diogenes* in London was to get me back. He wasn't expecting Wild to send us a message himself!'

'And now he doesn't want to tell the cops, because he's got a direct link.' Mai narrows her eyes at me. 'But Rachel, think about it. It's really not that complicated. Heroics in England aside, not telling the cops about Wild's message on the blog is a dick move.'

'Mai—'

'Rachel, Mycroft's my friend too, which means I get to rag on him for being an idiot.'

'The message on the blog doesn't matter. If Wild really wanted to find us, he wouldn't need *Diogenes*. He's a high-level criminal, with possible government connections. Me and Mycroft, we're just a pair of teenaged nobodies. He could probably swat us like flies.'

That message from Wild – *I know you* – is still there in the Comments field on the blog, squatting like a toad. I crumple inside every time I think about it. Fear is such a primal thing. It makes your heart pummel against your ribcage, your palms sweat . . .

I search for more words. Speaking them out loud makes my chest hurt. 'Okay, maybe Mycroft screwed up. But it's not like he did it for some malicious or trivial reason – he wants to find out about his parents. He's not selling his soul for Justin Bieber tickets or something.'

'This is your scale of justice?'

Controlling the shake in my voice takes some serious effort. 'Mycroft walked into that warehouse – for me. He got his ribs broken – for me. If I don't have the guts to see this investigation through to the end, then that's not his fault.'

Mai stares at me. 'Rachel, you need to go see him.'

'I don't think that's a good idea.' Wild's henchmen hound me through the nights; I don't want to discuss it over and over with Mycroft during the day as well.

'You should talk about this stuff with him. It might help with the—'

'Mai, *don't*. I mean it. I'm dealing with it.' I wave my hand towards the laptop. 'Can we just . . . talk about the dance, and clothes, and shit like that? I really need a bit of normal.'

'Okay – sure.' Mai exhales, long and loud.

We do normal for a while. We talk about holiday study sessions – about which I have practically negative interest – and movies, and books, and how Gus is busy with soccer season, and whether Mai should re-dye her hair for the dance. When the clock on her nightstand gets to five-thirty, I almost feel relaxed.

I stand up to go.

Mai grins at me. 'So was that enough normal for you?'

I swallow and look at her. 'You're a good mate, Mai. The best. I've told you that, right?'

'Oh, Rachel . . .' She reaches to hug me, but I flinch. She pulls back and peers at me strangely. 'What's that?'

'What?'

'The hugging thing. Every time I hug you lately, you—'

'I'll call you soon, okay?' I shoo her away, step through the bedroom door. 'Don't get too hung up about the punch.'

Mai insists on walking me out. She waves goodbye, standing in the hallway. Somehow this makes me feel worse. In the lift, I realise something: I am a shitty friend. I disappeared to England without letting Mai know, and since I returned, I've been a chronic downer. I dump all my crap on Mai, and expect her to put up with me. I didn't even ask how she and Gus are going with the date night thing, with her mum.

And I was in her room for nearly two hours, but right now, I couldn't tell you what picture she had on her T-shirt.

CHAPTER THREE

I have to wait for public transport, which is typical for a Sunday night, but I can't walk the distance with my knee. The Melbourne skyline glowers as I stand at the tram stop, jigging my feet against the cold. I'm wearing thermal leggings, thermal shirt, thermal everything, underneath an over-large pair of trackies – Mike's – and a sweatshirt and a woollen jumper – also Mike's. Despite the clothes layers, I still feel cold. I feel cold all the time lately, like my blood has turned to raspberry slushie.

The entire ride home, inside the bright flocked interior of the tram, I remind myself that I don't have to feel obligated. I can walk straight past Mycroft's weatherworn house, with the park bench still positioned forlornly under his bedroom window. Just keep walking along Summoner Street, over the cracked pavement, past the house across the street with the newly boarded-up windows, until I reach the stuccoed exterior of mine.

It's coming on evening by the time I reach the sagging wire fence outside Mycroft's place, and I implied to Mike that I'd be home for dinner. Mum and Dad will be watching the clock. I stand there, looking at Mycroft's weatherboard hovel, for a good two minutes.

I miss Mycroft like crazy. He's my best friend, my boyfriend, and being without him is driving me bonkers. The problem is that all my recent memories of us kissing, of him sharing the most intimate details of his life with me, are tainted with the same fear that wakes me in the night, sweating and nauseated.

Maybe I should be honest, tell him that his research scares the crap out of me. That I can't go through anything like London again. That I'm too gutless. Maybe I should explain about the nightmares. I could go in, right now, and talk to him, like Mai suggested.

My hand reaches for the gate, gives a tentative push. Talking to Mycroft. *Seeing* Mycroft. An uncontrollable buzz starts somewhere in my stomach and spreads through my entire body. I tell myself to calm down. The gate creaks. I'm about to step into the yard when another idea batters me out of the blue. I stop in my tracks.

It's not just discussing his parents' case that has me on edge. It's everything. Every time Mycroft comes near me, I push him away. If I care about Mycroft – and there's no question that's true – maybe I should do the right thing by him.

Maybe I should let him go.

The idea makes me blanch, because it makes so much bloody sense. It also makes me want to curl up in a ball and cry. But I need to be brave: to suck it up and make a clean break. At least then we'd both know what's going on.

The thought paralyses me for a whole minute, but I know I'm right. I need to put my feelings aside and tell Mycroft it's over. If I can't bear physical closeness, what kind of girlfriend am I – for

Mycroft, for anybody? And if I can't stand with him in the fight against Wild, I should have the guts to say so. He should be free to find out what happened to his parents, without my fears in the background conflicting him. He deserves that.

With a kind of numbness spreading through me, drowning the excitement of just a moment ago, I let the wind blow me through the weedy yard and along the squeezeway to Mycroft's back door. Opening it, I hear voices. I pause.

'. . . not like he'll talk to me about it.'

'No, I understand. I still think having you there will be good. Plus a break from his regular routine might help.'

'I'm just . . . worried. If he has an episode, we'll be miles from anywhere.'

'Actually, I don't think it's his mental health you need be so concerned about. He's sharper than ever in the lab. It's his physical health that's bothering me, but I thought I'd ask you before I had a word to him. If you think it might help . . .'

I freeze in place. I recognise the voices and I'm loath to intrude on the conversation, but I'm stuck. Mycroft's room is inaccessible except through the kitchen. I take a breath, clear my throat ostentatiously, then step into the house.

Mycroft's aunt, Angela Hudgson, and his boss, Professor Walsh, are sitting at the kitchen table over cups of tea. Angela is dressed in jeans and a thick sweatshirt, but she's not wearing her bandanna and she's *home*, which is weird. Normally she'd be on her way to work by now. She's saying, 'Certainly, if you'd have a go at talking to him, I'd be . . .' but when she sees me her words die away. She blinks at me as if I'm a mirage. 'Rachel?'

'Hi.' I make a tight little wave. 'Hi, Professor.'

Professor Walsh's hair has grown out a bit – it resembles grey seaweed floating around the desert island of his bare crown.

He looks tired, but his eyes are still bright and searching. He adjusts his glasses, smiles at me.

'Rachel, goodness, it's nice to see you. How are you getting on?'

'Fine. Good.' I think about saying 'great', decide not to push it. 'Nice to see you, too. Angela, I just came by to say hi to Mycroft – if that's okay?'

Angela's mouth opens. 'Of course.' Her nod starts slow, gets more vigorous. 'He'll be happy to see you.'

'Cool.' I shift from foot to foot. 'Well, I'll just . . .'

I wave again, then hobble down the hallway to Mycroft's room, the Stranger's Room. My eyes swim and my heart starts pounding as though someone's swinging a sledgehammer inside my chest.

Fronting up to his door, I realise that something has changed. Dead blobs of Blu-Tack decorate the spaces where posters used to hang. Everything has disappeared, except for the skull-and-crossbones sign. The door used to look cheerful and kooky; now it just looks ominous.

I steel myself and knock.

There's a delay, then I hear Mycroft say, 'Yup.' I rub my palms on my trackie pants. My hands are shaking. I take a deep breath, turn the doorknob, and step in.

The Stranger's Room is dim, the curtains drawn for late afternoon. But that's not weird – what's weird is that the twinkle of the Christmas lights is gone. It's also *cold*; the air in the room is icy on my cheeks. That's another weird thing, because Mycroft hates the cold.

But these are only my sense impressions: the most immediate thing I notice is that the room is absolutely *bombed*. Papers are scattered everywhere – on the floor, on the unmade bed, on the bookshelf – and boxes of books and detritus are placed willy-nilly. A stale smell hovers in the air, beneath the reek of old cigarette smoke.

Mycroft's backpack is on his low futon, half-stuffed with clothes. Mugs, in various states of mouldiness, are piled on the floor near the desk. The whole room looks grotty, misused.

Now I can see why the posters have been removed from the door: they've been taped up on the right-hand wall, their white backs facing out, to provide an impromptu whiteboard. Stuck all over them, in a display that rattles my world to the bone, are pictures and notes from Mycroft's Anniversary Book.

The album itself is lying against the wall, gutted. It's the folder where Mycroft keeps everything about his parents' case. He usually guards this private part of his history. Now half the contents are tacked up, with Post-it notes and texta lines connecting everything together in a bizarre spider web.

And in the middle of all this is Mycroft, like the eye of the maelstrom. He's sitting at his desk, which is still pushed into the far right corner near the window, as if he's waiting for me to visit him, to talk through the window the way we used to. He's hunched over his laptop – the cords and wires coming out of it seem to have reproduced and swarmed – in a gunmetal grey T-shirt and regulation black jeans. The black hoodie he's wearing is too thin for this cold weather, and his feet are bare. His toes must be freezing, but he doesn't seem to notice.

He hasn't noticed that I'm standing here, either, because he's so fixated on his screen. A cigarette burns between the fingers of the hand not holding his mouse. The column of ash on it looks ready to tumble. The giant plastic thermos is on the floor at his feet, and a steaming mug sits on his right.

Suddenly everything I feel for him comes crashing back. I can hardly speak. It's all I can do to breathe. But I lick my lips and open my mouth.

'Hey.'

Mycroft tears his eyes away from the laptop. When he sees me, he freezes. His eyes go huge, and his mouth opens. After a moment, he finds his voice.

'Hey.'

We stare at each other. His eyes are red-rimmed, deeply shadowed. The bruises from the beating he received in London faded weeks ago, but this is different – my god, it's like he's been punched in the face all over again. The blue of his gaze catapults into me.

My throat goes dry. I haven't seen Mycroft for weeks, only texted him now and again. It's horrifying to see what's become of him.

His hair is longer, tangled into some kind of curly miasma. Or maybe it's just more noticeable because his face is so gaunt. His cheekbones are like tribal cuts, scoring his shocked expression. His beautiful jaw is now a sharp angle, and he's got more than a five-o'clock shadow. He looks hollow, see-through, like a ghost.

His eyes run over me, taking in my listing posture. Then he fumbles to stand up, dumping his smoke in the overflowing ashtray on the desk.

'God, you probably want to, um, sit.' He swivels his chair in my direction – the action is made more awkward by the fact that he can't seem to take his eyes off me.

I clear my throat. 'I'm okay.'

'Oh.' He dithers for a second, waving his hand at the room. 'Sorry about the, uh . . . It's a bit of a mess. I just got home from work.' He says it like this is the reason the room is such a disaster, as if it's not obvious to even the most casual observer that the mess is the by-product of weeks of incidental neglect. 'The professor gave me a ride.'

I nod. 'I saw him. In the kitchen.'

'Right.' Mycroft bites his lip and I see the tiny silver scar there, where the stitch once was. Then he stills, like he's not sure what to say next. I've got the same problem.

I can't stop looking at him. His eyes are sharp, focused, intensely blue, but the rest of him is . . . Christ, I don't even know where to *start*.

'So how're you going?' I say, at the same moment he says, 'How've you been?' and the resulting confusion makes us both look elsewhere for a second.

I take a deep breath, straighten my shoulders. 'I'm . . . good.'

'Yeah?' Mycroft jams his hands in his jeans pockets. 'Me too. I'm good.'

We're so full of shit we're wading in it.

His gaze travels over me, taking everything in – my uber-glamorous trackie pants, limp hair, chewed nails . . . I want to cringe.

'Yeah . . .' Something in Mycroft's eyes changes. He stares straight at me. 'You look *awful*.'

I take a step forward, glaring at him. '*You* can talk.'

He matches my step. 'How much sleep are you getting?'

Oh for god's sake, why is everyone so obsessed with my sleep patterns? 'Enough.' I throw a hand out, hobble another step. 'What are you living on? Tea and cigarettes?'

Mycroft straightens. 'I eat stuff!'

'And you look half-frozen. What happened to the heater?'

'It broke. What do you care? And why are you wearing all your brother's clothes?'

'Mine are in the wash. What do you mean, *what do I care*?'

'Well, it's not like you've bothered to drop by before now. Or have you been sneaking in while I'm asleep again?'

'*Mycroft—*'

I stop, gasping. My internal temperature has risen, forced heat up my neck to bloom on my cheeks. My body is shaking. Mycroft is standing a hand's span away, and we're both buffeted by this waspish biting fury, like a cloud of gnats.

What the hell is happening? This isn't why I came. I don't want to fight with him.

My voice falls to a whisper. 'What are we doing?'

Mycroft shakes his head. He passes a hand over his face, his eyes shuttered like twilight by his purple lids.

'Jesus. I don't know.' He drops his hand and his eyes open. 'I've missed you.'

I nod blindly, because that's all I can do.

Mycroft takes a big, shuddering breath. Then he seems to get himself under control. He looks around to his desk, reaches to snag a sheaf of papers from the chaos. He shuffles them under my gaze.

'I've been working, you know. I think I'm getting closer. Cole replied to my emails. He said he's going to see if he can find another Home Office contact who knew my dad.'

My eyes skitter around the room.

'You were right, of course. About working backwards. Here, look.' Mycroft dumps the papers back on the desk and moves towards the wall tableau. Urging me closer, he points with his long fingers, eyes blazing with a zealous fire. 'The Shakespeare Folio wasn't the only case involving cultural artefacts – I've found links between *three* of the old carjacking cases and the theft of artwork or historical relics. And I've figured out the name of the guy who my father was visiting. The place we'd been coming from, just before the accident—'

'Mycroft . . .' I don't want him to go on.

'It's *this* guy – Robert Hannah.' He pokes at one of the Post-it notes on the wall, looks at me. The words are pouring out of him, as though he's trying to cram together all the news he's wanted to tell me for the past few weeks. 'It took me ages to work it out, but I finally remembered. Hannah had a place in Scotland, see? That's where we'd gone. I was researching my dad's work colleagues and I remembered my dad saying, *It'll be just like a mini-break, Jamie, wouldn't you like that?*, even though I'd thought it was weird, because we were packing to go so late in the evening . . .'

He's standing close enough for me to pick up his scent: beneath the whiff of cigarette smoke and stale sweat lives the familiar smell of Mycroft. It's making me dizzy.

'Your dad called you Jamie?'

'Yeah.' He swallows, stares at me. 'He used to . . . call me that.'

We stand there for a long moment. Some sort of electric charge ignites the air between us. Mycroft's blue eyes take up the whole world.

His next words seem to fall out of his mouth. 'Rachel, are we still together? Because I don't know what's going on. And it's kind of killing me, not knowing, but I've been too scared to—'

'Mycroft, I have to say something.' My tongue feels thick in my mouth. 'I have to tell you—'

'Actually – wait. Don't.' He closes his eyes, holds up a hand. 'Don't tell me. Not yet. I can hold on a little longer, I don't want this trip to—'

My back straightens. 'What trip?'

41

Mycroft drops his hand, clenches both hands into fists. 'That's what I needed to tell you. And I'm sorry. But I'm close, so close, and I . . . I'm going to Bali.'

'*What*?'

'Denpasar. I'm flying out tonight. This guy, Robert Hannah, he retired from the service and now he lives there. He runs a losmen there, like a B&B.' He turns to me, his eyes searing. 'He's tried to brush me off via email, but I need to see him. I'm going to ask him why my dad hustled us out of London in the middle of the night to visit him. He might know something about why my parents got murdered on the way home.'

I gape. 'You're flying out *tonight*?'

'Yeah.' He scratches a hand through his hair, steps over towards the bed. I see the mess of clothes, the backpack. Suddenly I get it. He's packing to leave. 'I was going to tell you. Call you. Or, you know . . .'

'Text.' I stand there, immobile. 'You were going to text me.'

'Yeah.' He can't quite meet my eyes.

I hug my arms around myself. He's leaving. Again. And he was going to text me about it. Just like last time.

And now I really am pissed off. Pissed off, and also – I don't want to think about this bit too hard – suddenly brought low. Did he figure out *nothing* from our disastrous trip to England? Did the last five weeks even bloody *happen*?

'So instead of *Going to UK with Walsh. Don't be mad*, you were going to say . . . what? *Gone to Bali. Have a nice life*?'

'No!' Mycroft dashes at his hair again. 'Rachel, it's not like the last time. Angela's coming with me. I've been wanting to tell you, but you're always at physio, or Mai's, or you're stuck at home on crutches, with your mum keeping guard—'

'So it's *my* fault that—'

'No, no, for god's sake, *listen*! I was going to say, it's not just you. I've been at work all the time too, or trying to piece together this . . . *shit*.'

He grabs a balled-up T-shirt from the mess of clothes on the bed, flings it at the desk. It hits the laptop screen, slides off, a sleeve sinking into one of the mould-experiment mugs lying on the floor.

I look at him – face drawn, thick eyebrows furrowed. He's being real with me. He's trying. It's just a collision of bad circumstances that has brought us to this point where I'm standing, bereft, in the room he's about to vacate.

'So . . . Bali.' My voice is croaky.

'Yeah.' He sighs, rubs his eyes with the heel of his hand. 'But I should be home in about five days. Then I'll be back, and you can say . . .' He stares into my eyes. 'You can say anything you want to say to me.'

I catch my breath. Five days. It's already been five weeks. What difference will another five days make? Maybe by then I'll have my head together about this. I might feel more solid. More brave.

'Okay.' I nod. 'Sure.'

'Great.' Mycroft's shoulders sag with relief. Then his eyes narrow. 'Hang on – do your parents know you're here?'

Oh *crap*. Real Life hits me over the back of the head with a giant hammer.

'No. Shit.' My panic must show in my face. 'I said I'd be home for dinner. God, I'd better go.'

'Yeah.' Mycroft nods. 'They'll tear strips off you.'

I take a step back, stumble on my sore leg, step forward again. 'Good luck with your trip.'

'Thanks,' Mycroft says.

43

I'm about to turn, then I realise: I can't leave like this. Not with this bare exchange of pleasantries. There's so much I want to say, only I'm out of time. But I need to start somewhere. We need to be kinder to each other. It's not an effort on my part – I *want* to be kind. Mycroft is, first and foremost, my friend, and it looks as if it's been a while since he was kind to himself.

I step towards him again. '*Eat*, okay? You should eat.'

He gives me his signature wonky grin. Then his grin disappears. 'I'll start eating if you'll start sleeping.'

My face falls. All my bravado floods away, and something thick and hoarse rolls in to take its place.

'I'm scared to,' I whisper. It sounds so raw, when I say it like that. I'm immediately embarrassed, like how I felt when Mai wiped the concealer from around my eyes, or after Harris saw me having a nightmare. But Mycroft is gazing at me, and I can't look away.

'Rachel,' he says, 'I'm so sorry.'

Then I do the thing I've wanted to do since the second I arrived. I push forward, fall against his chest, wrap my arms around his waist. I hug him, clinging on tight and desperate with my eyes closed.

It's been ages since I've touched him. He gasps and goes rigid in that first moment of contact. His body is warm, solid and real, if a bit bonier than I'm used to. I rub my cheek against his chest and make a small noise. I can't make my voice work, which is probably for the best: any louder and it would be a cry of anguish.

I feel his body soften. His hands settle gently, one on my shoulder, one on my back. He strokes me, these light tender strokes, as his face lowers onto the top of my head. His stubble catches on my hair.

I brace for the inevitable, and it doesn't take more than a moment: his arms curl around me. I revel in that initial contact. But I know it won't be long now, and I'm right – here it comes, as his arms circle and tighten around me, warming me up, keeping me in, squeezing me . . .

The knot tightens as my breathing starts to hitch, and then I'm sucking air at the feel of his arms holding me firm, holding me down—

I gasp and break away.

Mycroft looks at me, eyebrows snared together. 'Rachel—'

'I've gotta go,' I say, but I'm still hyperventilating from the hug, and my words are sobbed out. I hobble as fast as I can out his door, through the hall, out of the house, and out, and out . . .

I've got to get away. No one can hug me. No one. Not my parents, not my brother, not Mai . . . and not Mycroft. It's the nightmares, I *know* it's the nightmares, but I can't make them go away, I can't make them stop. I flee down Summoner Street, back to my house, and I wonder if maybe I'm going insane.

CHAPTER FOUR

Now we see what the meat is like inside, yes?

Four a.m. I'm quaking, covered in sweat.

I change my perspiration-soaked clothes in the dark, and have a little cry. Crying feels pointless, but it seems to release some of the tension. Or maybe I cry out of relief that it's over – until next time. There's always a next time.

Jesus, I'm so *tired* – every particle in my body is strung-out and exhausted. My knee aches. All my muscles are clenched. I lie in my cold bed, shivering, then I give up trying to get back to sleep. I turn on the lamp and grab my copy of *Australian First Aid*. I've got a St John's Ambulance class this morning – my certificate is up for a review – so I may as well study. The pictures of compound fractures and lacerations are gruesome, hardly ideal reading after a nightmare, but somehow I find them less confronting than the things my own brain can dream up.

Later, I go into the kitchen to make a cuppa. Mike is there, rubbing his hands through his hair and waiting for the kettle to boil. Harris must still be asleep.

'Hey, possum.' Mike nudges me as we crowd the bench together, positioning tea bags and mugs. 'Bloody hell, this house is freezing. One sec.'

Mike shuffles into the living room in his thick trackie pants and socks, turns on the big gas heater attached to the wall. By the time he gets back to the kitchen, I've made the tea.

'Good on ya.' He slurps from his mug, nods with his chin. 'Come stand in the warm spot with me.'

We stand in front of the heater, turning so the hot air hits our bums, the backs of our legs.

'Rachel, Rachel, Rachel . . .' Mike sighs and gives me the once-over. 'You look like hell, y'know.'

I sip my tea. 'It's been a bad week.'

'It's been kind of a bad life for the last month or so, hasn't it?'

Mike puts his arm lightly around my shoulders and gives me a gentle pat. He's figured out I don't respond too well to hugging at the moment. We stand leaning against each other in the backwash from the heater, like cattle huddling for warmth. I don't feel so frozen next to Mike's solid bulk. It's one of those moments when I love my brother more than life.

I breathe onto my tea. 'Tell me something nice. Is Alicia okay?'

'She's good.' Mike grins. 'Got an email last night. Said she's in Greece – she'll be home in three weeks.'

'God, that's great. She'll be back before you know it.'

'Yep. I've missed her like crazy. Tried not to be a sad sack in the emails, but it'll be bloody nice to have her home.' He glances at me. 'What about you, eh? When're you gonna come home?'

'What do you mean?'

'In here.' Mike moves his hand, taps the top of my head. 'Half your brain's still in London, I reckon.'

I clutch my mug in both hands, press the edge of it against my bottom lip.

Just say it. Just open your mouth and say it. Mike, I've been having these nightmares, and . . . they're getting worse—

But I don't get to say it, because Mum walks up the hall in her dressing gown and slippers. Her blonde bed-hair sticks up randomly, and her hands are hidden in her armpits against the cold.

I stiffen immediately, and focus on my tea. When I finally got home yesterday, the atmosphere was tense. Mike hadn't fore-warned Mum and Dad about Harris's arrival, but his presence was a distraction from the unmentionable argument. Mum kept looking at me sideways, like she was waiting for a private moment for us to talk. But I was feeling so sorrowful and listless after seeing Mycroft that I blew her off and went to bed.

Maybe Mum wants to apologise. I could apologise in return. Maybe we could both crash through the barriers we've put up between us. But I can't deal with it after another night of bad dreams. I'm exhausted and brittle, ready to snap.

'Morning,' Mum says. 'Did you two make a pot of tea to share, or were you only thinking short term?'

Mike shrugs. 'Nah, Mum, sorry. We just boiled the kettle.'

'Wonderful,' she sighs, and flip-flops her way to the kitchen.

We listen to her banging around in the cupboards, at the sink. Mike looks at me, and I look at Mike. Mornings are not Mum's forte.

I hand my mug to Mike, escape back to my room. If I can catch another hour's sleep before my first aid class, I might be able to make it through the day.

———

Low-hanging clouds give the city streets a surreal brightness as I look out the window of the tram on the way home from first aid. We spent most of class scribbling treatment notes. Fiona, the woman who teaches the St John Ambulance course, is a paramedic. Her short blonde hair reminds me of Patricia, the EMT who treated me in London. Fiona has the same calming manner, and answers all our questions smoothly.

We've already covered snakebite, heart attack, burns and broken bones. Today was compound fractures and penetrating wounds. I thought I'd be disturbed, seeing pictures that reminded me of what had happened to my fingers, but somehow I found it reassuring. We did the right thing in London – splinting my fingers with cardboard, that's exactly what you're supposed to do. Maybe I'm better at this medical stuff than I realise.

I sit in my seat, gnawing on a PowerBar and snatching glances at the other passengers. Two elderly ladies get on near ALDI, kick out the perfectly able-bodied boy slouching in the handicapped seat, and then talk together vigorously in what sounds like Serbian the whole way to my stop. I listen to the cadence of the language, the guttural consonants giving me chills, until it's time to press the button.

Mycroft's house feels quiet as I pass it on the way to mine. Just knowing he's not there is unsettling. Everything feels topsy-turvy.

Things at my house feel out of whack, too. Mike and Dad are at work, and Mum's running the taps in the bathroom. She might be having a shower after her shift, or preparing to leave, I honestly don't know. She and Dad have been playing some kind of Schedule-Sudoku to keep an eye on me.

I dump my satchel and wander through to the kitchen to put the kettle on. I'm half-expecting to see Harris lounging in the living room, watching daytime TV, but he's not there.

While I'm dunking my tea bag, I hear this rhythmic flicking sound coming from the backyard. Curiosity overwhelms my desire to huddle in bed, so I grab my hot mug and go out to investigate.

Of all the things I imagine I'll find, this isn't one of them.

Harris is skipping rope. He's wearing baggy trackie pants, a long-sleeved maroon T-shirt and a grey hoodie vest. He lands lightly on the balls of his feet, getting a bit of height on the jump.

I edge around the section of concrete path he's jumping on, until I reach an old stump. Then I perch myself on it and watch. Harris has thick socks paired with his runners, and he has gloves on, fingerless and a bit tattered. His movement is regular, even, practised. His hair is stringy and dark with sweat, his T-shirt pasted to his chest, drooping at the neckline. I can almost see the steam coming off him.

I raise my eyebrows at the skipping rope, sip my tea. 'Bit energetic for you, isn't it?'

Harris shakes his head at me as he skips, and his lips move silently. I realise he's counting.

So I wait. I watch Harris skip – it's hard not to, he's the only active thing in the backyard. Everything else is bedded down for winter: the garden plots, the compost heap. Dad's tools are in a pile over by the fence. A bare-rooted apricot tree sits in a tub of dirt, waiting for a weekend when Dad can plant it in the ground.

Harris skips for another twenty seconds, then does a little double-whip with the rope to finish.

'Not really,' he says. He's puffing, and I realise he's answering the question I put to him before. 'Keeps me fit. What happened – you get lazy in the city, sweetheart? You don't like being fit?'

'I like it fine, *Der-brain*.' I make a face at him, then look at my knee, stretched out in front. 'But it's not like I can do anything about it at the moment.'

Harris winds his skipping rope around one fist. 'You chopped wood in Five Mile. Went for walks. You could do stuff.'

'Like what?' My knee is throbbing now, stiffening in the cool air. I press my lips, rub the joint through layers of nylon brace, thermal leggings and denim. 'I've got limited movement in one leg and one hand. What exactly d'you imagine I could do?'

Harris shrugs. 'Good question.'

He slumps in a perspiring pile onto the ground beside me, grabs a water bottle resting near the stump. I notice that the punching bag he and Mike set up yesterday is still swaying gently under the eaves. If he's so breathless, the skipping must be the warm-down at the end of his workout.

Harris takes a long swig of water, smears his face against his sleeve and lifts his chin at my knee. 'You have an operation for that? Gonna have a scar?'

'Nah. No operation. I had one on my fingers though. They had to put wire in them to keep them straight. That'll leave a scar.'

Harris makes a face. 'Shit, it's a bit full on, isn't it?' He raises an eyebrow at me. 'I've got a scar. Better than that one on your fingers.'

'Where?'

'Here.' He pulls back the sleeve of his T-shirt and I see a jagged white line running up the outside of his forearm. Where it travels over his skin, no hair grows. 'Corrugated iron. When I was a kid.'

'Oh, I've got one of those.' I lean forward and tug up the hem of my left jeans leg, pull down the edge of my sock, to expose the bone on the outside of my ankle. 'There – not as good as your one, though.'

He pulls off one glove and shows me his hand. 'That's a roofing nail, about six years ago. Went straight through.'

'Jeez, you had a few prangs when you were younger.'

'Yeah.' Harris snorts and looks away. 'I guess.'

I point at another one on the back of his wrist, a perfectly round white mark, quite small. 'What's that one?'

'Can't remember.' Harris pulls his sleeve back down, yanks his glove on, covering the mark. 'Anyway, I've got one more. D'you wanna see?'

'Sure.'

He looks at me and grins. 'I've gotta take off my shirt a bit. Don't get carried away, all right?'

I roll my eyes. 'I think I'll cope. But you'll freeze—'

Too late. Harris has already pulled his hoodie and T-shirt up, just over his head, so his back and shoulders are exposed but the fabric is still covering his chest.

He angles his shoulder towards me. 'There, check that out. Dirt-bike accident. Came off near Furlough Creek Road, going about a million miles an hour, and copped the edge of the barbed-wire fence. Nice, huh?'

The twisting mark on his shoulder looks nasty, but I'm having trouble focusing on it because Harris's back is tanned and sleek, and the muscles under his T-shirt are not what I was expecting at all.

I thought he was just dicking around, play-boxing in the backyard when he was bored enough to give it a whirl, learning a few necessary skills for when he causes a ruckus at the pub on a Friday night. But I can see real muscle. Harris's back is developed in a way I know only happens when men work hard at a physical task for a long time. I can see the bulges at his trapezius when his shoulderblades flex. His waist is tapered, banded with muscle at the back and down either side of his spine.

It could be from his farm work or his job at the quarry . . . but I don't think so. I think Harris works out. A lot.

I don't remember Harris being this fit the last time I saw him – although that was at least a year ago. Since we met up again, Harris has been cloaked in winter clothes. God, he must be impressive in summer, in a singlet . . . I try to break my stare, refocus.

I never would have thought Harris could be disciplined enough to do something like this. It suggests that there's a controlled side of him, a side I've never seen.

And, y'know – the muscles. My god.

But I'm not going to give Harris the satisfaction of seeing me flustered.

'Yeah, I guess that's pretty good.' I clear my throat, pull up my own shirt sleeve. 'There you go. Not as impressive, but it's long.'

The silver slice down my arm *is* long – about thirty centimetres, from above my right elbow almost to the wrist. Harris pulls his clothes back over his head and grabs my arm to examine the neat scar close up.

'Shit, what *is* that? Looks like a—'

'Scalpel.' I shrug. 'Psycho guy with a scalpel.'

Harris stares at me. 'Bullshit.'

'No bull. And then we had to climb out of this lion pen . . .' I shake my head. 'Mycroft got mauled – that's a pretty cool scar, I can tell you.'

I blush after I've said it, because it seems almost rude to mention Mycroft. I feel as if I'm pointing a big neon sign at myself – *Boyfriend! Has a Boyfriend!!* – and that's not what I was intending at all.

Harris glances away, but he's still holding my arm when a holler spills out of the house.

'*RACHEL!*'

I jerk, look up. 'That's Mum.'

Harris's eyebrows lift as he releases me. 'She sounds kind of . . .'

Freaked, I think might be the word he's after, which perfectly describes the look on Mum's face when she appears in the backyard, damp hair curling and a tea-towel clutched in one hand.

'Rachel, there you are.' Her lips have gone chalky and she's holding the cordless phone. 'Detective Pickup is on his way. There's been a death.'

———

'Thank you for agreeing to come, Mrs Watts,' Detective Senior Sergeant Vincent Pickup says. 'This case has been playing on my mind, and I was in the area. I figured it was simplest just to bring Rachel to headquarters and have a chat.'

Pickup has said it's 'no one close' but not why he wants to see me. His glowering gaze in the rear-view darts between me and Mum. Pickup always looks serious – it's his default position – but now, with his compulsory detective's suit paired with a new, rather severe, orange buzzcut, the effect is particularly strong.

'That's all right, Detective,' Mum replies.

She and I are sitting at a careful distance from one another on the back seat of Pickup's unmarked sedan. This resolute, quiet tone coming from her is a total turnabout. When Mum talks to *me*, she's either scathing or screeching. Maybe I'm hyper-sensitive, but I'm suddenly aware of every detail about her, even her jeans, bleached pale blue from over-washing just like mine.

'We could've waited for Mike to get home,' I say quietly. 'He's done this before.'

'You're my daughter.' Mum looks at her hands. 'I should be with you.'

I don't have any comeback. Maybe Mum only came from this sense of obligation, not because she really wants to help. But Dad has said many times that simply isn't true. It just *feels* true, with Mum sitting stiffly beside me in the stuffy car.

'A death. My god,' Mum says in an undertone. The frown lines on her forehead are dark grooves. 'I honestly don't know how you deal with this all the time.'

A cold whip plays out from my stomach, down my legs, snap-freezing my toes. Despite what Pickup said, a worm of anxiety burrows into me: this new case might involve one of my friends. Or Mycroft.

I bite my lip. 'It's not as though I like it. You just . . . You just do it. And try not to think about it.'

'And Mycroft? He seems to enjoy dwelling on these sorts of things.'

I sigh. 'He doesn't *enjoy* it, Mum. He's a scientist. It's different.'

How can I explain Mycroft's state of mind to my mother? She has no frame of reference. To her, death is all about grieving and lamentation. How can I explain that to Mycroft, and Professor Walsh, and other scientists like them, a human body is the house of the spirit, a puzzle but also an answer?

I look over at my mother's anxious face. Confusion keeps my mouth closed, stoppers up the need to ask her why she's come along, why she's being civil to me. It bothers me that we've been thrown together here in the back seat of a police car when we haven't spoken about the argument, about the slap. I think it might bother her too.

'I'm sure it'll be okay,' I blurt.

'I don't know how a dead body can be *okay*,' Mum says. A bit of her fire seems to be returning.

I meant us. I swallow. 'I meant . . . y'know. It's not anyone in the family.'

She chews her lip for a moment. 'It's *someone's* family.' She looks out the window, her voice very level. 'Someone will be crying tonight.'

At the station, Pickup gets us through the lobby and up to an interview room in short order. As soon as he's got us arranged around the laminex tabletop and switched on the recorder, his voice goes deep and gruff.

'Right. Miss Watts, I've brought you here because the body of a young man was discovered in a street over in Croydon. Although the victim doesn't appear to have any connection to you, there are elements of the case that lead me to believe that . . .' He stops, frowns. 'Look, I think it might be better if you just see the photos.'

Pickup fumbles open a gold A4 envelope on the table near his elbow. The envelope is exactly like the one Mycroft used to hold the photos of Dave Washburn that he showed me in Mai's room one evening in March.

Suddenly I'm punched in the gut by a powerful sense of foreboding. I don't want to be here. I don't want to view these photos. Something bad is going to happen, has happened already. But before I can voice any objections, Pickup has slid a number of face-down glossy sheets out of the envelope.

He looks at me gravely. 'I'm sorry, Rachel. You might find these photos distressing.'

My hands ball together under the table. I agreed to come and now momentum has carried me to this point, and I can't stop this train. It's too late for objections. I swallow and nod.

Pickup turns over the first photo.

My gasp is loud in the quiet interview room.

The photo is a scene-of-crime shot. SOCO must have taken it. In the photo, a boy has his face turned at an angle. His jaw and cheekbones stand out sharply, and his eyes are open, staring. They look at nothing, or maybe everything, in that way dead people's eyes do.

The boy's hair is a cloud of dark brown curls.

Pickup lays another photo over the first. The same boy. He looks about eighteen, nineteen, and he's lying on something textured, dark. His collarbones are defined above the zip of his hoodie – I can see the elegant turn of his long neck. His mouth is open, as if he's just about to speak, and his face is pale, waxy, unreal. He has a leaf in his hair.

I have to blink sharply. My breathing sounds ragged and harsh in the interview room, but I can't control it.

Pickup lays down three more photos, and the scene is the same every time. A dead boy with dark curly hair. In some of the wider shots, a stain oozes out from beneath his head, haloing him in red. He could be a figure in a medieval religious icon: a blood angel.

My left hand reaches out automatically for the photos. I start sliding them around, looking. Looking for something I won't find. I want to use both hands, but I can't – Mum has my other hand clasped tightly in her own.

'It's . . .' I scrabble the photos together. 'He's not . . .' I make a breathless noise, as though I'm in pain. 'It's not him.'

The room swims, like I'm underwater. Suddenly I wonder if I'm asleep. Maybe this is a new chapter of the same nightmare . . . But my mother's hand feels solid. I'm solid, I'm sure of it. This is real. I look up at the ceiling, the only sane view in the world.

'No,' Pickup says softly. 'It's not him. Rachel, you know it's not him.'

My bark of laughter comes out cracked and awful. 'Oh god.'

'Rachel—' Mum says.

'Right.' I close my eyes tight for one second, open them again. I can't lose it in this room. I will not do that. I look back at Pickup. 'Okay.'

'I'm going to put these away,' Pickup says, reaching towards the glossies.

'*No.*' I've put my hand on his. I pull it back. 'Let me . . . Let me look again.'

So I look. The resemblance is striking, but it's not Mycroft. This boy with the dark curly hair, the one who is dead . . . He has the same long body as my boyfriend, the same alt-street look to his clothes, the same high cheekbones. But his eyes are hazel, not blue. And his skin is darker, olive-toned. His nose is bigger. Now I see it, I see it everywhere: how the resemblance is distinct, but only superficial.

Once my brain has reassured me that this is true, I feel a great settling of my shoulders. Relief thickens within me – thank god, thank god. But it's like a poison, seasoned with guilt. Mum was the one who said it: this boy may not be my boy, he may not be my family, but he's someone's. *Someone will be crying tonight.*

It's that awareness that makes me clutch the table, makes my voice strained but level. 'So it was the resemblance to Mycroft that made you contact me?'

'There were a few other things too,' Pickup says cryptically. 'You really don't know this boy?'

I shake my head.

Pickup frowns. 'You should understand that this is not officially my case. It's not being investigated as a homicide.'

'*Not* a homicide?'

'No. The body was found at the foot of a two-storey apartment building, below the balcony of a flat for let. The scene was . . .' He hesitates. 'It appears very much like this poor lad fell to his death. But when I read the case notes a few things sprang out.'

'Like what?'

Pickup starts shuffling the photos together. I'm glad I don't have to look at them anymore, but he's not meeting my eyes.

'*Detective?*'

'The body was found in Croydon,' Pickup says, and I nod impatiently.

'Yeah, I know that, you told me—'

'In Sherlock Road.'

I freeze. 'Right.'

'There was one more thing.' Pickup holds my gaze. 'He has a number of injuries from the fall. But there are also signs of a recent beating, including broken ribs. Mycroft suffered broken ribs in London, didn't he? On the left side?'

'Yes.' When the blood leeches out of my cheeks, I actually feel it – a drawing, tingling sensation under my skin. My hands go up to shutter my face. Behind my eyelids is nothing but blackness.

'Given the circumstances, I thought I'd better get you down here to see if you had any ideas about how he died, apart from the obvious one.'

'What are you saying?' Mum asks Pickup quietly.

I have to get it together. This might not be Wild. This might not be anything. It's not even a homicide investigation.

I drag my hands down, focus on Pickup. 'What was the COD?'

Pickup cocks an eyebrow at me. 'Know all the lingo now, do you?'

'I *date* a forensic scientist.' I try to be more cooperative. 'Please just tell me what the cause of death was.'

'He died from the fall.'

'Did anybody hear anything? See anything?'

'They did. A Mrs . . .' Pickup retrieves his police notebook from his jacket pocket, flicks pages. '. . . McShanagh heard a scream. Too scared to go out and check, called the police, end of story. Body was found under bushes below the building, near the top of the street.'

The leaf tangled in the boy's curls . . . I feel suddenly, wrenchingly sick. The sensation of iron bars around my lungs is claustrophobic – I focus on my breathing. Breathe in, breathe out. Pickup said 'obvious', but nothing is obvious. Paranoia is not my friend. I'm panicking because . . . shit, because I'm stressed, and tired, and every shadow is Wild-shaped to me now. Mum and Pickup are looking at me weirdly.

'Right.' With an effort, I keep my breaths even, smooth my palms down the sides of my legs. I don't know how long I'll be able to sustain the controlled facade, but I'd better give it a go, for Mum's sake at least. 'Has Professor Walsh come back with anything?'

Pickup shakes his head. 'Another pathologist did the examination, and it's still too early for results.'

Mum is tugging on my hand. 'Rachel, what does he mean? About the obvious reason?'

She looks anxious, frightened, and a bit green. I hardly know what to say, because I haven't explained everything about what happened in England.

No – it's not that I didn't explain. I lied. Mum only knows the official line, that Mycroft and I were involved in a car accident.

Dad and Mike backed me up – in fact, it was their idea to keep the truth from Mum, because they thought she'd freak out. I've had plenty of moments when I've regretted that decision, but none of them were as pressing as right now.

But how can I tell her? At this moment, it just seems too hard and confusing and mean to lump it all on her, all the—

'Rachel and James were involved in a police case in England.' Pickup speaks calmly and with rehearsed brevity. He must be used to giving the condensed version of events to people. 'One of the persons of interest in that case is still at large. Up to this point, we've believed that the geographical distance made the situation controlled and safe—'

'But now this poor boy is dead, maybe pushed out of a building, and you're not so sure.' Anger gives Mum's words an unsanded edge.

Pickup says nothing.

'So what are you going to do to keep my daughter out of harm's way?'

'Mrs Watts—'

'You don't really have anything, do you?' I butt in. 'I mean, it could be a genuine accident. Some random boy, who happens to look a lot like Mycroft, has tripped and fallen—'

Pickup sighs. 'His name is Benjamin Tonna. He was a nineteen-year-old street prostitute from St Kilda. We've found enough money in his wallet to suggest that he was paid to go with someone. He's a long way from home, and this is the only Sherlock Road in Melbourne.'

My stomach rises again, and I have to swallow it down. This boy, this poor sad boy, was lured to this particular street to die. But this is not my boy, not my street. Nightmares in the dark, and

61

the sound of Serbian on the tram, and jumping at loud noises . . . This is not who I am. This is not who I want to be.

When my voice comes out it sounds thin, as though I'm talking from high altitude. 'It doesn't mean anything conclusively, though, right? It could be a coincidence, or a—'

'Rachel, listen to me.' Pickup looks at me intently. 'The officer on this case is arguing for a ruling of death by misadventure. But I think it requires further investigation. It's not my show, but I'm trying to get people to pay attention. I don't believe this was a random act. From where I'm sitting, this looks like a carefully stage-managed event.'

'But you don't think Mycroft's in danger?' I blurt out. I have to say it quickly, or I'd be too scared to say it.

'I think Mycroft is overseas with his aunt. And I think this murder has happened here, in Melbourne.'

There – he used the word *murder*. Whatever the other officers on this case might think, it's clear that Pickup believes he should be investigating this as an official homicide.

Pickup sits back stiffly in his chair, rubs a rough-knuckled hand through his buzzcut. His expression is faintly surprised, as though he's not used to the shortness of it yet.

'Look, I don't know if there's a danger.' He looks at me, shakes his head as if he's disagreeing with himself. 'I can't speak with the authority of the department, but I'm going to advise you to keep yourself safe. Stay close to home. I'll talk to Mycroft too, as soon as he gets back.'

I speak softly. 'Detective, there's nothing concrete, no evidence—'

'*Yet.*' Pickup grinds it out. 'There's no evidence *yet*. Rachel, don't be foolhardy about this. Take precautions. Don't go off on your own, don't interact with people you're unfamiliar with.'

'Is that all you're going to do?' Mum grips my hand tightly and glares at Pickup across the table. 'Some crazy person could be running around Melbourne, and you're just telling her to watch her back?'

'Mrs Watts, I'm not authorised to do anything else. A boy has died. He bears a superficial resemblance to Rachel's boyfriend. His injuries are similar to ones that Mycroft experienced in England. That is all we have. And that is all we are able to do, until something else happens.'

'You mean, until Rachel gets murdered herself?'

Mum frowns. Pickup frowns. They play duelling eyebrows for a good five seconds.

I look away from both of them. My skin feels tissue-paper thin. 'I want to go home.'

Pickup puts all the photos away in their envelope. He sighs out his nose, scrapes his chair back to rise. 'Thank you for your time. I'll arrange a car to return you to Summoner Street.'

———

I'm sitting out in the back garden, in the half-dark, with Mike and Harris. We're grouped around the old tree stump, in the little 'easy corner' that Dad has thrown together as an organic outgrowth of his general gardening projects. The wide flat stump is edged under a tree, serving as a coffee table of sorts, surrounded by a collection of things to sit on: a milk crate, an ancient vinyl armchair, a fold-out camping stool, a bright pink plastic lounger that Dad has repurposed from someone else's hard-rubbish pile.

I'm slumped back in the armchair, Mike wriggles on the milk crate, Harris lounges. We're rugged up against the cold. It's just after dinner, which I couldn't eat, and there's a mug of tea in my hands – Mike said I looked like I needed something warming. I sit and watch the vegetable beds, snug in their winter coverings, through the clouds of steam rising from my mug.

'So, according to Mum, that's it?' Mike sips his own tea. 'You're just supposed to be "alert not alarmed" and hope this Wild guy doesn't come for you?'

'Detective Pickup said he's going to contact the Scotland Yard police we worked with in England, look into it more,' I say. My injured fingers ache in the cold. 'Mike, please don't make this into a thing. We don't know it's Wild. The other officers don't even think it's a murder.'

'Bloody pathetic.' Harris sneers towards some unfixed point in the back garden.

'Well, it's not like there are any real connections.'

Mike's mouth tightens. 'Jesus, what do they need? A big sign painted in blood saying *Rachel Watts, I'm coming to get you*?'

'Mike—'

'Don't tell me not to get uptight about this, Rachel. I'm uptight, okay? Wear it.' He looks at me, shakes his head. 'I don't know why you're not more stressed.'

I nearly snap back, but snapping would certainly qualify as a symptom of being stressed, so I bite my lip instead.

'I don't think this Wild bloke is gonna come for her,' Harris says suddenly.

Mike stares at him. 'What?'

'Think about it.' Harris is wearing a windbreaker of Mike's, and he's leaning back in the lounger in his jeans, booted ankles crossed. 'This guy's dead, who Rachel said looks a bit like her boyfriend. It's all set up like a scene from a movie – the look of the guy, the broken ribs, the name of the street. If this is Wild, he's just stirring. Playing with her.'

Mike glares at Harris. 'It's not a bloody *game*.'

It's exactly what I said to Mycroft in the plane on the way back from England. The memory kicks off a hollow ache beneath my ribs.

'Sure it is,' Harris cuts back. 'Think about it. Whoever did this is being clever. If there'd been something really smack-in-the-face obvious, there'd be a paddy wagon stationed out your front door before you could say "death threat".'

'There are no *death threats*,' I insist. 'There's nothing. Don't beat this up into some paranoid delusion, Harris.'

'*I'm* beating it up into a paranoid delusion,' Mike says. His bottom lip juts grimly as he frowns at Harris. 'Train her up. Do it.'

'Mate . . .' Harris's surfer hair falls over his face as he shakes his head.

'Teach her. Go on, I know you've got enough of that self-defence stuff from Westie to—'

'Teach me what?' I clutch at my mug, searching between them.

'*Harris*,' Mike says.

Harris exhales deeply. Looks straight at me.

'I can teach you some self-defence moves. If you want me to. It's not gonna make you kick-arse or anything, but it might help.' He holds my gaze, his eyes glowing emerald in the dim light. 'It might help with lots of things.'

I don't need to be a mind-reader to know what he's referring to. And I don't want the nightmare issue to spill out now – Mike'll be pissed that Harris knew about it before he did.

'Sure.' I plonk my mug in the dirt, spread my hands. 'Teach me self-defence. Knock yourself out.'

'All right,' Harris says quietly. 'But it won't be bullshit karate moves, okay? It's just plain street fighting. Nothing fancy.'

'Sounds perfect,' I grate out.

'It can't hurt,' Mike says, and I soften for a moment. Like he said, it can't hurt. And maybe it'll make Mike feel better, if nothing else.

'This guy, Wild . . .' Harris says. 'He's really got you goosed, yeah?'

I look away. Mycroft may have been right about Wild all along. I try to think about it in those terms. 'Wild likes the game. He likes moving the pieces around. It's how he gets his jollies.'

'So how is he moving *you* around, d'you reckon?'

I remember my reaction when Pickup showed me the photos of Benjamin Tonna – my clenched fists, my tight breathing, my sense of panic. I swallow hard. 'He's trying to upset me. Make me lose concentration.'

'That's right.'

I tuck my fingers into my armpits, look at Harris. 'It's working.'

And suddenly I'm glad Mycroft's not here. Because where my first instinct is to shrink away from all this, his is to throw himself in. He'd be out, walking down back streets and hunting for clues, before I could blink. And I don't want him to engage with this, I don't want him to engage with any of it.

It's exactly what Wild would want.

CHAPTER FIVE

'Jesus. Not much of a good-morning smile. You okay?'

I don't look up from my coffee to see Harris's expression. 'Tell me you don't actually need me to answer.'

'Another bad night, eh?'

I shudder. I lost track of how many times I woke up last night. My body is sore, as if I've been running in my sleep, the way dogs do.

'You need something to snap you out of it.' Harris, already dressed in trackies and a long-sleeved T-shirt, pours himself a cup from the coffee pot then adds dolloping spoonfuls of sugar to the blackness. 'Training starts now. Go get your kit on.'

'Harris, it's barely seven.' Sleeplessness has leached the colour out of my voice.

'No time like the present, grasshopper. Kit. Now.'

Because I agreed to this, for some fool reason, and because I don't have the energy to argue, I drag myself away from the kitchen table. I throw on my clothes; splashing water on my face in the bathroom is what I've got in place of alertness.

The backyard is still gloomy. Harris is already making a patter on the concrete as he jumps up and down on the balls of his feet. His hoodie has the sleeves ripped off, and his runners are so old they're held together with electrical tape. He chafes his hands for warmth, shakes his arms out, clasps his fists down behind his back until his shoulder joints pop. His breath comes out foggy. 'Ready for a bit of a tussle, are ya?'

'No.' I plop down on the stump. What I'd like to do is go back to bed. But I know I'd only wake up sweating again. 'Harris, honestly, I feel rooted. If Wild tapped me on the shoulder right now and said he was going to kill me, I'd cheer him on.'

Harris walks closer. 'Too bad. Cos apparently it's my job to make sure that doesn't happen. Stand up.'

'Why?'

He rolls his eyes. 'Jesus, I dunno – why do you have to be so snippy every time you open your mouth? Just stand up.'

I make a face, but decide that for once I won't fight with him, just to prove him wrong. With a lot of bad grace, I push off the stump and stand. 'Now what?'

'Make a fist.' He holds his hands up to demonstrate.

'I can't.' I take off my finger splints and ball my hands. My right hand curls up completely. The fingers of my left hand only go halfway before they hurt.

Harris nods. 'Okay, you need support. Hold still.'

He leans for the duffle bag on the ground, pulls the skipping rope out of the way, and comes back up with a roll of sports tape.

'Flatten your fingers out.' He examines my bad hand with a frown, then tears off a piece of sports tape with his teeth, wraps it firmly around my fingers. Rips off two more lengths of tape, winds them carefully. Where he touches my palm and wrist, his grip is warm, and a bit sweaty. 'There – try that.'

Securely bound in sports tape, my sore fingers feel stronger. I still can't make a fist, but they're firmer, more supported.

'That feels . . . better,' I say.

'Good.' He nods. 'Now take a swing at me.'

'What?'

He steps back a pace. 'Take a swing. Not with your left hand – hold that up, defensive. Keep your elbow tucked. That's it. Now belt me with your right.'

Feeling completely weird, I do it – I wind up and try to punch him. He pulls his head back easily, and my fist goes wide.

'That's okay,' he says, 'but you're not wailing at me. You're trying to hit me. Here, right in the chops.'

I swing again, feeling stupid. This punch feels more controlled, but it still misses.

'Not bad.' Harris taps his chin. 'Gotta get me right here, though. Or here, on the nose. What did Mike teach you about punching?'

'Just . . . make a fist, aim for the nose, don't bruise your knuckles.' I think. 'And if you're gonna kick, go for the balls.'

Harris nods. 'Yeah, well, that's all sound. But there's a bit of technique to a good punch. Lemme show you.'

He walks me over to the punching bag under the eaves and stands me in front of it. His hands are businesslike, economical; firm, brief touches at my waist and shoulders that angle me correctly. There's none of the jokey sleazeball talk that's his usual trademark: he's like another person when he's focused this way.

'Right,' he says. 'See the dot? That's roughly eye-height for me. So aim for that, or just below it.'

'What am I supposed to do with this?' I wobble my left hand. 'Just stick it up in front of my face?'

'Yep.' Harris nods. 'Not your hand, though – your forearm. Keep your elbow in. Now punch.'

I wind back and punch. My right fist *thonks* into the hard-stuffed bag, the impact jarring my wrist, surprising as a yabbie bite. But the leather makes a satisfying creak.

Harris nods. 'Good. But brace your wrist, and don't swing out. It should come from your shoulder – here.' He taps me on the right shoulderblade. 'And then it goes straight forward – bang. Try again.'

I punch the bag under Harris's instruction, enjoying the feeling of give when my fist pummels in hard. When my right arm starts to ache, and my left arm gets tired from being lifted up in the air, Harris shows me something new.

'Check this out. You can do this with your left arm.'

He steps in smoothly and delivers an elbow strike to the bag, like he's done this many times before. Then he steps back and pushes me forward.

'Okay, brace your left hand with your right, otherwise you'll feel it in your fingers. That's it. Don't use the point of your elbow – that's a great way to get a broken elbow. It's your forearm that does the connecting, and your shoulder that provides the swing.' He watches me deliver another elbow strike to the bag, starts nodding. 'Yeah, that's good. Do it again.'

I practise it a dozen more times. Harris gives pointers on swing, bracing, how to bend a little for more power, where to put my feet. I try a few combinations of punching and striking. For the first time in weeks, I'm doing something that makes me feel strong.

'That's good,' Harris says. 'You're really giving it heaps.'

I steady myself, breathing hard. 'I'm imagining it's Wild's head. It's very motivating.'

Harris sobers. 'Ready to give a bit of your own back, huh?'

'Sometimes.' I swallow. 'Other times I just feel panicked. Terrified. And then the rest of the time I'm so lethargic I can hardly move. Being scared all the time is exhausting.'

My cheeks go hot suddenly. What am I doing? I never talk about this stuff to anyone, and now I'm talking to Harris?

But Harris doesn't seem to notice my embarrassment. He nods at the bag.

'Well, this should help. Exercising gives you more energy. Okay, let's try something else.' He pushes past the bag, backs me up to a level area of dirt just off the garden path. 'A few grappling moves.'

'What's that?'

Harris's lips twist into a grimace. 'Easier to do a demo.'

Suddenly he steps in, right in my face. He grabs me by the shoulders with both hands – the fabric of my thermal shirt bunches in his grip.

I jerk back automatically, way out of my comfort zone. 'Hey—'

He tugs me nearer. Now we've gone from comfort zone to Twilight Zone.

My hands push against his chest. 'Harris—'

His breath puffs warm on my face. 'Here's me, I've just grabbed you. I'm a much bigger, heavier opponent, and we're in close contact.'

Too close, I think. I could count his freckles from here. Harris smells of sweat and, oddly enough, grapefruit-scented shampoo from our bathroom. His nearness paralyses me for a second. Then I break the spell, shoving against the corral of his arms, wriggling my shoulders to release his grip.

71

'Harris, this isn't *funny*—'

'It's not supposed to be.' He stands, impassive. 'How's that wriggling thing working for you?'

I grit my teeth. Harris's arms are all sinew and solid muscle – it's like bashing my forearms against two marble pillars. I struggle, but he pulls me right against him. Now I'm looking into his eyes at a scarily intimate distance. Brown flecks stand out in their green depths, and his eyelashes are long as a young calf's.

'Come on, Rachel.' He's not even breathing hard. 'You can do better than this.'

'I *can't*. You're too close—'

'That's right,' he says. 'I've got you wrapped up around the torso and shoulders. Your arms are no good. Consider your other options.'

I think for a second, then I kick him in the shins.

'Ow,' he says. But he's still holding me.

I kick him again, harder.

'Now you're getting it.'

Suddenly he releases me. I've been pulling so hard against him that when he lets me go, I stumble back. He snags my elbow with one hand, so I don't fall on my arse in the shrubbery.

'Congratulations – you've got legs,' he says. 'Go for the shins, the instep, or if you're in the mood, just knee them straight in the balls.'

I yank my elbow away. '*Right.*'

'You're also free up top. Give them a nice Liverpool kiss, just here.' He rubs a spot between his eyebrows. 'That'll make their eyes water. But it hurts, so I usually only do it as a last resort. Wanna try again?'

'*No.*'

'Cranky, are we? Well, that'll warm you up.'

My face is tight – I *am* angry. I know this stuff. I used some of it on Paul when he attacked me in the Bodleian Library. My instincts were good then, so why didn't I just go for it when Harris first grabbed me?

I guess . . . part of me froze up. Well, that's bloody stupid. I've got to get beyond that, I've got to unfreeze. If this was a real struggle, I'd lose.

I exhale. 'Okay. Fine. Again.'

We go through it three more times, and each time my responses get stronger, faster. I learn how to compensate for my sore hand, my leg. But the feel of Harris holding me is still a shock, every time.

By the time we exhaust all the retaliatory options, the yard is starting to steam as the sun hits the frost. I'm steaming too, with a mix of anger and exhaustion and tension.

Harris seems indefatigable. 'So that's what you do if they come at you head-on. But they might try to grab you from behind.'

He skirts around me, stands at my back. I don't like it. A cold prickle begins low in my spine.

'Harris, I don't—'

'Okay, usually if someone gets behind you, they'll try to grab you like this.'

He puts his arms around me. My back is suddenly pulled hard against Harris's chest; his arms lock around my upper shoulders, around my ribs.

I draw a fast, gulping breath.

'Now, what you can . . .'

His voice fades out. A light-headed feeling suddenly invades my whole body, my head. Gasping, I scrabble at his forearms, but they're like iron bands.

'Stop.' My voice wheezes as Harris's arms squeeze tight. 'No—' *Stop.*

But I don't know if I've said it out loud. I have passed into another country. I'm being held tight, held down. Everything is two-dimensional, and I am flattening out like paper – my chest compressed, my breathing tight and laboured. Monochrome sparks swarm in my eyes. A dry, keening cry builds in my throat, then something inside me goes into shutdown. I start thrashing, making weird animal sounds – whining, yelping – and I'm gonna be sick, and I can't—

The pressure is suddenly gone. Harris is in front of me, his hands on my shoulders. '*Rachel?*'

I bat at him and he releases me – I tear away, stumble over to the tree stump, my vision white. Leaning on jelly arms, I fight the urge to dry-retch.

'Ah, Jesus . . .' Harris says.

I lean on the stump. A strong bitter taste has flooded my mouth, like acid reflux. I spit and spit, trying to get rid of it. I can't speak yet.

Harris hovers next to me. 'Is this about the nightmares?'

'It's . . . related.' I've finally recovered my breath, but my voice comes out harsh.

I wipe my mouth on my sleeve, run a trembling hand through my hair. Like an old windsock buffeted in a storm, I'm deflated now. When I push up to stand straight, I have to grip Harris's proffered arm so I don't keel over.

'I didn't . . . Mate, I'm sorry.' Harris sounds mortified. 'I'm a dickhead. I didn't know it was like that.'

God – I've just lost the plot, big time. Blood rushes up into my face. The embarrassment makes me want to cry. 'It's fine.'

'No, it's *not*. Don't say that.' Harris tilts my chin up, brushes my hair out of my face gently. 'Nobody should ever have to say that.'

I turn my head away. 'When did I get so fucking *helpless*?'

'Rachel . . .'

'I used to be the tough girl—'

'You *are* the tough girl.'

'I used to . . .' My hands spasm as I look blindly around the garden. 'Oh god, d'you remember? When those blokes from Parilla were rustling stock all over the district, I stayed up all bloody night in the back paddock—'

'I remember,' Harris says. 'You fired the rifle over their heads, didn't you? Your dad bragged about it in the pub for a year.'

'I'm so fucking *sick to death* of being scared all the time!' I scuff my face on my sleeve.

Harris pats my shoulder gently. 'It'll be okay, Rachel.'

'I *hate* this. I *hate* it.'

'I know, mate.'

I wipe my face again. Maybe it's time to stop crying and *do* something. Something to get myself right. Something to prepare for what might be coming.

'We should try it again.' I say it quickly, forcefully, even though my throat is still clogged.

'What?' Harris squints. 'Rachel, slow down. You almost chucked your guts after one hold.'

'I know.' I adjust my knee brace under my trackies, hands shaking. 'And that's why we should do it again. I want to learn how to get out of it.'

'Well . . . okay.' Harris licks his lips. His shoulders straighten. 'But if you start freaking out again, you gotta say something, yeah? Cos I'm gonna be behind you and I can't see your face.'

I look at Dad's garden beds and say the first thing that pops into my head. 'Marigolds.'

'*Marigolds?* That's the code word?'

'Yeah.'

Harris shrugs. 'Okay, if it feels like too much, say *marigolds* and I'll let go.'

I stand in place. As Harris edges up quietly behind me, I get that uneasy feeling again.

Harris shifts, and now he's so close that his chest is against my back. I fight the urge to jump. The sweaty heat of his body seeps through my shirt layers, into my shoulderblades. My senses scramble to high alert.

'How's that?'

His breath is right at my ear, and I shiver. 'Weird.'

But I'm not sure whether the weirdness is from fear, or from the feeling of Harris's warm, muscled body tucked against mine. The only boy who's ever come this close to me before is Mycroft. I swallow, try to force the thought away.

'I'm gonna start slow, all right?'

Harris's hands settle on the top of my shoulders. The sensation is discomforting. I try to get a handle on it. But the feeling is too fresh, and I start breathing in that watery way again. 'Okay, marigolds, marigolds—'

I break forward before steadying. I *have* to learn this, I have to train myself to react differently. A boy is dead, and Wild is out there. I take a breath and step back.

'Again.'

'Rachel, if you're not ready—'

'*Again.*' I blow out a breath, wait.

A moment later his hands grip my shoulders. They're warm, only a little heavy, and I can feel each of his fingers. Harris's chest is firm against me. My body tenses, but I close my eyes and breathe through it. In, out. Nice and slow.

The pressure on my shoulders increases. I imagine exhaling the fear and panic like a noxious black cloud. Harris starts moving his hands. His left arm slides around my waist. I twitch automatically, but it's okay – his arm is just there, solid, warm, keeping me grounded. I breathe and breathe.

Harris slides his other arm around the top of my chest, near my collarbones. He squeezes gently. I have to suck back my reaction. It's right there, on the tip of my tongue – *marigolds*. I can say it if I need to. But I force myself to continue to the next few seconds, and the next.

I don't know how long we stand there – me, frozen in position and shaking like a leaf, and Harris, snug against my back with his arms wrapped around my upper body. His face is tucked behind my ear, and his left hand smooths my waist, like you'd gentle a spooking horse.

After what seems like years, Harris clears his throat quietly. 'Rachel . . .'

'It's okay.' Eyes closed, I have to focus to even gasp this out. 'It's working.'

'Awesome.' His words sound thick and breathless, like he's the one hyperventilating. 'I think . . . I'm gonna let you go now.'

'Oh.' My eyes open. The sun is glaring-bright as the garden comes back into view. A myna bird is pecking at the straw covering the seed beds. 'Okay.'

Harris's arms slide away, then his body heat, his presence, is gone. It's almost as disorienting as the initial contact. I stumble against him.

'Crap, sorry.' My whole body feels stiff and strangely placed.

Harris holds my elbow to steady me. 'That's, um, a good start. Probably enough for today?'

'Yeah.' I sound a bit odd, but actually I'm elated. I did it. I actually did it. Harris held me, and I didn't panic.

'You're still a way off fighting back.' Harris's eyes are large in his flushed face.

'But I didn't flip.' I laugh, still breathless. 'It's progress.'

'Baby steps, yeah?'

'Harris, thank you.' I put a hand on his. 'Really. I know Mike twisted your arm to train me, but this . . . it means a lot.'

Harris lets me go, steps back to get his training bag. 'You don't need to thank me. It's just the right thing to do.'

Is he *blushing*? But that can't be right. So far as I know, Harris has never learnt how.

I step closer, pluck at his hoodie. 'How do you know all this stuff? The self-defence stuff, and the grappling . . .'

'Told you. Westie – from the quarry – he got me into it.' He shoves his skipping rope and sports tape back into his bag. I can't see his eyes, and for a second, I feel like I don't know him.

'What, you got sick of not holding your own at the pub?' I say it lightly, but Harris turns back and frowns.

'Yeah.' He snorts, flicking his head to get his hair out of his way. 'At the pub. Anyway, the lesson's over. More advice from the master later. Now, the master is hungry. You gonna make me breakfast or what?'

I squint at him. 'When did that become part of the deal?'

'Right this second. Bacon, eggs, hot Milo – the works.'

'You want me to cook you breakfast,' I say, flatly.

'Bloody oath. Fair trade, I reckon. Isn't that what you city folk are always going on about? Fair trade, homegrown, low food miles . . .'

I sigh. It's low food miles to walk into the kitchen anyway. 'Just tell me you're gonna help with the washing up.'

'We'll discuss that later.' He hoists his bag onto his shoulder. 'Breakfast, woman! Get to it!'

'I'm not your bloody "woman", Harris!' I shove on his arm as he barrels past me for the kitchen.

Over breakfast, Harris complains that his eggs aren't organic and offers to share a shower with me to conserve hot water. I might have made progress with the hugging thing, but as far as understanding Harris goes, I'm back where I started. The next few days will be hard work – and I don't just mean the training.

———

Everything looks different. During my slow drift up to consciousness, I wonder why. Sunlight spills over my chair, my study desk, the clothes scattered here and there – god, my room is a complete tip.

Then I figure out what the difference is. It's not dark. It's morning – hence the sun. If I can see the sun, then it's past dawn. I snake a hand out to grab my phone and check the time.

Eight-eighteen.

I've slept all night again. Unbelievable.

That's three nights in a row. I feel ... refreshed. Last night I tried playing guitar for a while, like my physio suggested, exercising my wooden fingers on a Vance Joy tune. Then I stayed up reading, staving off sleep until after midnight. My book is still in bed with me, the cover and first few pages scrunched from me lying on them overnight.

Over eight hours of uninterrupted sleep is some sort of record. My body protests when I stretch. My knee and fingers ache in the usual places, and the rest of my muscles are stiff too: my waist, from twisting to throw punches; my forearms, bruised from hitting the leather bag. But they're just the normal aches and pains you get after training. Harris has had me shadow-boxing and practising punches for the last four days.

I remember this feeling from rough treatment at derby, and I know how to remedy it. I throw back the doona, wincing at the onslaught of cold air, and head for the shower.

Hot water, how I love thee ... Everything that was cold, that aches, is soothed under the rush of the shower. I wash my hair – *crap*, I had no idea it was so grotty. I have to use a brush to get the conditioner through it. Then I decide to go the whole hog, so I shave my legs and scrub my face as well.

I could stay here in the steam all day, but the water starts running cold – I'm not the only person in the house who's enjoyed the hot shower. I towel off, tug on my knee brace and yank on my clothes, then go out to dry my hair in front of the gas heater.

Again, I'm not the only brains trust to have had this bright idea – it's like a goddamn family meeting in the lounge room. Mike and Harris are milling in front of the heater, mugs in hand, and I can see Dad and Mum talking quietly in the kitchen. Dad's already home from work – no, not *already home*, just *home*. It's been weeks since I got up after he's returned from his usual shift.

'Oh my god, she's awake!' Mike's shaved and dressed in jeans and shirt, his typical janitor outfit. 'Bit of a sleep in, was it? And you've washed your hair. Shit, someone call *Ripley's Believe It or Not*.'

'Shut up.' I slap his shoulder.

'Hey, watch out for my coffee.'

'Move over, you linebackers, make room.' I shove in between the boys to get some heat on my legs.

Mike shivers. 'Bloody hell, it's cold as a witch's tit this morning.' He hands me his mug. 'Here, you take mine. I'll get another one,

Dad's put the pot on. Dad! Another warming beverage, if you don't mind!'

He heads for the kitchen, leaving me and Harris standing in warm.

Harris frowns, sniffs at me. 'You smell like grapefruits.'

'Then we match,' I say, nodding at his damp hair.

'Here you go.' He holds his mug off to one side while he flicks his hair in my direction, shaking his head like a dog after a bath. 'Sharing the joy.'

'Harris! You shithead!' I flick my hair back. It works better for me, because my hair is wetter, and there's more of it.

'Bugger off!' Harris sobers, slurps his coffee. 'Guess you're perking up now that you're getting a decent night's sleep.'

'Yeah. Feel almost human today.' I can't keep the smile off my face. I lift my chin towards his jeans and clean shirt, his unzipped but tidy jacket. 'So what's with the neat casual?'

'Mike's taking me in to the hospital. Gonna see if they'll take me on. Mike'll vouch for me, and they can call Westie if they need references.'

I slurp my donated coffee to hide my grin. 'Well, this is different.'

'What?'

'You. Applying for jobs. Model citizen. I thought you'd come to Melbourne and go out on a tear.'

Harris gives me an amused look. 'Thought I'd give it a burl. New city, new start, all that shit.'

I double-take theatrically. 'Who are you, and what have you done with the real Harris Derwent?'

'Shut up.' He squints at me sideways. 'Wow.'

'What?' I return his squint. 'Have I got something on my—'

'You're smiling.'

'Oh, that.' I straighten, try to control my blush. 'Hey, I smile. On occasion.'

'It's the first time I've seen you do it lately.'

'First time in about a month, I reckon,' Mike says. He's returned with the car keys. 'Rightie-oh, then, we're off. And no, Der-brain, you can't drive.'

'Your brother has a lead foot.' Harris calls over his shoulder as they head for the door.

I roll my eyes. 'Tell me something I don't know.'

'Philistines!' Mike shouts as he opens the front door.

I laugh, because I didn't think he knew what a philistine was. Turning back, I get a shock. Mum is standing in the warm blast of the heater. She has a crocheted blanket wrapped around her waist like you'd wear a sarong, and Dad's green taxi windbreaker on. The collar of her flannelette pyjamas peeks out at the top.

'Sorry. I stole your spot.' She blows on the surface of her tea, then shuffles to one side. 'We can share if you like.'

Feeling distinctly odd, I shuffle in beside her. Now I'm standing shoulder to shoulder with my mother. But this doesn't feel acrimonious. It feels almost . . . normal.

'Harris Derwent.' Mum sighs and shakes her head.

'Yeah.' I tuck my damp hair behind my ears. 'Were you surprised when Mike brought him home?'

'More just . . . ambushed.' She raises her eyebrows.

I nod in reply. This is weird. We haven't talked about us. About the mess that is us, the mess we've made. We haven't talked about the argument, the slap. But we're here, conversing.

'He's changed a fair bit, though, don't you reckon?' I gesture towards the door with my mug. 'Coming to the city. Applying for work. That's not the Harris I knew back in Five Mile.'

Mum considers her tea. 'He's different,' she agrees at last.

Maybe this is an avoidance strategy. Maybe Mum isn't going to talk about anything personal or relevant or close to home. Maybe we're going to just stick to these nice, safe, superficial topics, gloss over what happened, move on. Never mention it again. Just have a pleasant surface relationship where we don't make any pointed comments or receive any barbed-wire replies.

But Mum hasn't finished.

'He's grown up,' she says. Her voice is quiet, and her eyes seem drawn in my direction, like my face is a magnet to her emotional iron filings. 'It happens to everyone, I guess.'

I stand still. I don't know how to respond.

Before I even figure out something to say, she lets out a little sigh. 'Time to get ready for work.'

She heads off down the hall for the bathroom.

CHAPTER SIX

'God, you're really going to make me go to this thing, aren't you?'

'Yes. If you don't come, I'll cry and say you've hurt my feelings.' Ignoring my sighs, Mai waves the eyelash curler. 'Come on, Rachel – it's all arranged, and we've already gone to the trouble of getting you a dress. Anyway, have you got something better to do on the first Monday night of term?'

'Loll around in my pyjamas? Seriously, Mai, what am I gonna do – stand guard over the refreshments table?'

'It's a *dance*, Rachel. You're going to *dance*.'

'With a bung leg. Right. Who, exactly, am I gonna dance with?'

'Me. Gus.'

I'm touched by that, but I slump my shoulders anyway. 'Fine, then. But remind me again why you organised this gig for a Monday night in the middle of July?'

Mai rolls her eyes, which isn't the best strategy when you're putting on mascara. 'Wasn't my choice. I wanted a Friday, but

Conroy said he thought it would *encourage the attendees to get into a party mood by imbibing at the event.'*

'But it's the only chance seniors have to cut loose before exam prep starts.' I pull up the knee-highs Mai's lent me, do up my belt. 'They'll all just get pissed before they arrive.'

'Or scull from the bottles they've got stashed in their cars,' Mai agrees. She makes a final adjustment to her cleavage. 'At least there won't be any vodka in the punch – I threatened Karo with bodily harm if he did that. How do I look?'

She stands up and does a twirl. She looks gorgeous, of course. As the hostess, she can't be anything less than super-glam, and Mai loves to dress up anyway.

She's wearing a black baby-doll skirt, fluffed with tulle, over black fishnet tights and her most galumptious purple vinyl boots. Her bodice is like a goth Swedish dairymaid's, and she's certainly got the goods to make it work. Her hair is smoothed into a Louise Brooks bob, tweaked to one side with a red bow clip, and she's got red lippie on. I'm sure she's been saving all her best efforts for tonight, just to see the look on Gus's face.

'What do you think?' she prods.

I smile broadly. 'I think it's the first time I've seen you wear something without a pithy slogan on the front.'

'Ah. You didn't see my button.'

She leans so I can read the text on the badge she has pinned to one side of her bodice: *#SLAMDANCEBABYYOLO.*

'Classy.'

We're in my room, at my house, because Mai said she wanted to make sure I didn't chicken out. She also brought along a giant armful of things she suspected I would need, since I don't own an eyelash curler, or a hair dryer, or tights that match with anything.

There's another reason we're at my place, which is that after the visit to Pickup's office, Mum and Dad haven't wanted to let me out of their sight. My parents only gave me permission to attend the dance if I stuck to a certain number of rules, which included getting ready at home and Mike escorting me.

But apart from maintaining a slightly German shepherd attitude towards curfews and meal attendance, there's been a softening in Mum. That conversation by the heater last week seems to have kicked off a thaw. We've had two further exchanges of pleasantries, and numerous instances of actual eye contact. She even made me toast this morning. That's not just weird, it's disorienting.

I feel like there should be heavenly trumpets blaring, some kind of public announcement – *In BREAKING NEWS, Rachel Watts and her mother, Jenny, have resumed communication* . . . But there's nothing, of course. Nothing in the larger universe has changed. It's just an internal revolution, a series of small turnaround moments that makes you see everything slightly differently. They don't make public announcements for those.

'So,' Mai says, reeling me back to the present as she pulls on her long purple satin gloves, 'your mate. Harris.'

'What about him?' I experiment with putting my hair up in a twist.

'Hasn't exactly been thumped with the ugly stick, has he?'

'I guess not.' I let the strands I've pulled up flop back down. No time, and I can't be bothered. When I glance up, Mai's got her eyebrows raised at me. 'What? I dunno – Harris isn't bad, I s'pose. I'm not really the best person to ask.'

'He looks at you, y'know.'

'Well, yeah. He's living in our house. It's kind of hard to avoid.'

86

Mai sighs. 'Is Mycroft back? Didn't he say five days? It's been a week. When's he coming home?'

'Last text, he said *very soon*.' It gives me a pang to be reminded of him. I haven't told Mai about the other messages. Typical Mycroft stuff like, *I am in a rotisserie oven* and, *Where does black sand come from?* and, *Today I saw a man with a wheelbarrow full of ducks*.

Sprinkled through those messages, though, were the odd flash of his thoughts. *Nervous*, one read. A few texts later, *Are you sleeping?* That one gave me pause. I tried to text back, *Are you eating?* But for some reason it bounced: the line came up 'not delivered'.

Very soon. That message alone is enough to fill my stomach with butterflies. Actually, stuff the butterflies – the sensation's more like a stampeding herd of wildebeest. The past week has felt like a lifetime, but I still have no idea what I'm going to say when I see Mycroft in person.

'It's a bit of a tragedy he's not going to see you in your party gear. Hang on.' Mai dives for her handbag and emerges, after a scramble, with her phone clutched high. 'Stand still. I want proof that you have actually, at one time in your life, worn a dress.'

'Hey, I've worn a dress before. When I was . . . ten.'

'*Rachel*.' Mai shakes her head and points the phone.

The outfit I'm wearing feels a bit ridiculous, but I guess all dress-ups do. I haven't gone for the full vixen look, like Mai. The latte-coloured vintage cotton dress I found in Savers is loose on my shoulders. Mai's honeybee-striped tights go up to my knee – they cover the bottom edge of a diamond-patterned strapping of sports tape. There's probably an excess of sports tape, really. It's not as ugly as the brace, but it's still ugly.

At least the dress is nice. Tiny pearl buttons decorate the front, and a thin red belt cinches the material at my waist. It's sleeveless, so I'm wearing a red cashmere cardigan. It's a summer dress, but I liked the pattern of tiny white daisies, and the broderie Anglaise holes speckled on the fabric. I have to wear a slip underneath, because of the holes: the slip feels silky against my skin. It all looks kind of demurely sexy, with a little bit of thigh on view and a pair of ancient brown cowboy boots from the op shop and my long hair loose.

'Come on, it's quarter to seven,' I say, after we've admired ourselves in the mirror on my wardrobe door. 'Don't you need to get there early to organise the refreshment table?'

'I'm coming . . .' Mai dithers about with final adjustments, then shoves on her glasses and bundles towards the doorway.

When we get out to the living room, I realise belatedly that Mai's outfit might not exactly inspire my parents with joy. Mum lifts her eyebrows, Dad just nods his head.

'You both look lovely,' he says. 'Very, er, festive.'

Mai grins. 'Thanks, Mr Watts.'

Mike and Harris lurch into the living room, taking up every available inch of space. Both of them are dressed like they're heading off to the Five Mile B&S, in neat-pressed jeans and well-shined boots. Mike's hair appears to have had a visit from a comb. He looks embarrassed and awkward, and his shirt and windbreaker don't go with his tie.

Harris is wearing a black button-down shirt and a black leather jacket I had no idea he owned. He's *not* wearing a tie. His shirt is open at the top, giving all and sundry an impressive view of his tanned neck and collarbones.

'Whaddya think?' He smiles broadly and opens out his hands. 'Flasher than a rat with a gold tooth, eh?'

'What are you doing?' I stare at him. 'You don't have to dress to impress, you're not coming.'

'Yes, I am,' Harris says. The muscles of his shoulders bunch under the jacket as he puts his hands on his hips. 'Mike agreed. Two bodyguards is better than one.'

'But—'

'Your mum and dad think it's a great idea. Don't you, Mr and Mrs Watts?'

My parents nod obediently at Harris, while I gape. Have they gone completely mad? I distinctly remember my mother, a few years back, referring to Harris as 'that bloody layabout'. Now they're trusting him to escort me to a social event?

I round on Mike. 'Which one of you smarty-pants thought this up?'

Mike gives me the evil eye. 'You really wanna argue after Pickup's visit the other day?'

'Oh, for god's sake.' This is supposed to be a party night, and I don't appreciate Mike's reminder.

Harris is giving Mai a once-over. 'Those tights look good, but what's with all the holes?'

'They're fishnets,' Mai explains.

'Nice. So what are we waiting for?'

'Our ride.' Mai checks the time on the clock above the door to the kitchen. 'Gus said he'd be here—'

Right on cue, a car horn toots from outside. All four of us – me, Mai, and my two bulky escorts – say our goodbyes to Mum and Dad as we squeeze out the door of the house, heading for Gus's car.

When I see the car, I baulk. It's a *Mini*.

'I thought you were bringing your uncle's station wagon?' I say plaintively.

'There was, um, a change of plan.' Gus looks at Mike and Harris with confusion, looks at me. 'There are three of you?'

I raise my eyes to the heavens. 'Don't ask.'

It's freezing outside without a jacket. Gus looks incredibly dapper in a red shirt and black trousers. He stands on the pavement, holding the car door open for Mai – his eyes quietly fall out of his head when he sees her décolletage.

Mai takes the passenger seat next to Gus. Mike and me and Harris squash into the back. I sit between the two boys like a sardine pressed between thick slices of bread. My boots are crammed into the gearstick space. Mike is bunched up with his hands on his knees, and I catch Harris trying to look down the front of my dress.

I glare at him. 'You've done this on purpose, just to piss me off.'

'Now, Rachel,' Harris says, 'don't be rude. Me and Mike are worried about your personal safety.'

'So you guys are, like, Rachel's security team for tonight?' Gus says over his shoulder.

'*Mike* is my security team,' I call back. 'Harris just wants to ogle the chicks at the dance.'

Harris smirks. 'High school girls. What's not to love?'

'Harris,' Mike says, 'if you dump me in the corner, keeping an eye on Rachel, while you go off chasing tail, I will personally bang your head against the wall.'

Gus snorts and pulls the car out from the kerb.

We drive past Mycroft and Angela's house – they've left a kitchen light on, to give the illusion that someone is home, but apart from that the whole place looks grey, abandoned. I'm torn by twin desires: the desire to have Mycroft back, and the desire to have him stay in Bali, well clear of this murder business. Both these desires are equally strong, equally fierce.

We turn out of Summoner Street and Mai looks at me anxiously over her shoulder. 'Your dress is going to be crushed by the time we arrive.'

I grimace at her. 'You try sitting in the back of a Mini between two full-forwards.'

Harris has chosen to angle himself towards me. I'm pressed up against him in ways I'd prefer not to think about. I try to wriggle into a more comfortable position.

He grins. 'Is this what people in the city do for fun?'

I glare at him. 'I wouldn't call this fun.'

'Well, I'm enjoying myself.'

Mike glances over. 'Lay off, Harris, she's not twelve anymore.'

Harris checks out the length of my thigh, his eyes resting on the spot where my dress ends and the knee-highs begin. 'Yeah, I noticed that.'

Mai interrupts this frivolity with the tinkle of glass as she holds up three alcopops by their necks. 'Traveller? Our school principal has said no booze at the event, so it might be best to load up in the car.'

'Now you're talking,' Harris says.

He accepts one, passes me another. Mike declines – he's taking this bodyguard stuff very seriously.

Gus glances at us in the rear-view mirror as he navigates the traffic. 'At least if I get pulled over I can say that only two of the drinkers in my car are under-age.'

Harris takes a long gulp of his lemon-and-vodka and tips the bottle neck towards Gus. 'Where're you from, mate?'

Gus gives him a dry look in the rear-view. 'North Brunswick.'

I'd laugh, but I'm too squashed. And I'm sure this won't be Harris's last conversational faux pas in Melbourne. Five Mile is not a multiracial melting pot, by any stretch of the imagination. This is probably the first time Harris has ever met a Sudanese guy.

He seems to be taking it in his stride, though, peering out the window at all the action. 'Bloody hell, would you look at that. Mike, the city lights are calling to me.'

'Don't get too dazzled by the glare, mate.' Mike says. 'I want your head in the game tonight.'

'No worries.' Harris pats my shoulder. 'I'll protect this young lady with my life.'

I roll my eyes. 'Sod off, Harris.'

———

Silver paper hangs in curling strips from the ceiling of the North Coburg Secondary School indoor basketball court; it's a bit like peering through a jungle of fettucine. By nine-thirty, all the decorations are starting to wilt. By ten, half the seniors in the hall are dancing, and the other half are feeling up their dates in darkened corners of the room. Mai can chalk this up as a resounding success – in high school terms, the dance is a winner.

Zia and Gabrielle have arranged couches and just enough lights to make the place look clubby. The music is piped, but Mai got this Year Eleven boy, Terence Kim, to DJ: he's the only kid I've ever met who has their own set of turntables, and he sends away to the UK for house vinyl, so the music's actually really good. The food and beverages were maybe *too* good – the sausage rolls and Iced VoVos disappeared early, and all that's left by this stage is a half-empty bowl of punch and a few plates scattered with Doritos.

Everybody seems to be having an okay time. Even the teachers haven't butted in much. Principal Conroy is on hand: he made his presence felt earlier, when he ordered a couple of particularly drunk boys to leave. But the other two chaperones seem to have retired for a quiet smoke out the back behind the landscaped shrubbery.

I've danced, and I've eaten Iced VoVos, and my knee seems to be holding up all right, although my feet are starting to hurt in these cowboy boots. I sling back another plastic cup of mineral water and fruit juice, observe Mike looking uncomfortable over near the wall. Hanging out at a high school dance, when you're a lofty twenty-year-old, must be the height of embarrassment.

I stroll over. 'How's security detail going?'

'Awkward.' Mike grimaces, scans the room. 'Some of these birds are showing a lot of leg. I dunno where to put my eyes.'

'If it makes you feel better, I won't tell Alicia you spent an evening checking out a bunch of teenage girls.'

'Thanks,' he says, eyebrow raised.

Impulsively, I dump my cup and grab his hand. 'Come dance with me.'

'Rache, you know I can't dance for shit.'

'Me neither. Doesn't matter.' I grin at him. 'Come on, for old times' sake. Remember when we used to put Mum's Johnny Cash album on, and you'd spin me around in the living room?'

Mike smiles. 'You used to sing with the dog brush for a microphone. Gross.'

I laugh. 'What was I thinking?'

'You were eight. I don't reckon there was a lot of thinking going on.' He moves away from the wall, holding out both my hands. 'God, look at you now. Seventeen years old, finishing high school in a few months. My little sister.'

He shakes his head like he can't believe it, then reels me in. He holds me in a casual waltz grip, the way he used to dance with me when we'd all go to the annual bush-band roundup near Lameroo.

Tonight my left hand, free of its plastic splints, seems delicate on Mike's broad shoulder. We sway on the spot, smiling at each other.

'So what's your plan?' I ask him. 'Alicia comes home, you two keep working at the hospital in romantic bliss, maybe rent a little house one day . . .'

Mike laughs. 'Yeah, maybe one day we could rent a little house in, like, Sunbury. Costs a bomb to rent in Melbourne.'

My swaying slows. 'You're gonna move out of Coburg?'

'Relax, Rachel.' Mike pats my shoulder. 'Nobody's talking about moving anywhere. It's still early days. Alicia might come back from overseas with some moustachioed European bloke on her arm.'

'Nah, she's not gonna do that.' I peck his cheek. 'Because she knows she's got the real deal right here. My big brother.'

Mike grins, shakes his head.

The old song finishes and a new one starts while we do our elephant-sway dance. Then Mike gets a tap on the shoulder.

'Can I cut in?' Harris says. 'None of these chicks wanna dance with me.'

I roll my eyes. 'You're supposed to be guarding, not groping.'

'Yeah, well, the only suspect event so far has been me springing a couple of boys sharing a spliff out the back. Said I wouldn't dob them in if they'd give me a toke. Come on, Rache, I'm bored. Gimme a dance.'

'Well, I gotta go to the men's anyway . . .' Mike checks with me. 'Rachel?'

'Oh, all right.'

Mike's warm hands release me, and I exchange partners. Harris is a veteran of country bush dances as well: he holds me in the exact same way, my right hand in his left, his other hand resting smoothly on my waist. He spins us out a bit further from the wall, though, close enough to the main floor that I can see past the balloons and streamers to catch sight of Gus and Mai.

They're on the dance floor again – Mai's energy seems to be never-ending. Gus is twirling Mai around so her skirt flares out. He must catch an inspiring glimpse of her purple knickers because the look on his face changes to a combination of 'oh-my-god-how-did-I-get-so-lucky?' and something else that suggests he'd like to leave the dance with her immediately, like *right now*. Mai starts laughing.

I glance away, straight into Harris's grinning face. 'Seems like they're having a good time. Although maybe the good times will come later?'

'I guess so.' I blush, clear my throat. 'You look kind of hot in that jacket.'

'Why, thank you.' His grin broadens. 'You look pretty hot yourself.'

'That's not what I meant.'

'Ah, come on, Rachel, I'm just pulling your chain.' He eyes me, lips twitching. 'Don't you know how to take a compliment?'

'Sure I do.' I look away. 'But I feel kind of ridiculous in this dress, with sports tape everywhere. And my feet are hurting in these boots.'

Harris glances down. 'Take 'em off.'

'Are you kidding? God only knows what's on the floor in here.'

'You can stand on my feet.'

95

I laugh, but the look on Harris's face is totally serious. 'Well, I guess . . . All right then.'

I toe off my boots one at a time – the relief is immediate. Harris bends to scoop them up. He hands them to me, then shoves his own foot forward.

'Go on then.'

'I don't wanna crush your feet . . .'

'Rachel, you weigh about fifty kilos soaking wet. Just do it.'

So I do – I step lightly onto the tops of his boots, as he holds my waist secure. Now I really am flooded with memories: I remember dancing like this on Dad's feet when I was little. Mum and Dad loved the Lameroo bush bashes. They'd gossip and dance, Mike would hang with the teenage boys and pretend to be too cool to join in, and I'd spend all night running around, thrilled by the music and the strange excitement of having other kids to play with. Usually I'd fall asleep in the back seat of the car on the drive home, remembering the feeling of Dad's strong arms as he spun me on the floor.

But Harris is not my dad. We have to stand a lot closer, now his feet are carrying me. I'm clutching my boots behind his back, and our chests are snugged in together. A weird, nervy rush goes through me: am I sweating? Can Harris smell my perspiration? Which is a stupid thing to worry about, because surely he's already smelled me sweating in training.

In the space of a heartbeat, this acute awareness falls on top of me: Harris is nearly three years older than me, and he's a guy. I knew that. I mean, I *thought* I knew that. But why is it suddenly so important?

'Is that better?'

I struggle back to the conversation. 'Um, yeah, heaps.'

Harris grins. 'See? You should trust my good judgement.'

'Right. Because you have such a long history of it.' I cock my head at him. 'You're different here, though. Ever since you got here, you're like . . .'

'Like what?'

'I dunno. Maybe being in Melbourne agrees with you.'

'Maybe it does. If I can get some work, I'll stay for sure.' He smiles, almost wistful-looking. 'I like it. The action, the noise, the colour . . .'

'And the company? It must have been a bit quiet on the farm.'

'Yeah. The company is good.' Harris glances at me, looks away.

'So why'd you leave?'

'What?'

'The farm. Why'd you leave? You were set up there, you had a job . . . I mean, it sounds like your dad must've been pretty hard work, but—'

'Just got sick of it,' Harris says. A muscle jumps in his jaw. 'No real reason. Wanted a change of scenery. That's all right, isn't it?'

What just happened? For a second, I actually had Harris talking about himself. But there's something. It was there in his interruption, in the way his arms and his shoulders suddenly tense.

'Yeah, sure. Change of scenery is good.' I search for another topic. 'So I reckon I must be getting better with the training, if we're dancing like this.'

'Yeah.' Harris thaws by one degree, then melts a little further. 'I guess. No more panic attacks, eh?'

'Nup. Mike even gave me a hug today.' I beam. I feel quite proud of that. 'With a bit more practice, I'll be able to start breaking out of holds – fighting back.'

'A bit more practice?' Harris grins. 'How's this?'

97

Without any warning, he spins us both, and then bends me into a sharp dip. I drop my boots and yelp, clutching at Harris's shoulders as my body curves back. Harris's face is above mine, and his eyes are sparking with some strange intensity. His lips are parted, his hair ruffled and wild.

'We move pretty well together, Rachel, don't you think?' he says softly.

'Harris—' I'm surprised by how breathless my voice is, and I'm cut off when his head dips. His lips skim down the side of my neck to my collarbone. This is not what I was expecting *at all*. Suddenly my body is electrified. Before I can react, Harris's lips settle in the curve above my collarbone. He snorts gently against my skin, then—

He blows a giant raspberry, hauls me up.

My breath explodes out of me, when I hadn't even realised I'd been holding it in. '*Hey!*'

He grins. 'There's a bit of practice for you.'

'You shithead – what are you *doing*?' I push at his arms.

'Ah, mate,' Harris says, laughing. 'Your face!'

I'm so set on righting myself, tugging down my dress and whacking Harris away, that I don't immediately focus on the lanky figure in a white dress shirt and black trousers walking towards me through the crowd. It's several more seconds before my brain registers who it is.

Mycroft.

The trousers lengthen his legs, hug his slim hips. Thin black braces snap up from his waist. The white shirt and braces accentuate his height and his lean figure – he looks broad-shouldered and classy. His op-shop suit jacket hangs loosely over his shoulder by one finger. There's a cigarette tucked behind his ear, and his purple-laced Cons add to his outfit's offbeat allure.

He looks older, somehow, like a boho sophisticate, as though he's just stepped off the set of *Breakfast at Tiffany's*. He looks *good* – Jesus, he looks so goddamn good I've forgotten to breathe. He's smooth-shaved, and his dark curls are tumbling, and . . . and . . .

An instant glow puffs up inside me, widens my eyes and upturns my lips. Mycroft's supposed to be in Bali. He's not in Bali. He's *here*, right in front of me. And something suddenly clicks into place in my head, in my heart.

It's Mycroft – it's *always* been Mycroft. Forget stress-filled talks: we'll work it out somehow. But right now, my god, I want to feel his arms around me more than *anything*. My angst about him, me, us, it all scatters like so much vapour, floats away in the flood of good feeling that wells up at the mere sight of him.

The blossoming good feeling lasts for about three seconds. That's how long it takes Mycroft to stride closer, drop his jacket on the floor, and punch Harris Derwent straight in the face.

CHAPTER SEVEN

'*Fuck!*' Harris spins with the force of the punch.

'*Jesus!*' I stumble back, trip on one of my boots, grab for Mycroft's shoulder. He slips from my grasp like a fish, shaking out his punching hand, blue eyes locked on Harris.

A new song by Disclosure comes on over the tinny PA system as Harris staggers, recovers, turns. I see his expression go feral as he lunges for Mycroft, who brings up a fist at the same instant. Suddenly, they're both pounding each other.

Mycroft may have the height advantage and the element of surprise, but he's not a brawler like Harris. He doubles over when Harris sinks one right into his guts. They both lurch in tandem for the wall. Somebody in the crowd nearby screams.

'*Stop!* For god's sake!' I clutch at my hair.

I need a bucket of water, or a hose, like you use to split up fighting dogs. But neither of those things are on hand at the moment, so I have to wade in. My stockinged feet slip on the floorboards as I get a fistful of Mycroft's shirt, smack at Harris's shoulder.

'*Will you two fucking idiots STOP!*' They're not listening to me, or maybe they can't hear a bloody thing over the music.

Mycroft's so angry, he's shaking. Both he and Harris are breathing hard, flailing for each other. Thrown off balance, I misstep with my bad leg, swear hard, and go down like a sack of potatoes.

Suddenly there's a squirt of cold, and I jerk my head around to see Mike behind me. He's got a bottle of mineral water in his hands – he must've grabbed it off the refreshment table and shaken it – and he's giving Mycroft and Harris a good spray.

'*Enough!*' Mike bellows. '*Back off.* Both of you.'

Mycroft and Harris's faces swivel around. They've got their fingers in each other's collars, and mineral water dripping off their noses, and twin looks of astonishment. It'd almost make me laugh, but they're being such dickheads I can't. I'm so pissed off I can hardly see straight.

'You right, Rache?'

'Fine.' I accept Mike's hand, lever myself up off the floor, share out the glares. 'Do these two need another hose-down?'

'Dunno. Saw the circus coming back from the men's.' Mike glares at Harris and shoves his hand at Mycroft's chest as he separates them. 'Have you two clowns both lost your minds? It's a *high school dance*, for Christ's sake!'

Harris ignores him and pushes towards Mycroft, his eyes flaring. 'You wanna go for the title, mate?'

Mike grabs the lapel of Harris's jacket. 'Harris, shut it.'

Mycroft is panting, hands on knees and looking at me in confusion. 'You were hitting him . . .'

'He's a *friend*.' I sigh, push back my hair. 'He wasn't hurting me. He and Mike are looking after me.'

'*Gentlemen.*' Principal Conroy appears like magic, points at Harris, grabs Mycroft by the collar and hauls him up. 'Right, I want both of you off the premises. *Now.*'

'Mycroft, you're home!' Mai and Gus have arrived. Mai is beaming, Gus is trying not to laugh.

'Leave quietly, or I'm calling the police,' Conroy says.

Harris sneers at Conroy. 'Call them, then.' Blood and mineral water oozes from his nose onto his shirt.

'*Harris!*' Mike shakes Harris by the scruff of the neck. 'Mate, shut your trap.'

'He bloody king hit me!'

'He's her *boyfriend*, you fucking moron.'

'Mr Mycroft, welcome back,' Conroy says. 'I'll speak to you about your detention tomorrow.'

'*Detention?* I've only been back ten minutes!' Mycroft, whose jacket appears to have gone missing in the skirmish, rubs at a red mark on his neck where Harris's fingers must have dug in.

Harris mops his nose with a damp shirt cuff. '*That's* the boyfriend?'

'I'll get them both out, sir,' Mike says to Conroy, before he glares at Harris. 'What, the English accent didn't give it away?'

'He didn't say anything! He just came up and belted me!'

'Nice to see you, Mycroft.' Mai is grinning hugely. 'And thanks! No high school dance is complete without a fistfight.'

'Least I could do.' Mycroft straightens his clothes as Conroy releases him. Then he looks at me and his blue eyes get this intensity, like the way the air gets electricity in it after a big storm. 'Why do you need looking after?'

I gulp. 'We need to talk.'

'You wore a dress,' he says.

Harris looks at my face, looks back and forth from Mycroft to me. He shakes his head. 'Shit.'

I straighten my cardigan, which has fallen off one shoulder. One of my pearl buttons has popped, and Mai's knee-highs are laddered. I exhale slowly out my nose.

'Harris, meet James Mycroft. James, Harris Derwent. Now the introductions are over, could you do me a favour, Gus, and call me a cab? I think I'd like to go home.'

'You're right – we do need to talk,' Mycroft says. 'There's something I need to tell you.'

He's waited until we're all in the cab. The driver is playing Bollywood music down low; a string of beads hangs from the rear-view mirror, and a short garland of yellow flowers – marigolds, believe it or not – brightens the dash.

Harris is in the front passenger seat, and I'm squashed between two boys in the back again – Mike and Mycroft, this time. The cab is roomier than the Mini, but I don't want this discussion to happen here.

I cross my arms, squeeze my elbows. 'When did you get back?'

'Plane landed about six. Took ages to get through Customs. Rachel—'

'You look better. Have you put on weight?' He definitely looks more solid. The way we're pressed together, I can feel more muscle, fewer bones, although I'm trying not to dwell on it.

Mycroft grimaces. 'Seven days of rice. Look, maybe it'd be better if I show you the—'

'There's been a murder,' Mike says, over the top of my head.

Mycroft tenses. 'What?'

Harris twists in the front seat to look at Mycroft. 'She didn't tell you.'

I glare at his self-satisfied expression. 'It's none of your business who I tell!'

'This guy died last week. He looked like you.' Mike is ignoring me, his eyes fixed on Mycroft's with grim seriousness. 'He fell out of a building in Sherlock Road, and he had broken ribs and—'

'Jesus Christ.' Mycroft looks at me quickly. 'Rachel?'

'*I didn't want you involved!*' The words explode out of me; my whole body is like one giant fretwire. 'It's not even an official homicide case! And you were overseas. There was no point telling you—'

'An email? A text?'

Mike nods. 'Bit of advance warning would've been good, Rache.'

'Oh shut up, both of you!' I cup my hot cheeks in my hands.

'You should've told me,' Mycroft says mulishly.

'Well, now you know. What did you want to show me?'

'Best you come to mine.'

Mycroft sounds cagey. I'm suddenly very aware of how our legs are pressed together. I've got one now-booted foot on the vent near the cab's gear shift, and one in the footwell on Mycroft's side. The skirt of my dress has ridden up, exposing my sports-taped knee. The edge of my thigh looks incredibly pale next to Mycroft's black dress pants.

We don't talk anymore until we're back in Summoner Street. When we get out of the cab at my place, Mike and Harris mill on the pavement. The taillights of the cab cast them both in a red glow as the driver peels away.

Harris has a shirty, hangdog look on his face. He pulls at his collar. 'Rachel—'

'Don't even start. Tell Mum and Dad I'll be right home,' I say to Mike.

Mike raises his eyebrows. 'We're supposed to be keeping an eye on you . . .' He stops when he sees the look on my face.

'It's only twenty metres.' It takes a solid effort to make my expression neutral. 'Honestly, I think I'll cope.'

'Then I'm going to keep watch out front until you get back. Just so you know.' Mike gives me a significant glance, then grabs Harris's shoulder and pulls him towards the house.

I hug my arms around myself – it's absolutely glacial, one of those typical, snotty Melbourne nights. Almost worse than London.

'Here.' Mycroft walks towards me, shaking his jacket open. 'Put this on, or you'll freeze to death.'

I chew my lip for about one second, then relent. I burrow my arms into the sleeves – the jacket is warm from his body, and comes down to my thighs.

'So I'm assuming Pickup told you to stay safe.' Mycroft reaches out to ease a fall of my hair out of the jacket collar. 'Which would explain the trigger-happy chaperones.'

'Only one of them was trigger-happy. Mike has more sense. And *you* threw the first punch.'

'Yeah.' Mycroft rubs at his neck again. 'God, I can't believe I did that.'

'You could have told me you were flying back tonight, you know.'

'I wanted to surprise you.'

'Well, you sure as hell did that.' I sigh. 'Come on. It's freezing out here.'

We walk together under the streetlamps, maintaining an awkward distance. Back at my place, Mum and Dad will probably be having conniptions, and Harris will be borrowing a dry shirt. I can't think about all that. I'd like to recover the glow that bubbled up when I first saw Mycroft at the dance, but the fist-fight and the argument in the cab have got me frazzled. It weighs on me now, the fact that Mycroft is back, and we're supposed to talk.

I grab for a diversion, trying to martial my nerves. 'How's Angela?'

'Asleep, I think. I hope so, anyway. She's got work tomorrow night.'

'Was it all right – you and her in Bali?'

'Yeah.' Mycroft strolls along in his Cons, hands in pockets, considering the concrete. 'I thought it was a crap idea, but actually it was really good. She kind of force-fed me for a week. When I wasn't running around hunting for Robert Hannah, we spent a lot of time playing cards on the beach and . . . just talking, I guess.'

'That's great.'

'Yeah.' He glances my way. 'We talked a bit about what happened in England.'

'Oh. Right.' I swallow. 'So what'd you find out from Hannah?'

Mycroft's shoulders shift; he must have clenched his fists inside his pockets.

'Robert Hannah is a late-fifties retired British spook with a bad comb-over and a beer gut. He dodged me for as long as he possibly could, and then I had to delay my flight back just so I could meet him in a crappy bar near Ubud.' He looks at me. 'Tell me about Harris Derwent.'

'*Harris?*' My eyebrows hike up. 'There's nothing to tell. He's Mike's best mate from Five Mile. He hitched a ride with us to the city, and he's staying with us for a while.'

'At your house?' Mycroft tongues his back teeth, glances away. 'Well, that's great.'

'There are more important things to talk about than Harris right now, don't you think?'

Mycroft looks at me. 'Yeah. Yeah, I do.'

I press my lips together, look at my feet, realise we've reached the concrete path that leads to Mycroft and Angela's porch. Lamplight from the Stranger's Room glows through the blue curtain: of course, Mycroft and Angela would have come home before Mycroft ventured out to the dance.

'Come on, the message is on my laptop,' Mycroft says.

I'm not sure what he's talking about, but I nod. My stomach flip-flops, like I'm on the Octopus at the Ouyen Show.

We skirt past the side of the house to find his backyard washed in moonlight – some of the garden weeding has been done, I'm surprised to notice, and pea straw is bedded around plants for the winter. Has Dad been over here helping Angela, or did she do that herself?

Mycroft's room is in the same shambles as before he left, the mess cast with a mellow glow by the orange light of his bedside reading lamp. His backpack is against the wall, spewing dirty clothes – the Anniversary Book pokes out, along with other odd bits and pieces. Dresser drawers are pulled open, the bed is stripped – untouched for over a week – but the desk now holds an explosion of papers and Indonesian money and Mycroft's laptop, which seems to be in the process of downloading something.

One thing is different: an oil heater sits ticking in the corner. The room is warm again.

'Christ, it's pretty bad in here, isn't it?' Mycroft says quietly, as though he's only just realised.

I don't reply, which is probably comment enough.

'At least it's warm,' Mycroft says. 'Angela lent me her heater.'

I turn around, ignoring the disorder, ignoring the strange feeling produced just by being here. I look at Mycroft and try to pretend that this is all perfectly normal: me standing here in a thigh-baring dress and cowboy boots, him in an elegant shirt and trousers with braces. There's nothing surreal about this picture at all.

The room suddenly seems too small to fit both of us. A powerful awareness of Mycroft's presence overwhelms me again. Maybe part of it is because I'm still wearing his jacket, breathing in his scent from the material, but I know it's more than that. His looks, his energy: everything about him tugs me in.

I remember, years ago, Mum relating – to everyone's amuse-ment – how she'd always found my father irresistible. Mike and I had made jokes. Now I completely understand. What I feel for this boy hasn't diluted with familiarity, or weakened in his absence – it's only sunk deeper. This is more than simple attraction: even now, when I'm so conflicted, something about being near Mycroft makes my soul feel strangely, helplessly happy.

'Right.' I have to wrangle my brain to concentrate. 'What did you want to show me?'

Mycroft starts for his laptop. 'It's about *Diogenes*,' he says. 'Come and have a look.'

He nods me closer: when I don't move, he reaches to tug on my hands. 'Here. You don't have to do anything. You just have to see.'

It's the last thing on earth I want. But I let him draw me over to the desk, the laptop. He leans for the mouse and starts clicking, pulling up the window I designed myself, the one I've been too scared to look at for the last month. Since we discovered that Wild was communicating through the blog, neither of us has logged on to post or comment.

There's the electric-blue header, *Diogenes* – just seeing the name is enough to make me tuck my hands around my waist, as if I'm trying to hold in a bout of seasickness. And there's the article, with the long list of comments beneath it.

'What is it?' My voice has dropped to a whisper.

Mycroft scrolls down through the comments and I see a new one at the bottom, with the red letters of the profile name licking like flame on the left: *Moriarty.*

'A new message from Wild,' Mycroft says. 'It's dated from yesterday. That's why I raced out to the dance, because I couldn't raise you on the phone, and I thought maybe you'd seen it, that you'd be worried . . .'

'I didn't take my phone,' I say. I get a queasy feeling. 'Anyway, I haven't been checking the blog.' But my eyes are fixed on the message. '*You must drop it, Mr Holmes. You must stand clear, or be trodden underfoot. I know every move of your game, and I will have what is mine* . . . What is that? A quote?'

'Yes.' Mycroft's hand steadies my lower back. 'Almost verbatim, from *The Final Problem* by Conan Doyle, except for the bit at the end, about having *what is mine*. Don't suppose you know what he's talking about there?'

I shake my head, which gives me vertigo, so I stop. Lifting my face high, as if that will help me get more air, I turn back to Mycroft. 'Right. Do *you* know what it means?'

'No idea.' Mycroft looks back at the screen. '*Mr Holmes* . . . The boy who died . . . your brother said that was in Sherlock Road?'

'Yes. In Croydon.' I need to sit down, but my only options are the bed or the chair at the desk, squarely in front of the laptop.

'This is the first message Wild has sent since we left England, right?'

'Yeah. Look, I'm sorry to throw this at you now, but I thought you should know.'

'Keeping me in the loop, right?' I hiccup something that could be a laugh, but isn't.

Mycroft looks at me. 'We don't have to talk about it.'

'No, we should.' I almost gag, saying that. 'It's Wild. We should, y'know, talk.'

'Really? Because I got the impression it was the last thing you wanted to talk about ever again.'

There it is, right out there in the open. Mycroft watches me carefully. I want my reply to be composed, exact. Instead I open my mouth and find that nothing comes out at all.

'I just . . .' Mycroft glances around the room. 'While I was away, I had some time to think. I've always prided myself on being observant. But I haven't been very observant lately.' He looks at the laptop, then straight at me. 'You've been terrified ever since we left England.'

It's not a question. I just . . . stand there.

'And for five weeks, I've thought that the investigation I've been doing was something that was good for both of us. For me, because I'd get answers about my family. And for you, because I thought it would help . . . resolve your fear.' He gazes at me sadly. 'But it hasn't been like that, has it?'

'No.' It takes a lot of effort to get out that one word. I swallow past a dreadful pressure in my throat. 'No, it's just made it worse.'

Mycroft nods again, exhales deeply. 'I'm sorry. I've been a little obsessed since London. And I saw it. I saw you pulling away. I just didn't connect the dots – or maybe I couldn't.'

'You saw,' I say softly, 'but you didn't observe.'

Mycroft bites on his bottom lip, releases it. His smile is lack-lustre. 'I told you I was a shit detective.'

'You're not a shit detective.'

'Rachel—'

We just stare at each other for a moment, until Mycroft clears his throat. 'Right. So while I was away, I racked my brain trying to figure out how I can put this right. This new message changes things but I could stop the investigation—'

'No.' I shake my head. 'You can't.'

Mycroft's eyes go impossibly soft. 'But it's hurting you.'

'Mycroft, you deserve to get justice for your family, for yourself.' I press my feet down hard, like I do in training. 'And this message . . . Wild's really trying to intimidate us now.'

I realise that I've been wringing my hands together. I unclench, smooth my fingers down the sides of my dress before looking back at Mycroft.

'You're right. I have been scared. I've been scared for too long,' I say. 'But I'm working on it now. I'm doing self-defence with Harris—'

Mycroft's lip curls.

'—and it's *helping*. I can deal with it. If you keep investigating, I'll . . . keep dealing.' I let out a wobbly breath. 'So what did you find out in Bali?'

Mycroft frowns at me, as if he's trying to judge whether I can take it. 'Well, Hannah offered his condolences.'

'Bit late for that, isn't it?'

'Yeah. I dunno why he was avoiding me – he's a bit of a recluse, which could be a hangover from his years working intelligence. But when I finally met with him, he said that he hadn't learned any more about the accident than what the police knew at the time.'

'So the trip was a waste of time?'

'No. He told me something else. He said that my dad was contracted by the Home Office to write a report on corruption in the service. He said that my dad was dealing with "sensitive issues" but that was all he'd say.'

'A report on corruption *within* British intelligence? Did the police know about that seven years ago?'

'I don't know.'

'But . . . that report could have Wild's real name in it.'

'Yes.'

'You already suspected that Wild could be a member of the British government, or—'

'—the intelligence service, yes. So we don't know who Wild is, but the existence of the report strongly suggests that someone in those circles had something to lose. Something worth killing a whole family for.'

I absorb this for a second. 'There's stuff I don't get, though.'

'What's that?'

I tick off the chain of events on my fingers. 'Your dad investigates corruption in the Home Office. Wild gets nervous, because his name is probably in the report. He contracts the Colonel to kill your family . . .'

'Yes.'

'Then *we* start fishing around. Wild knows we're onto him. So why send us these stupid blog messages? Why doesn't he just have us killed?'

'I don't know. Maybe he's not sure how much we've figured out. Even Hannah didn't seem to know all that much – although he told me I should let it go. "Poking a hornet's nest" was the term he used, but I think he just felt guilty for not telling me about it earlier . . .' He squints at me. 'Are you sure you're okay talking about this?'

'Yeah, sure.' I see his expression, amend my automated reply. 'I mean, I'm dealing with it. To be honest, I'm just glad we're not breaking up.'

Mycroft gives me the full cobalt stare. 'Is that what you were going to say before I left? That things would be easier if we broke up?'

'Well, yeah.' I shrug, look at the grungy carpet. 'I thought . . . Actually, I don't know what I thought. Maybe that it'd be better for both of us. I wouldn't be confronted with the Wild stuff all the time, and you'd have the freedom to investigate properly.'

'Where'd you get that idea?'

'From . . . stuff.' I flail my hands. '*Us*. How we've been lately . . . I dunno. It sounds pretty stupid when I say it out loud.'

Mycroft looks at me squarely. 'Rachel, I don't want us to break up.'

'Good.' The word comes out so quickly it makes me snort. 'I mean, I don't want us to break up either.'

Mycroft's shoulders release as he smiles. 'Okay. Great. So we're not breaking up. We're just . . .' He gives me a quizzical look. 'How much do you know about quantum theories of intermolecular forces?'

'What?'

Mycroft takes a step closer, hands held up in demonstration. 'Think of it this way. There are two atoms, yeah? And they're held together by a covalent bond, a molecular—'

'I know about covalent bonds, Mycroft.' I have to work hard not to roll my eyes.

'Right. I thought we'd covered that, but Mr Knox has that really drone-y voice, so I—'

'Covalent bonds are a type of molecular bond formed by the sharing of a pair of electrons between adjacent atoms,' I recite.

'Yes! Covalent bonds are about the strongest molecular bonds in biochemistry, right? So you've got this molecule, it's very strongly bonded . . .'

Mycroft is close enough now that I can feel the warmth of him through his white shirt. He slips one of his hands into one of mine, and holds our joined hands high. Our fingers twine together, and some of the heat in his palm radiates out into my body. My stomach starts to do gravity-defying things again, and my cheeks flame.

His voice has gone low. 'But then the molecule comes into interaction with other molecules, where it can be affected by something called dispersion forces . . .'

'Dispersion forces. Uh-huh.' My heart is hammering.

'. . . also called London forces.'

'You're shitting me.'

'Totally not.' Mycroft's lips turn up at the corners as he rubs my palm with his thumb. 'They were discovered by this guy, Fritz London. Anyway, these London forces shift the electronic charges around inside the molecule. It's a type of fluctuation, which chemists call a *perturbation*.'

I'm feeling a bit perturbed myself at the moment, but I try to keep my face neutral. 'So . . . London forces disturb the electronic balance inside the molecule.'

'Yes. In fact, the closer other molecules get to our strong covalent molecule, the greater the perturbation forces become. But they don't destroy the molecule.'

'They don't?'

'No.' Mycroft shifts closer. He smooths the pad of his finger across one of my knuckles. 'They can't do that. Because London forces are much weaker than covalent bonds. Covalent bonds are stronger than anything.'

'Right.' I'm breathless, and I have to concentrate to get my next words out. 'So are you going to write a dissertation on this now, or are you going to kiss me?'

Mycroft smiles, tugs me into his chest, and all at once I see his eyes up close, the deep, enveloping sea of his irises. An incredible warmth swarms throughout my whole body. Then his head comes down, and his lips graze softly against mine. A fizzy sensation spirals up inside me, gaining momentum, as if tiny fireworks are going off under my skin. Mycroft's arms wrap around me, and for a moment I think everything will be fine. I can do this, I've been working on this . . .

But then, just as suddenly, the tightness of his arms becomes stifling. My breath starts stuttering. An instant later, panic starts flooding through me.

I break away. 'Sorry – ah god, I'm sorry. I can't—'

'Rachel—'

'It's not your fault. Really. It's not about you. It's just . . .'

'It's okay,' he says. 'I worked that out, too. While I was away.'

'What?'

'The no-hugging thing.' He stares at me. 'It's when you sleep, isn't it? Is it nightmares?'

I swallow thickly. 'Yeah. Night terrors.'

'That . . . makes sense.' Mycroft looks relieved. 'It makes a lot of things make sense. Because up until the point I put my arms around you, you're fine. And then when I touch you—'

'It's not like that.' I look away. 'I mean, you can touch me. But I just can't deal with . . .'

'Being held.' His expression is grief-stricken. 'So what can we do? I mean, can we work around this? Is there something I can do, that would make it—'

'I can touch you.' The thought popped into my head, and then out of my mouth, with no preamble. My cheeks tingle in a suspect way – I must be blushing like an idiot. But now that I think about it, I realise it's a good idea. 'I mean, if you can handle just standing still, and letting me get used to being held again, I could—'

'Come here,' he says softly.

He takes my hand and steps towards the wall, puts his back to it. He drops my hand once I'm standing in front of him.

'Kiss me again.' His voice is so low and rough that I melt a little.

I blink at him. 'And you're just going to stand there?'

'Yes.'

My lips quirk up. 'So . . . why the wall? Is that some sort of—'

'It's been a while,' he says. 'I don't know how my legs will go.'

And *that's* almost enough to turn me to mush inside. I feel a stirring, deep in my body that I haven't felt for weeks. It makes me brave.

'O-kay . . .' I move closer. Then my hands go up. 'But I might freak out a little, all right?'

'It doesn't matter.' He shakes his head, his curls tumbling. 'Just take it slow. I'll just stand here, I promise. No moving.'

That makes me laugh. I take a big breath, look down at my feet, look up again.

There's the ghost of a smile on his lips. 'Would it help if I closed my eyes?'

116

I laugh again. 'Maybe.'

'All right, then.' His eyes close, his long eyelashes feathering his cheeks.

I step in. Ease myself into Mycroft's circle. His back is braced against the wall, his feet pushed forward so he's closer to my level. His knees are apart. I step between them, look up at his face: his features are entirely neutral. But I can feel this energy emanating from him – anticipating. Waiting. Wanting.

The lovely line of Mycroft's neck, the strong planes of his face . . . I know it all so well, but I still find it mesmerising. I put my hands on his chest.

He swallows reflexively. 'You okay?'

'Shh.'

I look at his lips. I remember how soft they felt the first time we kissed. Mycroft licks them, pulls the bottom one – with the little silver scar like a sickle moon – into his mouth with his teeth, releases it. Just that simple unconscious movement sends a white-hot zap of electricity careering from my toes all the way up my spine.

I push against his chest as I lean in and press my lips to his.

Oh god, his lips are so tender. I sink in, like you sink yourself onto a warm pillow. Mycroft's breath catches as I move my mouth, brushing his top lip and bottom lip in turn, like the pull and return of the sea. He makes a tiny noise, and tilts his head so we can angle closer. His jacket slips off my shoulders, puddles on the floor at my feet.

I kiss him again, softly, like a whisper against his mouth. I slide one hand up to cup the back of his neck, move my other hand across to his shoulder and smooth down his arm; his muscles are taut beneath his shirt sleeve. When I glance down,

I see his hands flexing against the wall. He must be willing himself not to grab me.

The thrill that goes through me then is like fire. I'm the one holding the reins, controlling this, and I don't need to be scared. I ease closer, brushing against Mycroft's chest with my own. The feeling is so good I moan. I *want* this. I've wanted it for weeks. I've been kidding myself that I could stay away from Mycroft, because this need is so strong it's palpable.

Suddenly this incredible urgency floods through me. Like I've been starving for a long time, living on war rations, and now there's a buffet in front of me and I'm frantic. I want everything, the whole dinner. The whole fantasy.

I push the full length of my body against Mycroft's, close as static cling, deepening the kiss. Mycroft's entire body is reverberating with the effort of not touching me, not moving. When I slick his tongue with mine he makes this agonised groan, and his arms lift—

I tear my lips away from his. '*Don't.*'

If he hugs me now I don't know how I'll react, but I don't think it will be good. And I don't want to break this spell.

'Rachel—'

'You said you wouldn't move.' I squeeze his shoulders, lean in and bite his neck, little nips all the way down from his ear. 'You have to wait.'

'Okay.' His voice is hoarse. 'Okay.'

I'm losing it, badly. My hands are shaking as I slide them back to his chest. As I pull on the thin braces, testing.

As I undo the top button of his shirt.

There's a little pop, drowned out by the sound of Mycroft's gasp. '*Rachel—*'

I press a finger to his swollen lips. Then I undo another button, drunk on the feelings inside, on the sound of Mycroft's ragged breathing.

'I like this shirt.' My voice is trembling. I flick open another button.

Mycroft swallows hard. 'Y-yeah?'

'Oh, yes.' Another button. The buttons are small and white, and a bit tricky to undo with shaky fingers. I pull too hard, and the whole button pops off and falls on the carpet.

Now his shirt is completely, temptingly open. I slide one hand into the fold – the skin of his chest is soft and hard at once. Mycroft watches me as I ease back the rest of his shirt front.

His shoulders move rapidly as he breathes. With each breath, there's a play of muscle. I spread my hands wide across his chest. He groans and sways against the wall, his eyes going black, pupils completely blown.

Slowly, I push the shirt off his shoulders. The braces slip down to his hips. The fabric bunches around his waist, only held in place by the cuffs at his wrists. I run my hands up his bare arms, along his shoulders, down to his chest and back up again. Up and down, in tender sweeping strokes. The way Mycroft has his eyes scrunched up, the noises he's making, makes me feel powerful.

Our mouths connect as my hands move. His arms are trapped by the cuffs of his shirt, his big hands clutching the air. And now I feel a bit sorry that I can't feel his hands on me, so I move them until they're resting lightly on my flanks. Mycroft gasps. His hands squeeze hard, then travel down, touching places he doesn't usually have access to because I always wear jeans.

I think I should wear dresses more often.

The feel of his hands on my bare skin makes me reel. He slides his fingertips under the hem of my slip. Trickles his fingers down my outer thighs to my knee-highs, then all the way back up. My whole body is alive, burning with a kind of delirium.

The room is incredibly quiet. The only noises are the sounds we're making as we explore each other's surfaces. Mycroft's panting breaths, my little moans and sighs. Our lips, making the soft round vowels of desire.

Suddenly Mycroft loses patience with his shirt, tugs and shakes frantically at the cuffs as he kisses me, until the fastenings ping open and he can shuck the smooth cotton. He slides his arms completely around me, and I'm enveloped in warm muscle. His arms around me feel *right*. He squeezes me so hard I gasp, then he's hitching up my knee, curling me around him, and I want to climb up his body, feel every part of his skin against every part of mine, and—

The banging on the door is like an explosion.

We both jump. If Mycroft wasn't holding me tight, I'd have hit the roof. My heart jerks in my chest as the banging sounds again. Mycroft mutters an unbelievably rude word and unwinds his arms from around me.

A roar of frustration slams through my insides. 'For god's sake, can't people just leave us alone for *five minutes*? Is that really too much to ask?'

Mycroft rubs my arms. 'I'll deal with it.'

'You just got home!' I'm shaking at the shift of emotions. 'I'm gonna bloody *kill* my parents.'

'It's okay. Just let me talk to them.'

He pulls on his shirt and walks to the door, looking a lot like I feel – darkly irritated, his skin flushed with interrupted desire. I'm not sure how much leverage he's going to have, standing with his curls tangled and his shirt open, and me blushing with a combination of lust and anger in the background. But he swings the door open anyway.

I'm expecting to see my dad. He's there, sure, but he's not the person leading the charge. Detective Pickup has his fist raised, like he's just about to bang again. When he sees Mycroft, he baulks and frowns. Then he sees me. I pull at the hem of my dress self-consciously.

'Right,' Pickup says. 'Glad you're both here.'

What? My eyes lurch between Mycroft and Pickup and my dad, who is glowering behind Pickup's shoulder. Surely my parents haven't *called the police* because I flipped off my 'security' and walked Mycroft home? That would just be the absolute height of—

'Hello, Detective,' Mycroft says. 'I'd say it's nice to see you, but—'

'Button your shirt, son.' Pickup gives him a grave look. 'You need to come to the station.'

I think of my paranoid parents, and Principal Conroy's threat to call the cops after the fight earlier this evening.

'Why?' I step forward on shaky legs. 'What's this all about?'

Dad leans around Pickup's shoulder to look at me. 'Rachel, you both need to come. There's been another murder.'

CHAPTER EIGHT

They found this body in Thornbury, near the sports facility off St Georges Road. In Watt Street.

This time, the victim is not a boy, and not a prostitute. She is a homeless person. Her name is yet to be determined. But she is young, she frequents the areas around Thornbury station, and she's done nothing to deserve this helpless death, except that she looks an awful lot like me – brown hair with a touch of blonde, big dark eyes. She's even dressed in a flannie shirt and jeans.

Pickup explains it all in a dry professional manner as he takes the Queens Bridge exit, driving the back way into Kavanagh Street.

'I really don't believe you know this girl,' he says, as he steers between traffic, 'but given the situation, we'd like to go through the process of possible identification.'

'You think there's something we'll see that you might have missed,' Mycroft says softly.

Pickup glances at him in the rear-view. 'There's something else you need to know. I've been in contact with Scotland Yard – your

DCI Gupta. He briefed me on some of the finer details of the case over there, and it seems there've been a few developments.'

'Like what?'

'The woman in the Daniel Gardener case—'

'Irina.' I nod, remembering. 'Irina Addington.'

'That's her.' Pickup keeps his eyes on the traffic light he's waiting to change. 'She's gone missing.'

'But they had her in protective custody.' My voice is weak with dismay.

'Not anymore.' Pickup's profile is stony. Somehow I don't think he believes Irina has got lost on her way to the local shop.

The neon of the CBD seems too bright, too disco, this late on a Monday night. I'm still in my dress and honeybee tights and cowboy boots, with Mycroft's suit jacket around me to protect against the cold.

Mycroft is in his suit trousers, braces dangling at his hips. He's wearing his dress shirt with his old red and white trackie jacket that he threw on before we left his room – it's a bit of a weird combination, but time is of the essence in a murder investigation. Time is always of the essence, even when the person to whom the investigation matters most is dead and cold and used to waiting.

We enter the coronial services building from the basement, like we did with Dave Washburn, a million years ago. Like that last time, Mycroft touches my hand in the lift on the way up. But things are different now. I know this building well – it's Mycroft's place of work. And the feeling this time has changed. This time it's not about a man we knew, a case we're looking into. This time it's about *us*.

I shrink away from Mycroft's hand. I'm not ready for this. I'm not mentally prepared. If anyone enters my protective carapace, air and brutal reality might rush in through the gap and I'll be shocked into full alertness. I'm quite capable of dealing with all this, as long as I'm in my bubble. But without it, I might do or say something . . . stupid.

Pickup takes us down again to the morgue floor. Wafts of antiseptic cleaning fluid hit me when the lift doors open. I brace my hand against the side of the lift, and for a moment my feet won't budge.

'Are you coming, Miss Watts?' I hear a hint of pity in Pickup's tone.

'Rachel?' Dad says.

'I'm coming.' But I'm not. My body won't move for a second.

'Rachel.' Mycroft just looks at me.

It takes all my resolve to step out of the lift and join them. Once it's done, moving one foot in front of the other becomes automatic.

When we get to the viewing room, it's Dad's turn to have a spasm.

'No. Sorry.' He's gone quite green. 'I don't think I can do this.'

I'm quite sure then that he's noticed the same thing I did when we first arrived: that smell of decay, partly disguised with bleaching agents. We both recognise that smell. Only this time we know it's not dead sheep. It's dead people. And I don't begrudge Dad his cowardice about this, not at all.

'I'm really sorry, love,' he says to me, gripping my shoulder. 'But if it's a girl your age—'

'It's okay, Dad.' I rub his back.

'You've brought the young people this far, Mr Watts,' Pickup says. 'We won't be long. You can wait out here, if you like.'

I give Pickup a grateful glance. There's no denying the look of relief on Dad's face, mixed with shame.

We leave Dad behind and enter the viewing room.

'I should warn you,' Pickup says, as we cluster inside at the glass window, 'that there's a different pathologist on this case, Dr Stephen Rossi. He's been brought in as a locum.'

'Where's Professor Walsh?' Mycroft asks.

'On sick leave.' Pickup buzzes the intercom to let the pathology techs know we've arrived.

Before we can ask more about Walsh, a green-gowned man enters the room on the other side of the window.

He's pushing a trolley in front of him, and there's the body of a girl on it. She has no sheet over her, standard in forensic cases – nothing can be allowed to disturb the evidence before the post-mortem, not even a sterile drape – but the sudden wham-bam arrival of her is a shock. I gasp as real life rushes in to sandpaper its way over me.

'Bloody hell,' Pickup mutters, and then he says, for our benefit, 'Dr Rossi is a bit more abrupt than the Professor. I'm also not sure if he'll let us in to examine the body more closely. Let me talk to him.'

He hits the intercom button. 'Doctor? Could you tell us when you're ready, please?'

The doctor holds up a hand, then taps the clear plastic welder's plate over his face with one gloved finger. He steadies the trolley as if he's positioning it at the supermarket checkout, then strides over to the wall and hits the button.

'Yes, yes. All ready.' He's young, about twenty-five or thirty. His features are hard to make out behind the protective faceplate, but I see a clean-shaven chin, soft pink cheeks. 'I have notes – wait – ah, here . . .'

Dr Rossi waves a clipboard in the air and hits the button again.

'Okay, you want me to run through details? Post-mortem is about to be performed, on request from the department. The note here says this case isn't listed as wrongful death. Is that right?'

Pickup glowers. 'The case hasn't been listed as a homicide *yet*. Big emphasis on *yet*. That's why *you're* here.'

Rossi shrugs. 'Okay, that's fine. Initial findings—'

Pickup interrupts. 'Doctor, the young people here are familiar with examination procedures. Mr Mycroft works in the forensics unit with Professor Walsh. We'd like permission to enter, if you don't mind, to conduct a closer examination.'

'What?' Rossi turns to look at us, as if he's only just realised we exist. 'You want to come in?'

'Yes.' Pickup's voice is terse.

'That's outside of forensic protocols . . .' Dr Rossi says, and for a second I think we're going to be spared a closer look at this victim, this girl from whom I've deliberately averted my eyes. But Rossi relents. 'Okay. You all want to come?'

'Yes.' Pickup doesn't seem that excited about going in himself, but Rossi is buzzing the door open.

Pickup leads, and me and Mycroft trail behind. The smell in this room . . . That awful cloudy-sweet smell of preserving fluids; I'm so familiar with it, but it still makes my eyes water and the hair inside my nostrils curl.

Rossi stands there, staring, until he remembers he's got the faceplate on. He raises the visor, and we finally get a better look at his face.

He's closer to thirty, I see now, but his cheeks are chubby, full as a baby's, with the rosy underglow I noticed before. His eyes are brown, sharp, attentive.

Pickup gestures stiffly, like he doesn't want to swing his arms around in case he contaminates something. 'Dr Rossi, this is James Mycroft, who works with Professor Walsh. And Rachel Watts.'

I'm glad he doesn't say 'Mycroft's girlfriend', demoting me to an appendage.

Rossi's eyes slide over us, like you'd slide your eyes over a list of items on a restaurant menu – I get the impression he's examined us and found us less interesting than other things on display.

'Okay, here are the rules. No leaning over the body, no touching, and sneeze over your shoulder.'

He grins at this last one, and it makes me angry. Does he think this is some kind of joke?

'We understand,' I say roughly.

Mycroft puts his hand on my arm. 'We're familiar with protocols. Thanks for letting us in, Doctor.'

'You work with the professor? I only substitute for him, usually I'm at the hospital. But he's good, one of the best.' Rossi claps his hands together. 'Okay, let's get going.'

He moves back around the body on the table. Suddenly she's right there, and I have to focus. It's all too immediate. I think of the way Professor Walsh prepared Dave Washburn's body for viewing, with a drape he gently folded down. This is not the same experience at all. This girl is grey, and she's . . .

'*Jesus*,' Mycroft says, inhaling sharply. I know he didn't mean to speak – he would want to appear professional in front of Rossi and Pickup – but this girl has taken him by surprise.

She is not exactly like me. Her eyes are a tawny hazel, not brown, and her skin is a bit jaundiced. Her hair is deliberately streaked, probably with kitchen bleach, where mine falls to blonde, and her lips are thinner, pulled back from her teeth in a grimace.

But yes, she looks a lot like me. If I was wearing my usual clothes, you'd be hard pressed to tell us apart. Now we're all standing here, gazing at her, it seems even more obvious. Even Rossi does a double take.

'Ah.' He flicks his eyes from the dead girl to me. 'So, you're a relative?'

'No.' I'm glad I'm not – this guy's bedside manner is absolutely zero. I have a sudden longing for Professor Walsh's soothing presence.

'Wow, okay. You could be sisters.'

I feel sick. Is Rossi really this insensitive?

'They're not sisters,' Pickup says gruffly. 'Can we get on with the details, please?'

'Ah, right. Well, I've already checked for external trace – done the nails, taken scrapings, X-rays and so on.'

He pokes a gloved finger down on the dead girl's shoulder. It's stiff, unyielding. I make a little noise. Mycroft's hand grazes mine.

'I'd say she's been in rigor about two hours,' Rossi says, not noticing my gaffe. He consults his chart. 'She was found at a storm drain – that's probably why her hair's stringy, but I don't think she's had a bath in a while either.' He wrinkles his nose. I have to remind myself that he's seen a lot of death.

Pickup glares at him, then looks at us. 'It was called in by some kid who didn't leave his name.'

'You're sure it was a kid?' Mycroft says softly.

'Yes. I've listened to the tape. I'd say this kid was mucking around up by the sports ground, found her and then called triple-0.'

I just stand there, looking at the girl. Her head is propped on a block under the nape of her neck, her arms resting on the steel table. I stare at her feet – this seems easier somehow – and note that her shoes are old runners, the laces replaced with string.

Her jeans are loose, grubby, worn to holes at the knees – I can see her pale skin there. She's been sleeping rough, and she doesn't even have tights on under her jeans to protect against the cold.

Then I have to look at her torso, and this is harder. Her flannie and the thin T-shirt underneath have both been cut from hem to collar, in one long slice. She's not wearing a bra. Her breasts are smaller than mine. They fall to each side of her sternum in gentle planes, frozen in the position when rigor came upon her, pulling the skin over her breastbone taut.

I get this feeling like there's not really enough air in the room.

I look back to her head. It's easy to see how she died. There's a very deep, collapsed-looking indentation at her hairline. Something grey peeks out from behind the broken pieces of bone. Blood coats the top of her head, has soaked into her hair, flicked down onto her forehead.

'All right,' Rossi says. 'The SOC photos show her lying with her head against the edge of the concrete drainpipe. There was some falling away of the ground in front, which is why there's so little blood on her face.'

'So she was tipped down, headfirst?' Mycroft asks quietly.

'Yep. Now, you can see she's got a depressed skull fracture, focal at the hairline.'

'What does that suggest?' Pickup asks.

'That's a traumatic brain injury – it's quite likely she died of intracranial haemorrhage or severe contusion. It's consistent with blunt trauma.' Mycroft's voice is gluey. When I glance at him, his usual expression of studied seriousness when talking about forensics is absent. He looks a bit ill. But he presses his lips together and goes on. 'She was found facedown?'

'Yup.' Rossi nods.

'So, they're guessing she slipped and fell forward,' Mycroft says.

Pickup scowls. 'Does that rule out non-accidental death?'

'No.' Mycroft is studying the girl's head again. His lips have gone white. 'She could have been hit with a blunt object, or been pushed onto the drain-edge. But it's hard to determine if a head injury like this has been deliberately inflicted.'

'That's right,' Rossi says. He smiles at Mycroft approvingly, as if he's passed some kind of test.

Pickup presses harder. 'Can't you tell, then, if she fell or was pushed?'

'Maybe,' Rossi muses. 'Angles of fracture might tell us more. But, hey, I won't write it off as an accident for now.'

'That's good,' Pickup says. He glances at me and Mycroft. 'The Tonna boy was officially listed as death by misadventure.'

I nod automatically. Mycroft doesn't say anything.

I steel myself, look back at the girl. Her legs are painfully skinny. She's got a long, soaking stain on her jeans along the front of each shin. Through a hole in the denim I can see a fresh abrasion on her knee.

'There's . . .' I clear my throat. 'The scrape on her knee?'

'Yes,' Rossi says, nodding. 'If she fell, maybe she contacted at the knees first? Or maybe, you know, if it was an attack, then she was on her knees, before the assailant . . .'

He gestures again, towards her head, in a pushing motion. I get it. I think everybody gets it.

I scan down the length of the girl's body. She doesn't look country – the flannie and jeans are just practical winter wear. She looks city. The small details illustrate it clearly. The ear piercings, the tiny tattoo of a star she's got on her neck – I can see that where her hair has spilled away, just below one ear.

The girl has three black rubber wristbands, and her nails are bitten. They're dark, and I realise that she's used a Sharpie or something to colour them in, in lieu of nail polish. The skin around them is raw, as though she's chewed off some of the quick, like I sometimes do.

Then, as clearly as if someone pointed it out to me, I can see from the discolouration at her knuckles where three fingers on her left hand are broken.

'Her fingers . . .' My knees suddenly go wobbly.

Mycroft steadies me by the arm. 'I saw it.' He glances at Pickup, who nods, then at Rossi. 'The left phalangeal breaks?'

'Maybe she put her hand out to stop the fall?'

I shake my head. This girl didn't break her fingers in a fall. Just like the Tonna boy's broken ribs weren't a coincidence.

I've been denying what's been straight in front of my eyes. Pickup was right. These are murder cases – these are *Wild's* cases. And they are a message, as clear as that message on the blog.

You must stand clear, or be trodden underfoot . . .

An awful quaking begins inside me, somewhere down in my diaphragm, like the shuddering feeling I get after a nightmare. I squeeze my own once-broken fingers, trying to control it.

Mycroft looks at me, looks down at the girl again and swallows. 'She's very thin.'

'Junkie, I imagine.' Rossi shrugs. 'Be surprised if I don't find tracks on her arms once I get the shirt off. But see, here – fingernail marks on the right palm. So that might go towards a wrongful-death ruling, yeah? I'll have to check the cortisol levels.'

'What for?' Pickup says, his brow furrowed.

'Cortisol is an indicator of stress. Pain. A high level of cortisol means . . .' Mycroft leans back a bit to stare up at the ceiling, and he looks horrible. 'It means she had her fingers broken while she was still alive. Jesus Christ.'

Without any warning, Mycroft suddenly turns around and strides to the door, thumbs the button. The door buzzes, and he pushes himself through it shoulders-first. He's just a blur behind the glass as he walks swiftly out through the viewing area and into the hall.

Dr Rossi seems taken aback. 'Does he always do that? You can't do this job with a weak stomach, you know. If he wants to keep working with Walsh—'

'Thanks for your time, Doctor,' Pickup says. He tugs on my sleeve and we beat a retreat along the same path Mycroft took.

When we get out into the hall, the air seems fresher. I can breathe better. Dad is standing to the left, listing slightly, as if he's just straightened from leaning against the wall.

A sound distracts me, and I glance to the right to see Mycroft bent over a rubbish bin. He's holding on to the edges, with his arms locked and his head hanging between them. In his black dress trousers and limp braces, with the red trackie jacket, he looks like a guy at the latter end of a bad night on the town.

'He just came out and started with the dry-heaves,' Dad says, waving his hands helplessly.

I walk over to Mycroft. He's just spitting into the bin now. He turns away and reaches for one of the plastic chairs against the wall, eases himself into it. He puts his elbows on his knees and his head in his hands.

Pickup stands to one side. 'You all right, son?'

I've never seen Mycroft react this way in the morgue. Even when he helped Professor Walsh with the post-mortem on Daniel

Gardener, with all the memories of his parents' accident and injuries bundled up inside him, he wasn't physically sick. Something is different this time. Something has changed.

'Are you okay?' I whisper.

'I fucked up.' Mycroft's voice is muffled by his hands. He wipes his mouth on his sleeve, then runs his palms down the legs of his pants, staring at the floor. 'Oh god.'

'Mycroft?'

'It was a mistake. This investigation – it's all been just . . . emails, and research, and paper evidence. Not real stuff. And I thought if I left the site open, then we'd at least have a bit of warning . . .' He looks up at me, and his eyes are a desolate blue. 'You told me about the first murder, how that boy looked like me. But I didn't really get it. And now this girl is dead. I'm a fucking idiot. This isn't what I . . . *Shit.*'

'It's okay.' I take a step closer, my hand out.

'No, *don't.*' He stands abruptly, making space between us. 'You don't want to touch me. I don't know how you . . . How can you even want to be *near* me? *Fuck.*'

He looks at me desperately, then turns and starts pacing. He runs a hand through his hair and all the curls fly up, tumble back into place.

Pickup looks confused. 'Mr Mycroft, what's this all about?'

'It'll be okay,' I repeat, my voice shaking.

'*IT'S NOT OKAY!*'

Mycroft's words ricochet down the hallway, and we all jump. His expression is absolutely wretched.

'It's not okay.' He kicks at a chair, and it crashes into its neighbour. 'People are *dead*. Because I was stupid. A stupid, arrogant—'

'Don't say that!' I grab him by the arm. 'Look at me. *James.*'

His face is taut with anger. But it's guilt and despair that are making his eyes well up. I grip his arm more tightly.

'Yes,' I say firmly. 'Keeping the site open, not telling the police ... it was a mistake. But that's *not* why these kids were killed. That was *Wild's* doing. And maybe your investigation has stirred him up, but finding out Wild's real identity is necessary – it always has been. And I'm not going away, James. I'm not going anywhere.'

He makes a choked noise, and his face crumples just before he grabs for me.

His arms go around me. I jerk at first, then I slip my arms around his waist and breathe through the feeling of being held. And it works. The training I've been doing with Harris, the moment with Mycroft in his room, the way I feel about him – it all stirs together, makes hugging possible. Maybe the chains of the last five weeks have been broken. God, I hope so. Because Mycroft really needs this hug. He holds me so tightly my ribs mash together, and it's like he can't let go, or he doesn't want to.

He gasps into my hair. 'She looked *just like you*. Oh god . . .'

'I know,' I say. I clutch him against me.

Pickup clears his throat behind us. His voice sounds solemn. 'Mr Mycroft, I think you'd better explain what the hell's going on.'

CHAPTER NINE

'So this Wild character,' Dad says. 'You're saying he got in touch with you just before you returned from England?'

'Yes.'

'But you didn't tell Scotland Yard about this,' Pickup says, sighing.

'No.'

Mycroft cups the mug of tea that Pickup has given him. Dad clenches his hands around his own mug. I sit beside Mycroft at the morgue staffroom table and sip from mine. It's awful tea, bitter and lukewarm. Mycroft stares into the grey-brown depths of his as if it might reveal something really, really important.

It's nearly two a.m. and the staffroom is incongruously bright. My skin feels paper-thin and grimy, and my striped tights sag over my aching knee. This has been a much longer night than any of us anticipated. Only Pickup, who's accustomed to late call-outs, seems to have his head on straight. My dad looks knackered, and he has to get up for a day shift in four hours.

But I'm glad he's here. Dad's presence keeps me centred. His blunt fingers, roughened from work, remind me that there is a practical solution to every catastrophe, every puzzle. Now he's listening, brows furrowed, as Mycroft explains.

'I told Scotland Yard that the Colonel sent me a note directly.' Mycroft looks haggard. 'I didn't tell them that Wild's men – the Colonel and the others – made contact with me via *Diogenes* to negotiate for Rachel. Or that I left the site open for future contact.'

Dad leans back in his chair, his chest barrelled out. 'That was a bloody stupid thing to do, young man, if you don't mind me saying.' His mouth forms a terse line.

I reach across the table to squeeze my father's fingers. 'You understand, don't you, Dad? Wild's the one. The guy who called the shots when I was abducted in London. The guy who ordered Mycroft's parents to be killed. Mycroft was trying to get a bead on him. He was trying to *help*.'

Dad nods, but his face looks stormy, and the anger isn't directed at me. 'And you never considered just letting the police do their jobs?'

Mycroft looks at my father, his face flinching. 'Mr Watts, I'm sorry. But I've been waiting nearly eight years for the police to do something about my parents' murders. *Eight years*. It's just . . .'

'. . . a long time,' Dad concedes. He grimaces at the table, scratches at his jaw. 'I get it. Not saying I agree, mind you.'

'I knew the London police wouldn't keep me in the loop about Wild's activities. But not telling the police Wild had contacted me via the blog *was* stupid. Unbelievably stupid.' Mycroft looks at me, shakes his head. 'I *wanted* Wild to make contact again.'

'And now you've had this new message from him.' Pickup wrinkles his knobbly nose. He's just read the new comment on the blog on Mycroft's phone. 'But what does he mean by *I will have what is mine*?'

I shake my head. 'We don't know.'

'Well, obviously, not telling anybody about the messages was bloody idiotic,' Pickup points out. 'But I don't think that's what's caused this murder business.'

'These two murdered kids – they're *us*. They're a warning,' I say. 'You recognised that straight away, right?'

Pickup sucks his teeth. 'It still doesn't make sense.'

'He wants to intimidate us.'

'Yes,' Pickup says, frowning, 'but why wasn't the threatening comment on the site enough? That alone would have put you on your guard. This is more extreme, the action of a man under pressure. Something has happened, something's changed . . . What is it?'

I shrug helplessly.

'When did the first murder happen?' Mycroft asks.

'Tuesday evening,' Pickup says. 'Once I had a proper look at the file, I got Rachel down here Wednesday night to see the photos.'

'What happened before that?' Dad asks.

'Well . . . nothing.' I stare at the wooden table top, thinking aloud. 'I'd been in Five Mile, and then I came home . . .'

Mycroft looks at me, at Pickup. 'I flew to Denpasar a week ago.'

'What exactly were you doing in Bali, son?' Pickup asks.

'I . . . I got a lead. Rachel had this idea about chasing up the people my dad used to work with. So I went to see this guy, Robert Hannah.'

'So that's it,' Dad says. 'This Wild character knows you've contacted this Hannah fellow. That you're off searching for clues.'

'But how can Wild *know* that?' Mycroft's eyebrows knit. 'The only people who knew I was going to Bali were me, Angela, Professor Walsh, Rachel and Hannah himself.'

'Perhaps your Mr Hannah is more involved in this than you think?' Pickup suggests.

'So it was Hannah.' Mycroft's lips thin. 'Robert Hannah informed on me. To Wild.'

Pickup raises an eyebrow. 'That seems most likely, for my money.'

'Then ... that's probably what happened to my parents too. We went to visit Hannah, and the morning we drove back to London, that was when ...' Mycroft swallows, his face hardening, becoming adamantine. 'Hannah must have told Wild that my father was a threat. And Wild had them killed.'

Pickup leans forward. 'Why was your dad a threat to Wild?'

'Mycroft's dad was a political analyst contracted to write a report on corruption in the intelligence service,' I explain. 'We think Wild might be a member of the service, or the government, and that his real name could be contained in the report.'

Pickup glances between me and Mycroft. 'So what happened to that report?'

I shake my head. 'We don't know.'

Mycroft scrapes back his chair, goes to the doorway. His back is taut and his posture is unnaturally stiff as he stands there, one arm up, squeezing the jamb and staring out at the long, empty hall.

I watch him for a second, before looking back at Pickup. 'So what do we do now?'

Pickup sits back, shaking his head. 'Reports on British intelligence service corruption are a little outside my pay grade, I'm afraid. And yours too.'

Dad snorts. 'Rachel and Mycroft don't even *have* a pay grade.'

138

'I'm going to have to contact Scotland Yard again,' Pickup says. 'DCI Gupta told me there's some government bloke who's been involved in the case—'

Mycroft turns. 'You mean Jonathan Cole?'

'No, he was just the representative collecting the Folio. He hasn't had any further involvement, to my knowledge.'

'Worth.' The name comes back to me suddenly. 'When we were in hospital, in England, he came to see me.'

'I met him too,' Mycroft says. 'Skinny guy, kind of dour—'

'That's him.' I frown. 'The cranky one.'

'Whatever his disposition,' Pickup says, cocking an eyebrow, 'he'll likely have the information we need. Might even know about this report. Let me contact Gupta, see if I can get in touch with this Worth fellow.'

'But how do we know we can trust him?' My hackles are already rising. 'It could be *Worth's* name in the report, for all we know. *He* could be Wild, and we'd be playing right into his—'

'*Rachel.*' Dad bumps the table as he leans forward to touch my hand. 'The detective has to know more before he can do anything. He's gotta get info from somewhere. We might just have to take the chance.'

I meet Mycroft's eyes, and I can tell he's thinking the same thing as me: Pickup's well-meaning investigative methods could be a huge misstep. If Wild is connected to the government, he could be *anybody*. Taking this chance might be fatal.

But Pickup is going on. 'In the short term, I suggest you go home, lie low, and let me and the division figure out how to catch this guy. We'll monitor the blog in case he contacts you again. But don't reply to this new message, under any circumstances.'

Mycroft stands behind his plastic chair, gripping the back. 'Wild must be scared because he thinks I'm getting closer to the truth.'

Pickup nods. 'That might be right. But you need to keep yourselves safe. There's no point knowing the truth if it gets you both killed.' He checks his watch. 'It's after two. Gimme a minute to organise a car so you can go home, get some rest. I'll contact you again in the morning.'

'But it's the second day of term—' I start.

Pickup shakes his head. 'Don't go to school. Don't leave your homes. Contact me if you notice anything out of the ordinary. I meant what I said about lying low.'

———

Dad stands in Mycroft and Angela's chilly backyard, inspecting the mulch on the garden beds. I don't like making Dad wait, but I need to talk to Mycroft alone.

'Five minutes,' Dad says sternly. 'You do your talking, then we get straight back into the car.'

Using a police car to ride twenty metres up the road seems like overkill, but I'm not going to argue with Dad at the moment. Even the word 'overkill' would make him wince. I nod and go to catch up with Mycroft, who's already forged ahead.

By the time I get to the Stranger's Room, he's standing hunched over the laptop on his desk. The desk chair swivels awkwardly in front of him, so he shoves it closer to the window. Then the open front of his trackie jacket gets in his way, so he yanks that off as well, grabs for the mouse. His fingers make sharp, disjointed movements as he slides and clicks.

I step closer. 'What are you doing?'

'I should close down the blog.' His eyes flick across the screen.

'*Don't*. Wait.' I grab for his arm. 'Mycroft, you can't close *Diogenes*. Pickup's going to monitor the site. And if you still think that you caused those murders by keeping *Diogenes* open, then stop right now. If it was anybody, it was Robert Hannah, informing on you to Wild.'

Mycroft straightens and stares at me. 'I don't know if that's true.'

'Mycroft, it *wasn't you*, okay?'

'Okay. Fine.' He rubs the heel of his hand against his cheekbone, then leans forward again to click open a new window. 'But I'm sending a message to Wild.'

My eyes go wide. 'You can't. Pickup said not to reply, he'll see it—'

'*Good*,' Mycroft says. 'Then everyone will know where I stand.' He starts typing.

A clammy shiver starts at the nape of my neck, inches its way down my back, despite the warmth in the room. The sheer concept of contacting Wild against police orders fills my veins with ice water.

'What are you saying?' I whisper.

'That I'll drop it, just like he asked.' Mycroft's fingers fly across the keys. 'No more fact-finding missions, and no more emails to England. No more investigation. There.'

He clicks 'Send' before I have time to object further, before I can stop him. I see the message from *Diogenes_mod* spring to life in the comments list, right beneath the new one from *Moriarty*.

'Mycroft—'

'*No*.' He straightens to look at me. 'My mum and dad are dead. Robert Hannah sold them out to Wild, and they were killed. I found out how it happened, I don't need to know any more.'

'But you still don't know the *why*.'

'It doesn't matter. Not if it's going to hurt you more than you've been hurt already. Not if it's going to get us both killed.' He flings a hand out at the screen, around the bomb-site of his room, the papers on the wall. 'I used to think I could do all this – figure out this case, get justice for my parents – without any consequences. But that's just lunacy. I don't want anybody else to die over this. My family is dead, but *you're* not. I'm not going to let my *actual live girlfriend* get killed because I'm hunting some dead facts.'

Something swirls inside me, and it's heady, the idea that Mycroft is prepared to sacrifice so much for me. But I know it's not fair.

'James, don't give this up for me.' I clutch at his shirt, feel the tension in his muscles under the fabric. 'This is your *family*, your history—'

'I don't care anymore!' Mycroft twists to face me, squeezes my arms. His eyes burn like the damned. 'Rachel, *listen to me*. I'm not going down with your parents to identify your body in the morgue. I'm not going to stare at you lying on a steel table, like that dead girl. I . . . I think it would kill me.'

His grip hurts my arms. He breaks away, scrubs his hands over his face. Stares down at the desk littered with the soft pack of Indonesian cigarettes, the spray of rupiah and the stub of his Garuda boarding pass.

'I still can't believe it. Hannah.' He shakes his head, reaches a trembling hand for the smokes.

I touch his waist tentatively. 'You couldn't have known.'

'Yeah, but I just . . .' His mouth screws up. 'All those years ago, when my father took us to Hannah's house . . . Dad must've thought he could trust him. He was supposed to be a friend.'

His expression twists with disgust as he pulls out a cigarette, turns it in his long fingers. Standing there, clutching Mycroft's waist, I realise that I'm still wearing his dinner jacket. The smell of him in the fabric, in the room, reminds me that only a few hours ago I was sliding the jacket off my shoulders, pressing my lips to his . . . It's disorienting that we're back in the same space now, in such different circumstances, discussing an atrocity.

I start slipping my arms out of the jacket, but Mycroft reaches out to tug at the lapels. 'Keep it. You still need to get home.'

A sigh falls out of me. I feel as though I'm ripping him off: he's giving up his jacket *and* his family's mystery for me. There've been plenty of times I've given back, tried to be there for him, tried to be patient, not judging, just accepting him the way he is. Is it *even*, though? If he gives up this investigation for me, how will we ever feel balanced?

'It must have been something big,' I say suddenly. 'The report, or whatever it was that your dad shared with Hannah that he passed on to Wild. Something political, maybe.'

Mycroft blinks reddened eyes at the message he's just uploaded to the comments field on *Diogenes*. The black letters glow in the backlight of the laptop screen. 'I guess we'll never know.'

'But that's why Wild is *doing* this. He's warning us to stay away, because you're close. The truth must be just within arm's reach—'

'It doesn't matter.' Mycroft tosses his cigarette onto the desk and reaches for me. He folds me into his arms, presses his cheek against my hair. '*This* – this is true. This is the only truth I want.'

CHAPTER TEN

Harris slings one arm across my shoulders from behind, and I tense.

'Stop freezing up.'

'I'm not freezing up.'

'You are.' He pulls at the waist of my hoodie with his other hand, until my back collides against his chest again. 'Come on, we've been over it a million times – yank the arm to get your attacker off balance, stamp the instep, elbow in the guts, slam back your head. You've got plenty of options.'

If only that were actually the case. It's Wednesday afternoon, and I've been on lockdown at home since the dance – my parents' version of lying low. Unable to go to Mycroft's place, and him unable to come to me. Exercising my fingers on the guitar. Distracting myself with my medical textbook, getting some virtual hand-holding from Mai, reciting my processes at night to ward off nightmares. It hasn't been very successful, and the strain is like hot wires under my skin.

Harris took the news of the second murder like a declaration of war, and his obvious fury ignited my own anxiety. He's channelled it all into making sure I can defend myself from attack. He's been flaying me in training sessions, stepping up the retaliation stuff, working us both until we're gasping and stinking of sweat. That moment at the dance, when I was angsting about my BO, seems like a pathetic joke now.

'Okay. Options.' I brace my feet, yank hard on his arm.

'Rachel, stop fucking around and just hit me.'

'If I slam my head back I could break your nose.'

'Good. Then do it.'

'I don't *want* to break your nose, Harris.'

His chest moves against my back as he sighs. He releases me, skirts around so we're face to face. 'Come on. There's gotta be *something* to make you wanna hit me.'

'Actually, there isn't.'

'Remember the fight at the dance?'

I frown. 'That was a miscommunication.'

'Come on, have a whack. I deserve it.'

'You don't deserve a broken nose.'

'Your boyfriend's a dick.'

'Now you're just trying to wind me up.'

'I'm trying to get you in the mood to *belt* something. You've gotta have a knee-jerk response.'

'Here's your knee-jerk response.' I flip him off.

'Great.' He rolls his eyes. 'Babe, you're gonna need more than that in a fight.'

I don't know how I can explain it, what words to use. I've struggled with it in every slack moment, that image of the girl on the steel table, the memory of the wound above her hairline. Going to the morgue was a visceral reminder of all the horrible things people can do to hurt one another.

I've hurt people. Hurt them and killed them. Not by direct action, but I colluded in their deaths.

Today I really feel it, really remember it: it hangs around me like the pall of cold afternoon air hanging over the back garden.

I put a hand on his arm. 'Harris, I get that I'm not up to scratch. But I just . . . can't do it right now.' I unwind the tape from around my fingers, give him a nudge. 'Come on, I promise I'll do a bit more later. I'll get ninja. You'll see.'

His smile is tight in reply.

There's a clatter at the rear of the garden, and we both jerk around. A grubby backpack tumbles over the tall garden fence. I take a fast reverse step, my lungs backing up somewhere near my throat. Harris moves in front of me, arms akimbo, which would almost make me laugh if I didn't feel so suddenly panicked.

A pair of legs appears: long, grey, gawky. Then Mycroft's tangled head of curls appears over the fence palings. He wobbles, straddling the fence awkwardly. 'Ah, bit of help here?'

'The *fuck*?' Harris says.

I push past him and hobble over in a rush. 'Mycroft, what are you *doing*?'

'One sec.' He uses a grubby beanie to cushion one hand on the fence, grabs for my shoulder with his other hand to ease himself over. Something makes a rip as he descends, then he's dusting himself off. 'Yeah, okay. I've not really tried that before.'

Mycroft is not dressed in his usual gear. His jeans have the knees torn out, and are black in name only, as if the colour ran – far, far away – in the wash. He seems to be wearing about five layers of shirts and T-shirts, plus a hoodie that may have started out life dyed Gelato Orange but is now a sort of Infected Scab colour.

Everything is hem-frayed, stained, filthy, with an overpowering stench. The beanie he's holding is not something I'd want in contact with my head – in contact with my anything, actually.

'*Mycroft*. You know you nearly gave me a fucking heart attack, right?'

'Oh.' He finally notices how my fists are clenched. 'Shit, I'm sorry, I didn't even think about that.'

'Clearly. And what are you . . .' The words *doing* and *wearing* wage war in my mouth.

'Recon mission.' He has a long smear of brown along one cheek, but he's smiling. 'Wearing the appropriate. Sorry about the smell.'

'Why are you climbing over my back fence?' Through a gap in the shirt-layers I see his neck, filmed with a patina of dirt and sweat.

He waves his beanie at the fence palings. 'Dunno, really. Wasn't sure your mum would let me in the front. Did you know that the people in the house behind yours have an actual car body on stumps in their yard? Anyway, Pickup wants us – no emergency, but I thought I'd come over before he arrived. Maybe bot a shower?'

'You're not answering my—'

'Spent last night in the company of some useful friends. Very informative.'

Suddenly I recognise the clogged pong of drains, and it makes me twig. I feel my expression flatten. 'You were up near the sports ground.'

Mycroft shrugs. 'Pickup said a kid phoned in, so I went up for a chat. Had to look the part.'

'You're . . .' I'm trying to get my head around it. 'Oh my god, you're in *disguise*.'

He grins. 'Yeah. Clothes from the Salvos, then I jumped in the skip near the kebab shop.' His face goes sombre. 'Kids don't talk to cops – not these kids, anyway. Don't talk to anybody much, unless you've got something to offer.' He toes his backpack with a grotty runner – he's not wearing any socks – and I see the top of his thermos peeking out. 'The supernatural power of hot coffee and a smoke. Amazing, really.'

'Pickup told us to lie low.' My blood is doing the raspberry slushie thing again. 'You spent last night in a drain. You said you'd stopped investigating—'

'Watts, this isn't about Wild. It's about his man on the ground here in Melbourne. Whoever's got our ticket is still roaming around and I want this monkey off my back, don't you? Or do you *like* being stuck at home under house arrest again?' Before I can jump in with an angry reply, his eyes spear into me. '*They knew the girl*, Rachel. They knew her name. But that's not even the most incredible bit.' He squeezes my arm. 'I think they might have seen the guy who killed her.'

My shoulders straighten as Harris joins us.

He eyes Mycroft, glances at me. 'Your mum was wondering what had happened. I told her it was just this bloke, making a ruckus.'

'Thanks.' I frown at Harris. Mum might come storming out of the house now to chase Mycroft off, and I realise Harris probably told her for exactly that reason.

But then again, maybe that won't happen. Something funny has been going on with my parents since the second murder: there've been a lot of whispered conversations, and subdued, serious looks. Mum's attitude towards Mycroft appears to be undergoing a slow metamorphosis. Maybe she's discovered how he came to my rescue in London. I don't know what Dad or Mike might have told her, or what else she might have sussed out.

'Hello again,' Mycroft says to Harris. His voice is unnaturally neutral, formally British.

'Bit of a change from a dinner suit.' Harris squints at Mycroft's outfit.

I look between them. 'You two aren't going to bash each other up again, are you?'

'Well, that would be a bit immature, wouldn't it?' Mycroft says, but I can tell from his tone that he wouldn't mind. He swaps the filthy beanie to his other fist, sticks out his hand in Harris's direction. 'It's Harris, yeah?'

Harris stares at Mycroft's dirty hand for half a second before leaning forward to shake it. 'Yep. And you're . . . Mycroft?'

'Yeah.'

'Just the last name, is it?' Harris raises his eyebrows. 'Like Bond, James Bond.'

Something undefinable plays across both their features. I step between them. 'Okay, well, hand-shaking, there's a start. Mycroft, you said Pickup wanted us – please tell me that means good news.'

'Actually, Pickup's just the taxi service, sorry.' Mycroft rubs at his hair with the beanie, splicing out a collection of old cobwebs and adding more dirt. 'It's Professor Walsh who wants to see us. At his place. Apparently, there's some forensic detail he wants to hash out.'

'Bit ghoulish, isn't it?' Harris makes a face. 'Going over skin samples and nose hairs and stuff?'

'Sometimes the details are important,' Mycroft says, his back stiff.

It's strange, seeing them together. Harris is older, you can see it in the way he carries himself – the relaxed, louche posture, the confidence of a man. But Mycroft has a loose grace to all his movements, not to mention about ten centimetres of height on Harris. Even dressed in his ridiculous Infected Scab hoodie, he looks vital and cocksure.

It hits me hard then: a sudden vision of what Mycroft might look like in ten years' time, wearing the same nutmeg cords and reading glasses his father has on in the photos from the Anniversary Book . . . I wonder if I'll get to see that. I wonder if we'll live that long.

'Well, Walsh obviously thinks there's something we need to know.' My voice comes out hinky. I swallow and shake out the tension from my arms. 'I'd better go tell Mum. She'll have kittens if Pickup shows up unannounced.'

'I'll tell her,' Harris says. Maybe he's seen the way my eyes have clouded over. 'You go put your brace back on.'

The log stump is damp when I sit on it to roll up the leg of my trackie pants, wrap my brace around my knee. Mycroft stretches out on the lounger beside me, his backpack on the ground nearby. He seems oddly good-humoured, considering he's spent the night in a storm drain and is now lurking in the forbidden territory of my backyard. I still can't get over his outfit. It's a far cry from dinner jackets and braces. And I really *did* like that white shirt.

'You said the kids at the sports ground saw the killer.' I use brute force to do up the sticky velcro.

'Let's not get too excited yet,' Mycroft says. 'Their description was kind of vague. I'm trying to figure out a way to tell Pickup without getting yelled at.'

'Sorry to harsh your buzz, but I don't know if that's avoidable. And I bloody can't *believe* you went to the sports ground last night.'

'Little present to myself,' Mycroft says cryptically. He slings his legs either side of the pink plastic lounger and sits up. 'Sorry, Watts, I didn't mean to give you a scare. But who's gonna look for me in a storm drain?'

Half of me is freaked out by the risk he took, but the other half is just a little pissed off he didn't invite me along. I sigh. 'Christ, James, it's July. It must have been freezing up there.'

'Yeah – concrete in the dead of winter. Pretty cold.'

Something nags at the back of my mind. Something not murder-autopsy-conspiracy related . . . No, it's not coming to me.

'Glad I had the thermos,' Mycroft goes on. 'So, what about that shower? I've got a change of clothes in my bag.'

'Mum might take pity on you, because of the smell.'

Mycroft lifts his chin towards Harris's punching bag. 'I see Harris is still working the self-defence angle hard.'

'It's not an angle.' I tug the leg of my trackie pants back down, pick up the sweaty towel I abandoned on the stump earlier. 'He's dead serious about it. He keeps wanting me to beat him up.'

'Now, there's a training regime I can totally get behind.'

'Stop it.' I flick him with the towel. 'You two could both grow up a little, you know.'

'Where's the fun in that?'

And suddenly all the words – *little present, July, grow up* – jumble together in my head, and it comes to me. I sit up straight, my mouth falling open.

'Holy shit. It's the twenty-third.' Oh my god, I can't believe I didn't *remember*! 'Mycroft, it's your *birthday*. You're eighteen!'

He bites his lip over a grin, looks down at the pink plastic beneath him.

'Why didn't you say something?' I groan, throw the towel over my face. 'And I haven't even gotten you a present!'

'Hey, don't worry about it.' He reaches over to pull the towel off. 'Honestly, forget it. It's just a birthday.'

'It's not.' I get up and shift so I'm sitting on the lounger facing him, knee to knee. I grab his hands. 'It's important, it's your eighteenth. Oh god, I'm so sorry . . .'

'Well, we've had a few other things occupying our minds lately,' he says solemnly.

'I know, but still. Major girlfriend fail.' I feel terrible, but not terrible enough to stop myself laughing. 'Bloody hell. And I can't even kiss you right now, because you're too disgusting.'

He tugs on my fingers. 'I had a breath mint on the way over, if that sways you.' He smiles temptingly. 'It's nice to see you, after two days . . .'

'It's nice to see you, too.' I throw my towel at him, grab his backpack and pull him up, lead him towards the back door. 'Shower. Now.'

He pulls the towel away cautiously. 'Will this disguise get me past your mum?'

'You're joking, right? She's gonna smell you from the other end of the house.'

Tackling the situation head on seems the best bet. Yanking the door open, I pull Mycroft straight into the laundry, where Mum's sorting clothes from the hamper into the washing machine. She looks up and her eyes go wide as her forehead puckers. I open my mouth to start a heartfelt spiel about needing to meet with Walsh, and how it's Mycroft's birthday, but she beats me to the punch.

'Oh my god.' She holds one hand over her nose, waves the other in the direction of the bathroom. 'Shower. Now. For pity's sake . . .'

Mycroft has time to call out, 'Thanks, Mrs Watts!' before I haul him away. But Mum's reaction to Mycroft is enough to confirm everything I've suspected. Something is going on. I can hear the gentle drip of glaciers melting.

Fifteen minutes later, Mycroft reappears in the kitchen dressed in fresh jeans and a long-sleeved blue T-shirt from his backpack. He didn't have a clean jacket, so I've returned an old hoodie of his that I stole months ago.

Harris is crunching toast at the bench. 'So your cop mate is sending a car over to pick you up?'

'I don't like the idea of you going out. Either of you.' Mum hands me a steaming mug, then hands one to Mycroft with no fanfare at all.

'It'll be okay, Mum,' I say. 'We'll be with Pickup and Walsh, and we'll be together.'

'Great,' Harris says. 'So this nutter can kill two birds with one stone.'

'*Harris!*' Mum and I exclaim in tandem.

Mycroft holds his mug in two hands, like a penitent. 'I'll take good care of her, Mrs Watts.'

Mum smiles tightly, but she's not mollified. I can see it in her eyes as she leaves the kitchen when the doorbell's tinny ring sounds. I limp into the living room to grab my jacket and satchel. Voices from the kitchen still me.

'You'll take good care of her,' Harris says, sneering bitterness in his voice. 'Right. Like you did in London?'

From the clip of Mycroft's accent, I can tell he's got his hackles up. 'How has this got anything to do with you?'

Harris makes a disgusted noise. 'Rachel's solid. Last time I knew her, she was riding the quaddie and having a fine old life. Now she's here, getting in deep with you and being crapped on from a great height. I mean, *death threats? Murders?* How is this good for her?'

'Maybe you should keep your opinions to yourself.'

'Maybe I'm not a big fan of Pommy know-it-alls who put my friends in danger.'

Mycroft's snort is explosive. 'And you're the Outback Jack who's gonna fix it, are you? Jesus, you are so full of shit.'

'Mate, you're gonna wish you never said that—'

I hustle back into the kitchen, clearly just in time. Mycroft and Harris are standing eyeball to eyeball near the kitchen bench, hands clenched into fists.

'*Guys!*' The table wobbles as I slam my hand onto the yellow laminex surface. 'This is not a pissing contest! We don't have time for this – Harris, pull your head in. And Mycroft, if you start throwing punches again, I'll hit you myself!'

I turn just at the moment Mum and Pickup walk into the kitchen.

Pickup surveys the scene with interest. 'Missed something, have I?'

'Nothing worth talking about,' I say. 'Come on, Mycroft, let's go.'

CHAPTER ELEVEN

In the car on the way to Walsh's place, we check the blog on Mycroft's phone. There's a reply message. Mycroft swears, and Pickup's hold on the steering wheel falters.

'You'd better take a look, Detective,' I say, already wincing at the thought of Pickup's reaction.

Pickup pulls over on St Kilda Road, ignoring another driver's tooting horn. He takes Mycroft's phone and studies it. 'Yes, I saw your message from Monday night. I did tell you both not to make contact with him, correct?'

'It's my fault,' Mycroft says. 'I sent the message before Rachel could stop me.'

'This is what happens when you don't do as you're told.' Pickup refocuses on the phone's screen. 'Right. That's your message, saying you'll drop the investigation. And now Wild's replied, *I am quite sure that a man of your intelligence will see that there can be but one outcome to this affair. Surrender what is mine, or I will be forced to take extreme measures* . . . Part of that sounds like another quote. But are you positive you don't know what he's referring to? Because he sure seems to think you do.'

'If I knew, don't you think I'd tell you?' Mycroft says angrily.

Pickup's expression goes completely arid. 'Indeed. Because you have such an excellent reputation for sharing crucial information with your police friends.'

He turns around and pulls back onto the road.

At the metal-barred door to Walsh's apartment block, Mycroft presses the buzzer for Walsh to let us up. Someone's yappy little dog is barking non-stop from across the street. Pickup has let us out at the security entrance, and gone to park.

'Have you been here before?' Freezing wind from the bay whips strands of my hair into my mouth and eyes. It feels weird, being out of the confines of Summoner Street. It's become my whole world lately, and sometimes I have to look beyond the fence to the steel and glass in the distance to remind myself that I'm still in Melbourne.

'Never.' Mycroft scratches at his jaw. 'Didn't even know he lived in Albert Park.'

The door buzzes, and we bundle into a swish modern foyer with sound-deadening carpet. Up three floors, we eventually find the right door. A flicker at the peephole tells me that someone has checked it's us, then the door opens wide.

Professor Walsh looks a bit more drawn than the last time I saw him, and he's rubbing at his reddened nose with a handkerchief. He's wearing the same tweedy trousers he had on in London, with a cream shirt and a thin brown jumper. Warm air from the apartment – central heating – washes over me, and I shiver.

Walsh stuffs his handkerchief away in his pocket. 'Hello, goodness, it's freezing out there today. Come in, come in. Where's Vincent?'

'Finding a park,' Mycroft says.

There's an oriental-patterned runner in the hallway, and I feel an urge to take off my shoes – that's what you always do in nice houses – but Walsh ushers us on. We follow him until the tastefully decorated hall expands out into an open-plan kitchen and dining area.

I smell something delicious stewing. Wooden benchtops are paired with nice appliances, and there's a stainless steel fridge in the niche on the left. A man in a blue shirt is pulling out a stack of bowls from the cupboard and setting them on the bench.

'. . . wasn't completely sure you'd come,' Walsh is saying as I zone back in, 'but we made enough for everybody. Early dinner all right?' He gestures to the man, who's removing a thick handful of maroon napkins from a drawer. 'My partner, Douglas Givens.'

Douglas is in his late fifties, much stockier than Walsh, with thin ginger hair and a slightly florid face under his glasses.

'Nice to meet you both. Just sorry it had to be over something like this.' He makes an apologetic shrug as we shake hands in turn. 'I'd like to say I could contribute, but it's not really my area. Theoretical Mathematics Fellow, I'm afraid. '

'Nice to meet you, Mr Givens,' I say.

'Oh, just Douglas, please. Mycroft and Rachel, isn't it?'

'Yeah,' I say. 'Sorry to intrude. Detective Pickup said the Professor is still on sick leave.'

'Goodness, don't worry yourself about it. Emmett is a terrible patient, and a few juicy murders make a wonderful diversion for him.'

He grins before smothering it, realising too late that he's made a conversational gaffe. I'm reminded of a little kid who blurts things out with thoughtless honesty – it's the kind of thing I would do, and it makes me like Douglas straight away.

'You must be under a great deal of stress,' Walsh says. He checks his watch, even though there's a clock on the wall above the sink, then waves at the large dining-room table. 'Why don't we have a bit of a talk about it now, before Pickup arrives.'

Walsh collects two document folders from a sideboard, and sits at the head of the table. Mycroft takes a seat to his left, and I dump my satchel and sit next to Mycroft, as if having his body between me and the forensic evidence will shield me somehow.

'Stephen Rossi dropped off the PM report this morning,' Walsh says, opening the first folder and re-positioning his glasses. 'How did you find Dr Rossi, by the way?'

'Abrasive,' I say. 'Rude. Disrespectful.'

'Yes, yes, Stephen is all those things.' Walsh chuckles briefly. 'He's also incredibly thorough, which is why I asked Pickup to assign him both of these autopsies. He wasn't assigned the PM on the first case, the boy, but when I explained the circumstances he reviewed the file and arranged another examination.'

'So did Rossi find anything out of the usual?' Mycroft asks.

'A couple of odd things. Are you both going to be all right examining these photos again?'

I grip my thighs under the table. 'Show us.'

There are two gold envelopes this time, and Walsh removes the glossies from the second one. Douglas, who's been transferring bowls to the table, winces and glances away.

It's the girl. I'm hit again with that wash of sadness and despair I felt the other night when I first saw her body. But I'm not as badly affected this time – I can handle it, resign myself to it.

I hear Mycroft's sharp intake of breath, though, and when he sees the photos his whole body tenses like a coiled wire.

'Yes, I'm sorry,' Walsh says. 'If you don't think you can look—'

'No. I need to look,' Mycroft says.

Walsh pulls out the photos of the boy, Benjamin Tonna, and we study the two sets of autopsy shots. Walsh's lovely dining table becomes a Scene of Crime, complete with blood spatter.

The pictures are comprehensive, showing all the details of the victims' outward appearances when they died. Then we see the photos of them unclothed, cut open. I don't look at these ones for long, but it's the pathos of it that gets me. The quiet bodies, now here, vandalised.

My voice comes out with rough edges. 'So tell us what we've got.'

Walsh blows his nose again, tucks the hankie in his pocket. 'What we've got is someone who likes to conceal their activities under the guise of accidental death. If I didn't know there was a suspicion of homicide, I'd have been hard-pressed to tell that anything in particular had happened apart from two very unfortunate accidents.'

Mycroft looks up from the photos. 'So that in itself is a bit of a giveaway, isn't it? The fact that the murders are so rigorously staged to look like misadventure.'

'Most definitely.' Walsh selects a few photos to display. 'You see here, in both cases, we have a victim who appears to have fallen. But look at the hands – not the broken fingers, the sides of the hands.'

I squint at the picture of the girl. 'Are these bruises?'

Walsh nods. 'Yes. So we could be looking at evidence of the victim struggling with an assailant, even in a restricted way. '

The intercom buzzes and Douglas moves to answer it.

Walsh goes on. 'Of course, the most pertinent factor is the broken bones. Dr Rossi checked the cortisol, and there's a definite spike in both victims. Tricky to determine in the boy's case, given the height of the fall, but on closer examination it looks as though his ribs were broken with a brick or weight of some kind – see the faint marks here? We see similar marks on the girl's fingers.'

'Becky,' Mycroft says softly. 'The kids up near the sports ground said the girl's name was Becky.'

It's just bad luck that Pickup enters the room with Douglas the moment Mycroft says this.

'Since *when*,' Pickup says, throwing down his coat on a chair, 'do you go off on your own questioning witnesses? Especially after I told you to stay home?'

The exchange in the car has clearly already set them both on edge.

Mycroft holds Pickup's gaze. 'Look, your guys didn't have any luck chasing up those kids. I bet they scattered as soon as they saw the cops, am I right?'

Pickup seats himself at the table, still glowering at Mycroft. 'You're not a detective, son.'

'All the same,' Mycroft says, 'I got the girl's name, and a description of a guy lurking around asking questions. It's nothing you could take to court, but I'll write up the details if you like.'

Pickup makes a disgruntled sound through his nose.

Walsh clears his throat. 'If we could return to the matter of the evidence.' He indicates a spot on another photo I'm examining. 'Mycroft, I know you have some knowledge of forensic engineering, and there's something even more interesting in the girl's case – Becky's case. Becky weighed forty-three kilos.'

'God, that's light,' I say.

'Yes. So a forty-three kilo person, standing about five foot tall, falling with an estimated acceleration of standard gravity, hits the concrete rim of the drainage pipe. You should end up with a wound of roughly what depth?'

'That's, um, like an estimate of terminal ballistics . . .' Mycroft scrunches his eyebrows. 'What are the measurements again?'

Walsh tells him, then goes on. 'So the kinetic energy of a moving object is half the mass, times the velocity of the object squared—'

'Er, if I may . . .' Douglas, who's been sitting in a wing-backed armchair over by the large bay window, raises his hand. 'Velocity is the square root of twice acceleration times distance travelled, so in this case, about five-point-four-seven.'

Walsh nods at him. 'And consider that the depth of the wound would depend on the amount of kinetic energy transferred plus the nature of the tissue—'

'—and the impact on a curved surface will cause greater damage,' Mycroft says. 'So we should be looking at a wound of a relative depth. But that isn't . . .' He scrabbles through the photos until he finds the one he needs. 'It's not consistent. Half her skull is caved in.'

'That's right. Do you see where I'm going with this?'

Mycroft looks at the Professor. 'She contacted the drain edge with a much greater amount of additional force.'

'Come again?' Pickup asks.

'She was pushed, with considerable additional force, onto the edge of the pipe,' Walsh says. 'Also, Stephen noticed that there's a contre-coup injury – a contusion on the opposite side of the brain to the area of impact. It suggests a significant deceleration force. In other words, it appears that her head was supported from behind.'

It strikes me with such horror I want to get up and turn away from the table. Instead, I level my gaze at Pickup. 'So, all these little clues tell us that both cases were deliberate homicides.'

Pickup nods. 'Finally, something solid. I've been in touch with the English crew as well. Simon Gupta and that other bloke,

Mr Worth—' he catches my eye-roll, '—who I *know* you don't trust, but he's emailing me the details of the police interviews with your Colonel fellow, as well as a bunch of other material on the case. Now, son, what about this description?'

Mycroft sits up as Pickup catches his eye. 'Like I said, nothing that would hold up in court. A guy, perhaps in his thirties, with dark hair, slicked back. Jeans, a green windbreaker. They said he smoked, and that he had a lined face. That's it.'

'We knew about the smoking.' Walsh checks the notes in the SOC dossier. 'Hand-rolled Champion Ruby cigarettes. There were no butts, but testing at the site revealed fresh ash on the victim's clothes.'

I get a mental image of the killer standing over the bodies of Benjamin Tonna, of Becky, and casually rolling and smoking a cigarette before departing. It makes me shudder.

'The killer obviously thought to collect the butts,' Mycroft says.

'He's a pro, then.' Pickup nods firmly.

'Perhaps,' Walsh agrees, 'but he clearly didn't realise that we can identify the brand with certainty from ash remains.'

Mycroft leans his elbows on the table and spreads his hands over the photos. 'So Wild's done the same thing he did in England – hired a professional to do his dirty work.'

'Well, the guy's local,' I say. 'Champion Ruby – that's an Australian brand.'

'The killer could have changed brands,' Walsh suggests.

'I doubt it,' Pickup says. 'And if he'd flown over from England, he could have bought his own brand duty-free. Rachel's right, this is a local operator. The modus operandi gives it away. This is someone who knows the lay of the land in Melbourne. Who doesn't mind chatting around at street level to find the kind of victim he needs.'

'Someone who's skilled at making "accidents" happen,' Mycroft says. He pushes out of his chair and walks away from the table. Over by the bay window, a handsome wooden chess set sits on an occasional table facing Douglas in the wing-backed chair. The pieces appear to be in mid-game. Mycroft touches the endangered white king, rolls it on its base.

'All this cloak-and-dagger bullshit – sending us these messages, setting up these murder scenes in such an unnecessarily elaborate way . . . Wild must know where we both *live*. If he wants us dead, why doesn't he just . . .' His face screws up, and for a moment, I think he's about to throw the chess piece at the window. 'I feel like I'm being *jerked around*. Do you know what I mean?'

Douglas leans forward in his chair, watches Mycroft's fingers on the chess board. 'Do you play?'

'Pardon?' Mycroft looks at him. 'Oh. Sorry, no. Well, I mean I can play. I just don't really enjoy it. The set moves frustrate me.'

'You prefer looking outside the square.'

'Yeah. I have the same problem with most computer games.'

Douglas smiles. 'Chess is a good way of teaching strategy.'

'Maybe I should have paid closer attention when I was learning,' Mycroft says bitterly. 'I'd have a strategy now.'

'Well then, let's imagine,' Douglas says. He clears the board, rearranges the pieces. 'Emmett has explained some of the circumstances of the case to me – I hope you don't mind,' Douglas goes on. 'So, a good chess player always thinks a certain number of moves ahead. Now, your Mr Wild is obviously quite strategic, quite logical, despite his name. He's used his pieces to set you up, make you vulnerable.'

Douglas has arranged a black king in one corner of the board, surrounded by pawns and a select number of allies. On the opposite side, a white king and queen stand embattled.

'Wild is trying to anticipate your next move. He's making it easier for himself by choosing moves of his own that hem you in, to limit your choices.' Douglas looks up at Mycroft. 'So in a way, thinking beyond the set moves, thinking outside the square, could be an advantage. That makes you a whole lot less predictable.'

'One for our team,' I mutter.

'Yes,' Douglas says, sharing a smile with me. 'But you, in turn, have to think about what Wild is like, so you can predict what *he'll* do next.'

'But we don't know anything about him. We don't even know his real name.'

'Ah, but famous chess players know their opponents without ever meeting them before a game. They know them by studying the moves they've made in other games. So what moves has Wild already made?'

I rub the nape of my neck as I think. 'He's ... he's tried to frighten us by killing people who resemble us.'

'So, he's not above a bit of theatre. A braggart, then.'

'That's right – the theatre bit, that's true. He calls himself *Moriarty* when he contacts us, he uses Conan Doyle quotes ... And the set-up for Daniel Gardener's murder in England, with Irina Addington as a scapegoat – that was really elaborate as well.'

'What else?'

I squint with concentration. What other things do I know about Wild, without ever realising I knew them? 'Well, there's the fact that he *has* contacted us personally. And both here and in England, he's used other people to do his work.'

Mycroft's been gazing at distant palm trees out the window; now his eyes return to the room. 'He's not too worried about getting someone to torture a couple of teenagers to gain information – he ordered the Colonel to interrogate us that way in England. And he's had two teenagers killed just to send a warning.'

'So – a true king,' Douglas nods. 'He's ruthless and he's thorough. He delegates.'

'He's a collector,' Mycroft says. 'The Shakespeare Folio, the other cases in England . . . They're all related to artworks or artefacts.'

'Is that all we know?'

'I can't think of anything else,' I say.

Pickup is nodding. 'It's a good start.'

Walsh sniffs and stirs beside me. 'It would be easier, wouldn't it, if it really were like a chess game, or maybe one of the Sherlock Holmes stories. We'd understand the players, and there'd be an even greater element of predictability.'

I watch him slide the autopsy photos back into their gold sleeves. 'In the Conan Doyle stories, there weren't actually that many central players. Moriarty had his henchmen, and Holmes and Watson had Lestrade . . .'

I look towards Pickup as I say this. I don't mean to do it, but he certainly notices.

'So I've been relegated to fictional sidekick now, is that it?' Pickup cocks an eyebrow. 'Thanks very much.'

'The only other characters were the Irregulars,' I say, 'and Mrs Hudson, Holmes's landlady.'

Mycroft makes a sudden noise. His head turns sharply in my direction. 'Oh shit. There's something else. Don't you remember? The Colonel said it, he said . . .' He's fumbling for his phone, and his face has gone chalky.

'Mycroft, what—'

'*Eliminate this man, eliminate his family.*' He presses the phone to his ear. 'It's not just about the central players. Wild knocks down *all* the pieces.'

Which is when I remember Angela, at home alone. My expression shifts, I feel it – I must be almost as wide-eyed as Mycroft when I push back my chair to stand. 'Is she answering?'

Mycroft shakes his head, his lips stiff. He redials as Professor Walsh rises.

'Vincent—' Walsh says to Pickup, but Pickup has already dashed for his own phone in his coat.

He clicks his fingers to get my attention. 'What about your place?'

I press my palms onto the table, feeling light-headed. 'They're ... they're all at work. Mum will have left for her shift. Dad and Mike will get home before eight. Harris is at home, but nobody knows he's there—'

I'm cut off as Pickup starts talking in brusque officialese with someone on the other end of his line.

Douglas looks anxiously from Pickup to Mycroft to me. 'Do you think he'd really move on your families?'

'You said it yourself.' I squeeze my cold fingers. 'Wild is ruthless.'

Mycroft takes two steps towards the table. I don't think he's even realised he's still got a chess piece clasped in one hand. 'I can't raise her.'

I take one look at him, then turn to Pickup. '*Detective.*'

He's already finished his call. 'I'll drive you home,' he says, holding out his keys.

CHAPTER TWELVE

The whole way back to Coburg I keep my hand glued onto Mycroft's rigid shoulder. He tries calling Angela again and again, with no luck. Outside the car, wind swirls rubbish in the streets and yanks rudely at people's clothes. The darkening day reflects off all the city glass.

I clutch Mycroft's shoulder. 'Maybe she doesn't have her phone on her.'

He shakes his head. 'She's always got it with her now.' His face is controlled, but his eyes tell another story.

Mycroft and Angela are a funny pair. They treat each other more like distant housemates than family, with a peculiarly formal arrangement of words and gestures. But the small kindnesses – Mycroft making her the odd cup of tea, Angela taking greater care with the grocery shopping, both of them staying in contact with one another – reveal how things have improved. The trip to Bali seems to have drawn them even closer. And now I understand just how much Mycroft cares about his aunt, because the fear inside him is pulsing hot, even if it's tightly contained behind a wooden expression.

I lean towards Pickup in the driver's seat. 'Can't we go any faster?'

He checks me in the rear-view. 'One sec.'

He reaches down and presses a button. Even without the siren, traffic clears before us like the parting of the Red Sea, but the throb of the blue and red dashboard lights is like the ominous build-up to a bad dream. Maybe the reason Pickup offered to take us, instead of waiting for another car, was so he would be first on the scene – if Mycroft's home turns out to be a crime scene. And *my* home, *my* family, is only two doors down ... An iron fist is clamped around my heart by the time we turn sharply onto Summoner Street.

Pickup is still coming to a stop when Mycroft flings the door open and jumps out of the car. Pickup bangs his foot on the brake and swears; I have to throw up a hand to stop myself from whacking into the seat in front. Mycroft has vaulted the gate and started running up the side of his house before Pickup has even gotten out of the driver's seat.

I struggle to move quickly with my limp. When Pickup and I reach the back door we can hear Mycroft inside, yelling hoarsely.

'Angela!'

I find him in the kitchen, spinning in a circle as he takes in one rinsed plate on the drainer, one mug. I feel sick at how frantic his eyes are.

'*ANGELA!*'

He's in the hall, reaching for the handle of the frosted glass door to the living area that leads to Angela's room, and Pickup is saying, 'Son, why don't you let me . . .' when a shadow coalesces on the other side of the door and it opens to reveal Angela Hudgson, startled and a bit embarrassed. She's wearing her nylon dressing gown and her wet hair is slicked back. Her face looks flushed, fresh.

'I'm *here*, James, goodness. What's all the . . . ?' Her eyes travel from Mycroft, to me, to Pickup.

Mycroft makes this knife-sharp inhale and turns away, staggering a few steps down the hall towards his room. His hand clutches the wall, and his head hangs forward, like he's going to throw up.

'James?' Angela looks towards him, then back to me. 'I was just . . . in the shower . . .'

'It's fine.' My breaths are large and calming, and I nod a lot. 'He was . . . We were worried when we couldn't get you on the phone.'

Pickup elaborates carefully. 'We've had some concerns with this police case, that family members may be at risk. When Mr Mycroft couldn't raise you on the phone, he became anxious for your safety.'

Angela's whole face changes when Pickup says this. She looks back to Mycroft.

He's standing just outside the door to his room, with his back to us and his hand clamped on the lintel. He's leaning over, his other hand on his waist, as though he's got a stitch. When Angela walks over to him and puts a tentative hand on his arm, he shudders.

'James?'

He straightens and turns; his face shows a barely controlled combination of utter relief and terror. When he speaks, his voice comes out hoarse and deep. 'I'm fine, it's okay. I was . . . I was worried you . . .'

Angela doesn't say anything, just puts her hands on his shoulders. Then Mycroft makes a choked sound and his arms go around her, and they are *hugging*. I've *never* seen Mycroft and Angela hug. Mycroft clings to her, as if she's just saved his life. Angela reaches up and pats his hair gently like he's a baby. His face is buried in her shoulder, and Angela makes soft gentling sounds.

I don't know where to look. Pickup tugs on my sleeve and we back out of the house until we reach the rear step.

'Looks like everything's in order.' Pickup's face has relaxed into a standard frown. 'I'll head back to the station then, unless there's something else you need.'

I nod and shake my head, dazed. My legs are a bit wobbly as the adrenalin recedes.

'Do you think what Mycroft said was true, about our families being at risk?' I don't care that anxiousness has coloured my voice grey, pinched my vowels taut. I need to know.

Pickup scratches the orange stubble on his head, his normally cool eyes uncertain.

'Look, I'm not saying it's not possible. But everything that's happened so far suggests that the focus is on you two. Let's not get ourselves worked up yet, okay? I'll make some arrangements to keep an eye on your families, but there's a limit to our resources. Let's concentrate them in the place we know we definitely need them.' He glances one last time towards the scene of Mycroft and his aunt. 'Keep your heads down. I'll be in touch again soon.'

He pats my shoulder and heads back to his car. I'm left on the back step, wondering whether I should walk back to my place, when Mycroft appears in the doorway behind me.

'Hey.' He's red-eyed, but his voice is steady. 'Come back in. It's all right.'

Angela isn't anywhere in sight as I follow Mycroft to his room. I leave the door ajar behind me. Mycroft grabs a T-shirt from the pile of dirty clothes near his bed and wipes his face with it, before scrabbling for the pack of smokes in his hoodie pocket.

'Bloody hell.' He takes his time lipping a cigarette out of the soft pack, raking at his hair with his free hand. 'Bit of a scene, eh?'

I step closer. 'You feeling all right now?'

'Mm.' He gropes for a lighter in his jeans pocket. 'Probably need a cup of tea. Or maybe a stiff drink.'

'Probably.' I smile at him gently. 'Where's Angela?'

'I'm here.'

I turn to see Angela at the door to the Stranger's Room. She looks red around the eyes too, but otherwise her face – usually so closed off and tense – seems clear and bright. She looks younger: more like the thirty-eight-year-old she is, instead of the tired, middle-aged woman she typically appears to be. Her hands are clasped around a thick brown-paper envelope.

'Here.' She thrusts the envelope in Mycroft's direction. 'I was going to give this to you earlier, but ... Well, we both got a bit busy.'

Mycroft takes the unlit cigarette out of his mouth and tucks it behind his ear.

'Did you get me a birthday present?' He's looking at her as though this idea in itself is a bit of a miracle.

Angela shrugs. 'Actually, I thought you'd like a new printer for your birthday, I just haven't had a chance to talk to you about it. But this is different.' She proffers the envelope insistently. 'You should take it.'

Mycroft is half-grinning as he takes the thing, the brown paper crinkling in his hands. 'What, *two* presents? That's a bit—'

His words cut off abruptly. His grin dies as he stares at the package. He turns it over carefully, as though it might explode. 'This is my mum's handwriting. On the paper, my mum's . . .' His face is white.

I step closer. 'Mycroft . . .'

He stares at Angela, his eyes hardening. 'What is this?'

'I don't know what it is, but it's from your mum and dad. From their estate.' Angela stands there and takes his stare, cupping her elbows as she folds her arms tightly across her diaphragm. 'It was given to me with specific instructions that I should hold on to it until you turned eighteen. Well, now you're eighteen. '

My mouth opens, because this is completely unexpected. Mycroft seems to be utterly thrown by it. He sways on the spot for a moment before recovering, his eyes boring holes into Angela's face.

'You've had this . . .' He presses his lips. 'You've had this, from my parents, for eight years. And you never told me.'

'There was no point telling you,' Angela says. 'You couldn't open it until now. It just would have been a bit torturous, don't you think?'

Mycroft splutters. 'Well, yes, but . . .'

Angela steps forward, right into Mycroft's room. What she does next makes me gasp: she leans up on tiptoe and kisses Mycroft on the cheek. Mycroft is so flummoxed he shuts up straight away.

'Happy birthday, James,' Angela says.

She turns and is almost out in the hall before Mycroft finds his words. 'Thank you.'

Angela smiles over her shoulder. 'That's okay.'

Mycroft stares down the hallway for so long after she leaves that I think he's forgotten about the envelope, so I touch his arm.

'Mycroft.' He jumps and I squeeze his hand to settle him. 'Aren't you going to open it?'

'I . . .' He closes his mouth, blinks at the package, blinks at me. 'Yes.'

We end up sitting on the bed. Mycroft shuts the door first, comes back to sit beside me on the worn sheets, holding the envelope the whole time.

It's a plain brown-paper envelope, with a bit of white string tied around it. There's writing on the outside, which says *For James, when he reaches the age of eighteen*, and the whole thing already makes me sad before we've even seen the contents. I don't know how Mycroft can sit there so impassively, just staring. Then it occurs to me that he's scared.

'Just pull the string,' I suggest softly, and he does.

The paper is dry and it crackles delicately. Inside is a folded sheaf of papers and a small, flat circular object in a cellophane bag with a red-marked label.

'What is it?' I lean on Mycroft's arm to look.

He holds the bag up to the light, his hand faintly shaking. 'It's a . . . coin. An old coin.'

He unfolds the papers carefully. There are about six sheets, covered in symbols.

'That's my mum's writing,' Mycroft says. But then he finds another two sheets of paper that are of a different texture from the others, more like onionskin. When he opens them out, his breath catches. 'It's my dad. This is my . . .' And his voice disappears completely.

I don't know what to do except hold on to his arm. 'Aren't you going to read it?'

Mycroft looks at the first page, shakes his head and presses the onionskin sheets into my hands. 'You do it.'

I startle. 'I-I *can't*. It's from your parents. I shouldn't—'

'I want you to. Please.' His lips are dry, and his eyes dart all over the place. 'Please.'

So I take the sheets and turn them towards me. It feels almost like sacrilege, but I am doing this for Mycroft, who is leaning against me. Tremors run through his body, as though little lightning storms are going off inside him. His face is close to mine, and his breathing is shimmering and desperate.

I clear my throat and begin to read.

'*Dear Jamie . . .*'

That is almost enough to do me in, right there. I swallow and start again.

'*Dear Jamie. I hope you never get this letter. I really do. But if the worst comes, and somehow we all end up separated—*'

I glance at Mycroft. His eyes are closed and his thumbnail is digging crescents into the scar on his bottom lip. I go on.

'*—if we all end up separated, then you will need this to help you understand what went wrong and why. You will be eighteen when you read this – eighteen, my god. Maybe everything will be cleared up by then. I hope so. If not, you will need the things your mother and I have put aside for you, and you will be old enough to act on them.*'

I steady the pages: they're shaking in my hands. It feels as if I'm channelling spirits, and my flesh isn't enough to contain them.

'*The coin is an Athenian Owl dekadrachm, from about 460BC. It is what got me into trouble in the first place. The papers are from your mother. They are a coded transcript of a report I wrote as part of a larger analysis of British Home Office corruption in 2006. Please send both of these items to Mr Robert Evelyn Hannah – he is a friend from the Home Office. He will know what to do with them.*'

I pause here, because Mycroft has made a grunt. When I look over, his eyes are fixed on the papers.

'Hannah.' I frown at the onionskin, at Mycroft. 'He was the one. Your dad thought he was a safe contact . . .'

'My dad was wrong.' Mycroft's voice is a rasping whisper, as though it's crawling out of a hole in the earth.

I look back at the sheets, take a breath.

'Don't worry that this doesn't make a lot of sense. I would rather you didn't know any details, as it's not safe. But once the service has decoded the transcript they will act on it, and inform you of the result, which I hope will bring you some closure.'

Mycroft's face is in his hands. 'Keep going.'

I don't want to. I feel like I'm hurting him. He sounds muffled and broken. But I go on.

'Finally, I'm writing this quickly, but here's the part I need to say – Jamie, you are the most wonderful boy.' My voice catches, but I keep reading. *'. . . I know, and your mum knows, that you will grow into a wonderful and talented young man. We both love you more than anything, more than life. Please remember that. And if this is the last time we get to communicate with you—'*

Mycroft groans, deep in his chest. In one sharp movement, he pushes himself up to stand on shaky legs. Now I'm strongly aware of how *big* he is in this room – his height, the breadth of his shoulders. His whole body expands and contracts with each breath. He steadies himself at the desk, head low, propping himself up as I read on.

'I-if this is the last time,' I stammer, *'remember to hold on to that, the fact that we love you. I hope to be with you, I hope to destroy this letter once we are safe, but if that doesn't happen, then remember . . .'*

I can't go on then, because Mycroft starts making noises – terrible, choking noises. Suddenly he curls his hands into fists and sweeps them across the desk. Papers and rupiah and half a mug of tea go flying. His laptop is tugged away from its spot, following the wires of his printer, which tumbles onto the carpet.

'Mycroft!' I clamber up, still holding the onionskin sheets.

I try to put a hand on his shoulder, but he shakes me off. When he turns around his eyes are scrunched closed and his face is contorted, wild.

I barely have time to lurch out of the way when he gives another cavernous groan, and kicks over the bookshelf by the bed. Books tumble in a forest of page-litter. The orange-shaded lamp on top of the bookshelf bounces away – I hear the globe smash. Mycroft staggers sideways, throwing his hands along the wall, pulling down paperwork from the Anniversary display.

'Mycroft, don't!' I grab for his arm, but it's like cast iron. The sounds coming out of him are making the hair on the back of my neck stand up, so I do the only thing I can do – I keep reading.

'Mycroft, your dad said something else! He said *don't hang on to the past.*' I shake the thin sheets. *'Take our love for you and move forward with it, into your future. We will always be proud of you, whatever you do—'*

Mycroft sobs out a terrible sound, and pushes his desk chair away, hard enough for it to topple over. But his energy is deserting him. He drops cross-legged into the spot the chair occupied, clutching his head, looking so wretched I can only sink down onto the low mattress near him.

'Don't,' he gasps. *'Stop.'*

I put a tentative hand on his shoulder. *'Don't grieve too long.* That's what he says here. *Don't grieve too long.'*

He *wails* then, and rocks sideways. I slide off the mattress onto the carpet in time to catch him. And I read the last few lines like that, with my arms circling him, his head against my shoulder. My voice is very small and quiet.

'He says, *live life*. D'you see? Right here. *Live life. Find something that fulfils you. Fall in love.* He says, *I know you will give your best to everything, like always. I know you will shine, James.* James—'

A deep keening sob tears out of him, and he clutches me tight. Then it's like a cork has been wrenched out of a bottle. He sobs and sobs. His body heaves, and I feel like I'm in a boat on the sea. I have to hang on to him to keep us both from falling overboard.

'James,' I whisper. I hug him and hug him. 'Jamie . . .'

I have never done this before, never held a boy as he cried with his arms wrapped around me. It's gut-wrenching. The last time I saw a guy cry like this was my dad, when his brother died. This is even worse – it's eight years of suppressed grief, of stoppered emotion, eight years of anguish James couldn't express. And it feels as if boys cry differently, because they do it so infrequently, so when they let go it's like some kind of tectonic force, like mountains crashing together. I am moved by the power of it.

He is clinging to me, curled against me, and he is very heavy. I am weeping a bit too, although these are not my parents, this is not my pain. But it's impossible not to feel it, because the grief in this room is like something you can taste, thick and tangible.

I don't know how long James sobs against me, but after a while he starts to quiet. I stroke his hair. He is still shuddering, so I make those sounds I've heard my mum make when she's calming lambs or other people's babies, just little crooning sounds that come out of me automatically, and I rock him. We rock and rock, until the storm abates and the sea lulls into soft bobbing waves. It takes a while, and I wonder if he's gone to sleep, but then his hand squeezes my waist and he clears his throat.

'I don't think I can move.' His voice is thick and burred, like sheep's wool.

'Here.' I disentangle him. 'Come on.'

His face is a wreck. I give him a T-shirt off the end of the bed, and he wipes and blows and cleans up. But I don't think he has the energy to stand. He's a big pile of bones between my knees. When I reach forward to unzip his hoodie, he startles.

'It's okay,' I say. 'Let's get you into bed.'

He looks hollowed out, like his insides have been removed. When I pull back the blankets on his bed, he crawls onto the futon shoes and all.

The hoodie comes off easily, and the shoes. I spoon around behind him, propped on one elbow, and run my hand down his arm.

'You don't have to stay,' he whispers.

I lean forward and kiss him on the ear. 'I want to.'

He shudders one last time and grabs for my hand, pulls it onto his chest.

I lie there, turning everything over in my mind. When I'm sure he's asleep, I get up carefully and creep to the door.

Out in the kitchen, Angela is dressed now in trackie pants and thick socks and layers of jumpers. 'How is he?'

'Asleep.' I look outside the kitchen window; it's black, and I have no idea of the time. 'I'd like to stay, but my parents—'

'I rang them.' Angela scrapes her hair back. 'I spoke to your dad, explained what's going on. I told him I'd like to keep you for tonight, if that's all right.'

'You – you told him what happened?'

'I told him James received a bequest from his parents because he came of age and that it upset him a hell of a lot, and that you've been really good at calming him down.'

'I didn't do anything. I just let him cry.'

'That's enough,' Angela says firmly. 'But do you want to go home now? I can walk you back if you like.'

I think for a moment. 'I'd like to stay.'

Angela's smile is soft. 'Good. I won't ask where you're sleeping, although your father said something about keeping the door open?'

'Right. The door.' I feel a bit limp, and suddenly it's an effort to stand up.

'Thank you,' Angela says, and I know she's not just talking about staying the night.

When I return to the Stranger's Room, James is still sleeping. I slip off my shoes and angle the oil heater so it's closer to the bed. Then I lie down and pull up the blankets, tuck my face into the crook of James's neck, and I go to sleep too.

———

The night is very soft and dark. I wonder if there's been some sort of power outage, until I realise that the blanket is over my head. I push it off and look around.

Mycroft is sitting barefoot at his desk under the light of the Anglepoise; the printer has been returned to its spot, and the room has been tidied. Some of the papers on the wall are still hanging down where the tape has come loose; the excess is piled like autumn leaves on the floor below.

Mycroft has his hoodie back on, his head down, poring over papers at the desk. He looks pale but focused.

I push the blanket down to my chest. 'Hey.'

He swivels to look at me. 'Hey. Didn't mean to wake you.'

'You didn't.' I stretch my shoulders back onto the flannelette pillowcase. 'You okay?'

'Better.' He wets his lips. 'Thank you. For—'

'It's fine,' I say gently. 'It's not something you should have to thank me for.'

He swallows, nods. Then he angles his pen to tap it on the papers on the desk. 'I've been looking at the encrypted copy of my dad's report.'

I get out of bed and move closer, stepping around the heater and pushing at my untidy hair. When I lean on Mycroft to see over his shoulder, he reaches up without looking to hold my hand, rub his thumb over my fingers.

'Have you found out anything about this?' I ask, plucking the cellophane bag with the coin out of the furore of papers. I hold it towards the lamplight. The label on the bag says *Do Not Handle!* in faded red marker, and the weight of the silver disc inside surprises me. 'It's heavy. Your dad said it was an owl?'

'Yeah. An Athenian owl dekadrachm. It's an extremely rare and valuable coin.'

'How valuable are we talking?'

Mycroft takes the bag carefully out of my fingers. 'I can't be completely sure, unless I get it assessed. But the last coin like this, sold at auction, went for nearly half a million US dollars.'

'Ah. Okay.' I laugh nervously. 'Crap.'

'This is my mum's writing.' Mycroft taps his pen to draw my eye. The writing on the papers is neat and precise, quite different from Mycroft's looping scrawl.

I squint at the sheets. 'Mycroft, these aren't words. It's just a whole lot of numbers and letters.'

'Yes, but I know this. It's a list of International Chemical Identifiers – a way of encoding molecular information about chemical substances. They describe chemicals in layered terms, with data about atoms, tantomeres, isotopes, stereochemistry . . .'

That makes sense: his mother was an organic chemist. When Mycroft's dad asked her to encode this for him, she went to the things she knew. Mycroft doesn't look happy about it, though. He shoves his pen into his hair.

'Anyway, it doesn't really matter, because they're not correct – like this one, see? *InChI=1/C2H6O/C1-2-3/h3H,2H2,1H3* should be ethanol. But she's listed it here as calcium carbonate. And they're all wrong like that.'

'So this is the code? Your mum used these . . . chemical identifiers to encrypt the information from your dad's report, and if you give this to the Home Office—'

'We can't. We can't give it to the Home Office, because we don't know who to trust. Don't you see? My dad wrote up the corruption report. Before he submitted it, he went to see Robert Hannah, who must have leaked word of it to the person Dad was going to expose. That's what got my parents killed.'

'But your dad knew the report was dangerous. He asked your mum to encrypt it as an insurance policy. For you.'

'Yes. Only now I can't give it to the Home Office because we don't know who the report names. We don't know if Wild himself works for the Home Office. If I gave it to them, I could be putting it right into his hands, for all I know.'

'Well, you can't give it to Pickup either,' I say. 'He'll just pass it on to Worth, and he already gives me the creeps.'

'You think Worth is Wild, don't you?'

'I don't know. Worth just gives me a bad feeling.' I glance at his laptop. 'What about Jonathan Cole? We don't know that much about him. You said he's been exchanging emails with you—'

'Which I stopped doing after that second murder. Cole's info wasn't really getting me anywhere, and I might even be putting him in danger by staying in contact. I've got to be more cautious now. Wild could be anybody.' Mycroft gnaws at the side of one nail. 'That's it, then. I'm going to have to figure out Wild's real name before I take the information to the authorities. I'll have to decrypt the message myself.'

'Mycroft, that could take ages.'

'Yeah, I know.' He spreads the first page with his thumbs and long fingers. 'But see this? The first bit? It's only one paragraph, and it's just a stream of letters. I think this might be the instructions for decrypting the rest of the cipher text. Only I don't know what cipher my mum might have used.'

'Could it be chemistry-related? She used chemical identifiers for the next section.'

'I don't think so. I mean, I tried using numbers from the periodic table, to see if it's a simple substitution cipher, and then I tried a few other things, like birthdays and anniversary dates, but none of them work.' He sits back, chafing the nape of his neck. 'What I need is a key. Every cipher has a key . . .'

Mycroft chews his lip, eyes diving through the squiggles on the page, the last message from his mother, which has turned out to be a puzzle. She knew his talents, even back then, eight years ago, when they were still just developing. She knew him well enough to give him a puzzle – did she also know he would try to work it out himself?

'What else do you have of your mum's?' My eyes go automatically to the pictures tacked up on the wall, the papers on the floor.

'Nothing.' Mycroft shrugs. 'I mean, there really wasn't anything. The executors sold the furniture, the jewellery, the house . . .'

I remember watching Mycroft grip the iron railings outside his old house – the one that got torn down – on a freezing London night, a slip of paper clutched in my fist. Then I remember something else.

'Mycroft—' I start.

'The key,' he finishes. We've realised at the same time. 'The *house* key.'

I move quickly to the Anniversary Book, lying abandoned on the carpet among the diaspora of paper, and carry it back to the desk. The album, with its solemn blue cover, is not as heavy now that Mycroft has dispersed half the contents onto his walls and floor.

Mycroft starts flicking pages.

'Here.' He leafs back to a point soon after the news reports of his parents' deaths and separates two pages stuck together. On the left-hand page, under a film of bubbled cellophane, is a normal brass key. The key that was sent to Mycroft by the executors of the estate – under instructions from Mycroft's parents.

Mycroft tears the cellophane in his hurry to get it out. One side bears the brand inscription *Yale*. The other side has four incised numbers.

'Three, twelve, seventeen, nine.' He moves the album to stare at the letters on the transcript again. 'But she hasn't used an easy substitution. It's more like . . .'

He grabs for one of the sheets he's been making notes on, hunts for a pen until I give him the one he has stuck in his hair. He starts

183

scribbling a series of long rows of letters in alphabetical order, with a column of numbers in the front.

'I think it's a variation of Vigenère's cipher.' His hand moves furiously. 'It's a very simple polyalphabetic code, but you need a cipher table. Okay – yeah, that's it. *Yale* would be *BMCN*. Which would make this beginning part read . . .'

He sucks his bottom lip between his teeth. I pick up the small brass key, trace the pad of my thumb over the incised numbers, watch Mycroft's face. His expression opens and he smooths down the page in front of him.

'The first words are *Clever boy*.' He looks up and smiles at me, and it almost breaks my heart.

CHAPTER THIRTEEN

This isn't how the dream is supposed to go.

Even right in the middle of it, I recognise that something is changing. It's the same chair, the same cool dark resonating outside the window, the same heat emanating from us. But the texture of everything is different. This time I am the one who moves, kissing down Mycroft's throat, unbuttoning his shirt, touching my lips all the way from his neck to his chest.

I'm wearing something different as well – my cotton dress and the honeybee tights from the dance. There's no sports tape anywhere, though, and the bare skin of my thighs, between the hem of my dress and the tights at my knee, is smooth and sensitive to Mycroft's touch.

We're doing things we haven't done in the dream before. Mycroft slowly unbuckles the red belt at my waist; it unfurls and slips away. My hands move on his body with a sure confidence. There's no tension except the anticipatory kind, like warm, slowly spreading honey.

I feel a vague concern that I shouldn't get completely undressed. I don't want to be that vulnerable when the next scene happens. But the next scene just keeps receding further and further away, until I'm not sure what will happen anymore.

At the crucial moment, someone shakes my arm. At first I think it's a new part of the dream, but then I open my eyes and realise that I'm awake, and it's my mum who's doing the shaking.

'Rachel. Wake up, love.'

'Wha—?'

'Rachel. Come on.' She's gazing down at me with concern. 'You were thrashing around, having some kind of nightmare . . .'

'Oh.' I'm not sure what sort of thrashing she saw me doing. There has to be some sort of law against being woken from a sex dream by your mother. 'Okay. Right.'

I push up, realise that I've crashed out on my bed with my clothes on. Textbooks and papers are scattered in lazy disorder around me. I can't remember when I decided to take an impromptu afternoon nap, but by the looks of things I didn't get very far with the whole 'trying to study' idea.

First, I grab my phone and check for news from Mycroft. We worked on the decryption nonstop last night – that teasing 'almost there' feeling was hard to resist. Finally, at about six-thirty this morning, I shoved some toast and tea in his direction and let myself out of his house to run back to mine.

There are no texts. Hopefully he's getting some sleep. Right now, though, Mum is competing for my attention.

'This nightmare business,' she says. 'It's been going on for weeks—'

'I'm all right, Mum.' I really don't want to explain that this wasn't a nightmare. I scramble to standing. 'How about I shower, and you make us both a cuppa? I'll only be a minute.'

'Sure.' She nods, obviously surprised. The look on her face is anxious, but it's also tentative, hopeful.

I brush my teeth standing under the hot spray, then dress in warm layers, wondering all the while what's made the dream change from the regular sequence of cold-sweat events. What's happened to make a difference? Is it just a matter of thinking about it? Not thinking about it? I don't know.

I walk out to the kitchen, still pondering.

'Here you go.' Mum pushes a mug across the table in my direction, then returns to peeling potatoes. Her own mug is on the bench beside the sink. 'So is Mycroft all right?'

She says his name stiffly. But she's turned side-on to the bench, so I don't have to talk to her back. It's just a subtle thing, but I read a lot into it.

'He's okay.' I sip my tea slowly and try to put the dream from my mind, refocus. 'He got a letter from his parents – Angela gave it to him as part of the bequest.'

'And it upset him?' Mum asks it softly.

'Well, I think he needed to be upset about it, y'know? The way his parents died ... I think it took something from him. And now ... well, I think he's starting to grieve properly.'

'He can let it go now,' Mum suggests.

'I don't know if it's something you completely let go of. I mean, if I'd had the same experience ...' I examine my mug. 'If you and Dad had died like that, I don't know how I'd cope.'

'Oh.' Mum looks at me, her face very sad and soft.

'But yeah, he can move forward now. He can ... have room to grow.'

Mum turns back to the potatoes, and her voice, when it comes out, sounds muffled. 'I've been very worried for you, Rachel.'

'Oh.' I don't know where this has come from – we were talking about Mycroft, not me. I'm not sure how to respond.

'And I know you and the boys didn't give me the whole story about what happened in England.'

Uh oh. I swallow, because we're on shaky ground here. 'Dad and Mike . . . They didn't want to upset you.'

'I know,' Mum says firmly. She lays a peeled potato in the sink and turns with the peeler in her hand. 'And I've spoken to your father about that. I'm not a child. I don't need to be protected from the truth. I'm an adult. I'm your mother. The boys did the wrong thing by not telling me.'

Eyes wide, I nod my head.

'Anyway,' Mum says, sighing, 'it's done. But I'd like you to tell me what happened to you over in London – not now, maybe, but one day. I'd like you to feel that you can talk to me about it.'

This makes me blink. 'I do. I mean, I didn't . . . But I'd like to. I've wanted to.'

How much I've wanted to! And even though now doesn't feel like the right time, the door has opened, and I know that Mum is willing and able to bear anything with me . . . The thought makes my chin wobble.

'You've grown up, Rachel.' Mum lays aside the peeler and wipes her hands roughly on a tea-towel, lifts her head. 'It seems to have happened overnight. I mean, I know it hasn't been like that, it's been a process – one I've been trying to pretend doesn't exist.' She lays the tea-towel on the bench. 'But all I see, when I look at you, is the little girl I raised. D'you understand? I see you taking your first steps in the yard, and your father sitting you on a sheep's back, and you and your brother playing in the paddocks . . . *That's* the girl I see.'

She's holding herself so stiffly I have to get up and go to her. But once I'm standing in front of her, I don't know what to do.

I place my mug next to the potato peelings in the sink. 'I'll be eighteen in five months.'

'I know.' She reaches a hand out, tucks a lock of my damp hair back behind my ear. 'It's not an age thing anyway, even though I've been insisting on it so hard.'

If I'm going to say it, now's the time. 'Mum, I'm sorry I called you a bitch. You're not.'

She laughs shortly, touches my hair again. The weird thing is, I can see myself in her face. Not just reflected in her eyes: I can see my own face in hers, the way our mannerisms are mirrored, the set of her lips so very like mine.

'I *can* be a bitch,' she says. 'When it's called for. But I'm sorry I slapped you. More sorry than I can say.' Mum's eyes are tender, even though her mouth is firm. 'You'll get through this, Rachel. You'll get through, and you'll win.'

My words sound very small. 'I hope so.'

'I know you will,' she says. 'I know you. My stubborn girl.'

She hugs me then, and it's as if something unlocks inside me. Like I can breathe properly for the first time in months.

'C'mon, Mum.' I wipe tears out of my eyes, onto my shirt sleeve. 'I'll help you with the chopping up.'

So I help Mum make dinner, and we end up doing that very country-woman thing of talking over the cooking. Suddenly I'm back in the normal groove of things. It's only when Mum does something casual, like asking for the oven mitt, or passing me the compost bucket, that I realise how much I've missed her.

The boys all get home around seven, and we sit down to eat. How do these things happen? How can a simple conversation make such a change? Life hasn't returned to 'normal' – I'm not the girl I was when we first moved to Melbourne, I'll never be that girl again. But somehow I'm back on track with my family. Even Harris looks relaxed sitting with us, laughing with Mike over dinner. And tonight, I feel like I can brave any challenge.

The feeling spills over into the long text I send to Mycroft, outlining these new parental developments and hoping he's going okay with the code. It lasts long enough to send me into sleep without fear – with a smile on my face, in fact.

So it's a shock when I'm forced to swim upwards into the cold of too-early morning. Mycroft is calling my name; I feel his hand touch my shoulder.

'Rachel. Rachel, wake up. This is important.'

Not a dream. Real Life again.

————

Mycroft turns on my desk lamp – the light slices through the gloom – and strides over to the window, unlocks it, pushes it open. He lights a cigarette, blows his long initial suck of smoke out into the ether.

'What is it?' I'm foggy-eyed, with hair in my mouth. 'How did you get in here?'

'The back door, but forget that. I've cracked it, Rachel. The report cipher. I've figured it out.' He should look elated, but he doesn't. He takes another hasty, dragging lungful, sends it away. 'I've translated the whole thing. The first paragraph had the instructions for—'

'Slow down.' I shove off my doona and sit up. 'Stop smoking and come over here.'

'Hang on.' He gasps out into the night and grabs onto a window bar with one hand to steady himself. 'I'm just . . . getting my head around it.'

'What?' My weak knee jerks under me as I stand, as if my body is still half asleep. 'You figured out who Wild is, didn't you? Is it Worth? That skinny bastard—'

'It's Cole.'

'What?' The black night air freezes me in place.

'Bloody *Jonathan Cole*. That's the name my dad specified in his report.' Mycroft flicks his cigarette out the window; it hits the next door neighbour's fence and showers sparks. 'The guy I've been trusting to get me in touch with people in the Home Office. The one I've been *emailing*. The bloody cultural attaché who's been so fucking *helpful*—'

'*Cole* is Wild?' A strange buzzing sensation unfurls inside me, like a hive of bees mid-murmur. 'Cole is . . . Are you *sure*?'

'*Yes*.' In the harsh light of the desk lamp, Mycroft's mouth is pinched. I thought it was anxiety, but that's not it. He is *angry*. It sharpens his features, makes his body hum.

Jonathan Cole. Okay, I remember him from that day in Pickup's office: expensive dark suit, hawkish grey-green eyes suspended in the corn-paleness of his face. He gave us his card, shook our hands, thanked us for finding the Shakespeare Folio, commiserated about our injuries . . .

The buzzing feeling inside me is very hot and white now.

'Jonathan Cole is Wild.' Mycroft turns, brandishing a sheet of paper he's snatched from a pile he's dumped on my desk. 'Here's the last email he sent me, with a bunch of useless contact info for the Home Office . . . He's been playing me for a fool this whole time. He's . . .' He can't keep going; his eyes are tearing up with frustration and anger.

Mycroft wipes his face roughly on his sleeve and grabs the rest of the papers. The whole six-page report has been transcribed in Mycroft's distinctive handwriting. I can see the scratchings-out and crossings-off.

'It's all right here. Here's where my dad first mentions him by name.' He shuffles through the sheets, pointing bits out. 'And this is where he details Cole's connections to underground operators in London and Europe, and some of the items he's "procured". Cole's a cultural attaché, so when artefacts went missing or were stolen, he was the man they'd go to . . .'

'Right.' I examine the pages, but I don't touch them. My hands are shaking.

'And here's the proof.' Mycroft digs around in the front pocket of his unbuttoned red shirt, pulls out the cellophane bag with the coin inside. 'The Athenian owl. Fewer than fifty examples left in existence. My dad found this in Cole's house when he went to interview him, soon after a collection of them went missing from a British Museum transport. Cole's fingerprint is on it – that's why it's marked *Do Not Handle*. As far as I know, it's the only solid evidence that links Cole to the theft, and to the death of Verner Plebisch, the museum administrator who died in a carjacking earlier that year.'

'So you were right,' I say. 'Wild is a collector – of artefacts. That's what the blog messages about having something of his meant. He was talking about the coin.'

'Yes.' Mycroft looks at me. 'He must think I've had it this whole time. And I can see why he'd want it back, if his print is on it. My dad's report also mentions something about Cole's stash of artefacts . . . But Dad never found out where he was hiding it.'

'A private museum.' I make a strange-sounding laugh. 'A nice little personal collection that Wild can admire . . .'

'Cole's been collecting for years,' Mycroft says. 'His position made it very easy.'

'Right.' The numb buzzing inside me is spreading – into my shoulders, up my arms. 'I have to stop calling him Wild now, I s'pose.'

'Rachel—' Mycroft puts the papers down and reaches for my hand.

'Don't.' I jerk, step back. 'Don't touch me, please. Just for a minute. I'm just . . .'

I honestly don't want anyone touching me right this second. There's a great energy under my skin, and I'm scared it might do something. I could explode, a human volcano, and anybody standing too close would get hurt in the conflagration. I could go nuclear. My body is shaking with the need to hold this energy in. I feel like kicking something, a chair. Or maybe I could wrench the door from its hinges, or pull the bars off my window.

I have to move, before I self-combust.

Pushing Mycroft aside, I grab my laptop and boot it up with the jab of a button. I open the window for my email, snatch up the paper with Cole's last email to Mycroft, check the address. Start typing.

'Rachel . . .' Mycroft shifts around to meet my eyes. 'Rachel, what are you doing?'

My eyes blur as my fingers dash across the keys. 'I'm sending an email.'

'What? To Cole?' He looks at the message. 'Jesus, Rachel—'

'No. It's bullshit. All *this* – this fear and stress and worry, and it's all over *him*.' The pads of my fingers slap the keys down hard. 'Well, fuck him. *Fuck him.* We know who he is now, and *he* should be the one who feels worried. That'd make a nice change.'

Mycroft pulls at my shoulder. 'Rachel, it's not safe—'

I whip around and thump my hands on his chest.

'*It's never bloody safe!* Don't you *get* that?' I feel my eyes welling up. 'I'm still limping around, and my fingers are still aching, and *I never feel safe*, not even in my head! Not even when I dream! I'm fucking *sick* of it!'

I fling back to my laptop and type a final line – then I hit 'Send'. When I turn again to Mycroft, he looks horrified. But he reaches for my shoulder and pulls me against him. My next words are muffled into his shirt.

'Let him *know*! Let Cole know that we found out who he is! And I don't *care* if he tries to kill me again. Because *I can't live like this anymore.*' Mycroft squeezes me and I squeeze back. 'James, I *can't*. I'm sorry. But I—'

'I don't know why you're apologising.'

'Because . . .' I know why. I understood it even as I was typing, but saying it aloud makes it real. 'Because this could put you at risk too. So I'm sorry.'

'I'm the one who put you in danger in the first place, by dragging you into this.' He rubs his face into my hair. 'So you don't have anything to be sorry for.'

I clutch at him, and he strokes my back. After a while, the buzzing fury inside me slows, settles to a dull hum, fades further into a liquid sensation permeating all my muscles. I'm jelly-limp and quivering.

When I've settled, Mycroft unpeels himself from me and leans over my computer. 'Okay, so let me see what you said to Mr Cole aka Wild . . .'

I know what he's seeing: my email isn't particularly subtle.

You know who we are, is that it? Well guess what, MR BLOODY JONATHAN COLE we know who you are too, so FUCK YOU, you murdering arsehole. We have the coin with your fingerprint, and the report, so you can go to hell.

Mycroft pales. 'Jesus. That's pretty unambiguous.'

'It's done now, isn't it?' I scrub my hand against my face. 'Oh god . . .'

'It's done, all right,' Mycroft agrees, but his face looks slightly panicked. 'Shit. Okay, we'd better contact Pickup first thing in the morning. This is . . . This is kind of bad, Rachel.'

My eyes tear up again. I cross my arms against my chest. 'At least there are no lies anymore. All that subterfuge – the cover-ups, and the bloody aliases, and the Secret Squirrel bullshit, it's all over. Cole's got nowhere to hide now.'

'It's okay. Shh, it's okay. We'll figure it out.' Mycroft tucks me against himself. His touch gradually works on me until I soften, uncross my arms and slip them around his waist.

'God, I feel exhausted. Just from typing a few lines on the computer.'

Mycroft cups my cheek. 'Rachel, come back to bed.'

He closes the laptop, ushers me towards the bed, lifts the doona as I slide in. Then he toes off his Cons and slides in with me. He's still fully dressed, but my body jumps in contact with his warmth.

I sigh. 'What, you think I can get back to sleep after all this?'

'I think you've been running on empty for about a month, and you need to rest.' He runs his hand down my arm. 'And I think that you helped me last night. No, really – you were a rock. And I needed you there. I felt like . . . like I was going to break into bits, but you were there for me. And now I'd like to be here for you.'

I look at him. 'So . . . you're feeling all right?'

'It's . . .' He stops and rephrases. 'I feel different. I mean, I still feel sad, but I don't feel hollow anymore. Does that make sense?'

'I think so.' I close my eyes, open them. 'Oh crap. Mycroft, I've done something stupid, haven't I? I feel better now it's all out in the open, but . . .'

Cole is ruthless. I knew that before I sent the message, but the knowledge sinks into me in this moment, makes my throat dry.

'We'll definitely talk to Pickup about it first thing,' Mycroft says. 'But it's three in the morning now. You should try to sleep.'

Mycroft's still stroking my arm, the way you'd stroke the pelt of a cat. His breath is smoky, and his jaw is rough, unshaven. I don't care about any of that.

I close my eyes, feel my lips curve up. 'I-I can't sleep when you do that.'

'Well, what if I do this?' He moves his hand from my arm to my head, smoothing my hair under his palm, feathering the strands back off my neck.

'That's nice.' I tuck my sore knee against his, yawn into his chest. 'Yeah. That's . . .'

That's when my mind goes as limp as the rest of me. But it follows me down, into the deep well of sleep: the knowledge that I'm right, that Cole has nowhere to hide . . . but neither have we.

CHAPTER FOURTEEN

When I wake up, the first thing I notice is that Mycroft is gone. The side of the bed he was on is still warm, and smells like him, so I snuggle into it. I lie there, relishing it for a moment, until I remember what happened.

Jonathan Cole is Mr Wild. He is the spider in the web, the chessmaster. The man who arranged the assassination of Mycroft's parents. The man who had me tortured in London. Who had those kids murdered purely to intimidate and terrify us.

And I've just shown him our hand. He's probably hard at work right now, figuring out how he'll kill us.

I curl into the doona, feeling suddenly nauseated. What made me *do* that? There was rage, like a flock of screeching birds inside me; I remember feeling buffeted by it. But I didn't realise anger could make you temporarily insane like that.

The only positive is that I've slept without nightmares. Which is crazy, considering what's happened. But the luxury of it, the relief from tiredness, is some consolation.

I need to pee, badly. I haul myself up for the dash to the loo. Mike snags me by the arm when I emerge from the bathroom.

'Jesus, are you up? Mycroft said to let you sleep, but it's midday and—'

'You saw Mycroft?' I feel my face go hot, hug my arms over my brushed-cotton pyjamas.

'Yeah, he just left, and don't get that look. He had all his clothes on, so I figured there was no harm in it. And Dad might have peeked in when he got home from work . . .' He nudges me, snorts. 'C'mon, Rache. If you wanna start getting all grown up about this, you're gonna have to stop blushing every time I mention your boyfriend.'

'Right.' I glance at the hall carpet. 'Anyway, did he tell you what's been happening? About Cole, and the report—'

'Yeah, he filled us in. I told him he'd better get on the horn to Pickup in a hurry . . . So it's the UK guy you saw here after the Folio palaver?'

I nod. Mike starts working his way through every dirty word he knows, so nodding is all I can do for a minute. Then Harris appears in jeans and a long-sleeved black T-shirt, his eyebrows raised at Mike.

'Dulcet tones, eh? Glad to know you don't protect your little sister from all the choice material.' He lifts his chin towards me. 'Come and have a coffee.'

I get dressed, then club around the yellow table in the kitchen with Mike and Harris, listening to the boys talk about a little medieval justice.

'You can't.' I slurp my coffee – it's too sweet, Harris made it – and gesture with my mug. 'We have to let the police work it out. Pickup will have enough evidence now to get things moving – the report, the coin, they both tie directly back to Cole.'

'But won't he have some sort of diplomatic immunity?' Mike asks.

'I don't know,' I confess. 'But if they can link Cole to these thefts, connect him to the related murders, like Daniel Gardener's, it could blow open something huge.'

'But you're still on Cole's shit list, aren't you?' Harris frowns at me. 'And he's got some guy offing kids in Melbourne.'

'Yeah.' I don't look at him when I reply. It doesn't sound as if Mycroft has told them about the email I sent, and Harris and Mike don't need to know how shitty Cole will actually be with me, after last night. 'I s'pose we just lie low and hope the police catch up with him soon.'

'At least you know who the bad guy is now,' Harris says. 'Should be a matter of point and shoot.'

'I reckon Detective Pickup'll make short work of him,' Mike says, stretching hugely and standing up. 'Meanwhile, I've gotta get a shuffle on. Stuff in town. Harris is gonna stay on guard here.'

I peer up at him. 'What stuff?'

'Errands.' Mike shrugs in a cagey manner. 'Ah, all right, it's something for Leesh, for when she gets home. I found this shop, sells these amazing—'

'Oh, can you do me a favour?' I interrupt him shamelessly. 'It was Mycroft's birthday on Wednesday, and I haven't even had a chance to get him anything.'

'You want your brother to go shopping for your boyfriend?' Harris makes a face. 'Seriously?'

'The thing I want to get is in the city, Der-brain.'

'Oy, kiddies, settle down.' Mike waves a hand at me. 'Write down where you want me to go and what you want me to get, then you and Harris can enjoy arguing over whether the sky is blue or something.'

I poke my tongue out at Harris, because I really am that mature, before scurrying to my bedroom for paper and a pen. Once I've written down the address of the hat shop under Flinders Street station and what I want from it, I go back into the hallway. Mike is already half out the door, pulling on his windbreaker.

I hand him the paper, follow him out off the porch into the front yard. 'Can you read it? Sorry, I know my handwriting is—'

'—bloody shocking, yes.' Mike squints at the paper as he pulls his car keys out of his pocket. 'Is there a size? Do deerstalkers even have sizes?'

'Shit, I didn't think.' I grab the paper back, squiggle a note. 'I've got no idea. About the same size as one for you, maybe?' I go to hand him the paper again, and the wind plucks it out of my fingers. 'Oh, bugger,' I say, ducking to fetch it off the concrete path.

Mike is standing right in front of me.

'You right there, butterfingers?' He grins. 'You sure you're not—'

A sharp whip-crack sound breaks his sentence. Lots of things happen at once. Mike arches back. I see the line of his throat. Something warm and wet, like a spray from a hot tap, flicks me in the face. And my brain makes a sudden connection between the whip-crack noise and a memory of me and Mike fox-hunting in Five Mile – the report, the kick of the rifle, the echo it makes on the air.

That sound.

'Mike! *Drop*, Mike, it's a—' I grab my brother's arm as he drops, but he drops onto me, and this is all wrong. He's flopping against me, bearing me down – I stagger under his weight as he falls forward. My knee spasms sharply, and I buckle. I have to use

200

both hands to wrestle us to the ground. Another whip-crack snaps on the air above us.

I push against my brother, shake him. '*Mike—*'

He's half-sprawled on top of me. God, he's heavy. He's like a bale of hay. I roll him to the side. Now I'm kneeling over him, which hurts my knee.

Mike's lying on his back. A red stain spreads on the front of his shirt, and I can't process this for a second, I can't get it right. This is my brother, my brother with his eyes shut. His face, so animated just a second ago, is blank and slack.

'Mike.' I shake him again. 'Mike.'

I hear a voice yelling, somewhere to my side. I press my hands down onto Mike's chest, which feels hot and damp. Then, other hands are grabbing at me, grabbing at Mike.

'No.' I struggle. 'Don't.'

'. . . *gotta get behind cover*,' Harris yells urgently. 'He could fire again, Rachel!'

I shake him off.

Harris seems to realise that the only way to get me to move is to take us as a package deal, so he clutches Mike under the arms and half-pulls, half-drags him backwards, onto our miniscule porch and behind the decorative concrete balustrade. I crawl on my hands and knees, trying to stay with my brother, stay connected, because it's important for reasons I can't fathom.

That stain on Mike's shirt is important too. I hear Harris curse in this strained, bawling whisper. But I'm ignoring him now, just concentrating on the stain. I touch it, see how my fingertips change colour, then I reach forward and pull on either side of Mike's shirt. I yank all the buttons free in one sharp movement, exposing the thermal shirt underneath, shoving that high.

Mike's chest is pale and strong – he's always been a bit barrel-chested, like Dad. Now his skin is sponged with red, and I can see the nasty black-red hole that has flayed open on one side of his ribs. It looks remarkably like he's been gored by a bull – it's bigger than a fifty-cent piece and the skin around it is white. A pinkish froth bubbles from the hole.

Behind me, Harris is muttering to himself as he hunkers down and peers over the top of the concrete barrier.

'Shush,' I say. I can hear something.

Then, a familiar figure comes barging through our open front door, from inside the house, except he's not barging so much as skidding his way through. Mycroft almost falls on top of us, and I push him clear of Mike's prone body just in time.

'*Rachel*,' he says to me, but I shake my head, put my finger to my lips, because I'm still trying to work out what the sound is.

'Heard the shots from my place. I've called triple-0,' Mycroft says to Harris. 'That was quick, getting them behind cover. Are you hit?'

Harris doesn't answer.

Mycroft grabs his arm. '*Harris*. Are you shot?'

'No,' Harris says, his voice hitching. 'No, just – ah, *fuck*.'

'Keep a lookout,' Mycroft says, and he turns back to me. 'Rachel, what is it?'

'Whistling,' I say. I cock my head. 'Can you hear that?'

Mycroft listens. 'Yes.'

I can hear it properly now, that sound that's coming out from under my hand and I think I know what it is. I don't recognise it, but I know of it. It's the sound of a sucking chest wound. I press down hard, hard enough that I can hear the creak of bones, and the sound stops. When I release the pressure, it starts again.

All I can think about is Fiona, the first-aid course paramedic, and the way she tucked her hair back behind her ears as she explained the procedures for chest wounds, shock, response times.

'I need cling wrap,' I say. 'Or a plastic bag. Something to make a seal. *Now.*'

Mycroft looks, I look – there's nothing here on the porch. But only a few steps away, in the exposed front garden, is a green plastic plant shield, held in place around a westringia seedling with three bamboo stakes. Before I can say anything, Mycroft crawls off the porch, lunges for the plant shield, grabs it, returns.

I snatch it off him, use my teeth to tear the shield apart. Now I have a piece of plastic wrap about thirty centimetres wide. I slap it down onto the hole in Mike's chest. There's a gaspy sound, and I see the plastic pull into the hole, just a little – I haven't done this before, or even seen it done, so I flatten my hands on the edges of the plastic, in case it sucks in too far.

Then I just sit there, with my hands on my brother, watching the way the plastic turns pink, then red. I listen for whistling sounds, but I can't hear anything more. I watch my brother's chest – it rises and falls with such delicacy, it's fascinating. I run my cold fingers down Mike's cheek, see the way his head lolls to the side at my touch. His dark hair falls across his forehead.

I don't know how long I sit there. Things start happening around us, around me and Mike. There are sirens, and people moving. A man with an orange-fluoro-striped jacket kneels down beside me. He takes control of the plastic on Mike's chest with such sureness and efficiency, I feel as though it's okay to let go.

CHAPTER FIFTEEN

'We've searched a five-block radius – all of Summoner Street, the corner of Sydney Road, further back past the train station,' Detective Pickup says. 'Some signs of disturbance in the vacant house opposite yours. Nothing concrete – no shell casings – but there's some cigarette ash. We're canvassing neighbours for information right now . . . Someone will know something.'

The chairs in the waiting area are upholstered in this weird burgundy microfibre, and the magazines are old. There were other waiting areas; I've had plenty of time to examine this one in detail. The chairs; the magazine table; the pot plants; the water dispenser with the tiny plastic cups. A little wooden kid's table in the corner holds drawing pads, pencils in a ceramic mug – looking at them makes me feel leaden, for some reason.

Pickup is leaning forward in the chair opposite me. I'm not sure how he wants me to respond, so I just nod.

'We'll catch this bastard, Rachel, all right? I've got the department on my side now. They're finally listening.' He seems to twig that I'm not, looks away. 'Mr Derwent?'

'Yeah.' Harris has been leaning by the window, staring into the black. He comes back, stands near my left shoulder. 'You need me to answer some more questions?'

'No, son, you're all done. Are Mr and Mrs Watts—'

'They're in talking to the docs again. I think they're here for the night.'

'Right. What about tonight? Where are you staying?'

'Dunno.' Harris's voice muddies as he rubs at his mouth. 'I don't . . . We should take Rachel home, give her a chance to rest.'

'Front yard is still a crime scene.' Pickup glances at me, looks back at Harris. 'And I'm not comfortable with you being in the house. It's the obvious place to find you, and there might be investigators, media . . .'

'She can stay at mine.' Mycroft slides into the chair beside me on the right, a polystyrene cup in each hand. One he passes to Harris, and the other one he puts into my good hand. 'Here, just sip it. It's hot chocolate.'

He helps me guide the cup to my lips, and I take a sip. The liquid is lukewarm, and it doesn't seem to have any taste at all.

'What about a mate's place?' Pickup suggests. 'Yours is only two doors down from the scene of the . . .' He trails off, looking at me.

'I'd have to make a call,' Mycroft says. 'And we'll have to go back to Rachel's, collect some things.'

'I'll make sure there's a police presence at the Watts house while you're there,' Pickup says. 'I've stationed officers at Angela's place, and Rachel's family will be protected here at the hospital.'

'Thank you.' Mycroft sounds relieved.

'Look, there's something you should know. Robert Hannah's body was found on a Bali beach earlier this afternoon, about two kay from his residence . . .'

Mycroft leans back in his chair. I hear him exhale – he sounds winded.

'. . . although the Indonesian police aren't following it up as a homicide,' Pickup continues, 'because it looks very much like an accidental drowning. But you can see what's happening here, can't you?'

'Yeah.' Mycroft's voice is very quiet. 'The circle's closing. All the potential links are dying.'

I flinch when he says that, and he returns his attention to making sure I don't drop the polystyrene cup.

'One more thing,' Pickup says. 'I spoke to Theo Worth earlier today. He's flying in from the UK, should touch down tomorrow. He seems to be the best authority on Wild and his outsourced operators, so at least we'll have someone here on the ground who can advise us.'

'Worth is coming to Melbourne?' Mycroft asks.

'He seemed pretty interested in the fact that this Wild character thinks you have something that belongs to him. I don't suppose you've figured out what that something might be?'

'No.' Mycroft shakes his head slowly. 'Not a clue.'

Pickup's eyes narrow. 'All right, then. But remember what I said. I'm putting a car on you. On all three of you. Don't separate, don't lose contact, d'you hear me?'

'Any word from the doctors?' Mycroft says to Harris.

Harris stops chewing his thumbnail. 'He's out of theatre. They won't say anything except he's been down-listed to "critical but stable", whatever that means.'

Mycroft releases a deep breath, lets his chin drop. 'It means he's gonna be okay.' He lifts his head, looks at me. 'Rachel, Mike'll be okay.'

'Give her some more hot chocolate,' Harris says.

Pickup frowns at both of them. 'You heard what I said, didn't you, about the car?'

'Stay together, stay in touch – yeah, we got it,' Mycroft says.

'Then you should take her home. It's been eight hours, and she looks . . .' Pickup shifts forward in his chair, gives my shoulder a little squeeze and a pat. 'Rachel, the boys are gonna take you back to Summoner Street to get your stuff.'

'Okay.' It's the first time I've spoken in a while. My voice sounds faint and tired, like it's run a marathon.

'Your brother's going to be all right. He's tough. We're going to look after things now, me and the department, okay? Just get some rest, we'll talk again tomorrow.' He's frowning, his fox-tail eyebrows wrinkled up.

A garbled announcement comes over the hospital PA system. The carpet in this room seems new. It has that new-carpet smell. Or maybe they've just shampooed it.

'Right,' Pickup says. He looks away.

―――――

Harris and Mycroft are wedged either side of me in the back seat of the taxi.

'. . . really think Cole will come all this way? For a stupid coin?' Harris says quietly.

'I'm sure of it,' Mycroft says. 'In the reply to Rachel's email he said he was *looking forward to seeing Melbourne again*. He's coming here. He could be halfway to Tullamarine by now. That's why I withheld the evidence from Pickup, why I didn't tell him about Cole or Rachel's email.'

'So, what, you meet Cole at the airport and give him the coin, and he pinkie-swears that his hired bloke won't off you when he leaves?' Harris says quietly. 'Sorry, but that just seems bloody stupid.'

'I don't *know*, okay?' Mycroft rubs at his neck. 'The police haven't managed to protect us so far, and this gives us some breathing room, at least. And it's not just about us anymore, is it?'

'Was he *aiming* for Mike? Or did Mike just get in the way?'

'The result is the same,' Mycroft says, and his arm goes around me.

I lean against him, but this isn't comfort. Mycroft is just keeping me upright. All my limbs feel weak, and my head is throbbing.

'It was my fault.' My voice has found itself. I sound croaky – sick, or something. 'I sent the message to Wild – Cole, I mean. I did this.'

'It *wasn't you*.' Mycroft takes my hand. 'This is part of Cole's play for the coin. He's been trying to intimidate us into giving up his property all along.'

'No. I sent the email, and Cole retaliated.' I don't look at him. I look out the window. I can't remember when night came, but it seems to have happened too suddenly. 'Cole's got us cornered now.'

Reflected in the window, I see Harris grimace, shake his head. 'Well, you've gotta change the game plan somehow. Don't just wait for Cole to get off the plane and have you executed, that's *bullshit*.'

'Please don't swear in my cab,' the taxi driver says. He's an Ethiopian guy with a short beard.

'Sorry,' Harris says. He squeezes my arm. 'Rachel, you can't let him win. There's gotta be something we can do—'

'Our families,' Mycroft says softly. 'He's targeting our *families*, Harris.'

'Then . . . take them out of the equation.' Harris's eyes get this fire. He twists in his seat to take us both in. 'Get out of town. Go up to Five Mile.'

Mycroft stares at him. 'What?'

'*Think* about it. Come on, it'd be perfect. You've got the whole property up there to work with.'

'We've got the coin, plus my dad's report.' Mycroft's reply is slow, considered. 'We'd have to dodge the police . . .'

'So, dodge them. They've been useless anyway. Head north. Take the coin with you – that's the physical evidence against Cole, that's what he really *wants*. Cole will think you're running, but you'll be leading him away.'

'We'd be isolated,' Mycroft says. He thumbs his bottom lip. 'But that might work in our favour. It's definitely a move outside the square.'

'Rachel knows the territory. You'd have the home-ground advantage.' Harris's eyes gleam in the flash of the streetlamps. 'It'd take the heat off your folks, if nothing else.'

There's a long pause.

'We'd need supplies,' Mycroft says.

The boys do some more talking. Out the windscreen of the cab, blue fairy lights flicker in the trees near the Westgarth Cinema. I study all the people gliding about, even this late at night, like goldfish in a bowl.

I don't quite know how we get inside my house. It seems to happen while I'm absent. But now the boys are moving around, collecting things – sleeping bags, food, other things. All the lights in the house are blazing, making me squint. I stand in the middle of the living room holding my backpack while Harris stuffs my sleeping bag into it.

'What about clothes?' he says. 'Rache, come on, you need socks and shit.'

He leads me to my room, where I consider random clean clothes. I'm already wearing my thermals, my jacket, my boots. He returns from the bathroom with my toothbrush and a packet of ibuprofen, and they both go into the bag. I'm contemplating my novel for English, and the dress I wore to the dance – it's hanging off the door of the cupboard – when Mycroft walks in.

'I've been in touch with Mai and Gus.' He sounds a little breathless. 'We've worked it out, to tell the police we're staying at Mai's place.'

'Mai's place would be good,' I say. I brush my hand lightly across the fabric of my dress, lift my first-aid notebook off my desk and pass it to Harris. He takes it, examines it with a frown, thrusts it in.

'Help me out here, would you?' Harris says. He's not talking to me, and his voice has a plaintive edge.

The two of them take over my bag, shove in socks, a pair of jeans, T-shirts, my old silver torch. Mycroft notices the other backpack Harris has slung over his shoulder – the tail of the orange sleeping bag is poking out the top.

'What are you doing?' Mycroft says. 'You're not involved in this. You should stay.'

'I'm not *staying*. Mike's my best mate, and Rachel's . . .' Harris glances at me, stares back at Mycroft. 'You *need* me. I mean, look at her.'

'I can take care of her,' Mycroft says through his teeth.

'I know the country, I know the land up there.'

'Jesus. This isn't an option.'

Harris shakes his head. 'You're really not thinking straight, are you, mate?'

'What are you talking about?'

'I wasn't joking when I said you need me. Far as I know, I'm the only one of us with a driver's license. Unless you're planning on catching the bus.'

Mycroft doesn't say much of anything after that.

Harris takes the corner of Summoner Street and turns left onto Sydney Road. Streetlamp light spills into Alicia's car, making square-edged flickering pools, as I huddle in the back.

Mycroft rides shotgun, giving directions. 'Third right after the traffic light, but you'll have to cross the tram tracks.'

'Got it.' Harris dodges traffic like he's been driving in Melbourne for years. In the rear-view mirror I see his eyes flick in my direction. 'You holding up back there?'

I notice something out the back window of the car. 'The police are tailing us. About two cars back.'

'That's fine,' Mycroft says. 'I went out and told them what we're doing. We're not trying to shake them. We're going to stay with a friend, it's all good.'

He gets on the phone and I know he's receiving instructions from Mai, in a one-sided conversation that I don't have the brain-energy to concentrate on. This is what it must be like to be an astronaut floating in space. Tethered to the ship with one of those loose umbilical cords of cable, spinning in this strange amniotic fluid that cushions you and stoppers up your ears and throat. That's how I feel – like I'm stoppered up, even though I don't know what there is left to contain.

All the street life out the window seems like a film set. This bizarre man-made environment, so detailed, right down to the garbage and the pocked windscreens on the parked cars. Except I don't know what my role is in this movie. I don't know what I'm doing here.

When Harris drives us into the parking area beneath Mai's block of flats, I realise that something is about to happen, and I have to act, and I don't know if I can even do that. But there are enough cues for me to play along: Harris and Mycroft grab the bags, and Mycroft takes my elbow gently and ushers me up to the lift doors, where he punches the button and we stand and wait.

He leans over to look at my face. 'Rachel. Mai's waiting for us upstairs. Are you okay?'

'She's not bloody okay.' Harris's nostrils flare. 'Would you be okay?'

'I don't know,' I whisper. I fix my eyes on Mycroft's anxious face. 'I don't know what I'm supposed to do next.'

He hugs me with one arm. 'It's all right. Come on, let's just get you to Mai's.'

My legs move on automatic; there's the lift, and the walking, and knocking, but I'm not concentrating on any of it. I seem to be concentrating on something else, but I'm not sure what it is.

The next thing I know, Mai is standing in the open doorway, and Gus is looming behind her, which is odd, because every other time I've visited Mai's mum or aunty has opened the door. Where are the rest of Mai's family?

'They're at church,' Mai says, and I think *wow, she's reading my mind*, but then I realise she must be answering Mycroft's question.

She pulls me through the doorway of the apartment, which seems even more crowded now with three huge boys in it, and tugs me into her room, leaving the boys in the kitchen.

Now, in the quiet light of her desk lamp, she holds me at arm's length.

'Right,' she says. 'Rachel, take off your shirt. You can't wear that.'

I just stare at her. 'I don't know if the police will notice my shirt if I'm hiding in the car—'

'Sweetie . . .' She sighs and shakes her head. 'You need to change your shirt.'

So I bring my fingers up and unbutton my flannie, and Mai helps me slip it off my shoulders. She looks critically at my long-sleeved navy thermal underneath, then hands me a yellow T-shirt with 'Pie Flavour' written on it and a funny graphic. I put it on. Mai bundles up my flannie, as if she's about to put it in the bin.

'Don't chuck my shirt, Mai, okay?' I say.

'I won't chuck it,' she says. 'But I don't know if you're gonna want to keep this one.'

Instead of binning my shirt, she hugs me. I feel stiff and strange inside her hug.

'It's my shirt,' I say. 'Of course I want to keep it.'

Mai looks at me weirdly. She puts the shirt into my hands. 'Look at it, Rachel.'

But I don't want to. I just stand there with the wad of stiff fabric in my hands.

Mai is still looking at me. She puts one hand on my shoulder and squeezes. 'Rachel. Go on. I'm right here.'

I feel strangely scared, but I open out the shirt in my hands. A wide brown-red stain has dried across the front of it. Spatter marks stipple the collar, as well as big blot-marks on the ends of both sleeves. But none of it means anything, because it's mixed up with the plaid pattern. It could almost be part of the pattern, except that it's not, it's too irregular.

213

And then I realise what I'm looking at.

A noise comes out of my mouth, like a dying rabbit noise, this high-pitched moaning. Suddenly the air in Mai's room is too thick, or too thin, or something like that, because it won't go into my lungs properly. Holding my shirt makes it worse, so I drop the shirt; no, actually, I shake the shirt onto the floor, as if it's stuck to my hand.

Because that is Mike's blood, on that shirt. My brother's blood. From his lungs, and his chest, and it's supposed to be *inside his body*, not on a shirt somewhere. Not anywhere but within him, not outside of him.

My brother . . . my brother was shot. Now he's in hospital, maybe dying. I list on the spot and I stagger closer to Mai's bed. A whole shelf of dolls sits there above it, really weird ones, with sewn-up cross-stitched eyes and button mouths and black clothes. I look at them and I can't stand the sight of them for some reason, and I don't think, I just lift my hand and sweep half of them onto the floor.

I hear something smash, and I immediately feel bad.

'Oh, I'm sorry, I'm sorry,' I say, and Mai shakes her head.

'It's okay, mate.'

'I think I broke your dolls,' I say, and I make the noise again, and I stuff my fist in my mouth, but the noise keeps coming out, and then I scream, because I can't make it stop. Then I can't make anything stop, and I see and feel the whole thing again, on a kind of loop – the whip-crack of the shot, the way Mike jerked, the look on his face as he fell, the weight of him . . .

'He was heavy,' I say. 'Oh god, he was so *heavy*. Mai—'

I reach out for something and Mai takes my hand, hugs me again, and suddenly everything I haven't been able to feel for the last nine hours spears into me like shards of glass, and *god, it hurts so much*. Mike's been shot. Because of me. And I tried to help him, but it didn't matter, and he might die.

I howl. Crying feels like something being pulled out of me with a bailing hook, but I have to do it. I do it for a long time, until I feel like puking. My face is a red, pummelled mess, and my nose is full of snot.

'I tried to control the bleeding, but—' I bat at my eyes with the back of my hand.

Mai hands me a tissue. 'Mycroft says you probably saved Mike's life.'

'*I don't know.*' I start crying again. 'He was just . . . Oh god, there was so much blood . . .'

'Yeah, I noticed,' Mai says, and she tugs on me again. 'Rachel, come to the bathroom.'

'Why?'

She sighs. 'Just come.'

On the way to the bathroom, we pass the kitchen. Mai looks in on the tableau of Harris, sitting at the table looking haggard, and Gus touching Mycroft's shoulder as they talk. Mai gets this scathing expression as she looks at Harris and Mycroft and says, 'Stellar job, guys. Unbelievable.'

She shakes her head, ushers me through the bathroom door. The tiles in here are glaring white; kids' toys are stuck to the wall of the shower. I look at myself in the mirror and baulk. Red-brown smears cover my neck. There's even a delicate spatter pattern on my face.

Mai shakes her head again as she runs hot water into the basin. 'God, I can't believe they didn't even help you clean up. Here.'

She wrings out a washcloth and starts wiping my face. Still shaky, I wash my hands with soap. I take the washcloth from her and scrub at my neck. By the time we're finished, the water in the basin is a soapy terracotta colour, and I can't reach in there to pull the plug, so Mai does it for me.

'You look better,' Mai says. 'Are you feeling better?'

My eyes in the mirror are bloodshot and huge. 'I don't know. I was feeling nice and blank before. Now everything hurts.'

'Yeah, but you seem more normal. More like you. You looked like a shop mannequin when you arrived.' Mai gives me a squeeze. 'Don't fade out again, okay? You've got a long road ahead.'

Somehow I do feel better, like when you're sick, and after you've thrown up, you feel immediately improved. I've cried enough. I don't know why, but it just feels like enough.

I look at Mai. 'We don't have a lot of time.'

'I know.' She hangs the rinsed washcloth over the shower curtain rail, which is such a homely gesture that I almost smile. 'Come on, let's go see what the boys have cooked up.'

———

When we get out into the kitchen, Mycroft and Harris both look up at me. I'm not sure what they're seeing, except for my red-eyed, blotchy, post-crying face, but they both make these matching sighs, and their own faces relax in different ways.

'Here, come and sit down,' Mycroft says, patting the wooden chair next to him. 'We're going to swap cars, so the police won't know we're leaving.'

'You know we're going away?' Harris narrows his eyes at me, like he's worried I might freak out again.

I nod. 'Yeah, I heard you talking before.' I sit, and Mai squeezes in on my left.

'I suggested we hit Five Mile,' Harris says, 'but your mates here have said there's a place in Keilor no one knows about—'

'My uncle's flat,' Gus says. 'It's empty, and it's not a place anyone else would think to look. You're welcome to go there. You could contact your folks and let them know you're okay, and you'd be close to your brother—'

'Thanks,' I say. 'Gus, it's a good idea, but I've decided. We should go to Five Mile. It's the best option. It's not close enough for Pickup to drag us back easily, if he finds out we've gone. And it's isolated enough to buy us some time – Cole will have to drive all the way up. He'll follow us, if we have the coin. And everyone will be safer if we get a bit more distance.'

Harris nods, quietly vindicated. Mycroft looks at me, and I feel his hand settle on my back, supporting me. I need it: the idea of driving away from my brother is making me nauseous. But I know this is the right choice.

'We'll text Pickup, and our families,' Mycroft says quietly. 'Tell them we're hiding at Mai's, that we're not coming out. Pickup himself suggested staying at a friend's place, so if we keep in regular contact nobody will worry. We don't want anybody to get suspicious about where we are.'

'Okay.' I swallow. 'But when Mum and Dad find out the truth, they'll be ropeable.'

There's nothing I can do about that. The further away I am from my family, the safer they'll be. I'd hate to make them angry, especially Mum – oh god, *Mum*! But I can do this. I can make this choice, because it's in her best interest, even if she doesn't understand. I would rather she was angry with me till the day I die than put her in Cole's line of fire.

'Right,' Harris says. 'So, Five Mile it is.'

'That's a hell of a drive,' Mai breathes.

'The cops have seen us drive into the underground car park in Alicia's green Toyota.' Harris picks at the edge of the wooden table with his thumbnail as he talks. I don't think he's even aware he's doing it. 'We'll load up Gus's uncle's station wagon, hide Rachel and Mycroft in the back. I'll drive out, head for the Calder Freeway, then bob's your uncle.'

'You'll want a cap or something, for your hair,' Mai says to him. 'Your hair is kind of distinctive. And maybe a different shirt.'

'We'll do a swap.' Gus looks down at himself, then at Harris. 'We'll figure something out.'

'What will you need? Food, yeah?'

'Tea,' Mycroft says. His eyes look tired. 'Tea would be good.'

'Is your uncle's car fueled up?' Harris asks.

Gus nods. 'Yep. I'm assuming you can drive a manual. Just watch the clutch – shove it right to the floor when you change gears or you'll stall. Will you be the only one driving?'

'Rache can run an engine, but she's unlicensed. We'll see how we go.' Harris scans my face, then Mycroft's. 'You got any driving experience?'

'Yes. Mostly bad,' Mycroft says. 'I can hot-wire, but I don't really drive. Long story.'

Harris nods. He knows enough of the story to understand.

'You've got sleeping bags, yeah?' Mai asks.

'Blankets,' I say. My voice sounds a little rusty, so I clear my throat. 'If you have blankets, Mai, we might need them too. And an extra torch. There's no power on at the old house.'

Mycroft looks at the tabletop. 'And Mai, I hate to ask but—'

'Shut up.' Mai waves a hand. 'Just ask.'

'We're going to need to borrow some money.'

'I've got some cash from my last pay,' Gus says quickly. He looks at Mai, and their eyes seam together with an almost audible zip, before he looks back at Mycroft. 'You can have it, don't worry about it.'

I feel my breath leave me a bit fast, grab for Mai's hand and squeeze. 'Your rental deposit . . .'

'Sweetheart, chill.' Mai's face is so fond and sympathetic it makes my chest hurt. She leans, so our foreheads make gentle contact.

'We'll pay you back,' I say softly.

Mai grins. 'You'd better.'

Mycroft stands, scraping back his chair and leaning a heavy hand on the tabletop. 'Okay, Harris says it's about a seven-hour drive, including stops, so we should try to get away by ten-thirty. I'll get online now and contact Cole.'

I look up at him. 'What are you going to say?'

'That we're leaving Melbourne. That we've got the coin and we'll send further instructions. If he wants to collect his incriminating evidence, then he'd better come find us.'

'Why is the coin so important anyway?' Gus asks. 'Shouldn't that report from Mycroft's dad be enough?'

Mai shakes her head. 'It's an old, unsubmitted report from a man who's died. Maybe not enough for a judicial case. But a fingerprint on a piece of material evidence that links Cole to the report, to the British Museum theft . . . That's more like the business. No wonder Cole's so nervous.'

'I don't think it's just that.' I wet my lips. 'The coin's been missing for eight years and now Cole's finally sure we have it. He wants it bad.'

'No point having a stolen collection if it's not complete.' Mycroft scowls.

Harris pushes out of his chair. 'Well, if you're contacting Cole now, we better get moving. Time to get out of Dodge.'

Gus takes Harris out of the kitchen to hunt down some blankets, and Mycroft goes to use Mai's laptop. I reluctantly pull out my phone and text my dad: it's a short, vague message about how we've decided to hole up at Mai's, with lots of reassurances to Mum and promises to stay safe – basically more lies than you can poke a stick at. When Mai gets back from setting Mycroft up, I'm sitting at the kitchen table staring at my phone, still wondering if I've made the right decision.

'Come and help me with this,' Mai says, thrusting a green shopping bag at me. 'I'm gonna give you stuff that Mum probably won't miss immediately.'

I stand up and follow her. When I'm moving, doing something, I feel more like myself. 'When will your mum and aunty get home with the kids?'

'Soon.' She wets her lips. 'There's always a pot-luck dinner on Friday nights after the service, but we've only got about half an hour. Rachel, listen to me for a sec.'

'What?'

She pulls me closer, so we're huddled together near the kitchen cupboard. 'This is probably the worst possible time to be saying this, but it's all the time we've got. Your friend, Harris. You know how he feels about you, right?'

'He – he's a mate.' I stare at her. 'He's supported me through this whole thing.'

'*Rachel*.' Mai tilts her chin to the ceiling and sighs deeply, looks back. 'Okay, fine. Harris is a good guy. I mean, obviously a little fucked up, but good at heart.'

'Mai, I don't—'

'Rachel, darling Rachel.' Mai leans our foreheads together again as she rubs my arm with her free hand. 'You and Mycroft make a great pair – you're both smart as anything, and thick as bricks. Take care of each other, okay? Try not to get yourselves killed, because I'll be really pissed off if you . . .'

She bites her lip, and I can see how her eyes have gone all wet. I ditch my shopping bag to pull her in, and I'd like another set of arms right now so I can hug her properly.

'We'll come back,' I say thickly.

'Yes, you bloody will.' Mai sniffs into my shoulder, leans away. 'Now, you finish with this shopping bag, and I'm gonna get you some clean undies for your backpack, because I asked Mycroft specifically, and he said he was too embarrassed to go through your drawer.'

'Mai.' I hold her hand with my bad one, the one that's gone through so much, the one that feels more sensitive now. 'Thank you. For everything.'

She just nods, turns towards her room. Turns back to give me a pale smile.

'I'll pack you something nice.'

CHAPTER SIXTEEN

Harris flicks the headlights on. 'All right, I'm turning out of the car park onto Sydney Road. You lot right there in the back?'

'Yep.' Mycroft reaches for my hand, and I squeeze back. His voice is muffled by the blanket over his face. 'We're good.'

'Okay, then. Onward to the stars,' Harris says, and he shuts up, so the police monitoring the apartment block don't get suss.

The dusty car floor beneath me is vibrating and a dark grey army blanket is covering me. All my skin feels tense, and it's not just because Harris has cranked the radio to eleven. There's a bump, a number of bumps, as the car I'm cocooned in revs and moves. This is the moment of truth: if the cops on point nab us here, as we're heading out, this whole trip is Game Over.

I hold my breath, feel the awkward way I'm positioned, huddled in the back footwell of Gus's uncle's Ford station wagon. Mycroft must have it worse than me, because he's taller. The car heater makes everything stuffy. I'd like to throw off the blanket and get some air, but I don't move a muscle until I feel the car pick up speed as it enters the traffic.

We're doing it – we're really going. Dread compounds in my throat, a thick paste of fear and grief that I have to swallow past. I'm leaving Mike. I'm leaving my brother, and I don't know yet if he's really all right. My parents won't forgive me for it. They might understand, but they won't forgive me.

We drive – ten seconds, twenty.

I don't hear sirens, I don't hear Harris swearing. There's only the thrum of the engine beneath me, and the sound of traffic noise and the beat of the radio. A weird flat-tyre sound echoes up as our car wheels pass over tram tracks. Edging the blanket down, I see a corner of the window; through the glass, streetlights emit a static flare, the city's own morse code flashing at inconsistent intervals.

The radio is throbbing and I don't like it. There's already too much going on in my head. But I recognise this song: 'Wolf' by Pyramid. I feel just like that, like a wolf sneaking out of town, creeping along on its belly. The song's beat builds into a driving tempo, as if it's exciting, the fact we're leaving like this. Which is wrong – it's not exciting. It's awful, and painful, and there's a dull dragging heaviness in my chest, as if something is sitting on my breastbone. My head is full of ashes, and my ribs ache.

Mycroft squeezes my hand again, and I realise he's still holding it.

'You okay?' he whispers.

My eyes are watering, but I sniff it back. 'My head feels . . . crowded.'

Mycroft doesn't say anything in reply, but his hand moves to grasp my wrist. I hold on to his wrist in turn, feel the twitch of his pulse under my fingers. We're holding each other in this monkey grip: two acrobats on the high wire, feeling the last touch of something human before we begin falling.

A few minutes later, Harris lowers the volume on the radio by a fraction.

'Okay, people, I think we've done it. I'm on Bell Street, and I can't see any flashing lights. You wanna come out and get some air?'

Cautiously pushing back the blanket, I struggle up onto the back seat of the car. I poke my head above the window ledge, as Mycroft tentatively does the same on the other side.

'I need someone to help with navigation here,' Harris says.

I clamber over Mycroft's legs into the front passenger seat, push my hair out of my eyes. 'You're fine, just head for the Calder. You got it.'

'We did it.' Harris is wearing a Richmond Tigers beanie over his hair. It makes him look like a bank robber. His voice is shaky, not as jubilant as I thought it would be. 'Jesus, we just ditched the cops and cut out of town.' He blows out his lips, keeping his eyes on the road. 'Okay. Rache, you gonna stay on point?'

'I can direct you from Maps,' I say, tugging my phone free. 'I drove this way last time.' I don't say *with Mike*; I can't do this and think about my brother at the same time.

'Follow the signs to Bendigo.' Mycroft leans through from the back. I smell the blanket-dust scent of his hair, plus the tang of nervous sweat. 'I checked the directions before we left. You'll pass the Calder Raceway. From there, it should be about half an hour to Macedon.'

I touch his knee through the gap between the seats. 'We did it.'

'Yeah.' He exhales heavily. 'I didn't think we'd make it. Shit.'

'Everyone sit back and buckle up,' Harris says. 'There's still plenty of Five-Oh on this road.'

So Mycroft sits back, and we both buckle up. And here we are, just a bunch of kids off home after a big night out on the town, or maybe a posse of law-breaking youth evading the police, or maybe just three scared teenagers on the run from a killer, on the road to nowhere.

I wonder what Cole is doing, if he's still on his way, or maybe touching down, walking through Tullamarine arrivals lounge right this minute . . . I roll the window down a crack to let some of the cold night in, and loll my head back against the headrest. Then I close my eyes, and try not to think of anything at all.

———

I wake up as we pass a sign for serrated tussock. Stones jut like jagged giant's teeth along the road edge. For a moment I'm disoriented, panicked—

'Mike! Drop, Mike, it's a—'

—then awareness comes back to me. I stop clutching my chest, let my hand fall into my lap.

'He'll be all right, babe.' Harris's voice seems disembodied in the dark of the car. 'He'll be okay. Told him I'd punch his lights out if he didn't pull through.'

I nod, even though Harris can't see me.

Harris drums his fingers on the steering wheel, flicks on the interior light. 'Glad you're awake, anyway. Pass me a coffee?'

I check my phone – it's just after twelve-thirty a.m. 'Sorry, I didn't mean to flake out like that . . .'

'Relax.' Harris glances between me and the road. 'You looked like you needed a snooze. Coffee?'

'Oh yeah, sorry.' I fumble around for the thermos at my feet, unscrew the lid and pour him a black brew.

Harris has ditched the beanie, but his hair is still a little flat. His eyes are bugged-out after two hours of fending off the attack of oncoming headlights. The car is moving smoothly and the rumble of the engine is soothing. Mycroft is sleeping behind me, kinked sideways on the back seat, his shoulders flopped on top of the load of gear.

'Just trying to decide whether to go into Bendigo and tank this bastard up before I take the turn-off,' Harris says. 'Is there a servo in Lockwood?'

'No. But don't go into town – remember the truck stop in Bridgewater? That's about twenty minutes away. There might be one in Marong too, that's even closer.'

'We're not in the red yet, and your mate said there's about thirty kay in that.'

'Gus is a good guy,' I say simply. I'm still quite overwhelmed by the generosity and kindness of my friends. It makes me feel proud and amazed to know people like that.

There's kindness all around me. Right beside me, in fact. Mai said it, but my tongue feels clumsy in my mouth as I acknowledge it. 'You're a good guy too, Harris.'

'Well, thanks, Rache, but come on. What was I gonna do?' He sips his coffee. We pass a sign informing the world that today's Fire Danger Rating is low. 'Mike's my brother. I mean – he's not my brother. You're feeling it worse. But he's always been there for me.'

I make a wan smile. 'So does that make me your sister?'

Harris just looks at me and snorts.

The night is grim and silent, punctuated by the *blat* of semis' engine brakes, the glare of their lights. Old gums stand sentry by the roadside, seeming to reach towards us as we pull forward.

The panels of the solar array before Bridgewater all glitter in the moonlight, their curved caves lolling like daffodils waiting for the sun. Harris eases off the accelerator. We cruise past the post office and the farm machinery shop, bump over the Loddon River.

Harris gives a discernible sigh of relief when we see the all-night truck stop. As he turns the car in, Mycroft stirs in the back seat.

I fill the tank while Harris goes to the men's room. Mycroft exits the warm car, makes a noise, dives back in to retrieve his jacket.

'Oh my god, it's fucking freezing,' he says when he emerges. He comes around to my side, pulling on a pair of black fingerless gloves, then a thick pea coat I've never seen him wear before. 'Where are we?'

'Bridgewater on Loddon.' Fog comes out with my breath.

'Which is . . .'

'About twenty minutes west of Bendigo? We're doing okay.'

'Right.' He opens his coat on one side and slips it around me, hugging me in. 'Are *you* doing okay?'

I look at the car and nod. He kisses the top of my head, which makes me smile, before releasing me to gaze at the untidy collection of houses pooled in shadow nearby.

'Wow – the country.' He picks grit from his eyes, tucks a hand into his coat pocket and pulls out a pack of smokes. 'Have I got time for a gasper before we start again?'

I look at the numbers flicking over on the bowser. 'Maybe half a one.'

Harris walks back from the men's, raises his eyebrows at the sight of Mycroft sticking the cigarette in his mouth. 'Don't light that up near the petrol, mate. Big tank go *boom*.'

'Thank you, yes. I was just getting an idea of where we are.'

'We've left your reality and entered the Harris Zone,' Harris says, 'where time and space fold into bumfuck nowhere.'

Mycroft just looks at him, then turns around to go smoke on the road shoulder.

————

'We're leaving old gold country,' I explain to Mycroft. 'The roads are reasonable quality, not much traffic, you get a pretty good run. It's just a bit hairy at night with the trucks.'

Mycroft shakes his head as we go past a town marker. 'Why has this place even got a name? It's just one house.'

'This is what it's like, all the way until you hit the desert. We're entering the Mallee wheat belt, and there's a few bigger towns along the Murray River, but . . . yeah, this is pretty much it.'

Harris is suffering in the driver's seat, trying not to wince when another Kleenheat Gas truck or double-barrelled semi bears down in our direction. Electricity poles take turns swapping from one side of the road to the other as we pass through each town. A sign warning that *A Microsleep Can Kill* flashes away to somewhere behind us.

I check on Harris. 'Are you flagging? I can drive for a bit, y'know.'

He smothers a yawn, shakes his head. 'Yeah, that sounds great. Sorry, officer, I know she doesn't have her Ps, or even her Ls actually, but I wanted a nanna nap.'

'Come on, what are the chances?'

'High enough. And your knee is stuffed. So not on your nelly.'

Past Wedderburn, with its lonesome cricket green and Dunlop tyre centre, the homesteads start to look like something out of *Wolf Creek*. It's too dark to see properly, but I don't need to:

I know these places, with car parts in junkyard heaps and broken tin sheds. Embellishing the dirt frontages are collections of old machinery, usually dark red with rust, now black in the midnight air, like everything else is black.

Harris is flicking between local radio stations and the ABC, anything to keep him alert. There's nothing but static on AM, and FM only yields someone talking about cars, someone else talking about football, or the hissing of barely audible country songs.

'So what's Five Mile like?' Mycroft asks.

'It's small,' I say.

'It's a shithole,' Harris says at the same time.

'Harris!'

'Well, it is.' He shrugs. 'Bottle shop-slash-pub, post office, general store – that's pretty much the whole show.'

'There are good people there,' I say firmly. I hold Mycroft's gaze. 'It's isolated, so people have to help each other out.'

'Yeah, right.' Harris stares out the windscreen. 'People help each other out . . . Jesus, Rachel, you're such an innocent.'

My hackles rise. 'Well, people do!'

He snaps me a glance. 'People help those who help themselves. They help with harvest, or lost stock, or if there's a fire or an accident. But if you're just a pisshead, making the whole place look untidy, they avoid you like the plague.'

I know exactly who he's talking about, but that doesn't mean I won't call him on it. 'I know plenty of farmers who get on the sauce on a Friday night—'

'Yeah, on a Friday night. Go into Ouyen or Murrayville with the missus, have a big knees-up. Go back to work the next day. My dad was never like that. He never had any interest in farming, and everybody knew it.' Harris jabs the radio buttons, grimaces over the static. 'You've gotta at least *look* like you give two shits about reading *Stock & Land* or which irrigation boom works better. If you don't have that thin veneer of respectability, you can go get rooted.'

The bitterness in his voice stills me. I know Harris was happy to leave the country – the way he flipped the place off on our way out of town last time was a pretty good indication – and I understand now that a lot of that was to do with getting away from his dad. But I had no idea this rancour ran so deep in him.

'So . . . that's what it was like for you?' Trying not to watch him too obviously, I look ahead at the road. A family of silos – Mama and Papa silo, two teenaged silos, and a twin pair of baby silos – shine past in silver under the moon.

'Shit, I'm not saying that everybody was bad.' Harris's mouth twists. 'I mean, your brother was always there. Things'd get rough with my old man, and Mike would . . .'

He stops; I can hear him breathing over the thrum of the engine. Something feels odd, a dark vein running beneath the surface of this conversation. I don't think it's the mention of my brother, or our awareness of his current circumstances, or even that Harris is opening up to me with Mycroft listening from the back. Harris's hands are squeezing the Ford's steering wheel like he's moulding it into a different shape.

'What d'you mean, "rough"? I know you and your dad used to argue—'

'*Argue.*' He laughs, short and harsh. 'That makes it sound pretty civilised. We used to *argue*, yeah.'

'Harris, what are you trying to—'

'Before I grew up, got a bit of meat on, there were never any "arguments". I just used to cop it. When I got taller, things changed. Didn't have to hold back anymore, did I? I could give as

230

good as I got. But the way things were going . . . Well, when it got too ugly, I called Mike about getting out.'

I sit beside him in the dark of the car interior, feeling a seismic shift. Feeling like an idiot. My memory of the day he showed me his scars – the relics of the 'accidents' he had as a kid, the small white mark on his wrist, the size and shape of a cigarette burn – suddenly returns with a wallop.

My voice comes out shaky, quiet. 'You didn't learn self-defence because of fights at the pub, did you?'

His eyes skitter sideways, not quite meeting mine. 'Nah.'

'Jesus.' I put my hand on his shoulder. 'Harris . . .'

Watching his face in the glow from the dashboard, I feel guilt spin its way through me. Harris has been giving me clues all along, but I've been blind to this.

'I'm sorry.' I try to pour everything I finally understand into my voice. 'Harris, I'm sorry. Mike never said anything. I didn't—'

'Look, forget it.' Harris's lips press together as he focuses on the road. 'Can we just . . . Can we talk about something else?' He reaches to change the station again, then his shoulders ease back. 'Let's just get there first, worry about the locals later.'

I sit back too, my nerves jangling. Through the car speakers, a woman sings plaintively of being carried away by a moonlight shadow. The lit-up highway ahead seems like the foreground of a dream, and it's as though we've forgotten that Mycroft is perched in the back seat, listening to our every word.

———

We get into Wycheproof a half-hour later, where the rail line for the grain silos is a thin blade of steel that bisects the main street of town along its length.

It's going on for two in the morning. I'm pretty sure Harris has had enough of driving. He stretches his legs by the side of the road, along with me and Mycroft, all of us feeling that dull sciatic ache from too much sitting down. A ghostly fog swirls over the paddocks on the other side, where cattle make zombie moans in the dark.

'Let me drive from here to Sea Lake,' I plead to Harris. 'Just an hour, tops. No one's gonna pull us over now.'

'Nice try, Rache,' Harris says. He looks at Mycroft. 'So you're sure Cole will follow you this far?' And you've said he's the only person you'll give the coin to?'

'Yeah, I told him if he wants it, he'll have to come fetch it himself.' Mycroft jerks at a nearby sound, but it's only a possum's death-rattling call from a tree across the street. He stubs his cigarette butt into the gravel. 'We meet, trade the coin for our safety, Cole drives away – then *bang*, the police grab him on the way out of town.'

Harris straightens. 'You're setting him up.'

'Mai's ready to contact Pickup on my instruction.'

'So that's the plan?' I chafe my hands against the cold.

'Mai kind of insisted on that part,' Mycroft admits. 'And I'd very much like to see Cole in court.'

'But you're meeting him without police backup?' Harris frowns. 'What's to stop Cole from taking the coin with his left hand and shooting you with his right?'

'I've got no intention of showing myself. We'll direct him to find the coin while we disappear. Plus, I've told him I've got a friend holding on to the report, as insurance, and it will be passed on to the police if anything happens to us. I'm hoping the threat will be enough. Once he's arrested, I can give the report to the cops.'

'But even if Cole gets busted, his local boy could tidy you up later.'

Mycroft runs his tongue over his bottom lip. 'It's not a perfect plan, no. But killing those kids and shooting Mike has drawn a lot of heat, so hopefully Cole's arrest will void any short-term contract and force the local agent to back off. Anyway, it's all I've got. At least he won't be attacking our families.'

'Yeah, like you said, it's not a perfect plan.' Harris sighs and scratches at his neck.

'If you think of another one, feel free to share.'

'Shit . . .' Harris shakes his head. 'My plan is to get us as far as Five Mile. I can't think further ahead than the next two hours of driving.'

'Then we'd better get moving.'

CHAPTER SEVENTEEN

It's about five a.m., when night still cups the world gently in its hands and the air feels cold and damp, like the insides of clouds.

My eyes are hanging out of my head, but we're bare kilometres away. The dormant excitement inside me begins to fizz and flutter as I see things I'm familiar with – Dog Netting Road, the turn-off to the Lake Tyrell saltworks, the zigzagging arms of jacarandas set against silo walls.

Suddenly we're driving up past the Victoria Hotel in Ouyen. The livestock exchange yards speed away to the left, and then we're bumping over the rail line. The sign to Patchewollock flashes past, the spear of our headlights making the salt flats glow. This road is a bitumen track to my heart.

I sit up higher, scan the road shoulder as Harris squints into the distance. Mycroft stirs in the back, edges between the seats.

'Are we close?'

'We're close.'

'So what are you looking for? Landmarks?'

'It's nearly dawn. I'm looking for roos.'

Mycroft scrapes a hand across his jaw. 'Kangaroos? Sure. I'd like to see kangaroos.'

Harris snorts.

'No, Mycroft,' I explain gently, 'we don't *want* to see kangaroos.'

'Oh,' he says, confused. 'Okay.'

Harris gives him a look in the rear-view. 'You don't get out much, do you?'

'Harris, stop,' I say quickly. 'There's one.'

Harris slows the car to a crawl. Mycroft peers through the window as we pass the twitching grey shape.

'Wow,' he says. 'A real live kangaroo. They're quite big, aren't they?'

'Yeah,' Harris drawls. 'They look *really* big when they go through your windscreen at a hundred kay an hour.'

'*Harris.*' I turn away from him, touch Mycroft's hand. 'You can't drive too fast at dusk or dawn. That's when they're most active.'

'Crepuscular,' Mycroft says thoughtfully. 'They're crepuscular animals – I remember that.'

'Jesus, there's a name for it?'

'There's a scientific name for everything,' Mycroft says. He cocks an eyebrow at Harris. 'You, for instance, would have the scientific name—'

'*Mycroft.*' I glare between the pair of them, turn back in time to see the first house. Then the road widens, and there's the Five Mile Post Office, beside Metcalfe's grocery. The red brick pub, the Five Flags, stands solid, almost brawny-looking in the moonlight. Gums tower over the footy ground on the right, and then we're through town, heading further, for the place I used to call home.

Mycroft squints out the window. 'Why don't any of the sheds have walls?'

'Because if you stack the hay without any airflow, when it's too green, it can spontaneously combust.'

'No way.'

'It's true. Harris, slow down, you're gonna miss the turn.'

'I'm not gonna miss the turn,' Harris says in a condescending tone. 'I could find your place in the dark with my eyes closed. Actually, I think me and Mike did that once, coming home after—'

I grab his arm. 'Turn *here*.'

The house looks different. I don't know whether it's because we're coming on it like thieves, in this early hour, or whether it's something else. But seeing the house is like the balm my heart needs – there's this instant relief when I sight the verandah, the wide square windows, the corrugated roof. I feel safe, which is crazy, because we're no safer here than we were in Melbourne.

My family will be safer, though.

Mycroft reaches through the gear space to squeeze my hand. 'There it is, yeah?'

'Yeah.' I exhale softly. 'There it is.'

I get out and unlatch the gate. It's absolutely frigid in the yard – I hop from one foot to the other. Harris drives the car up and into the machinery shed. The red glow of brake lights illuminates the inside of the shed, like the whole interior has been bathed in blood. The motor stills.

The first thing I notice is . . . silence. The soft whooshing roar of the car, the bustle of the city – all that is gone. Only a faint tinnitus lingers in my ears. Beyond that is absolute quiet. I close my eyes for a second, welcome the quiet like an old friend, take it into myself, breathe it out.

The boys come closer, and the moment disappears. Harris looks as if he's sleepwalking. Mycroft glances around, trying to take in as much as he can in the dark. He seems a bit twitchy, and I wonder if it's the result of being in the car for so long or if he finds the silence unnerving – it's certainly not something he's ever had a chance to get used to.

We each take the bags and haul them up the side verandah stairs to the double doors.

'Come on in,' I say. It seems polite somehow, to be inviting the boys inside.

The living room, with no furniture, seems vast to me again. In the kitchen, the primus and gas bottle still squat on the bench – we'll be able to cook, at least.

I immediately fall into familiar habits, dropping my bags in the corner and walking to the hearth to crack kindling. The floorboards creak under my feet in the old way.

'I'll get the fire on. Mycroft, boil the billy, would you? There should be water in the taps, from our last visit.'

Mycroft eyes the primus, the billy. 'Like boiling in a saucepan, is it?'

'Yep. Pop the lid on, it'll go faster.'

Harris rubs his neck. His eyes are so red and tired they're watering of their own accord. 'Plenty of firewood, anyway.'

I look at him. 'Aren't you glad now I did all that woodchopping?'

He sighs. 'I'll bring in a few big bits.' He goes outside for the wood, and probably to pee in the agapanthus.

The kindling catches, and the crackle of flame makes everything seem homier. The way the living room heats up so fast on a cold night is one of the best things about this house – Mum was always obsessed with the insulation – and five minutes after I light the fire, the room is a haven of warmth. Soon after that, Mycroft is handing out mugs of strong, sweet tea.

Harris slumps on his sleeping bag, tugging off his boots. He scorches his fingers on the tin of his pannikin before he shifts to holding the handle.

'One cuppa. Then I'm gonna crash.' He sucks his thumb, takes a sip, and makes a face that'd be more caustic if he wasn't so tired. 'Does this tea have condensed milk in it?'

I wave a hand. 'It's a thing, just go with it.'

'Well, we're here.' Mycroft stands by the kitchen island, sipping from his mug and rolling his shoulders. 'But we've got a bit of organising to do.'

Harris sighs deeply, and I echo.

'Let's get some rest first,' I say. 'We can work out a plan in the morning.'

'It's already morning,' Mycroft points out gently. 'But yeah, you guys should rest. I got some sleep in the car on the way up, I'll keep watch.'

I realise what he means. It's not over yet. This is just the start. I put my mug on the hearth bricks, push up from the floor and dust off my bum. 'Oh, right. Come on, then, I'll give you the twenty-cent tour.'

I grab the torch from my backpack and walk Mycroft through the dark house, opening doors, pointing out the toilet, the bathroom. When my hand falls on the door of the room nearest mine, I stop.

'This was Mike's room?' Mycroft asks softly.

'Yeah.' I don't say *it was* – I don't want to use past tense to talk about Mike.

'Rachel, he'll be okay. When they say "critical but stable" it's a sign that—'

'I know. But I won't be there if he wakes up.'

'*When* he wakes up.' Mycroft reaches up and runs a finger over my furrowed eyebrows, until they release.

I nod, my breath fluttering out, and move to the next door.

'And this is your old room?' Mycroft's eyes flare in the backwash of the torchlight. 'Wow.'

'Well, it's not exactly *Home Beautiful* right now . . .'

Before I can elaborate on the general dustiness and disorder, Mycroft feels for my waist, pulls me into a sideways hug. It takes me a second to respond: there's still some strange disconnect between my body and my brain. Then I feel Mycroft's hands move, turning me in to face him, positioning my body with gentle firmness. He lifts his hands to my head, smooths down from my crown to my nape. He squeezes my shoulders, opening his fingers and digging into the muscles there.

My first instinct is to stiffen – the events of the past eighteen hours have rubbed my soul raw. I feel excoriated. But Mycroft keeps moving his hands, taking fistfuls of my muscles: along my shoulders, my arms, from my neck down the tense ridges either side of my spine.

The waves of panic I'm expecting don't come. It's such a relief that I soften further. Mycroft squeezes and rubs until my bones loosen here in the dark, until I start to feel as if I'm coming back into my body again.

My head has fallen against his shoulder. 'Thank you.'

'I-I don't know how else to help,' he says.

'This is helping.'

The torch hangs loose in my hand, beam pointed at the floor, so we're standing in a puddle of watery light. In the gloom of my family's old hallway, I see Mycroft's head dip. Then I feel his lips on mine, so swift and soft it transports me into another world. With a jolt, I realise that this is a world I've imagined: kissing Mycroft here, in Five Mile, in my old house. This is a world I want to be in.

My nose is cold, but my hands are warm on Mycroft's chest. When we break apart, I feel a wrench inside. I clutch at his arms. Liquid lightning has suffused my whole body, and I still want him.

'Come on,' he whispers. 'We should go set up our stuff near the fire.'

When we get back to the living room, I stop worrying whether Harris has heard us kissing in the hall: he's crashed out in his sleeping bag, still in his unzipped windbreaker, his arms thrown up behind his head like a baby. He looks vulnerable in his sleep, his face unguarded, lips full and tender.

I pick up his abandoned mug and move it out of the way, in case he stirs. Mycroft collects our sleeping bags from the corner.

'I'll do this.' His voice is still low, for Harris's benefit. 'You look stuffed.'

'Thanks. I'm going out for a pee.'

'You just showed me the toilet!'

I shrug and smile. 'It's sort of traditional to pee in the agapanthus when you first get home. I'll only be a second.'

I *do* pee near the agapanthus, but then I climb back up the stairs and stand on the edge of the verandah in the dark. I've switched off my torch: now it's only me and the night sky, spread out like a flying carpet across the heavens. Each pinpoint of light is crisp and clear in the freezing air. It's like the planets have aligned to put on a show, in celebration of my return.

I'm back in Five Mile, and it's just like I'd thought: things have changed, *I've* changed. But my love for this place is still true. It will always be a part of me. My breath fogs out in front of my face and my fingertips go numb, but in this moment I can let go of my body and feel myself lifted up. My consciousness is just a mote absorbed into the dazzling stars, and these are *my* stars, *mine*. I know them, and they know me.

Beneath these stars, my fear doesn't matter. Cole doesn't matter. None of it has any importance. What we do in this situation has no more significance than any other trivial moment on the face of the earth – where a snake sleeps, or the wing feathers of a bird, or a momentary footprint in the dirt. Mycroft and Harris and me, we have no more permanence than water, and I am just one of the many animals absorbed by the minutiae of my life under the cold finger of the moon.

I look up. I want to jump into the sky. I want to suck in my breath and howl it out, just to release some of this feeling.

The verandah doors open. I glance over, surprised to see Mycroft. He pulls on his coat, his head tilted up, chin high. His Adam's apple moves as he swallows in the sight of all these stars.

'Is it always like this?'

I breathe out. 'Not always. But when it's clear – yeah.'

'My god.' He smiles up, like he's three years old. 'This is incredible.'

'Haven't you seen stars before?'

'Not this way. Not so . . .' He opens out his hands. 'It's so *big*.'

'Yep.'

He looks at me. 'You're jaded, aren't you? It's all old hat to you.'

'No,' I say. 'No, I still feel it.'

He looks at me, back to the stars. His face holds that same wonder. Without turning his head, he reaches for my hand. I smile at his touch. We just stand there in the dark, looking at the stars, until we get too cold. Then we go inside.

CHAPTER EIGHTEEN

The verandah doors open, and I jerk awake. For one horrible moment, I confuse the creak of the door with the crack of a shot.

Then I see Mycroft edging inside with a few lengths of firewood, my torch balanced on top. There's a glow beyond the windows: sunrise here is like a miles-distant explosion, radiant pink and orange bleeding over the sky. I guess I've had less than two hours sleep, but it was solid: no nightmares.

I unzip from my sleeping bag before Mycroft wrecks the fire.

'Hi, sorry,' he whispers. 'I was hoping you'd rest a bit longer.'

'I'm okay.' I rub at my cold arms, hunker down beside him to take over. 'You've gotta pull the baffle out, to air the coals. Now just this bark and twiggy stuff first, to get it going again. See?'

Mycroft adds his own handful of twigs, watches me as I yawn. 'Coffee?'

'God, yes.'

He pads over to the primus while I feed the coals. The air inside the living room warms. I pick my way past Harris's huddled bulk to take the mug Mycroft's offering.

My eyebrows twitch up at the sight of him with the spoon. 'You put condensed milk in instant coffee, too?'

'Everything is improved with condensed milk. You should try it on Weetbix – magic.'

I sip my over-sweet coffee. 'So it's about seven-thirty?'

'Spot on.' He looks at me over the edge of his mug. 'You know this place like the back of your hand, don't you?'

I glance out the glass doors, towards the paddocks shawled in lacy fog. 'I know that in July, first light comes at about seven. And we'll lose the light at about five-thirty in the afternoon. Long winter nights. We'll have to bring in more wood.'

'And wake up your little friend.' Mycroft lifts his chin towards Harris. 'We've got to get organised for Cole's arrival.'

But Harris manages to get in another hour of sleep before the clattering of the stove and the smell of frying bacon and sausages rouses him. It doesn't bother me that he's getting a sleep-in: last night's driving effort was heroic.

He rolls over and groans. 'Fuck. I feel hung-over.'

There's more swearing. Harris scratches at his hair before accepting the mug and bread-wrapped sausage and bacon I pass him.

He rubs a hand across his lips. 'Breakfast of champions, is it?'

'We've been talking about the quarry,' I say in reply. I stand with the backs of my legs towards the fire, cupping another coffee.

Harris looks between me and Mycroft, who's settled on one of Mai's old blankets with his sausage-in-bread handful. 'You two been scheming?'

'We need somewhere neutral to direct Cole.' Mycroft licks pan juices off his knuckles. 'Rachel says the main street of Five Mile is too public.'

'And the salt lakes are too exposed – there'd be nowhere for us to hide,' I say. 'But the quarry might be good. You know the place, and it's close.'

'Bit early. Hang on, get the old brain working.' Harris slurps, bites off more of his breakfast and talks through a mouthful. 'The quarry – yeah, I guess. Shitloads of gravel, dirt mounds, sheds, so there's cover. Walk to it from here, if you don't mind the walk.'

My nods pick up speed. 'So it should work.'

'If you can be sure it'll all go down tomorrow, it'll work. Sunday – all the blokes are off. Otherwise you're in trouble. Machines, people – everything switches back on first thing Monday morning.'

'Tomorrow?' I bite my lip. 'Will we be ready?'

'Question is, will Cole arrive by then?' Harris raises his eyebrows at Mycroft.

Mycroft shrugs. 'I don't know. It's about six hours' drive from Tullamarine, if you hammer it. But we've got his precious coin. You'd have to say he's highly motivated.'

I look at him. 'If we go in closer to town you can get internet reception. Send Cole a new message with a specific time and place. See if he's replied to your last one.'

'That's the best we can do for a guarantee?' Harris asks.

'As far as I can see, that's our only option,' Mycroft says.

'I really don't want it to happen here.' I wave a hand to indicate the house, my old home.

'So the quarry, then,' Harris muses. 'Yeah, okay. Let me think for a bit about what we can do there. Finish me coffee.'

While Harris polishes off his no-frills breakfast and Mycroft cleans up in the kitchen, I wander back down the hall to the toilet. On the way back, instead of passing by my old room, I walk in and look around.

It's very dusty – there's a faint smell of dry rot and salt. Cobwebs festoon the ceiling corners, and indentations score the floorboards where my deep old wardrobe used to plant its feet. All my mementoes are still on the windowsill, like exhibits in the museum of my childhood: three smooth rocks, a dried wildflower, a curled-up leathery thing that I know is the tail of a frill-necked lizard. I'd forgotten these things, forgotten I'd left them here when we left. I have a strong urge to crack the window up and push them all out onto the ground.

I didn't come into my room when I last visited. It seemed wrong, an empty nod to my old life. Now I notice the space of it – how much room I had! Here I could withdraw from the world and dream, doodle, play music, read, live in my imagination. Here I was work-hardened but soft, sheltered. Here I was safe.

But that kind of protection didn't do me any favours. Nothing could touch me, but I, in turn, touched nothing.

'Rachel?' Mycroft's footfalls sound in the hallway.

I turn to see him at the door. Dull blue eyes, reddened from rubbing and lack of sleep. Tousled hair, pall of dirt on his face. A cigarette is tucked behind his ear and his fingertips poke out from his cut-off gloves.

His hand squeezes the lintel. 'Rachel? You okay?'

My heart contracts as I look at him. 'I'm good. I'm ready.'

'Come on out, then,' Mycroft says. 'Me and Harris have a plan.'

———

'What do you mean, "booby traps"?'

'Like it says on the tin.' Harris glances at me over his shoulder. He turns the wheel of the Ford to the right, and everybody's teeth clack as we go over a pothole. 'Traps for boobies. Cole and his goons—'

'We're assuming he's got goons,' Mycroft says.

'He's got at least one.' Harris flashes a look at Mycroft in the passenger seat, cranks up the heater. 'Mike's shooter. Same guy who killed those two kids. And Cole's not gonna come here all on his lonesome, now, is he? He doesn't know which way's up, for starters. He'll need someone to show him around. Someone to point and shoot, so he doesn't have to get his own hands dirty.'

Harris's expression is pretty dirty when he says that: he looks like someone's challenged him to pistols at dawn. I'm more worried about how far we're going to have to take things to keep ourselves protected from Cole. When I try to explain this to Harris, though, he thinks I'm worried about getting my halo broken.

'Rachel, you can't give a shit about what's gonna happen to them. Cole is the one who's shifted everything up a rung. Him and his pet assassin – *they're* the bad guys.' His green eyes pierce me through the rear-view. 'They shot Mike. C'mon, don't tell me you're not pissed off.'

I frown at him while chewing my thumbnail. 'I just don't want to be picking through body parts to get out of this.'

Mycroft is looking out the passenger window at the pale, tattooed tracks rising up the side of a catchment dam, where sheep have laid a trail in the packed dirt.

I touch his shoulder. 'What's your take on all this, anyway? '

'I don't know. I don't exactly want to rain down fire and brimstone on Cole's head, but we don't know what he's got planned.'

His face shows a grim anxiety. It was Mycroft who built the bomb in the warehouse in London – the bomb that got us out, the bomb that killed two people. He feels the weight of that, I suddenly realise. Has felt it for weeks.

Harris looks disgusted. 'So what're you gonna use, then? Bad language?'

Mycroft shakes his head. 'Some sort of firepower would be good, to stop Cole from getting too close. Let's just find this stash of goodies you're talking about. We'll work out what we've got, and figure out what we can use without a guilty conscience.'

Harris sighs, but I let my gratitude flow through my fingers into Mycroft's shoulder. He looks over and gives me a tired smile.

Minutes later, we pull up at the bore station beside the dirt road bare kilometres from Harris's place. The collection of battered tin sheds here looks almost ready to be reclaimed by the earth, but there's a new green bore tank on stilts with shiny fixtures.

Harris grabs the ancient fold-out army shovel I scrounged from the house, then he jumps out of the car and walks to the bore tank. He stands between the metal struts that elevate it, scuffs at a spot there in the shade with his boot heel, starts digging.

Mycroft and I walk up to watch. The earth is sandy, strewn with moon-rock chunks of gypsum. I try one of the bore taps: the trickle of water that comes out is cloudy with salt and iron.

'Need some help?' Mycroft asks.

'Nah, it's just sand here. I'm good.' Harris's hair blows in his face as he ploughs away with the shovel.

'So this is your hidey-hole?' I look around. 'Foils of pot, booze cache and stolen blasting caps from the quarry?'

'We don't say *stolen*, we say *borrowed*. I was a trainee, yeah? I was just doing a little training out of hours.' He winks at me.

A minute later, Harris exhumes a sand-covered blue and white canvas sports bag.

'Right, here we go.' He blows sand out of the zipper, opens the bag. He holds up a small bottle of whisky and grins. 'Enough to wet your whistle.' He inspects the rest of the contents critically. 'I let off a couple of the caps a while back, but there's still enough to do a reasonable job. There's pliers, and a few metres of blasting wire, too.'

Mycroft nods casually, but I can see by his eyes he's keen to get his hands on that bag. He's been out of his element since we arrived in Five Mile – a foreign environment, limited phone reception, none of his usual resources – but this is something understandable, something he knows.

'Okay, so we've got materials. We'll need a few other bits and pieces – electrical tape, batteries, flour.'

'We can stop at the grocery shop in town on the way back,' I say.

'Weapons.' Mycroft squats, touches the tempting bag with Harris's tools. 'We've got this, as a deterrent, but nothing obviously threatening if they surprise us. They'll have guns.'

'I can get one.' Harris stands up and dusts himself off. 'Dad's rifle.'

'You'll have to go back home.' I check his face. 'Do you really wanna do that?'

'No problem,' Harris says, eyes low.

When we get back to the car, though, he pauses before starting the engine. At the turn-off to Sandbag Road, the road into his place, he jerks the wheel roughly.

I've been to Harris's house before – with Mike, long ago – although I've never been inside. It's like those places we passed in the dark on the way up here: the garden of rusted car bodies, graveyard of old tyres, falling-down corrugated sheds, coils of useless wire.

Harris parks near the gate, like he doesn't want to get close enough for a proper inspection. He stares through the bug splatter on the windscreen, gazing at the house. Suddenly he cracks into action, shoving open the driver's door.

'Right. One sec.'

'Do you want us to—'

'Stay here.' He frowns at me in the back seat. 'There might be words, so just . . . stay here.' Then he's gone.

Mycroft leans forward. 'Want to tell me what's going on?'

I consider what to say, opt for brevity. 'Harris and his dad don't get on.'

'I gathered. Not the loving home of memory, then.'

'Fair way from that, I think.'

If there are raised voices, we don't hear them. But a few minutes later, Harris strides out of the house, slamming the door behind him.

The rifle is in his hand. He opens the driver's-side door, shoves the gun stock at me, gets inside, pulls the door shut. He keeps his head down as he twists the key, revs the engine hard, backs us roughly off the sandy edge and out onto the road. Mycroft and I rock in our seats as he floors it.

'A three-oh-three.' I hold the rifle carefully. 'Not loaded, is it?'

Harris's hair flies around as he shakes his head. 'Box of rounds in my pocket.'

I check anyway, keeping my attention on the weapon as Harris sniffs, clears his throat. His hands on the steering wheel are shaking.

'Your dad was okay to lend you the rifle?' Mycroft asks from the passenger seat, looking over at Harris.

Harris makes a harsh laugh. 'Not exactly. Tough luck.'

He's keeping his chin down, and I smell a rat. I reach between the seats and push back his hair. A dark red bloom is rising on his cheekbone, although the rest of his face is pale. He'll have a bruise there by lunchtime.

I swear.

'It's fine.' Harris shakes my hand away.

Mycroft's voice is strangled. 'Your dad did that?'

Harris clears his throat. 'Ah, y'know, he gets on the piss . . . That's pretty much his life story.'

'Fucking hell.' Mycroft – for whom memories of family are grief-tinged but nonetheless happy – looks appalled. His voice hardens. 'D'you want us to go back and have a word with him?'

Harris ducks his head. 'Nah, mate. Leave it.' He wipes his nose on his sleeve in the pause, then glances at Mycroft. 'Thanks for offering, though.'

We stop at Metcalfe's grocery in Five Mile. Harris slips inside with a short list that Mycroft has written on the back of an old envelope from the glove compartment.

While he's gone, Mycroft and I walk up to the top of the hill behind the shops, so we can get decent phone reception. Mycroft texts Pickup, saying reassuring things about staying out of sight at Mai's. I send a similar text to my parents, with an additional query about Mike. Then Mycroft prepares another email, to Cole. I look away. From this vantage point, I can see a wedge-tailed eagle circling high. A breeze ripples through the rows of wheat in distant paddocks like a great green Mexican wave.

'Okay, Cole has replied to say he's in Melbourne. I've said we'll meet at nine a.m. tomorrow, and I'll contact him again later to say where. And I've texted Mai, told her to call Pickup at eight – he can contact the local police here to grab Cole on the way out.'

'The local cops are Jared and Derrin,' I say. 'I've known them since I was a kid, I could call them tomorrow morning—'

'You might not get reception at the quarry. And I don't want them barging in while I'm negotiating with Cole. Let's just get Pickup to handle the police end.' Mycroft looks at me. 'You sent a text to your parents – do you want to wait for a reply?'

'Not really.' I rub my arms through my jacket sleeves, enjoying the sun in this spot. 'I'd like to know about Mike, but Mum and Dad will be stressed, and I don't want to deal with that.'

'Fair enough.'

He switches off his phone and tucks it into his pocket as we meander back down the hill towards the car. His chin lifts as he surveys the street I'm so familiar with. I see it through his eyes suddenly: pub, post office, general store. Tatty houses intermixed with scrubby gardens. No pedestrians.

'Well, it's a bit different from Melbourne,' Mycroft says. 'A few more utes, for one thing.'

My lips drift up. 'Yeah, Toyota Hilux has basically cornered the market up this way.'

Mycroft looks around. 'Now I understand why it was such a shock for you, arriving in the city.'

'Five Mile *is* tiny.' How did I not realise before? I shake my head, still coming to terms with this. Mycroft grins.

By the time we get back to the car, Harris is already revving the engine. The radio is blaring 'Jessie's Girl' by Rick Springfield. Harris changes the channel with a rough jab of the button. 'You two hopping in or what?'

'Did you get it all?'

'I got the stuff on the list, plus extra wire. Had a bit of trouble with the styrofoam cups, but turned out they had some out the back in a packing crate.' He makes a face as we slide into the car. 'Had to put up with Bev Metcalfe at the checkout. And then Jared Capshaw's dad spotted me. *Does your old man know you're back in town?* What a lot of dipshits.'

'Word gets around fast.'

'No bloody kidding.' He turns in the driver's seat to reverse out.

———

Harris carefully lays out the equipment – borrowed and bought – on the kitchen bench. He and Mycroft stand over the stuff, positioning items.

'Here's the styro and the oil. We can get petrol from the jerry can for the pump. So that's five detonators, the flour, tape, batteries, wire—'

'You got clothes pegs?' Mycroft asks.

'Yeah, wooden ones.'

'That's perfect.'

'So you're thinking a pressure-firing device? Something they can step on? Or maybe a trip-wire?'

'Probably a trip-wire. We're looking for pyrotechnics more than anything. It'll be small – I don't want to take their legs off, I just want to block off certain areas, and stop them from getting too close.'

'If you lay it in scree, you'll get a nice little avalanche as well, which should complicate movement.' Harris smiles at the idea.

I don't know if I can listen to any more of this. The whole conversation is giving me chills. I'm scared of Cole and the guy who shot Mike – I feel that. But I really don't want to start blowing people up again. It was horrifying enough the first time around.

I find a bucket under the dusty sink, fill it with hot water from the billy on the Coonara, and go to the bathroom to give myself a cat's-lick wash. I feel refreshed afterwards, more clear-headed. Thank god for Mai, and fresh undies. Picking the porcupine grass out of my socks, I sling on my clothes and boots.

Out the window, the sky is beginning to darken with the promise of rain. When I get back to the living room, the boys are still sorting through their booby-trap components.

'We should walk to the quarry,' I point out. 'Have a look at the layout.'

'Scope out the terrain.' Mycroft nods, thumbing his bottom lip. 'I told Cole I'd meet him at nine, but I need to be at the quarry—'

'*We*,' I say. '*We* need to be at the quarry.'

'Right. Anyway, we've got to be there before Cole, and I don't trust him not to try a sneak attack. It'd be good to know when he arrives. But it's not like we can set up CCTV cameras down the main street of Five Mile . . .'

'It's Kennedy Street,' Harris says absently, then he looks up at me. 'Hang on.'

I've understood his look straight away.

'We just want an advance warning of Cole's arrival, right?' I look at Mycroft.

'Yeah. But—'

I cut him off, look back at Harris. 'Is the old Meary house still empty, out on Furlough Creek Road?'

'Yep.' Harris nods.

'Well, that's perfect.'

'What's perfect?' Mycroft is glancing between us both.

I'm trying to restrain my grin. 'The house on the corner of the approach road. Local kids . . . us, I mean. We used it for camp-outs some nights. Anyway, the house is on a rise. It's the perfect lookout spot.'

'So one of us could be the lookout? But even if a mobile works up there, we can't get reception here or in the quarry. They won't be able to send a warning,' Mycroft points out.

'Yeah, but whoever's there will have a view for miles because the rest of the district is so flat. If they see a Melbourne car approaching – something they don't recognise, that looks too clean for local – they can drive to the quarry and let us know.'

'That'll be me,' Harris says.

'Why's it always you?'

'Licensed driver, hello? And I'll recognise whether a car is local or not. Plus I could get binoculars at the quarry – I know where they're kept.'

Mycroft nods. 'Well, if we want to make sure Cole doesn't sneak up on us in the early hours of the morning, you'll have to keep watch overnight.'

Harris shrugs. 'I can set up the charges and grab the binoculars at the quarry late this arvo, go back and settle in at the house, catch a nap around sundown, be ready to go for the night. Then when I see Cole's car in the morning, I'll motor hard for the quarry to warn you.'

'What if Cole arrives before sun-up, in the dark?'

'Even better.' Harris grins. 'I'll practically see the headlights from Ouyen. And he'll have to go slow because he won't know the road.'

'You too,' I point out. 'You'll have to watch out for roos.'

'I'll do the old duck'n'dodge,' Harris says, winking.

'But if he comes before eight-thirty in the morning, you'll be driving *here* to warn us, not to the quarry. You'll have to drive like a bat out of hell to get back in time.'

'You've seen me drive, yeah?'

'Great.' Mycroft looks a bit baffled, but he's happy to go along with it. 'So, are we still walking to the quarry?'

'We should drive,' Harris says. 'Heaps quicker.'

I shake my head. 'I need to walk.' I glance down at the components. 'I just . . . need to work some of this off.'

Harris nods: he knows what 'this' is. I'm sure he and Mycroft are both feeling the steadily building tension too. It isn't like pre-exam nerves, or some kind of performance anxiety. This is more hollow.

The outside is what I need: the feel of cold air on my face is a momentary reprieve, like massaging a cramp. We go cross-country, cutting across Thorny Gap Road and over what used to be our east paddock. Trespassing on Pat Righetti's land, we walk briskly along the tractor track beside her waving wheat.

Choughs screech and fly off at our approach. My knee throbs a bit, but it's a good throb. Chunky piles of dry pink dirt rise on each side of the track, like caked fondant, and Harris points his shooting finger at the occasional dashing rabbit. I sigh, try to settle into a steady walking rhythm.

Mycroft catches my eye. 'What is it?'

'I miss my dog,' I admit. 'Tilly would love this. She loved going on big walks, chasing rabbits on the way.'

Harris smiles. 'I remember Tilly. Man, she was dumb as a bag of hair.'

'She was a lovely dog!'

'I'm not saying she wasn't. She was a great dog. Me and Mike used to play that old joke on her, y'know? We'd scratch under her chin and say, *Who's a good dog? Hey, girl, who's a good dog?* And she'd look up at us with those big brown eyes, like, *Is it me? Am I the good dog? Maybe it's me?* and we'd just laugh ourselves stupid.'

'She was kind of goofy,' I concede. I duck my head.

'Hey.' Harris reaches over to ruffle my hair. 'You made a tough call, Rache, putting the dogs down. But what's done is done. You can't dwell on it.'

He strides forward, scouting ahead. When I glance up, I see Mycroft look at me, then chew his bottom lip as he looks at Harris.

We're not excluding Mycroft on purpose – it's just that I'm back here, in the place I used to belong, and Harris is a part of that belonging. But I don't want Mycroft to feel left out. I nudge him with my elbow as we walk. 'See that mound of dirt over there?'

'Yeah?'

'Mallee fowl nest. The male and female mate, then dig a giant hole and fill it with sand and leaf litter to incubate their eggs.' I suddenly realise that maybe a local ornithology lesson isn't what he needs right now. 'Sorry, you probably think it's stupid . . .'

'No, no. Not at all.' He lifts an eyebrow as we pass the nest. 'Mallee fowl. Right.'

'I guess it's not that interesting.'

'No, it is. C'mon, tell me more.'

'Oh . . . Well, they're kind of funny. Fluffy, about as big as a cat. And they have this nest obsession. After they've dug the hole, the male moves something like a tonne of sand every day to keep the temperature constant.'

'That's a lot of sand,' Mycroft says. 'So . . . they dig themselves a hole to climb out of.'

'Yep.' I look at him and snort. 'The analogy didn't exactly elude me.'

Mycroft looks back at the nest. 'How do they know they can work together, though? How do they know they're compatible? Is it some sort of chemical thing – bird hormones?'

I shrug. 'I dunno. Maybe it's something to do with the way they ruffle feathers.'

'Feather-ruffling. Sounds good.'

'They mate for life, you know.'

'Right.' Mycroft grins, looks me square in the eyes. 'A bird after my own heart.'

I laugh, give him a push on the arm. 'Crikey, now you're sounding like a local.'

Half an hour later, the high-packed rise of the Ridgeback Falls Quarry looms up in front of us. Harris leads us across Marilla Road, past the Hazchem notices and twenty-kay speed signs for trucks, away from the general entrance and around to the far side of the hill.

'Here you go, slide under.'

Harris pulls up a length of fence wire for us to slide through, ushers us along the boundary until we reach a scrubby spot near the hilltop. We all hunker down on our stomachs, peering at the site. The ground beneath us is damp. Kangaroo grass scratches my face, and my hands are freezing.

'Right, there's the site sheds on the right, when you first drive in, and the weighbridge.' Harris·nods with his chin. 'You don't wanna set up there, it's too open. Get past the first set of crushing mills, then you're closer to the pit.'

From this distance it's easy to see the huge front-loader tyres that hem in the edges of the road, the mounds of pale scree. Old machinery and shipping containers are dotted around like pre-historic debris. Sagging lines are strung high from power poles. Men move around the space, close enough for us to make out their high-visibility jackets, bunched socks and boots, hard hats.

Everything is labelled *Keep Clear*, or *Warning*, or *No Entry* – this is not a place that people are encouraged to wander into.

The entrance road takes vehicles past the site sheds and the crushing mills, funnels towards a mill shed at the top of a rise, then down to two neighbouring pits. There's the new pit: a shelf of chalky clay, the clear path running in for machines and trucks. The cliff face is on the left side, and piles of sand, boulders and sized gravel lie on the right. Dropping away on that side is the old pit, descending further into the earth; a crescent-shaped cut, shadowed and deep. An old road, dark from disuse, splits off the main path and runs into it, and a chain is strung across to block off access. Nobody goes into the old pit.

Down the bottom of the old road lies a wide pool of brackish black water, where the run-off consistently fails to drain. We were all warned about the old pit as kids – not to go near it, and never to swim in that deceptive pool. The surface is cloudy with sediment; it's impossible to tell where the deep places lie, or where the bottom is scant inches deep. Diving into it would be an invitation to kill yourself, or maybe just become a quadriplegic.

Harris is squinting at the new pit, pointing. 'See? There's your vantage point, at the back of that pit. Get in there and you'd see everything that walks in.'

'A nice little corral,' Mycroft says contemplatively.

'Yep. You've got those rocks and mounds for cover. Station me above you, on the top of the cliff, and no one can come at you from behind.' He motions to the dirt roads that travel a curving course either side of both pits, to the top of the cliff face. 'Put something about halfway up each road. If you tried to go in either direction and something blew up in your face, you'd think twice about going on, wouldn't you?'

'That's two down,' Mycroft says. 'And we'd need at least two more – for the gravel near the drop-off to the lake on the right, and near the working cliff face on the left. I don't want anyone thinking they can skirt around me on either side.'

'What's all this *me* stuff?' I give him another elbow nudge, a less friendly one this time. 'I'll be there with you.'

'No, you won't,' Mycroft says. 'Because you'll be stationed there, out of sight near the mill shed.'

'That's not—'

'Slow down, tiger. You'll be watching there to make sure Cole collects the coin. Because I'm going to hide it in that pile of scree in front of the mill shed. A blind handover – he'll have to double back and collect the coin on his way out.' He looks at me. 'You need to stay out of sight. If something goes wrong, you're the only one who can run back to warn the police.'

I open my mouth, wanting to protest, wanting to say, *I won't let anything go wrong.* But I can't say that, because I don't know if it's true. Anything could happen. Plans go awry. I mash my lips together.

'You'll wanna set another trap near the entry to the mill shed,' Harris says quickly. 'In case anyone tries to come at her. She won't have a weapon. Or better yet, put Rachel on the cliff top and me at the shed. Then if there's a problem—'

'I can be at the shed.' I firm my chin when I say it. 'No one will know I'm there. It's no more dangerous than the cliff top – that's exposed.'

Harris pulls something out of the inside pocket of his jacket. I recognise it as my first-aid notebook, the one I gave to him to pack before we left Melbourne. With an unapologetic grin, he tears a page out, retrieves a pen from his jacket pocket and rests the page on the cover of the book so he can start sketching. It's a half-arsed map of the quarry, all flat lines and hieroglyphic circles and blobs.

'So that's it, yeah?' He talks as he sketches, gesturing with his pen at the map and then to the actual locations in turn. 'Cole will enter at this point, he's corralled towards you in the pit. Stay outta sight – he'll hear you well enough if you call out. You tell Cole where to find the coin on his way out. He does a smart reverse, Rachel checks he's got what he came for, and then he leaves. By that stage, Mai will have called the cops. Then Jared Capshaw and Derrin Blunt nab Cole on his way out on Marilla Road – job done, bad guys caught, cheers all round. And we all go back to the Five Flags for a beer.'

'Sounds easy,' Mycroft says, and he looks at me. I can almost hear what he's thinking: *too easy.*

'There'll be hiccups.' Grass tickles my cheek as I lean my arm against his. 'We don't know how many men Cole will bring. And there's bound to be something that doesn't go right. But the police will be backing us up. And it's a huge improvement on the last plan we had, in London.'

'What, the "blow up a microwave and hope we don't get killed" plan?'

I'm practically obliged to grin, even though my nerves feel frayed. 'Okay, so that's it. What time have you got?'

Mycroft checks his phone. 'About eleven-thirty.'

'Right. We need to get back and build the booby traps, check that the old Meary house will be okay as a lookout spot. Send Cole a message with the location. Text Pickup again, to say we're still at Mai's. And we should run the pump, bring in some firewood. And eat.'

'And sleep,' Mycroft says. 'You look knackered.'

On the way back, it hits me. We are really doing this. Confronting Cole aka Wild, the man I've come to fear as an amorphous malign presence, whose existence has shadowed my life for so long. The peaceful certainty I felt last night, looking up at the stars, is gone. My nerves aren't obeying me anymore – they're racing on ahead to tomorrow, the confrontation, the unknown outcome.

Suddenly I want it all to be over. I want to be sitting outside the Five Flags, eating roast beef and gravy rolls with Mycroft and Harris and sinking a sneaky beer, without this weight pressing me down. Then I want to drive back home to Melbourne – *back home*, that's what it is now – and walk into my brother's hospital room to see him sitting up, pale-faced but chirpy.

My legs get a juddering tremble. I feel like running, only I can't run properly. I jam my hands into the pockets of my windbreaker and start a hopping jog. Mycroft and Harris, talking about explosives, fall away behind me.

The sights on the route back – the dirt and scrub, the rotted posts of Mrs Righetti's fence, the black-trunked trees from the last burn-off – they all seem very clear and singular and remarkable. Every small detail around me has its own significance now. A silver bottle cap lies in the dust, hunched flat. I snatch it up, worry the thick ridges between my fingers as I go.

Back at the house, I go straight to the woodpile. The stack of cut wood is still generous, but we'll go through a lot tonight – there's already a chill in the air. I take another split into my arms, and another. Someone touches my shoulder, and I startle.

'I can take some of that,' Mycroft says, grabbing the chunk I have in my hand.

Harris comes around from my other side. 'Stack me up too.'

The two boys gather the firewood out of my arms, help themselves to a few more splits. By the time they're done, they're loaded like pack horses and I'm only carrying the kindling.

Harris shoos me towards the house. 'Come on, let's get you inside.'

The house has cooled while we were out. Harris settles his armful of wood beside the Coonara, heads for the kitchen bench. I'm about to kneel down and restart the fire when Mycroft dumps his own load of wood and takes the kindling off me.

My hands flail wildly as he steers me over to the sleeping bags piled near the hearth. 'But the fire's gone out—'

'I'll start it again.'

'You're hopeless at the fire!'

'Fine. Then Harris can start the fire.'

'Yes, Harris can,' Harris says, from over at the bench.

'And I'll put the kettle on,' Mycroft says. 'You need to get some rest.'

'I can't rest.' My fingers pluck at his sleeves, my hair, the old bottle cap from my pocket. 'I'm too buzzy.'

'Rachel.' He takes the bottle cap from me, lifts my chin gently so I'm looking right into his eyes. 'There's only so much sand you can move in a day.'

With absolutely no warning, exhaustion powers over me. Mycroft lays my sleeping bag out, helps me with my boots, while Harris breaks up kindling nearby.

Once I get into the sleeping bag, it's as if my entire body starts dissolving. All my processes are forgotten, my limbs weak and heavy. I hear the fire starting to crackle in the hearth. A tiny *tap-tap* at the window makes me look over: a willie wagtail is perched on the sill, rapping its beak against the glass, like it wants to come in.

Stay out! I think. *You don't want to get caught up in what's going on in here . . .* then my mind loses traction and I float away.

———

A distant familiar chugging brings me slowly awake. The fire snaps softly and the house is warm in the afternoon light.

I roll over in my sleeping bag to see Mycroft sitting on the floor, left foot tucked under the thigh of his extended right leg, as he leans towards something. Wisps of smoke rise from the cigarette pegged in the corner of his mouth. As I watch, he removes the cigarette with two pinched fingers, lays it butt-end out on the edge of a brick sitting beside him, and picks up a pair of needle-nose pliers. He lifts the thing he's got in his other hand and makes two neat cuts – *snip, snip* – with the pliers. Glistening strands of wire fall away.

He's doing that slouching thing that boys do: knees open, arms loose at the wrists and shoulders. His abdominal muscles are hidden beneath the folds of his long-sleeved T-shirt. His cheeks and chin are shaded with stubble, and his curls tuft up at the back, from wearing his hoodie. Where the neckline of his T-shirt falls away, the skin at the base of his neck is pale.

I know I should be thinking of other things – the plans for tomorrow, the preparations we have to make. I should be focused on these essentials, or I should be thinking about my brother, willing him to get well, expending my mental energy by winging positive thoughts in Mike's direction.

But all I can think about, right this second, is how *good* Mycroft looks. Good in a deep way, low down in my stomach. Good in a way that makes me want to creep over to him, press my cheek into the back of his neck, run my hands around to his front, tilt his head to the side and . . .

'Are you perving on me when you're supposed to be sleeping?' Mycroft takes his smoke off the brick to have a quick drag.

I rub at my eyes lazily. 'How'd you know I was awake?'

'You haven't figured it out yet, have you, Watts?' He looks at me, and his eyes are a tempting ultramarine beneath his thick brows. 'If you're nearby, I know exactly what you're doing at any given moment. It's my superpower.'

'Really?' I lean on one elbow and slide my other hand down, under the nylon where he can't see, to squeeze my boob. 'So . . . what am I doing now?'

Mycroft scans the down-stuffed nylon, and his mouth opens at the same moment his cheekbones flush a bright pink—

The door to the verandah creaks. I move my hand away quickly, only just realising that the background chugging has disappeared. Harris steps into the house, shaking raindrops out of his hair.

'Right, I've just shut off the pump. That should give us enough water for about—' Harris glances up, sees me. 'Oh hey, you're awake. Good timing. I'm gonna take the car to Furlough Creek Road, find a good spot at the Meary house to keep watch.'

I scrape my hair off my face and sit up properly, try to curry my features into something approaching normal. 'Make sure you're somewhere dry, on the verandah maybe, so you don't get pneumonia overnight.'

'Yes, Mum.' Harris shuts the door, walks to where Mycroft sits and squats down. 'How's it going with these?'

'Three down, two to go.' Mycroft's cheeks still show the remnants of his blush.

I clamber out of my bag and come closer. 'What time is it?'

'About three.' Mycroft grabs his phone off the floor and nods to confirm the time, before handing the phone to Harris. 'Take this with you. The email to Cole with the quarry location is prepped to go.' He takes the phone back for a moment to show Harris. 'As soon as you're in a spot with reception, hit "Send". There's a reassuring text going out to Pickup as well – here, see that?' Once Harris nods his understanding, Mycroft returns the phone. 'You'll need to charge it in the car, the battery's low.'

I squint at Mycroft as he straightens, winces, stretches his back. 'Have you guys slept?'

'Napped,' Harris says. 'Got up a half-hour ago.'

'I'm gonna finish these, and then sleep.' Mycroft glances at me, sitting on the floor near his knee. 'You look better.'

'I feel better.'

I examine the equipment in front of Mycroft – batteries, wire, square packages of flour, electrical tape. Further away are the blasting caps, plus something else. Laid out on greaseproof paper are blobs of an off-white gooey substance that looks like greasy cake icing.

I lean forward to see, reaching out a hand. 'What's that?'

Harris blocks me with his arm. 'Yeah, maybe don't touch that.'

'It's homemade plastique,' Mycroft explains. He points to the blackened saucepan on the primus. 'Had to wreck the pot to make it. But Harris said all the commercial explosives at the quarry are kept in a locked room in a safe. And they're emulgents – mixtures of reactive chemicals, incredibly dangerous if you don't know exactly what you're doing. We had to make our own alternative. We've got the caps, but they're useless without some primary explosive.'

Mycroft points as he elaborates. 'We'll lay the charges under gravel, run a trip-wire from the peg jaws, with a cardboard wedge instead of the Blu-Tack. Bad guy trips the wire, the peg snaps shut, closes the circuit. Blasting cap fires the plastique – *boom*. It's just flour, instead of shrapnel, so it's not going to seriously hurt anyone. But with a bit of luck the flour dust will ignite and we'll get a nice little fireball as well. That should put Cole off.'

'A non-lethal bomb.' I nod my approval. 'That makes a nice change.'

'You could rig these as grenades as well,' Harris says, considering.

'Yeah, you don't really want to start throwing them around.' Mycroft waves at Harris with the pliers. 'Do you understand how to lay these?'

'Yeah. Trip-wires will be a bit fiddly.'

'Take your time with them,' Mycroft says. 'I'm hooking the batteries up now, so don't take the Blu-Tack out from the peg until you're sure you've got it right.'

'I'll be careful.' Harris tugs a square of paper out of his jacket pocket, unfolds it, hands it to Mycroft. 'I've drawn up a proper map – here's your copy. Not really to scale, but close as I could make it. Check here – the circles show you where the gravel piles sit, and the crosshatching is the quarry face. There's the mill shed. We talked about placement here and here, in the new pit, then up either side of the road to the cliff top. Can you follow that?'

Mycroft nods.

'Be sure. I'm gonna be stationed at the old house after I've laid the charges, so I won't see you until we meet at the quarry. That'll be right before Cole arrives, so we might not have time to go over this again.'

'Don't forget the one in front of the mill shed.'

Harris glances at me. 'I won't.'

'Then we're all set.' Mycroft exhales, a little trembly and low.

'Okay, well, I'm off.' Harris tucks the paper back in his jacket pocket; his knee joints pop as he rises. 'Don't blow up anything without me. And Rachel, we'll need to bring in some wood.'

'Will do.'

Harris gives me a grin, backtracks to the door. I see his hair bobbing down the verandah stairs, and then he's gone.

Mycroft is still snipping when I turn back. His hands, without the gloves, are dextrous, but only now do I notice the almost imperceptible shake in his fingers.

'You should get some sleep.'

Mycroft makes a noncommittal grunt. A pad of tattered cloth is secured with electrical tape over the flesh at the base of his left thumb.

I point at the makeshift bandage. 'What's that?'

'A reminder not to be stupid.' He flexes his thumb, frowning at the joint. 'Cut myself on the wire. Harris laughed till he cried.'

'He's not all bad, y'know.'

'I'm aware.' Mycroft focuses on his work, connecting wire to pegs and batteries. 'And he's not as dumb as he makes himself out to be. At all. I just don't like the way he looks at you.'

The possessiveness in his voice surprises me. 'Doesn't matter how he looks at me. What matters is that I'm not looking back.'

'He speaks your language.' Mycroft's eyes still won't meet mine. 'He knows the jokes you like, the old stories, all the history . . .'

'Yes,' I say. 'He's part of my old life. But I've got a new life now.'

'With a guy who's so smart he got two innocent people killed.' Mycroft twists wire around a peg viciously. 'Who's dragged you into some crazy smackdown with a spy and an assassin—'

'*Mycroft.*' I lean forward and take away his pliers. 'Don't you give me that shit. You didn't kill those kids, and you didn't drag me into anything. Blame *me* for falling for you, for getting myself kidnapped in London, for getting caught up in—'

'I'm not gonna blame *you.*'

'Well, you shouldn't blame yourself either. Cole started this. He killed your folks, he was the one who set you on this path in the first place.'

Mycroft blinks at the components in front of him. 'I guess I should be grateful to him. Cole's the one who made me what I am. Cole's the man I've got to thank for all this.'

His hands are flopped in his lap and his shoulders are slumped. It cost him, to say that. But he's only speaking a part of the truth.

'No,' I say firmly. 'Cole sure as hell doesn't deserve a thank you. And now's the time to take him down, put him away where he can't hurt us or our families ever again. '

Mycroft looks at me. I reach for his left hand, the one with the cut; hold it in my left hand, the one with the recent breaks. The one with permanent damage. I raise his hand up and kiss his palm.

'Now, give me some pegs and wire,' I say, 'and show me what to do.'

———

Standing on the verandah with the gun is something I'm familiar with. I check the stock and examine the barrel, blow off some dust and clean the magazine with the tail of my flannie. I click it back together and dry-fire it a couple of times, checking the sight.

'It pulls to the right.' Harris closes the verandah doors behind him. 'Aim a little out.'

'Okay.' I give him a nod.

'Cartridges are in the duffle. Those messages went through – here's Mycroft's phone.' He passes it to me. 'Everything's sorted on Furlough Creek Road. Now I've just gotta go lay the charges, then keep watch.'

'You've done so much, Harris. And I can't even make you breakfast.' I smile, then tilt my head a little to see the bruise he's trying to hide under his hair. 'How's your cheek?'

'I've had worse.' He puts a hand up unconsciously. Over the last few days, his stubble has taken on a deeper golden cast.

'Shit, Harris.' I shake my head and sigh. 'I wish you'd told me what was going on when we still lived here. Dad would've been onto it like a shot.'

'It's not that easy.'

I frown at him. 'Actually, it really is. We could've helped, y'know. My parents, everyone in the district . . . we always thought you were a deadshit.'

'I *was* a deadshit.'

'I'm glad you used the past tense. But come on – extenuating circumstances.' I touch his cheek, wincing for him. 'You shouldn't have had to put up with that. You could've had a better life.'

Harris pushes my hand away gently, but his eyes have gone crystalline. He turns before I have a chance to see more, exhales a shaky breath.

'I could really handle a joint right now.' His words are thick.

'Except we don't have any pot.' I aim out with the rifle, bring it down. 'And we need you on the ball, so I would go completely apeshit at you.'

'Yeah, you would.' He laughs, then quiets as he looks out towards the paddocks. 'I still can't believe it. I worked my arse off at the quarry to get the hell outta here, and now I'm back.'

'And I wanted a quiet life,' I counter, 'and look at me now.'

He glances at me. 'I always thought you guys were nuts, y'know? You and Mike and your folks. Working like dogs so you could stay here, when I just wanted to get the fuck out. I could never understand why you wanted to stay so badly.'

I look at the paddocks too, probably with more fondness than Harris. The sky is darkening rapidly, and sunset is a fiery cordial stain on the horizon. Clouds are torn scraps of fairy floss, tinted pink in the fading light.

'I loved it here,' I say. 'I still love it. It's kind of in my bones . . . in my soul. But it's crazy, because it doesn't really feel the same. It didn't when I came up with Mike, either. Maybe it's because I'm not living here. Or maybe it's because I always think of it as the place where my family lives, and my family's not with me now . . .'

'Family.' Harris snorts. 'I used to get jealous of you guys. To me, family is just . . . Well, I guess that's one thing me and Mycroft have in common.'

'What's that?'

'Neither of us got family. Mine is too hopeless, and his is too dead.'

The mention of family has made me feel cold. I lean the gun on the verandah railing, butt end down with the muzzle pointing towards the roof, and rub my arms over my windbreaker. 'I wish I knew how Mike was.'

'He'll be okay. He's a tough bugger. Like his sister.'

The look Harris gives me then is different. I think he means to comfort and reassure me, but there's something else. Admiration? Suddenly I'm very aware of how close we're standing, shoulder to shoulder.

I make my voice casual. 'Is Mycroft still asleep?'

'Yeah,' Harris says quietly, 'he's conked out in front of the fire. I've packed all the charges into the car.' Harris wets his lips. 'Rachel—'

'Don't,' I say. I'm not sure what I mean when I say it. Don't spoil the moment? Don't speak it out loud? Don't make this strange tension between us real?

'You don't even know what I'm gonna say!'

'I think I do.'

'Look, I know you don't rate me, but . . .' He clears his throat. 'You're a good chick, Rachel.'

'Gee, thanks.' I try to keep my tone light.

Harris turns towards me. 'No, seriously. You're a good person. And I like you. A lot.' He sighs. 'Look, I don't have the toff accent or whatever it is that you go for in Mycroft. I'm no good with words and stuff, but . . . I wanted to tell you.'

The way he's said it makes me soften, makes me want to honour the way he's opened up. 'Thank you. For telling me.'

He nods, almost businesslike. But then it's as if something inside him won't be reined in, won't be ignored. His gaze is drawn to mine, like a compass needle pulls due north.

I see his eyes up close – the brown flecks, swirling deeply with the green – as he raises a hand and lifts my chin with his fingers. The contact makes me shiver, because I know what's going to happen next.

271

'I'm only gonna do this once,' he whispers, as though he's making a promise he doesn't think he can keep. Then he leans in and kisses me.

It's a soft brush of skin and warmth. My eyes snap closed with the shock of it. His lips are supple, coaxing – what surprises me is how delicate, how gentle, he is. I don't know why I'm surprised: Harris up-ends my expectations every time. Then, when I've barely had a chance to register the sweetness of it, the kiss has ended

'God, you taste like sunlight,' Harris sighs shakily, breaking the moment. 'Guess I left my run too late, didn't I?'

I stare at him. 'The whole time we lived here, you never . . .'

'Yeah. I was worried about what Mike would think.'

I don't know what to say, except the obvious. 'I'm in love with James.'

'I know.' He rubs the back of his neck, turns away quickly. 'I'm gonna go set up the stuff at the Falls now.'

'Harris—'

He half-jogs down the stairs. 'It's after five – we'll lose the light soon. Everyone at the quarry will've gone home.'

Working to make my voice come out, I follow him down as he walks away. 'Harris, you're gonna keep watch all night. You'll need a thermos of coffee, a sleeping bag—'

'All sorted.'

'Come back at midnight,' I say desperately. 'You'll be exhausted. I can take over—'

'No.' He shakes his head. 'I'll be all right. If I see anything, I'll drive straight back.'

I open my mouth – God, there's so much I want to say! – but Harris cuts me off with a look.

'Y'know, these last few years, I've really gone in hard. Smoking, fighting, getting on the piss . . .' He swallows, as if there's something bitter in his throat. 'I've found plenty of ways to fuck myself up.'

I understand what he's trying to say, and it hurts. 'And maybe I'm the best way so far?'

He looks from me to the house, where my boyfriend sleeps, then back to me. 'That's the thing, Rachel. I don't wanna be a fuck-up when I'm around you. I just thought you should know that.'

'Harris . . .' I step in close, cup his scratchy jaw in my hand, smooth his cheek with my thumb. When my voice comes out, it sounds gravelly. 'I rate you, okay? I rate you high.'

CHAPTER NINETEEN

After spending half an hour chewing my nails and brooding, I decide that it's better for my mental health if I do something productive.

I spend a while revising the scribbles in my first-aid notebook – it helps calm me down, and who knows when I'll need them? I bring in the wood. I make more housework for myself – tossing out the ruined saucepan, tidying up the remains of the bomb-manufacturing process, setting a billy of tea to brew on top of the Coonara. Our food supplies are running low: we're down to three packaged cups of instant noodles, tea bags, one tube of condensed milk, half a block of chocolate and a packet of trail mix. The boys have eaten their way through our only loaf of bread, and the sausages are long gone. Two bruised apples roll in the bottom of the green bag.

'It's night.' Mycroft sits up, scratching his chest through his T-shirt.

'Yeah, it's about eight. Welcome back.' I start putting all the food away, hesitate. 'You hungry?'

'Maybe.' He runs a finger into his mouth with his eyes closed. 'God, my teeth feel disgusting. Gimme a minute.'

While he pads off down the hall, I load the fire. The night seems to press in without curtains on the windows. Frost is misting and forming on the glass as the bitter external air hits the warmth.

When Mycroft returns, he checks his phone.

'Okay.' He glances from the screen to me and back again. 'Those messages went through. It's on. Nine a.m. tomorrow.'

I try not to show how this news dismays me. 'That's good, right?'

Mycroft nods, eyes downcast. He pulls on his shoes and another long-sleeved T-shirt out of his pack, tugs the pea coat around himself. 'Come outside with me.'

'Mycroft, it's gotta be about three degrees out there.'

'I want to see the stars again,' he says.

Beyond the doors, the cold pounces on us. My toes ice up straight away, so I jig on the spot. God, Harris must be freezing in the old Meary house. But maybe he's got a fire going, keeping himself warm . . . I try not to worry about it. I don't want to think about Harris right now.

'This really is amazing, y'know.' Mycroft stares high to where each star flashes its facets. He hugs his pea coat closer and tugs me down the stairs, so we have a better view 'Living here, growing up here . . . You were lucky.'

'I *was* lucky,' I say. 'Hopefully I still am. Hopefully some of that will rub off tomorrow.'

'No. Don't . . .' Mycroft looks away, frowning. 'Don't talk about that now. Tell me something else. Something nice.'

It's what I said to Mike that time, barely two weeks ago, when I was feeling particularly low.

'Okay . . .' I pull my jacket tighter, point with my chin. 'Well, there's the chopping block. It's actually the stump of a massive gum Dad cut because it was too close to the house – I wasn't even born at that stage. Dad always likes to tell the story of how he and Errol Davies felled that tree. They misjudged the line cuts, right? So when it finally came down, it missed the lambing shed – and Errol's car – by about a hair's-breadth.'

'Good. More.'

Mycroft follows me as I take a few steps across the lawn-poor allotment. My breath clouds out as I speak.

'Um . . . well, there's the machinery shed. And behind that is the stockyard. You can't see it very well at the moment. But I used to do the yarding there with Dad and Mike.'

'What about your mum?'

'No, god, she hated yarding. Said listening to all the lambs crying made her depressed. She used to deliver sandwiches and water. You get really thirsty when you're yarding. All the dust.'

'Okay. More.' His face looks strangely lost.

'More?' It seems like pretty boring, ordinary stuff to me, but if it dispels Mycroft's melancholy mood, I don't mind. 'Well, if we walked down towards the gully we might see the winter creek flowing.'

'Bit cold for swimming, though.'

'A bit.' I turn and see Mycroft, galaxies reflected on his cheeks in the moonlight. It takes me another second to realise he's crying. My heart leaps up fast and I grab for his hand. 'Oh god, are you okay?'

He turns his head away. 'Sorry. Sorry, I didn't mean to—'

'James . . .'

Finally my tugging hand makes him turn back.

'I miss my mum and dad.' He uses the collar of his T-shirt to wipe his face with rough strokes. 'Weird, yeah? I never used to be able to cry about them. But since my birthday, I get this . . .'

I put my hand on his arm, squeeze hard so he can feel me through the layers of shirts and coat. 'James, it's not weird. You miss them, and you cry. That's normal. It's way better than writing yourself off once a year on the day you lost them.'

He looks up to the heavens. 'Do you believe we go somewhere after we die?'

'I don't know. I think . . .' I glance up at the stars, too – when I'm outside, when they're this close, they pull on me constantly. 'Maybe, yeah. Do you?'

'I used to think there wasn't anything. I'm a scientist, y'know. I'm only supposed to believe in provable facts and logic.' He snorts, quiets. 'But now . . . I kind of hope there's a place. Somewhere you meet all the people you love again.'

'But you're not sure.'

'I don't believe. I hope. There's no knowing, is there? Only anticipation.'

Something about the way he says it, or the expression on his face, creates a seed of fear down in my diaphragm. Within seconds, the seed has swelled, expanded to fill up my body, to fill the whole night. I'm reminded of that revolting brown stuff my dad used for repair jobs around the machinery shed, the way it foamed and inflated to smother everything in its path. The analogy is so stupid I almost choke on a laugh, but I can't laugh now.

'You're frightened about tomorrow, aren't you?' I stand very still. 'Mycroft, please just tell me. You don't have to bullshit me.'

'Yeah, I'm frightened.' Mycroft looks at the ground, picking his words carefully. 'I've been trying not to make decisions based on fear, or anger. But it's hard. I think . . . I think Cole wants the coin, but he wants us dead too. And he's smart – he might already be a step ahead. He might enter the quarry by a different route, or bring more troops, or . . . I don't know, there are so many variables. So much of our plan depends on timing, and the bombs are just a diversion, and we're just a bunch of kids . . .'

Suddenly I realise what Mycroft must have suspected all along: we may not survive this. Me and Mycroft, the old dream of Baker Street, the share-house, my medical degree, his forensics training . . . We might not get to do any of those things, because chances are we won't all make it out of this unscathed.

Panic swarms up within me suddenly, hits me like a punch in the guts.

'Then . . . let's back out,' I say, my voice thin and pleading. 'We can let the police handle it, tell them where Cole is going to be, tell them—'

'If we don't show up at the quarry tomorrow, Cole will take off.' Mycroft looks straight at me. His resigned posture speaks volumes. 'He'll disappear, and we'll be back where we started.'

The truth of it makes my eyes tear up. I make a short, tight laugh. 'Okay, I changed my mind. Give me the bullshit. Give me platitudes and lies.'

'Rachel, I'm sorry.' Mycroft pulls me into a hug. 'Shit, please don't be upset. I'm just scared. We've got crap odds, but . . . we've got to try. Whatever happens, I'm not going to let you get killed. I'm not going to let Harris get killed. But I'm just worried I won't have the guts to . . .'

Words fail him, but what he's said is enough to chill me to the bone.

'Mycroft, it's okay.' I cling to him, taking comfort, giving it in return. 'We don't have to be tough about this. Our decisions aren't based on fear, but we can still *feel* scared.'

'Fucking hell,' he whispers.

We clutch each other, and I think of the first time I met Mycroft, when Mai introduced us at school. I think of the moment I realised I cared about him, the moment I admitted it to myself. Everything that's happened since, it's all been in the space of months, not even a year. A blink of an eye.

I can't stand out here in the freezing dark anymore. The energy inside us, inside the containment of the house, might be unbearable, but at least it's warm in there. 'Come on,' I say. 'Let's go back inside.'

We boil a billy of water for pot noodles. It's not real food, just hot water and over-seasoned mush, but at least it warms us.

When we're finished, I fish out the bottle that Harris stashed in the bottom of his duffle bag. It's not a big bottle, and there's only a few mouthfuls left – Harris has already helped himself, it seems – but the liquid inside will be fiery, and that's what I need.

I pass the bottle to Mycroft. 'Here, take a swig of this.'

'Dutch courage?'

'At this point, any kind of courage is good.'

Mycroft takes a pull, hands the bottle to me, and gets up to go to the window. I drain what's left. The taste of noodles is banished as the whisky lights its own way down my throat.

Mycroft is staring out the glass of the verandah doors like he's expecting to see the marauding hordes of the Persian army come rolling over the plains, but it's pitch-black out there. I stuff another log into the Coonara, sit back on my sleeping bag and watch the fire through the glass. The flames pop and shimmer, start a little dance party inside the wood stove.

With Harris's camping lantern turned off, the fire is the only light in the room. Somehow it settles me, makes me feel less like spinning into a million bits. I could stare at it all night, but the way Mycroft is shifting on his feet near the doors is distracting.

'Mycroft.'

He doesn't even turn around.

'*James.*'

'Yeah?'

'Stop looking. Nothing's happening, and nothing will happen until morning. Just . . . come and sit down, you're making me nervous.'

'I can't.' He takes a big breath, lets it shiver out. 'I can't stop thinking . . .'

'You can. You have to.' I pat the sleeping bag beside me. 'Come here. Let me look at your hand.'

He pulls himself away with an effort, strides over and plonks himself beside me. His face is drawn, his plush lips pale. When I take his left hand and pull it into my lap, he runs his other hand through his hair.

'Jesus . . .'

'Calm down. Just . . . think about something else.'

'How do you even do that?'

'I don't know. Watching the fire is good. Let me look at this.'

I unwrap the bandage on his hand and examine the wound by torchlight – the skin is a bit swollen, pink around the cut. It looks tender, but not like it will get infected.

'It's fine,' Mycroft says.

'Mm. We'll put something on it when we get home,' I say automatically. Then I realise the assumptions behind that statement. I wrap the bandage firmly around his hand again, secure it with another piece of tape, click off the torch.

Mycroft sits, staring at me. He wets his lips, opens them to speak.

'Don't say it.' I put my hand up and cover his lips with a finger. A tidal swell in my heart overwhelms me and I look away. But I'm sure he's already seen my eyes go damp, heard the thickness in my voice.

Mycroft curls his good hand around mine. 'I keep thinking, *it's not fair*. We should have had more time.'

I shake my head. 'There's never a perfect time. This is it – just us as we are, with all the mess inside, in the only time we have. This is all we get. I think that's all anyone ever gets.'

'It's not fair,' Mycroft repeats.

'It's just life.' I laugh, but it comes out awful. 'I mean, our lives are particularly screwed up, but—'

'Rachel.' He shakes my fingers gently. His other hand touches my knee, makes soft warm circles there. 'Do you remember that day when you fixed my broken nose? I got into a fight with Gary Cumberson about something, and you—'

'I remember. And your nose wasn't broken.'

'It *felt* broken.' He gives me a tired grin. 'I conned you into going to the zoo with me that night.'

I smile, until I recall the details. 'The night Dave was killed.'

Mycroft's grin fades too. 'It wasn't supposed to be like that. It was supposed to end differently. I was working up the guts to finally say something to you, and I thought maybe there, in the dark near the zoo . . .'

'What were you going to say?'

'I don't know.' He glances away. 'Probably something mushy and stupid. Most likely I would've started to say something and then screwed it up, turned it into a joke of some kind . . .'

'You're very good at that.'

'I know. Look at me now.' He laughs, blushing. 'Yeah, this is ace. I've really got it together.'

'You dag.' I smile at him, brush at my eyes, my voice very soft. 'What do you want to say, James?'

'Everything.' He looks right at me. 'You make me want to speak it out loud. All the real stuff.'

'So say it.'

Mycroft's voice breaks a little. 'I don't ever want to let you go.'

'Then don't,' I say.

He turns me gently then, curls my back against his chest and hugs me. His face drops into the vee of my neck and shoulder, and his breath is hotter than the fire in front of us. His arms squeeze me so tight, I feel as if my heart is going to rise up out of my chest.

I push his arms out a little and turn myself inside them, so we're facing each other. I drop my hands to the hems of my T-shirt and thermal, and I grab the hems and pull the shirts up, over my head. The air in the living room is warm, but it still feels strange when my hair spills down onto my bare shoulders and back.

Mycroft – *James* – draws a soft breath at the sight of me in my bra and jeans. He takes off his own shirt, then it's only our two bodies, lit by the fire, and I wouldn't trade this for a lifetime of anything else.

And we are really doing this. We're kissing, moving our hands over each other, slowly at first, then more urgently. I kneel up and dip my mouth onto his again and again. It takes James a few tries to get my bra undone, and I have to help him in the end, because his hands are shaking too much. Every place he touches, every place he kisses, shivers with the contrast of the warm air and his cool lips, but pretty soon his lips warm on my skin, and then everything is warm.

We stand up to shuck out of our jeans, and that moment is the most memorable one, when we're both standing in front of the fire, and the fire is inside us just as much. James's body is lit with the red glow, and his shadows are the deep smooth of caves and tree trunks, and I am the soft tone of sand dunes, or the curve of a riverbank.

This is not at all like the fantasy. Neither of us have done this before. And it's awkward with the sleeping bag, and we discover that there's a big difference between knowing *what* to do with those little foil packets and *how* to do it.

But the whole thing is also filled with these strange incredible moments that are like miracles. James's backbone. The fine silk of his skin, the graceful masculine shape of him. The way my entire body is sensitised to the point of aching. His lips and hips on me, and the way we give instructions to each other – 'Like this?' and 'Yes, yes.' The way James's face looks, how much it changes and how quickly, the way his eyes hold onto mine the whole time. The surprise of textures – soft, slippery, sticky. The laughs we make when we forget to be quiet. The way background noise fades out. How we lose and find ourselves as we settle into our own rhythm.

So it's not at all like the fantasy. It is somehow even better.

————

Later, we lie snugged in the sleeping bag in front of the slowly ebbing fire. Even though we're mostly naked, our body heat inside the nylon keeps us from feeling cold.

'Why weren't we doing this sooner?' I ask.

James laughs and runs a hand down my back. 'I've been wanting to do this for a long time. Probably since the day I met you.'

'Why didn't you? You could have at least kissed me. All that time in your room . . .'

'I know! I told you, I was . . . I was shy.'

'Oh my god!'

'No, it wasn't that.' He smiles at me. 'I've been besotted from the start. I've just been waiting until I was more . . .'

'More what?'

'Just *more*. Better. I wanted to be a better person for you.'

'James, you're a great person. You don't have to be perfect for me. I love you the way you are.'

He looks at me. 'You love me.'

'Yes.'

He laughs. 'I'm glad you said that.'

I get up and search through the green shopping bag for something to eat. I chase an apple around the bottom of the bag until I catch it. Even bruised, it makes a satisfying crunch. It's kind of weird, standing here in Mai's purple undies with the black daggers embroidered on them, but I don't think to feel self-conscious until I see James grinning at me.

'What? I'm hungry.' I look down at the apple juice on my fingers. 'Does sex make you hungry?'

'Apparently, yes,' he says, but he's got this look on his face like he can't believe we're getting to have this conversation.

I finish my snack and wipe my face and hands, go back to the sleeping bag. Because that's where James is, and it's where I want to be. I tuck down beside him again, and look at him, how gorgeous he is. His shirt is still somewhere on the floor with mine, and he's slipped his boxers back on, but they're loose, dishevelled . . . I run my fingers lightly down from the hollow at his neck, down his chest and stomach, all the way to his hip, just because I can.

'Seriously, though. We could have been doing this ages ago.'

James smiles. 'All the time we've wasted, and we could have been shagging like rabbits for the last eight months—'

'*Yes.*' I squeeze his hip, look right in his face. 'And now this is all the time we've got. And tomorrow—'

'Shh.' He kisses my lips. 'Don't talk about tomorrow.'

'It's today now. We could die today.'

'But we're not going to die today,' James says, with greater certainty than before. He tucks a fall of my hair behind my ear with a warm finger.

'Because you will it so?'

'Because . . .' he says, and he's looking deep into my eyes, 'because the world is very beautiful.'

CHAPTER TWENTY

At some point, I fall asleep. Some crazy part of me brims with the anticipation of waking up next to James in the sleeping bag, our bodies pressed together, soft and a little sweaty.

So it's a shock when I wake up in a different way. Someone shakes my shoulder, hard, and I nudge my eyes open and see Harris's face.

'Rachel, get up.' He squeezes the shoulder he's shaking. 'Wake up. Now.'

I blink at him, slow and languid. 'Hey.'

'Rachel, wake up. Where's Mycroft?'

'What?'

'Your *boyfriend*, mate. Come on.'

Part of me registers that it'd be too much to ask, that Harris might actually chill out and respect my lazy morning-after glow. Can't he see that the world is a slightly different place to what it was last night? Can't he let me enjoy it?

But then I realise that he shouldn't be here. He's supposed to be at the quarry – we're supposed to meet him there. And I see his expression, the way his eyes dart around. The tension in his face, as if this is valuable time he's wasting on waking me up when he really needs to be elsewhere, doing something more important.

'What is it?'

'Big flashy car coming in on the Ouyen road. About five minutes ago – I drove as fast as I could. You wanted the show – well, the show's coming. Right now.'

'Now?' A slap of awareness hits me. I fumble up, suddenly realise I'm shirtless in the sleeping bag. I scrounge around on the floor for my clothes, holding the nylon bunched over my breasts. 'What . . . How close are they? What time is it?'

'Dunno, and seven o'clock-ish. Jesus.' He turns away abruptly when I start putting my bra on. 'Give a guy some warning.'

'Sorry.' I struggle with the clasp, pull a T-shirt on – it's not mine, it's one of James's long-sleeved ones, and it still smells like him. I yank my hair out of the collar, all askew. 'It's cold in here. Why is it cold?'

'Fire's out. Your fella. He's not outside getting wood, Rache, so where the fuck is he?'

I shake my head, struggle up and hop my feet on the warm insides of the sleeping bag while I pull my jeans on. 'Check the toilet? We have to get to the quarry before Cole.'

Harris has the rifle in his hand. I see him start for the hallway, pull up short near the kitchen bench. He concentrates on something, starts swearing a mile a minute, turns fast to thrust it at me. It's a piece of notepaper, torn from my notebook. A sour-milk feeling curdles in my guts.

'He's gone,' Harris says.

'What?' I grab at the paper, recognise James's looping scrawl, get a chill deep in my lower back. He can't have gone. He wouldn't have abandoned me, us. He's just—

I read the note aloud.

'*Gone to the quarry. Stay here. Stay safe and let me deal with it. I know what to do, tell Harris thanks* . . . Fucking hell, James!' I wave the paper in the air. I didn't read out the last part, which says, *Love you.*

Harris is only just keeping a lid on his frustration. 'Yeah, it's a nice thought and everything, but we had a fucking *plan.*'

Of all the times that James has been spontaneous, unpredictable, erratic, I wish that now had not been one of them. But we don't have time to dwell on it.

'Right.' I dash wet out of my eyes. 'Shit. Okay. W-we take the car, head for the quarry, find him—'

'I think it's too late for that.' Harris has walked over to the verandah doors to look out. He turns back. 'Rachel, I can see dust on Thorny Gap Road.'

'What?' I stumble over with my socks still in my hand.

'Fuck. I think they're coming here.'

I don't want to believe it. But I can see it with my own eyes, so it must be true: a meagre dust plume tracing the line of this road, to this driveway, this *house.*

'Oh, shit.' I spin to face Harris, who's checking the gun. 'Harris, what—'

'At least he's left us the gun, that's nice.' Harris grabs his duffel and searches for the shells, tucks them into the pocket of his shirt, scoops the rest of the stuff around inside the bag. 'He's taken the pliers, and . . . yeah, he's taken the map of the quarry. Right. Well, I can't say I don't understand his motivation, but I guess he wasn't thinking they'd make this place their first port of call.'

I'm still standing here, barefoot. There's grit in my eyes from sleep. 'We've got to get out of here.'

'No time.' Harris reaches over and grabs my jacket, tosses it to me. 'Put that on. And your boots.'

'This wasn't . . .' I can feel my breaths starting to pile up on top of each other. 'This isn't how it's supposed to . . .'

Harris is still holding the gun, so he can only shake my shoulder with one hand. '*Rachel*. Forget supposed to, okay? This is it. We're on. Come on now – jacket, boots.'

I nod. My jacket – I need my jacket. But when I pull it on, the cold remains, because it's underneath my skin, not just outside it. I get my boots on, go over to the doors again. The dust plume is getting closer.

'They were supposed to go to the quarry.' I can hear the panic in my voice, am powerless to stop it. 'They weren't supposed to come *here*.'

'Rachel, chill.' Harris stands beside me. 'It's unexpected. You knew there'd be hiccups. We've just gotta adapt. Are you getting me?'

'Right.' I nod. 'Right.'

We should hide. I feel it strongly in my gut. But where? All the bedrooms are bare of furniture, there are no crawlspaces, and underneath the house is dirt. We could run. But where would we run to? I don't know. I don't know.

'This is what we wanted, remember?' Harris pushes his hair out of his face as he loads the rifle. 'To meet the charge. Confront them. Play them. This is what we planned, with a minor change or two.' He squeezes my arm with his free hand. 'When they get up here, we've gotta stall them. Give Mycroft a chance to get ready. Then we get them to take us to the quarry.'

James, I think. His name is James. I can't think of him as Mycroft anymore. 'What?'

He must see the terror in my face. 'Deep breaths, okay? The important thing is that we get them to take us to the quarry.'

I manage a jerky nod. My hands are shaking.

There's the sound of car doors opening, the crunch of gravel underfoot. They're coming up the steps.

'Get behind me,' Harris says.

I shuffle backwards until my boots hit the sleeping bag. James and I were naked together inside that bag just last night. My body is still sore from it, still resonates with it. I can't think of that now.

Shoes on wooden boards. I glance back to get my bearings and see something through the glass verandah doors. A short, wiry man in a dark green windbreaker is taking the steps up onto the verandah.

'Harris.' I tug at his sleeve, and he looks.

'Shit.' Now his attention is split between the front passage and the verandah. He brings up the rifle. I squeeze myself in behind him, and things happen very fast.

The man in the windbreaker opens one of the glass doors and steps into the house. He has black hair, oil-slicked, and a handgun in his right hand. His body is small, compact, and his lined face is hard and blank.

Two more men walk into the living room from the front passage. One of them is tall, with a black leather jacket and a broad build. The other one is Jonathan Cole. He's wearing a dark grey overcoat over a suit, which seems utterly out of place, and he's holding grey leather gloves. His eyes are like pale green stones, milky jade, and his hair is a little dishevelled, probably from the rigours of the drive. He's not exactly the same as when I last saw him, in Detective Pickup's office seven weeks ago, but near enough.

Harris angles me further back with his body, assesses the level of threat. He swings the barrel of the rifle, takes one step towards the guy with the gun, who is shutting the glass door with his free hand.

'Close enough,' Harris calls. 'Don't come any—'

The guy in the windbreaker shoots Harris in the leg.

That's it – no preamble. The sound of the shot reverberates in the hollow space of the living room, cut through by the sound of Harris's scream. He falls to the floor, and the guy in the wind-breaker just walks forward and grabs the rifle out of Harris's hands.

I drop to my knees, hands flailing, reaching for Harris, whose scream turns into a loud pain-filled obscenity. Red blood is spilling out everywhere, onto the floor, onto my hands, through Harris's fingers as he clutches his thigh.

'*FUCK!*' Harris roars.

'*Jesus.*' I clamp my hands onto his leg.

Harris writhes. I grab the nearest piece of clothing on the floor, which happens to be my T-shirt from last night, and stuff it over the wound. The blood is gushing. I press and press, and Harris's face contorts, and he gasps and cries out, swears again.

'Fuuuck!' He groans and leans into me. 'Oh, you fucking . . .'

The guy in the windbreaker is holding the rifle with one hand and covering us both with the handgun in the other. His expression hasn't changed the whole time.

I feel myself starting to cry, just blinking out tears the way you do when you're in shock. I press on Harris's wound as he pants and groans on the floor. It was that easy. They got us so quickly. It was that easy for them.

When I look up, it's to see Jonathan Cole's icy little eyes staring back at me.

'Miss Watts,' he says. 'So, here we are.'

I should spit in his face. I should swear at him, pummel him with my fists, but I can't. I'm completely frozen. The shock of the shot, Harris's groans, all form a maelstrom inside my head, and I can't say a single word.

The tall beefy guy walks back into the room. I hadn't even noticed he'd gone. He shakes his head at Cole. Cole looks back to me.

'Where is James Mycroft?' he says.

His accent is so proper, so bracingly English. Harris groans again, clutches at my sleeve. *Stall them*, he said. We were supposed to stall them, to give James more time.

My voice is a whisper. 'I don't . . .'

Cole glances at the guy in the windbreaker, and the guy steps forward, places the muzzle of the handgun at my temple.

My mouth dries up in an instant. I hear Harris gasp, but I don't look down at him. All my senses are consumed by the touch of the metal on my skin. The mouth of the gun is hot, and strands of my hair fall over it, onto my cheek.

Dad always said you should never point a gun at anything unless you're about to shoot. That's why you always angle your gun at the ground while at rest, because as soon as you raise it, you're aiming to kill.

This gun is loaded, cocked, and pressed to my head.

This is not how it was supposed to go. This is not anything. I'm about to get my brains blown out. I can't remember the plan. Did we have a plan? Nothing registers in my mind except that the gun barrel is still warm from shooting Harris.

'I will ask one more time,' Cole says. 'Where is—'

'*The Falls.*' I've said it so fast it comes out like a sob. 'You *know* he's at the Falls, the quarry. That's where *you* were supposed to go.'

I don't have time to wonder whether I'll regret telling him later. The whole of my consciousness is focused on the feel of that gun. It is the sum total of my existence, the sum of everything divided.

'Thank you,' Cole says.

He steps back and starts pulling on his gloves. The gun is still glued to my temple. It doesn't waver, the guy in the windbreaker has extremely steady hands. And I know suddenly that this is it, this is all the chance I'm going to get, so I do the only thing I can think of to keep me and Harris alive.

'Y-you have to bring us.' My words croak out, gluey and broken. 'You have to take us there. James will bury the coin if he doesn't see us, and you'd never find it under all that gravel . . . James will want to know we're safe.'

Cole pauses, considering. The metal at my temple doesn't move. It is hard and uncompromising against my skin, and I wonder if I've done enough, said enough. I'm looking at Cole, and Harris has gone quiet under my hands.

Cole looks at the guy in the windbreaker, and suddenly the gun barrel is gone.

'Bring them,' Cole says, as he turns away for the front door.

The relief batters me so hard I almost spew up, right then and there.

CHAPTER TWENTY-ONE

We're bundled out of the living room, down the steps, into a large heavy car, a Statesman. Harris gasps again and I have to put my arm around him to help him get into the car. Before we left the house, I wadded up my T-shirt over his wound, which is above the knee, and tied it in place with my flannie. In the time it took me to do that, Cole looked impatient. I moved very fast.

Once we're in the back seat, Harris leans into me heavily. He looks horribly pale. I'm pressed up against the door, Harris slumped against me, the guy with the gun on his other side.

I try to keep my glances at the gunman subtle. This guy must be the assassin that Cole hired to take us down in Melbourne. The guy who killed Benjamin Tonna and the homeless girl, Becky. This is the murderer of children. The man who shot my brother down like an animal.

He is a small, neat. Even his black T-shirt and jeans are neat. Maybe he pressed them last night, before getting into Cole's car for the long drive to come and kill us. He's wearing squeaky clean runners, some expensive brand. His face is lined, just like the kids from the sports ground said, and his forehead is high, made more prominent with his hair slicked back. He looks like a predator animal of some kind: a ferret, sleek and smooth, with the same inhuman ruthlessness.

Ferret's eyes are unreadable behind his sunglasses, and he doesn't look at us. Harris's soft groans, my hitching breath – none of it seems to draw his gaze or interest. It's like we don't exist. He doesn't point the gun at us. He doesn't need to. The gun rests on his thigh; he holds it with a relaxed, competent grip, a man used to guns and the damage they can inflict.

The big guy in the leather jacket drives us out along the dirt access track, then onto Thorny Gap Road, heading for Five Mile. Cole sits in the front passenger seat.

'You might be wondering,' he says, in that cultured English drawl, 'why I went to your house first, instead of the quarry.'

I don't reply. I'm still too scared: it would only take a glance from Cole to make Ferret raise his gun and shoot Harris or me in the face. There would be no warning, no hesitation. Ferret doesn't hesitate, and I've just seen how he uses the hesitation of others to his own advantage.

'It's very simple, really,' Cole says, answering his own question. He's relishing this, I can tell. 'There was an arrangement. But I decided that it was in my best interests to have a little insurance policy.'

It's like Cole is speaking another language and my brain isn't working fast enough to translate. The only thing I'm not confused about is that Cole found out about the house. I'm sure he knew about that. I'm sure he knows every place that James and I have ever been to.

'Young Mr Mycroft cheated, you know,' Cole goes on. 'But that's quite all right. I've cheated too.'

I force myself to speak. I've spoken to this man before, but that was when I thought he was on our side. 'W-what do you mean?'

Cole turns in his seat so he can see my face. He looks delighted that he's gotten me to talk back. 'He changed the time of our meeting.'

All the blood in me drains down to my feet. Puzzle pieces finally click together in my head. That's why James was so scared last night. He'd planned to meet Cole earlier, on his own. He knew Harris would see Cole's car arriving early and drive back to the house to warn us, instead of to the quarry. And it would all be over and done with before me and Harris even showed up to help. *I'm not going to let you get killed . . . let Harris get killed. But I'm worried I won't have the guts . . .* Now his words make sense.

And what chance would he have had against Cole and these two men alone?

Oh, James . . .

'Yes – I don't imagine he told you.' Cole says. 'He shifted our meeting to eight a.m. So I've cheated a little too, by arriving an hour earlier again. This is how the great game is played, Miss Watts. Move and countermove. Really, my dear, you must learn to keep up.'

He gives me a sly smile. The awareness that I'm somehow two steps behind – and have no idea how to make up lost ground – blows a hollow pit in my stomach.

'I must say, I wasn't expecting this fellow here.' Cole gestures dismissively towards Harris, who is sweating and dark-eyed beside me.

'He involved himself,' I say tightly, 'when you shot at his best friend. My brother.'

'Well, that's very unfortunate.' Cole frowns at me. 'You were rather rude to me in your email, my dear, which I suppose is only fair. But I have to say that disappointed me. You had such pleasant manners at police headquarters, last time we met.'

Maybe it's my mention of Mike, or maybe it's just Cole's smarmy face, but I feel a spark flare to life inside me. 'I was only calling it like I see it. Didn't I say you were a murdering arsehole? It's the truth.'

'What spirit.' Cole smiles at me, almost paternally. Then he looks over at Ferret. 'Shoot her in the head, in front of the other boy, once we've finished business at the quarry.'

Harris grasps my hand, and I startle.

'Rachel,' he says, and I can see the effort it's taking for him to keep his voice level. 'Loosen the bandage? It's cutting in . . .'

I swallow and nod. But when I check the makeshift bandage, I change my mind. The T-shirt I used as a compress is soaked with blood; it's leaching into the flannie, which will soon be soggy, useless.

'I can't,' I whisper. 'You need to keep pressure on it.'

'Rachel . . .'

'Harris, you'll bleed out.'

He's pouring with sweat in the heater-warmed car. I press against the bandage, can't decide whether to press harder to halt the flow of blood, or more gently, in case I'm hurting him. Harris turns his head right in, against my shoulder. I guess any pressure is bad.

Cole is shaking his head at the view out the window. 'My god. What a desolate place.'

That makes me baulk, but I say nothing. I refuse to see my childhood environment through Cole's eyes. The green wheat bobs in great shining rows in the distance. The land looks fertile, bountiful. To me it looks beautiful, maybe more beautiful right now, when this view might be my last.

But I can see things that might make this place look uninviting. The clouds glower above us, threatening rain. We're passing the shuttered shops in town, and all the pollarded trees along Kennedy Street look like desperate supplicants, their stumpy branch-stripped arms reaching for the heavens. I notice stray rubbish on the road shoulder – chip packets, old cans. Further on, past the wheatfields, I know what Cole is seeing: burnt-looking marginal salt-flat land, with clumps of mould-like vegetation in shades of sage and mission brown.

I tie my hair back in a knot at my nape. Keeping my right hand on Harris's bandage, I put my left hand as far around him as I can manage, trying to comfort him. His hair brushes my nose. We bump over a pothole in the road and he moans, mashes his lips against my shoulder, his eyes squeezed tight with pain.

'Harris, I'm sorry,' I whisper. 'Oh god, I'm so sorry.'

He just squeezes his fist into my shirt-front. I don't think he can make words right now. My own words dry up. The fear inside me, and the anger that this is the way things are playing out, have sucked all the moisture out of my throat. I watch Cole, watch the other men in the car, and flick my eyes constantly out the window to catch glimpses of a world that I might never get to see again.

We're past the limits of town now, and the car is bumping over Marilla Road, the road that takes trucks and heavy traffic through to the Falls. The mallee on the road shoulder here looks particularly tortured, twisting its straggly branches through the dust and contorting high, reaching for fresh air. This early in the morning, frost still whitens every surface.

But this is all I've got. I don't have time to prepare myself by meditating, or looking at rainbows or crystal waterfalls. Nobody gets to prepare for death like that, not really. We get the inside of hospital rooms, or ambulances, or if we're lucky, the comforting familiarity of our own bedrooms. So in a way I'm grateful that this is going to happen outside, where I can see the sky, in a place I know, a place that is part of my heart.

The Statesman rolls through the open gate of the quarry. This is one detail I don't miss: if the gate is open, it means James has cracked the bolt and pulled it open himself. That small mark of his presence makes me immediately alert.

I see the old signs stuck up along the fenceline: *Ridgeback Falls, Hard Hats Must Be Worn, Report to the Office on Arrival.* Cole's driver pulls up into the wide space just in front of the small portable shack that serves as the site shed and idles there.

'Well, my dear?' Cole twists in his seat again to look at me. 'I'm sure you know directions better than I.'

I bite my bottom lip. 'Go further into the quarry. To the top of the pit.'

Cole waves at the driver, and the man cruises the big car further on. We come level with the mill shed, near the top of the road leading into the quarry, and the car finally stills.

Cole and the driver both open their doors to exit the car, Cole straightening his leather gloves. Ferret turns so that Harris and I can see ourselves reflected in his sunglasses. He raises the gun off his leg and points it at Harris's chest.

'Out.'

I get out, then help Harris out. The terrified shake in my legs has started again, and my knee is aching. Ferret exits from the other door. He leaves Harris's rifle in the back footwell of the car and walks over to me. With clinical proficiency, he pulls my hands away from Harris and claps my wrists together. He wraps a generous length of silver gaffer tape around them – the tape squeals coming off the roll.

Harris swears, holds on to my shoulder. He doesn't get any gaffer tape: he's not much of a threat with his leg injury, white-faced and barely able to stand.

I watch Cole, as he and the driver walk to a place where they can see down the short road into the pit. The sound of wind in the underbrush on the cliffs around the cutting is like the rustle of ten thousand plastic bags. Cole scans the area, makes an annoyed-sounding noise, shoos the driver with his head.

The driver walks straight up to us, pulls Harris away from me. I cry out, and Harris stumbles, grunts. Ferret grabs my arm, holding me fast, the handgun loose at his side. My wrists sting where the gaffer tape sticks to the hairs on my skin. Harris is only a few metres away, but it seems like a mile. The pain in his leg must be agonising.

The driver gives Harris's arm a shake. 'Okay, where is he?'

Then I get it: they can't see James. He must be hiding behind the boulders near the cliff face. I want to shout, *Stay hidden! Please, James, stay hidden*, but of course I can't do that.

'Where's who?' Harris says, with this sick grin.

The driver slaps him across the face. It's an open-handed slap, but it's hard and very fast. An efficient slap, not like my mum's react-without-thinking effort. Harris's head whips around so he is looking at me. He doesn't gasp or anything – I mean, he gasps a little, but I think it's just because he's not used to how fast these guys are.

But he's used to being slapped. I see that in the way he collects his breath, the way he licks the blood off his lip with almost no change of facial expression, the way he turns his head back so calmly.

'He's probably hunkered down somewhere, checking you guys out,' Harris says. He sneers at the driver, who turns and raises his eyebrows towards Cole.

Cole sighs, as though it's monumentally inconvenient that the people he wants dead won't just line up quietly to be shot. 'Then I suppose we will have to go down further. Hold that one here. Bring Miss Watts in front.'

Ferret pulls at my arm, but I'm not going to leave Harris alone. '*No*. You have to take us together, you can't—'

'Rachel.' Harris looks at me. 'It's okay, mate.'

Cole waits until Ferret has manhandled me forward, then he extracts a pistol from the pocket of his coat and grabs me by the chin with his gloved fingers. Looking into his eyes is like falling into icy water.

'That's enough now, Rachel. It's time to go and see James.'

I make a desperate sound, but Ferret is pushing me forward. I manage to catch one last glimpse of Harris's face, partially obscured by the shoulder of the beefy driver, before I'm dragged down the road.

———

The road is a wide track of packed red earth descending in a straight line into the bowels of the pit. Boulders and sandy orange dirt line the shoulder. Each step down is colder and darker than the one before: the road has frosted overnight into a chilled swathe of crunchy, tyre-marked mud. I nearly slip half a dozen times; Ferret hauls me up by the arm.

Sunlight hasn't risen high enough yet to give colour to the inner sections of the quarry. To my left is the glistening rock face of the working cliff, and a few heaps of mixed earth and stone. To my right are shoulder-high piles of gravel and sandy dirt. Behind those piles is the drop-off for the old pit, and the evil black lake at its bottom.

Straight ahead lies the dead-end wall of the quarry. There are a few boulders scattered there, but I can't see James. I don't want to see James – if I can't see him, then Cole can't see him, and if Cole can't see him, then he can't kill him.

But the gravel piles ... I give my brain a good kick in the pants. Try to bring up a mental map of the quarry. When the boys were talking about the charges, I took note of where they were laid, which circles were marked with X. Hidden somewhere to my right, in those piles, is a booby-trapped charge.

The problem is that out here, every gravel pile looks identical to another. Harris has done his job too well. There's nothing to indicate whether the gravel at the bases of certain piles has been disturbed, dug up and then tamped down. And if I'm not careful, I'm going to give everything away to Ferret and Cole, just because I'm looking around so much.

I start angling my path towards the right of the road. Scanning the piles, I *see* something – just a subtle bump in the dirt, a sweet glimmer of copper. The sizzling spark that fired me to backtalk Cole in the car suddenly flames to life again. I've *found* it, Harris's charge. Now if I can continue twisting my walk gently to the right ...

It would be a great plan, if Ferret was just a bit less observant. But he's not. He hauls at my gaffer tape restraints, redirects my steps to the centre of the road. Then it's too late, we've passed the copper flash, we're walking on. The lost opportunity gouges me with sharp nails as I stumble forward.

My lips are chapped from the cold. I lick them, but the spit dries stiff on my skin, making the feeling worse. Ferret grips my arm and Cole's striding footsteps echo behind me. I don't know if I can keep walking like this, knowing there's nothing but death at the end of the path. I think of French royalists, walking to the guillotine – did their legs get tired and weak too? I don't know. History textbooks never tell you the important stuff.

Then a voice pulls me up short.

'Please stop dragging Rachel around. I'm here.'

CHAPTER TWENTY-TWO

Ferret stops dead, yanks me towards him. Cole walks forward to come level with us.

James's voice isn't raised. You don't have to raise your voice in this rocky amphitheatre, where every sound is bounced back at you. I hear every inflection – and it sounds too close. My head turns slowly until I see the boulder collection to the left, about fifteen metres away, near the new cliff face.

James has eased out from behind it. He's standing there with his hands stuffed in his pockets, his shoulders squared inside his pea coat, dark brown curls being tugged into his eyes by the stiff breeze.

My throat fills up with airy fear. My nostrils feel cold with it, my shoulders and arms are stiffened tight. What James said last night is true: it's not fair. We should have had more time. I can't stop looking at his windblown curls, remembering how I tugged on those curls myself last night, sank my fingers deep into them.

'Mr Mycroft,' Cole says. He is smiling.

'You went to the house. You weren't supposed to go to the house.'

'I've not survived in the service so long without being a cautious man.' Cole spreads his hands out to his sides. The gesture would seem more genuine if he didn't have a gun in one fist. 'I wanted some assurance that our arrangement would be honoured.'

James doesn't reply. Cole's eyes narrow. 'One thing for another, James,' he says softly. 'The coin for your friend. Very simple.'

For a long moment, there's only the sound of the wind.

'It was supposed to be simple,' James says finally. 'But you've made it complicated.'

I can't panic now. I can't do that. I have to think. If James has done what he said, and texted Mai before he arrived, the police should be on their way. In the meantime, there must be something I can do. Giving James information about the situation would be a start.

'There's three of them!' I call. 'They've got Harris, he's hurt but—'

The side of my face suddenly explodes with pain as my head is knocked sideways. Ferret has struck me, belted me hard with the heel of his hand. It's the hand holding the gun, and the extra weight is as effective as a knuckleduster.

'*Rachel!*' James's cry echoes off the rock face around us.

But I'm not putting up with that shit – I list back, use the momentum to shove into Ferret, rocking us both as I yell, 'Fucking *OW!*'

Ferret grunts and grabs for my hair, shakes my head. I wince. Something wet slides down the side of my face.

'Settle her down,' Cole barks.

'*You didn't need to do that!*' James's face, in my watery-eyed vision, is like a mass of thunderheads. His fists are clenched.

'Do you have the coin?' Cole asks.

James glares at him.

Cole glances at Ferret. Ferret shakes me by the hair again, lifts his gun and presses the muzzle against the side of my neck, just under my ear. The gun metal is cold in the freezing air.

'As I was saying,' Cole goes on, 'you shall give me the coin, and I shall hand over the lovely Miss Watts. Do you have the owl?' Cole's expression is that of a man who knows he's won.

'It's . . . safe,' James says. 'I buried it.'

'Then dig for it, my boy,' Cole says. He adjusts his gloves, as two tiny birds flit past: their movement is free and graceful, everything our little group is not. Cole gives them a brief smile. 'Charming . . . And I trust I won't walk out of here to find a police car waiting?'

James's eyes seem to glow in the strange, burnished early-morning light that tints everything around us. 'I told you I wouldn't contact the police, and I've kept my word.'

My mouth drops open. For a moment, the hand in my hair and the gun at my neck is forgotten. 'What?'

Cole looks at me with amusement. 'Ah, yes. Something else I imagine he conveniently failed to tell you.'

I am staring at James. 'You said Mai *insisted*. You said—'

'Rachel, I'm sorry.' James looks stricken.

'Tell me that's not true!' I shake myself in Ferret's grip. '*Goddamnit*, James!'

'I didn't contact Pickup,' James says softly. 'There were no instructions for Mai. This is it. Just me, and . . . Just us.'

He transfers his gaze to Cole, who's grinning now – a fox's grin, all wicked, sharp cunning. Did I think Ferret was the predator animal? I was wrong, so wrong.

My voice is so choked I can hardly get the words out. 'James, why would you *do* that?'

'Because he wants to ask me about my treasures,' Cole says, glancing back and forth between us as if this is the most entertaining thing in the world. 'Aren't I right, James?'

The *collection* – Cole's personal cache of artefacts. The one that Edward Mycroft never found. The one that would nail Cole to the wall. I knew James wanted to find out about it. But I didn't know he'd take things this far.

I think there might be a lot I didn't know, which fills me with a dreadful despair. I've felt scared from the moment Cole arrived at the house, but it's only in this moment that I feel defeated.

'That's what you want, isn't it?' Cole adjusts his grip on his gun. His grin has widened, overtaken his whole face. 'So why don't you ask me? Go on, James . . . ask!'

James stands there, paralysed.

My exhale comes out like a sob.

'I don't think it matters,' James says suddenly. He bites down hard on his bottom lip, releases it. 'You won't tell me now. Concealment and secrets . . . That's what you love, even more than your artefacts, maybe – you just love *the game*, don't you, Mr Cole?'

Cole's face suddenly takes on an iron cast. 'You're a very insightful fellow, my boy, but don't confuse insight with understanding. Don't presume to know me.'

'Was that it?' James asks. He looks like he's bracing himself for the answer. 'When you gave the order to have my parents killed, was that all part of the game?'

Cole lifts his right hand, his gun hand, in my direction. 'You know, all this talk is becoming tiresome. James, I gave you a chance to ask about the collection, but I think you're under the mistaken impression that this is a negotiation.' He shakes his head ruefully. 'So like your father. Edward was always so *rigid*. There was no bending of the rules with him. The law was the law. He never understood that some things fall outside society's laws. Things like beauty, and history, and art.'

James pales at the mention of his father. 'And you're the only one who appreciates those things, is that it? Everything you stole belonged to public collections—'

'*Yes!*' Cole jabs a finger at the ground. For a moment, his jaw clenches in a rictus. It's a tiny thing, but it's the first time I've seen him falter. 'Priceless antiquities housed in dusty museums, viewed by people who had no understanding of what they were looking at. You think the general public really *appreciates* something as extraordinary as the First Folio? They understand that it's important, on an intellectual level. But they don't value it like I do. It broke my heart to return that book to the Bodleian.'

He sighs at this admission. Just like the time in Pickup's office, I'm hit by the idea that Cole looks almost like someone's kindly middle-class grandfather. Maybe he *is* a grandfather, I don't know.

Then his sigh disappears, and the illusion is gone. He's exactly how I described him to Mai: one guy, one crazy guy, who thinks he can do whatever he likes.

James is looking at Cole as if he's thinking the same thing. His voice, when it comes out, is very soft. 'So where is your collection, Mr Cole?'

'Oh, James, my dear boy . . .' Coles smile starts small, grows bigger and bigger. 'Maybe one day I'll show you.' He winks, then straightens. 'Now, you've put me to an incredible amount of trouble, not to mention a very tedious car journey after a dreadfully long plane trip. We have a task to complete, yes? The girl for the coin. Or the coin for the girl. Which is more valuable, do you think? If we were to weigh them both on a universal scale, then—'

'The girl,' James interrupts. 'The girl is more valuable.'

My breath catches. James doesn't look at me. I don't think he can do this, conduct this conversation, and watch me bleed at the same time.

'I'm sure you find her so.' Cole cocks one eyebrow. 'Well, as you can see, she's right here. You merely need to dig up the coin, and—'

'I'm not giving it to you before you let Rachel leave.'

'James, James . . .' Cole says sadly, 'you will have to trust me, like it or not. It is along the bridge of trust that we proceed, or we shall be standing here into next week. Retrieve the coin, and I will let her go.'

Cole sounds so calm, so *reasonable*. He tilts his head, and I remember he made the same gesture in the car, right before he said something. Something significant.

Shoot her in the head, in front of the other boy, once we've finished the business at the quarry.

He's not planning to give me to James. There's no trade. It's all just bullshit. And while I'm sure James suspects this, he doesn't *know*.

Ignoring the sharp pain from my hair, I wrench myself forward. 'James, *don't listen*, he's—'

Lying, I'm about to say, but Ferret has slung his arm around my neck and slapped a hand over my mouth. I fight, but he squeezes his thumb and fingers into my cheeks, bruising my lips together, keeping me gagged. He cocks the gun near my temple.

James takes an involuntary step closer. His face is terrible, full of ash and fury. I can see the struggle going on behind his eyes.

'James.' Cole's expression darkens. 'Listen carefully. I am an old man. And I am standing in a filthy hole, in the middle of this dreadful countryside, with a gun. I am tired, and I am losing patience. Give me the coin now, please, or Rachel will die.'

James's eyes move between Cole and me, no matter that there's no decision to make, no matter that whatever he does the outcome will be the same.

He takes a deep, shuddering breath. 'All right.'

No, no, no!!! I yell beneath my gag. I wriggle and strain. Ferret squeezes me tighter. His hand is clamped over my mouth, his gun at my head. I am pulled back against the chest of the man who shot my brother.

Gut-churning panic rises in me, bubbling up like stomach acid. My arms and legs tremble.

Then Ferret makes a soft sigh out his nose. For some reason that quiet sound strikes inside me, somewhere deep. It's as though he is annoyed with my struggling, and bored, as though he would like this all to be over so he can do something more interesting.

And I remember: I don't have to let fear control me. I've worked hard at this. I've *beat* this.

Fuck him – if he thinks I'm going to sink down and cry and wait to be shot, he'd better think again. I tense my muscles. I'm going to make this messy. I'm going to make this so bloody messy, he's going to wish he—

Suddenly a deep-belly sound reverberates through the chasm we're standing in, an echoing *BOOM* that sinks into my guts like syrup. I've never heard this sound before, but I know exactly what it is: it's the sound of a kilo of flour being blown up with homemade plastique.

Harris Derwent, I bloody *love* you.

Cole jerks, looks left towards the car. Ferret's hand falls from my mouth to my shoulder.

I don't wait to think about how: Harris has given us a span of seconds. We're not going to get another chance – this is it.

I can hear Harris's voice in my head: *Yank the arm to get your attacker off balance, stamp the instep, elbow in the guts, slam back your head.*

I reverse the order. The back of my head smacks into Ferret's face. He makes an *Agh!* of pain. Can't do the elbow with my wrists restrained, so I lift my left leg and stamp down on Ferret's fancy runner as hard as I can with my boot-heel. I reach up with my joined hands and grab his flailing forearm, *yank* as hard as I can, use that momentum to push him into Cole.

The two men collide and fall.

'*Rachel!*' James yells.

'*Run!*' I scream.

Then I spin, and take my own advice.

Ferret makes a furious, nose-clogged roar behind me. A sharp report clips the air high above, and I duck on automatic, but I keep running. I know exactly where I'm headed. Please god, let James have made it behind cover.

My hair lashes my face. Past one pile of gravel – having my hands taped is a pain in the arse, and my knee is hurting. Second pile – there's feet behind me, thumping and scrabbling on shale.

'For god's sake, *catch her!*' Cole's outraged bellow.

Something chips at the ground to my right, so I swerve. I have no idea what Cole is doing, maybe hunting for James. I risk a glance over my shoulder – Ferret is barely a body-length behind me, gun in one fist, blood streaming down his chin. His sunglasses

311

have fallen off, and he's lost that detached ruthlessness. He looks like a red-eyed rodent now, teeth bared for the kill. Maybe he'll stretch things out when he catches me, put a few bullets in tender places, listen to me scream before he puts the gun in my mouth. But I won't let that happen, because I—

I trip over a rock.

I go sprawling, and with my hands taped I can't throw out my arms to protect myself. My knees bear the brunt, and then elbows, forehead, and it all *hurts like fuck*. I slide on gravel, hear my jeans rip.

My brain clonks back and forth inside my head, but I don't have time to be dazed. I roll. Hard feet strike my hip – Ferret goes sprawling over *me*, which is so bizarre I almost laugh.

I curl onto my side, stagger upright. The world tilts crazily for a second; I glimpse the pit edge. Ferret is on his stomach, searching for his gun in the gravel sprayed out around him.

Suddenly I see a bright coppery gleam at ground level and give a gasping cry. In all this chaos, I've somehow managed to find Harris's charge again.

I lurch sideways, towards the trip wire. Ferret's hand snaps out, almost snags my ankle; my foot skips higher. Then he's up, grabbing for me. I react on automatic, striking with both hands in a sideways hammer blow.

The strike hits his chin. Ferret yells, clutches for my hair. I shriek – oh shit, I'm gonna trip the wire myself by accident. I swing around and—

I don't know what I'm expecting, but it isn't this ear-splitting spray of noise and light.

The explosion bursts up from the mound of gravel, a gout of flame rising faster than my scream – I twist side-on as tiny stones slam into my exposed skin. My knee crimps, and my elbows fly up from my body. I rear back with the concussion.

Ferret's hands on me are thrown loose; his body is thrown against mine. Fire and stars are superimposed on my eyelids as we fall. Instead of thumping into hard ground, we keep falling, Ferret and I are falling together. We fall and fall, a long way down, into stillness, and silence, and there's a moment when everything seems to make sense, before we fall into the black lake of the old pit with a hideous smash of ice.

———

Air slams from my lungs.

Everything slows down, becomes viscous, like my dream: bands of iron around me, my limbs moving hard but sluggish, the tension, the fear. My cries of protest come out like bubbles. I kick my legs, thrust with my arms, but my hands are held tight. I make another cry: it emerges with a *glub*.

Then the cold shocks me awake. All I know is that the treacly light is *up*. Light is up, and air is up, and I kick again, through and out of the dream, and my head breaks the surface of the lake with a rib-bursting gasp.

I thrust my hands high; they're still stuck together. Everything is numb. My legs are barely working. I mince on the thick mix of fluid and sediment around me until I've shimmied forward, and there's the rising ground, under my feet. I catch it with my toes, with my whole foot. Another foot; closer, closer. I stagger up out of the lake, like a creature from some primeval swamp.

Brackish liquid sloshes out of my boots. I'm almost out on the road. I look behind me. Ferret is floating on the surface of the pool, facedown and silent. Not floating: his body is snagged on a pillow of pale sediment, the edge of a sandbank disguised by a thin layer of water.

He's dead – no one can lie like that for such a long time in water – and the water around him is tinted pink. He is dead because I fell on him. He cushioned my fall. Which is amazing, and ironic, and funny, but I'm not sure what those words mean right now.

I should go back into the lake, find Ferret's gun. But I don't think I can do that. I don't think I can do anything but stand here. Everything is vaguely aching. Water streams off my hair, dribbles off my hands, my face. Rivers trickle from my clothes onto the dirt. I lick my lips: they taste salty.

My body feels very heavy. I lean my head down and raise my hands up, then I bite at the gaffer tape around my wrists. My teeth feel wobbly, but I bite and spit out bits of plastic until the tape is just a thread that I can snap apart. Okay, that feels better.

Hair strands like wet rope on my face and neck. My jacket feels cumbersome, so I shake it off. I turn to face the road. I should go up there. I should go up and find James, help Harris. Christ, that's a lot of hard work. I don't even know if I can walk up this road.

But I'm thinking about it, and my feet are moving, giant anvils inside my heavy boots. My right leg keeps giving out. I weave up the incline of the road. My body is coming back to life. I am cold. The cold starts in my shoulders, where my wet T-shirt is plastered to my skin. It crackles out, like one of those time-lapse sequences of ice forming over plant life.

By the time I get to the top of the rise, I'm shivering so hard everything looks blurry. Lifting my legs over the chain blocking the road, I nearly fall over. But I can't do that – if I fall over now, I won't get up.

There's the Statesman, parked on the edge of the rise. I should be sneaking, in case Cole or the driver is nearby, but I can only stagger. I shiver and stagger my way to the car. It takes two goes before my fingers can lift the door release.

The inside of the car is warmer than the outside, but my body temperature is set on Frigid now. Apart from sitting on top of the Coonara, nothing could make a dent in how cold I feel. So I reject the scratchy-looking black scarf in the well near the gearstick, and just grab for the rifle. *The rifle is loaded* – yep, remember that. I check the safety switch, and keep it pointed away. The rifle shakes in my hand, but gripping it makes me feel more solid.

Right. I fell into the lake, but I've made it up here, and I've got a rifle. What's my next move? My brain, oh god, my brain is as frozen as the rest of me. James – I need to find James. And Harris – I don't know where he's disappeared to, he's supposed to be here but he's not. Cole might be close, or dead, I've got no clue, and his driver could be anywhere.

This is hopeless. I can't be limping around, freezing my arse off and waiting for people to come find me.

The mill shed is right there, on the far side of the car. If I can get high enough, I'll have a view of the whole quarry. I just have to climb onto the shed roof.

Fuck.

I clutch my lovely rifle and limp around the front of the car, using the bonnet for support. I'm almost at the shed when I see something – it's the driver. He's lying on his front, lapels of his jacket sprawled around him. A light spray of sand has settled on him, like a chalky rash. The back of his head is red and wet.

Gravel is disturbed nearby, fanning out from a burnt-looking depression. I see a glint of silver and a plastic gleam – something is flashing at me from the ground nearby. It makes as much sense as anything else just to lean over and pick it up. It's the cellophane bag, with the coin in it. I've found the coin, where James originally buried it. *Go me.*

It looks like the driver is dead. I don't know how it happened, but I don't go to check – he's out of commission, which is all I need to know right now. Clutching the cellophane bag, I limp gingerly past him, a few steps further until I'm at the side of the shed. I suck salt off my bottom lip. How can I get up to the roof? A forty-four gallon drum stands beside the wall, but it's a long stretch from there to the top. I stagger back a pace, breathing heavily. Have I got the energy to jump up from the drum and haul myself onto the roof? Then I see the metal maintenance ladder set into the back right corner of the wall. That makes me laugh.

Climbing a ladder with a rifle and a bad leg and the bone-shaking shivers isn't easy, but it's a lot easier than trying some crazy parkour manoeuvre with the drum. When I get to the roof, I flump down on my stomach and crawl my way across to the front. My clothes make black marks on the corrugated surface and the tin creaks disconcertingly beneath me. I am heavier in these wet clothes. I am also colder up here – there's nothing to stop the wind from stripping across my face, wiping icy hands over my body. But at least I can see.

What I see nearly stops my heart.

No more than thirty metres away, Cole stands in the middle of the road bellying into the quarry. He looks ruffled in his overcoat, turning in a circle, his right arm pointed straight out, the gleaming dark gun in his hand. The wind lifts his silver hair, carries his words to my ears.

'. . . doesn't help anybody if you don't cooperate, James.'

And there's James, hunkered down behind a huge pile of sand near the edge of the new pit. He's kneeling, and his hands are covering his face. He leans forward for a moment, like he's prostrating himself. Then he sits up again and drags his hands down so they flop in his lap. He is looking towards the place where Ferret and I went over.

'Why should I . . .' He stops, clears his throat. 'Why should I cooperate with you now, exactly?'

His words are quite soft, but like before, I can hear every syllable, every flat, dull tone. Oh god, he thinks I'm dead. He thinks I'm dead, and it will change everything he does, every decision he makes, and I can't tell him, I can't shout to him, because I'll expose myself here on the roof.

Suddenly, I see Harris. He is down in the new pit, far to the left, behind a giant mound of pale gravel. His back is pressed to the gravel, his head tilted, eyes closed, face white as the chalk around him. His mouth is slack.

For a moment, a terrible pain burns in my chest – then Harris's mouth closes and his eyes flick open. He leans around the gravel mound to see what Cole is doing.

Cole is pointing his gun in the direction of James's voice, and he's taken a step closer to the spot. James is still slumped behind the pile of sand. Cole's back is to me, and I've missed the first bit of what he's saying.

'. . . terrible thing, and I'm sure you feel responsible. But she's gone. You should think about your own life now. Think about what your parents would want. They'd want you to live, wouldn't they?'

'You won't let me live,' James says, so quietly. 'That was never part of the plan.'

'It could be.' Cole takes a step. 'I admired your father, you know. A brilliant mind. Such a shame—'

'I think you should stop talking about my father now,' James says.

Cole looks over the sight line of his gun. 'Give me what I want. Then I'll go far away, and this will all be over.'

There's a pause.

'Over,' James says. 'Yes. I'd like this to be over.'

He just sits there. Oh god, I want to *shake* him. Then hug him, then shake him again.

'That's right,' Cole says.

James, don't listen *to him*.

Cole takes another step. I'm shivering so hard, I jerk the rifle next to me. *The rifle.* I almost smack myself.

I bring it closer, into position. My line of sight wobbles and judders. Oh fuck, this shivering won't stop.

I see Harris edge carefully to the side of his gravel-mound cover. A dark stain smears the gravel he leaves behind. He's looking at something at ground level – a patch of dirt, a touch more colourful than the surrounding earth.

Another charge. It has to be. But Harris can't get to it without revealing himself to Cole.

I'm shocked by movement when James stands up. He pushes himself off the sand and walks slowly around the pile until he's completely exposed. My breath catches and I fumble with the rifle. If Cole shoots him now, if Cole hurts him now—

But Cole won't hurt James, because Cole hasn't got what he came for yet. Cole straightens his back, relaxes his gun arm until it's by his side.

'You've made the right decision, James,' he says.

'It's the only decision, isn't it?' James's voice is dead and empty and awful.

'Yes,' Cole says. 'Yes, it is.' I can hear him smiling.

I don't know when James notices Harris, but I see his posture change: his shoulders lift and set back a little.

'The coin is . . .' James glances at the dirt away to his left.

Cole ushers with his gun hand.

So James walks to the left, heading for the place where Ferret and I struggled for the honour of falling first. Cole turns to follow him. Now Cole is facing away from Harris, but James is utterly, utterly vulnerable.

Oh god, he is making a chess move. It's a simple one: expose the King to give the Knight an opportunity to shift into position. Harris does exactly that. He wriggles out of his spot, starts moving towards the hidden charge.

And the Queen is lying here, up on the roof of the bloody mill shed, rifle in position and unable to fire because of this *goddamn shaking*. If I shoot now, I could take Cole out, or I could blow off the top of James's head. Over this distance, with the tremors in my hands, my accuracy will be rooted.

I breathe. I huff and puff, try to slow myself down. My fingers are like ice cubes and my nose is running. I fight it, *willing* my body to warm. But that just seems to make things worse.

Then I realise: I don't have to shoot from here. Harris is working on the charge. James has dropped to his knees, preparing to dig for his life. And *I've* got the coin. I've got the thing that Cole wants. And the Queen doesn't lie stationary: the Queen advances.

I get off the shed roof by falling, basically, halfway down the ladder. For the second time, I hobble down that stupid, slippery road. I hold the rifle in a two-handed grip. When I reach a point, about fifteen metres away from Cole and James, where they can see me, I drag the rifle up to my shoulder, chamber a round.

James sees the movement first, and then he sees me. His eyes turn into big blue moons. Cole sees me, recoils, lifts his gun in my direction.

James's mouth moves, and nothing comes out for a moment.

'You fell,' he finally gets out. 'I saw you fall—'

Cole blinks at me; I think he's weighing up the relative merits of his pistol versus my rifle. Then he swings his arm around so the gun is aimed squarely at the back of James's head.

Sunlight glints on the bag with the coin as I hold it up. 'Is this what you're after?' My voice comes out hoarse. 'This is it, right? Does this mean we're back at square one?'

'You're really not just his Watson, are you?' Cole says softly.

'And you really talk a lot of bullshit.' I don't take my eyes off him for an instant. 'James? Get up and come over here.'

'James, don't do that,' Cole says immediately.

James is still kneeling, hands by his sides.

'Rachel,' he says, sounding dazed. He clears his throat, raises his voice over the wind. 'Rachel . . . what time is it?'

'What?'

My eyes flick to his, which is enough time for Cole to move. He steps forward, grabs James by the back of the neck and hauls him up. Now Cole is mostly shielded behind my boyfriend's body, holding a gun to his head. This is not what I had in mind. I firm my aim down the rifle sight, but that doesn't help: James is still blocking any chance I might have had of a decent shot.

James's arms are half-raised, elbows up, as if he thinks he's under arrest. He's looking at me like he can't believe I'm real. 'Help me out here, Rachel. What time is it?'

'Time to give up the coin,' Cole says firmly. His voice is slightly muffled from behind James's collar. He's keeping his head down.

I don't know why James is asking me about the time. But then I think back to what he said to me yesterday: *You know this place like the back of your hand, don't you?* That's true. I thought it was an off-the-cuff comment. But maybe it's important. Maybe this isn't just some last-gasp distraction for Cole. At least stalling will give Harris some more time to work the charge.

I flick my eyes up at the sky. The light above the quarry cliff is faintly pink, the rosy cheeks of a new day. Still early, although the birds have settled.

'It's eight-thirty,' I say to James.

He smiles.

'It's funny,' he says, and I don't realise at first that he's not talking to me. 'I don't know what I expected to get out of this meeting. Although, I've been anticipating it. Like I felt it was necessary. Like I suppose that first meeting in Pickup's office was necessary to *you*.' He's looking up. It's as though he's not really aware that he's standing there, with a gun at his temple, acting as a human shield to the man behind him.

'*Mr Mycroft*—' Cole starts.

'But then I finally figured it out,' James continues. 'What I was hoping would happen. What I really *wanted* from you, Mr Cole. Only you're not in a position to give it.'

He swallows. There's a moment when I think he's not going to say any more. But he does.

'What I really want . . .' James says. 'What I would really *like* is to have my parents back. That's what I want. And you can't give me that. So I've been kind of wanting the impossible, all these years.'

321

He laughs. It doesn't sound happy, or melancholy: it's a relieved laugh. 'You can't give me anything, Mr Cole. There's nothing else you have that I want. So there's no trade, is there? No exchange, no negotiation, no move or countermove. There's nothing. No game.'

I'm standing here, pointing a rifle at him, but a blush of pride in my boyfriend rises up my neck in that moment. Which is crazy, because he seems to have said exactly the wrong thing.

Cole pincers his hand more firmly, gripping the hair at James's nape. 'You stupid boy—'

'And that really sticks in your throat, doesn't it, Mr Cole?' James goes on. 'Because you set it all up so we could play. So if I refuse to join in, then that bugs the crap out of you, because – do you know why? Because that's how I win, isn't it? By refusing to play the game. That's how I win.'

Cole's eyes peek out from behind the top of James's shoulder, and I suddenly remember something else Harris said: *He'll need someone to point and shoot . . . so he doesn't have to get his own hands dirty.* Cole's never been a killer. Sure, he arranges people's deaths, but he never deals with the mess himself. Now he's the one holding the gun, and I can see he's rattled. He shakes James in his grip, the way Ferret shook me, like a cat with its prey in its mouth.

'It's not enough to *concede defeat*,' he hisses.

'No, it's not, is it?' James says. 'To concede, the King has to be taken out of play. The King has to fall.'

And James looks straight at me then and mouths three words. Not the sweet, clichéd ones – three other words.

I trust you.

'Oy!' Harris calls. '*Marigolds!*'

Cole jerks, half-turns.

'Now!' James yells, and he covers his head with his arms as Harris throws his makeshift grenade.

The package arches through the cold air.

Cole cries out, snaps his gun arm up. He fires, and the charge explodes before it hits earth – the fireworks display of powder spraying out in all directions, the *BOOM* filling up the quarry, making the gravel shudder, the dragon-fire ball of flame *whoomping* upwards.

Despite best intentions, I flinch, my teeth coming together with a snap. Smoke is clearing, gravel spattering down. Harris has fallen to one side. Jonathan Cole is waving his gun, clearing the air. His face is a mask of fury as he trains his gun back towards James.

Flour and sand have whitened James's hair, and his eyes are open, so he can see that he's about to die.

And I have bare seconds to find myself. I reach deep inside. I don't fight the cold anymore. I let it fill me, let it turn me icy and unyielding. I have made tough calls before. Muscle memory lives in me. I think of those things – those memories. I think of sleeping bags, and James's backbone, and Summoner Street, as I level the rifle, my breath panting loud, my hair in my mouth and my heart in my throat as I sight—

Aim—

Fire.

CHAPTER TWENTY-THREE

I know I've made a mistake right away.

James and Cole are thrown back together in a tangle of limbs, as if they've been punched by a wrecking ball. Voices echo somewhere, but they could be figments, aural blowback from the explosion and the report of the shot. Only the voice in my head is clear, and it sounds a helluva lot like Harris saying, *It pulls to the right, you dickhead, it pulls to the right.*

One tiny detail, which I forgot in all the tension and terror. Now I lurch forward, gasping, and I can't get to James fast enough. There is blood, oh god, there's blood everywhere, and Cole is crabbing his hands over the wound in his gut, his gloved fingers daubed a sickening red. James has rolled over, and I can't see, I can't see—

Voices nearby. They are real, not figments, not Harris.

'Careful!' one of them yells, and I hear movement behind me – I spin, raise the rifle and pull the bolt so fast I nearly dislocate my shoulder.

'Bloody hell!' somebody says, and another voice says, 'Easy, lass – Rachel, it's okay. You can lower the gun now . . .' and it takes me a second to realise that I know this voice, I know this face, and when awareness filters through I sag with relief.

Detective Pickup is wearing a flak jacket, which makes him look even more hulking than normal. People are coming down the quarry road behind him. Pickup is holding a service revolver in one hand, his other hand extended as he edges closer.

'That's it, lass. Come on, let me get in there, okay? Can I have that? Good girl.'

He takes the rifle and passes it to another officer, who is – incredibly – Jared Capshaw. Jared is a long drink of water in uniform, with a head of orange hair, and I have known him since I was nine, and it seems bizarre that apart from their wildly disparate builds, he and Pickup almost look related, because of the hair.

'James . . .' I start, and then surprise myself when I sob out some wretched noise. I clap a hand over my mouth. Pickup steadies me at the shoulder.

There's groaning behind me, and an officer in a flak jacket with a Red Cross patch comes into view, pushing past police.

'Can I get in now?' she asks, but Pickup holds her back.

'One sec,' he says, and he walks past me towards Cole and James, kicks Cole's pistol away along the ground, points at Jared Capshaw then at the weapon. 'Secure that. Right, you're good.'

The police medic jumps into action, and I move with her.

'Gunshot wound from a three-oh-three,' I say.

'Good to know,' the woman says. She ignores Cole's horrible moans for a moment and squats down besides James, gently turns him onto his back.

My voice is thick. 'It pulled . . . oh god, it pulled to the—'

'Mm,' James says, and then, 'Aargh,' and I feel tears spring out immediately, scuff them away to see the damage.

James's hair blows around his milky face, and his eyes are closed. He's lying arms akimbo, his pea coat belled out around him. Dark blood has clotted his T-shirt at his waist, spilled onto the black wool, the denim of his jeans.

The medic tugs up the T-shirt, uses latex-covered fingers to prod. James gasps.

'Through above the iliac crest. Not much more than a flesh wound.' The medic pulls me down to kneel beside her, places my hands into position above folded white gauze. 'Pressure here, and here above his hip. *Firm* now, that's it. Don't go anywhere.' She gets up and moves quickly to Cole.

'I'm not going anywhere,' I say belatedly, then I realise James is looking at me.

'You know,' he says, a little breathlessly, 'I've been thinking of giving up smoking.'

I can't say anything for a moment. My chin wobbles.

James grins. 'You shot me.'

'It was an accident.' I press firmly, sniffing. 'I forgot. Harris told me it pulls to the right, but I forgot.'

'You *shot* me,' he says again.

'It was an *accident*,' I say. 'No police. You said you didn't—'

'I lied.' James winces, grins again. A little more washed-out, this grin. 'Professor Walsh was the one I emailed with instructions, on the walk over. Told him to alert Pickup. Get Worth and everyone else here by eight-thirty.'

'I take it back,' I say. 'You're not a genius. You're an idiot.'

'You're crying.'

'No I'm not.' I smear my cheek against my shoulder – my hands are occupied.

'I knew you weren't dead.'

'No you didn't.'

'No,' he says. 'I didn't.' The look he gives me then almost kills me. He catches his breath. 'That hurts.'

'Stop wriggling, then.' I lean forward and put my forehead on his chest, because I suddenly feel really dizzy. James reaches up a hand and pats my hair.

'Call ahead to the hospital,' the medic says nearby, and I hear the snap as she removes her gloves. More uniformed police are arriving. 'Quickly. Watch how you move him. Detective, I need to stay with this one.'

'That's all right, I've got the next case,' a familiar voice says, and Detective Pickup growls, 'I thought I told you to stay in the car?' and I startle, look up.

'Vincent, I'm a medical doctor,' Professor Walsh says testily, and he looks utterly different in some kind of dark blue jumpsuit over his clothes, which I realise is a Tyvek, and he strides over towards—

'Harris!' I finally remember.

Harris is sitting up on the gravel, his legs sprawled out in front of him and his hands behind, keeping him upright. But even as Walsh reaches him, his hands lose their grip. He slides back onto his elbows, then towards the ground.

'Some assistance here, please,' Walsh calls to me, but I can't move because I'm putting pressure on James's injury. Then Pickup is leaning over James from the other side.

'I've got this one. Go and help Professor Walsh with Mr Derwent.' Pickup's face looks mottled, as if he's still calming down. His hands take over confidently.

'Oh god, you're gonna ask me why I didn't contact you sooner, aren't you?' James says weakly as I get up, and Pickup says, 'That would be in contravention of standard rules for witness questioning, although I bloody well *should*,' but I've already listed away by then until I'm kneeling beside Walsh.

'Stats, please,' he says. He's using scissors.

'Um, a handgun, small calibre, I'm not as familiar – maybe a nine millimetre. The match'll be at the bottom of the lake.' I glance over my shoulder at the pit edge, can't help it. 'It's been about an hour. There's an exit wound.'

'Hold here,' Walsh says. 'Hard.'

I do as I'm told, until Walsh takes over. While he works, I prop up Harris's head with my other arm.

'Jesus, Rache, don't,' Harris complains. 'You're all wet and festy.'

I'm still shivering, and now anxiousness is making me shiver even more, because Harris's left leg is completely red from his thigh to his foot, and his boot is full of blood. He shifts in my arms.

'*Hold him.*' Walsh frowns. 'This is why I gave up treating live patients, they move around too much.'

Harris grunts. 'Aren't you a doctor for dead people? Am I dead?'

'Not if I can help it,' Walsh says determinedly.

'Rachel. Babe,' Harris says. 'You shot your boyfriend. That's hardcore.' His eyes roll a little, drift closed.

'*Harris*,' I say.

'Keep him talking.' Walsh pushes his glasses back towards his nose with the back of his hand. His gloved fingers are red. 'You're doing well, Rachel.'

'Yeah, Rache, you're doing good,' Harris slurs.

But it's not good, because this wound, shit, this wound has been bleeding for a long time. Harris looks awful.

I keep my hand on the bandage. 'You blew up the driver, and then you blew up Cole—'

'Yeah,' Harris says. 'Yeah, that was cool.'

'If you were still working here, they'd have to upgrade you from trainee.'

He chuckles. 'Reckon so.'

'And now you're going to squeeze my hand, and we're going to get you to hospital in Ouyen. They're gonna give you a blood transfusion, and lots of drugs—'

'Awesome.'

'—so just stay with me now, Harris, okay?'

'You're gonna be a good doctor, Rachel,' Harris says. His sun-bleached hair drifts over his cheek. His lips have gone softly blue, like wax lilies.

'Come on, Harris,' I whisper. 'Squeeze my hand.'

'All right, that's the best we can do here. Time to go,' Walsh says, and there are other people around now. 'Rachel, they're taking him to Ouyen now. Let him go. That's it ... Let him get to hospital. Your friend with the red hair, Mr Capshaw, is driving, they'll make good time. Let me look at you. You don't seem to have got off completely unscathed.'

I shake him away. 'I want to get back to James.'

'Which I quite understand,' Walsh says. 'But there's no reason you can't lean on me a little as we walk.'

'How did you get here?' I ask dazedly.

'Vincent commandeered a helicopter from Essendon Airport, then we drove from Ouyen with the local authorities. I'm afraid I bullied Vincent into letting me come along. Said I was already involved, and he might need me.' Walsh makes a small smile at the ground. 'I've never flown in a helicopter before.'

James is being taken care of, and another man is there, a painfully skinny man who I last saw in England wearing his government-official suit. Now he's wearing dark hiking trousers and a khaki shirt. His hair is still thin and flattened the same way, and his features are sharp, but he looks more human now.

'. . . from our own evidence-gathering, plus all the documents from the email you had forwarded to Detective Pickup,' he's saying to James. 'But the case against Cole won't be solid without—'

'I've got it,' I say, reaching into my front pocket for the cellophane bag with the coin. I dangle it in front of Theo Worth.

Worth lets out an unmistakeable sigh. 'You have no idea how long I've been looking for that.'

'Look harder,' James says with his eyes closed.

So I do. The silver disc inside the cellophane bag is large, flat, irregular. It's the same size as the dekadrachm. But something isn't right. Then I notice the weight.

'Hang on,' Worth says. He takes the bag, holds it up to the light. 'This is a bottle cap.'

James is laughing now, wincing and snorting.

'Here we go.' Pickup rolls his eyes.

'My coat,' James says, and it only takes a cursory look in his coat pockets to find the ziplocked sandwich bag with the heavy disc inside.

'Weren't the tea bags in this?' I ask, and James looks up at me.

'That bloody coin,' he says. 'It's been in my pocket the whole time.'

CHAPTER TWENTY-FOUR

I get to see my brother the day we arrive home, which is on Monday, but I don't get to see him properly until Tuesday, after he's been moved from intensive care. I go in during visiting hours. Mike's asleep, so I just sit by the bed and hold his hand until his eyes open.

'Damn. I was kind of hoping you were Alicia.' His voice is a little sloppy from the drugs.

'Thanks very much.' I smile. 'But no – that's not till tomorrow.'

'Yeah.' He looks pretty happy about that. 'I can't believe she's coming back early.'

'I can believe it.'

'What's the word on Harris?'

'He's still in Ouyen,' I admit. 'He's gonna be in the hospital for at least five days.'

'Will he come back to Melbourne?' Mike asks.

I shake my head. 'I don't know. Dennis Derwent's been nosing around, apparently, but I've asked Dad to go up and have a chat with Harris, see if he needs anything. I feel shitty about it, but it's the best we can do right now.'

'And Mycroft's gone back to London?'

'Yes.' I press my lips. 'Worth is arranging for Cole to be repatriated, but there are some loose ends that need tying up. James has recovered okay, and he finally had the chance to explain his research to the police. Plus, he kind of wanted to be there.'

'Jesus,' Mike says. 'Y'know, I'd pretty much forgotten that he had a first name.'

I smile tightly.

Mike lifts his chin at me. 'Your cheek is healing up all right.'

I nod. I had to spend a while in Outpatients, having gravel picked out of my cheek and jaw. I have a new brace on my knee. My physio, predictably, was very unhappy.

'Rachel, Rachel, Rachel . . .' Mike looks different in the white hospital gown – older. Or maybe being shot in the chest has aged him. 'You look a bit funny. You going okay?'

I look down at our joined hands. You're supposed to be strong for people in hospital, put their wellbeing above your own.

'I feel like I've come back from a war,' I say softly.

'You silly sod.' Mike pulls me in to hug me properly. 'Just have a cry, tough girl. You'll feel better.'

And I do.

———

The night sky is pretty here. It's not a patch on Five Mile, of course – the streetlights create too much light pollution. But it's not bad. The apartment building is on the edge of Keilor, and the land beside it spills down into the wide rolling expanse of Brimbank Park. From the second-floor balcony, I listen to the late-night sounds of wind in the gums and imagine I'm in the country again.

I stood under the shower – the shower here is hot as blazes, which was about perfect – until all my skin was pink. After drying off and dressing warm, I somehow didn't want to be inside: the balcony seemed like the best option, and there were two white plastic chairs already out there. I've been drinking tea and sitting here, ignoring the cold, for the better part of half an hour.

Now I hear a key turn inside, at the front door. I don't move. I'm too nervous. I just sit and wait for James to slide open the glass door to the balcony before I twist to smile.

'Hey.'

'Hey.' He's wearing jeans and a black thermal T-shirt, with his pea coat over the top. 'I made it. Last leg of the flight was intense, but it's staggering how fast you get through Customs when you're holding papers co-signed by the British Home Office and the Australian police.' He dumps his backpack inside the door. 'Are you drinking tea?'

'What else would I be drinking?'

James holds out a small bottle. 'Some really excellent scotch, purloined from the minibar of a London hotel?'

I extend my hand for it, but he doesn't come any closer, and I remember. 'Oh, right. I forgot we're on the second floor.'

'How can you forget that?'

I walk over and take the bottle – the liquid inside is spicy on my tongue, clashing with the temperature of the air.

I pass back the bottle, shaking my head. 'How do you fly in a plane, if you're that scared of heights?'

'You're *inside* a plane. You're contained. It's different.' He takes a swig, looks at me. 'Nobody ever said phobias were *logical*.'

I can actually see him mentally screwing himself to the spot, so it's a complete surprise when he speaks again.

'Can I sit out here with you for a bit?'

I squint at him. 'You don't wanna go inside?'

'No, no. Here is good. And look – there's chairs. We could just sit here, in the chairs.'

'D'you want me to move them back so you can—'

'Yes, if you wouldn't mind.'

I snort, push the plastic chairs back against the wall. James eases himself off the balcony step and into one of the chairs. I sit beside him, put the bottle down on the concrete floor.

'Are you okay?' I bite my lip over a grin. 'You look a bit pale.'

'I'm perfectly fine,' James says. He pauses. 'Do you think Mai and Gus sit out here sometimes, when they're—'

'Yes,' I say firmly.

'It was nice of Gus to lend us the key for tonight.'

'Yes, it was.' I don't look at him. I look out past the balcony railing, at the stir of the trees down the hill. 'James, please just tell me.'

'Okay.' He keeps his eyes on his hands. 'Well, I was right. Cole had arranged for an accomplice to move the collection in the event of his arrest. Worth had a few suspects, so they tailed them, and bingo – one of them led the police straight to it. It was in Maida Vale. I didn't see all the stuff, but it's at least a couple of million pounds of—'

'Not that,' I say. 'I mean, hooray. But that's not what I'm asking about.'

James wets his lips. 'I know Theo Worth kind of cornered you after Cole was taken from hospital, before we left for England. I don't know what he said to you—'

'That he'd offered you work with the Office, when you felt ready.' I clasp my hands together and say it all in a rush. 'That he'd been through your files on the Cole case and he was satisfied – *satisfied* was the word he used – that you had considerable talent for the kinds of investigative . . . blah blah, something blah. I kind of tuned out at that point.'

'Right,' James says. 'I don't suppose he mentioned that I turned him down.'

My heart stutters. 'What?'

'Yes. I politely declined his offer, here and again in England.' James rakes a hand through his curls. 'He got a bit cranky about it, then he tried to sweeten the pot. Said the Home Office could fund my forensics training, and your medical degree. In Britain, of course. But I said I couldn't accept on your behalf, and although we hadn't ruled out a future trip to the UK, we don't want to live in England right now because all our family is here, so—'

'You didn't,' I whisper. I stare at him.

'I did. I hope that's all right. I felt kind of bad, knocking back a paid tertiary education for you, I hope I did the right—'

I barrel into him with my hug. My arms fly around his neck, and we both tip in our chairs.

'Whoah, hang on,' James says, and he wheels his free arm to straighten us both up. He's wincing, smiling. 'Watch the bandage. And please don't push me off the balcony.'

I keep clinging to him. 'I can't believe you *did* that.'

'Well, don't start celebrating yet. Worth he'll stay in contact. He said he'll keep asking me until I say yes.'

I pull back to look into his face. 'It's a pretty amazing offer. Are we crazy not to accept? Did you *want* to stay in England? You were born there—'

'But I grew up – *really* grew up – here.' James holds my hands. 'Maybe we'll go back again some day – and I'll give you a proper tour of London – but England isn't my home anymore. This is where I belong.'

I don't know what to say. I put my arms around his waist and mash my face into his neck, before I start crying.

'So that's a *yes*, I did the right thing?'

'Yes. Oh yes.' I give him one more giant squeeze, then I let go, blot my eyes.

'Good. Have you been worried about that all this time? My god. I mean, I felt okay about it, except for the funding part. But the British Museum said they'd like to show their appreciation for the return of the coin, so that might help.' He blushes a little. 'It's quite a lot of money.'

'How much?'

'Well, it's nothing like the actual sale value of a dekadrachm on the—'

'*James.*'

'About ten thousand.' He clears his throat. 'Pounds.'

'Oh my god.'

'Yeah, that's pretty much what I said. So Mai and Gus's rental deposit is sorted. And that should help with the tertiary education business.'

'I don't care about that,' I say.

'Well, your mum seemed to care. I spoke to her about it on the phone. She seemed, um, happy.'

'You mean she threatened to hug you.'

'Yeah. And then she asked me to come to dinner tomorrow night, which I said I would do, once I've checked if Angela can come too.'

I lace my fingers with James's fingers, my right hand in his left – the cut he got from the wire has healed – and smile at him. 'You're still a bit uncomfortable with the "extended family" thing, aren't you?'

'I'm . . . dealing.' He looks at our joined hands, then into my eyes. 'Are you still uncomfortable with the hugging thing?'

'I don't think so,' I say quietly. 'I've talked about it with Alicia a few times, since she got back. I still get the odd flutter, but—'

James stands up carefully from his chair.

'Let's test it out. But it should be a fair test, so we're both out of our comfort zones.' He nods towards the balcony railing. 'Right there.'

I frown. 'James, you don't have to—'

'It's not about *having* to do anything. It's about *wanting* to.' He looks at me again. 'Do you want to?'

'Yes,' I say softly.

I stand up and tug on his hands, bring him two careful steps towards the railing. He gulps a bit, but he takes those steps. When he's close, I turn so my back is against his chest, and I take a deep breath.

James wraps his arms around me, squeezes me against the long line of his body. I don't feel any flutters, just an all-over rush of warmth. It feels so good that I adjust us both, so the front lapels of his pea coat are wrapped around me. Now I'm tucked into him like a second skin. It's almost like being in a sleeping bag.

His face is low, his breath hot on my neck. He's trembling a little. 'Are you okay?'

'Yes. Are you?'

'I think so. It's a bit scary. But I'm okay.' He raises his head, so his cheek is next to mine. 'This is it, isn't it? Can I say it now?'

'Definitely.' I press my own cheek in. 'You're finally free—'

'Yes.'

'—and I'm finally grown.'

'Really?'

'My parents know where we are. I told them.'

'Fucking hell.'

'Such enthusiasm.' I laugh. 'James . . . can I ask you a question?'

'You can ask me anything at all,' James says softly.

I squeeze his arms, which are snugged under my breasts. 'Why are you afraid of heights?'

That makes *him* laugh. 'I . . . I don't know, really.' He pauses. 'It always just seems like a long way down.'

'I came back from a long way down,' I remind him.

'You did.' James looks at me. His eyes hold that same amazement from the quarry. 'You're a miracle.'

'Are you ready for another miracle?'

I shuffle us both a bit nearer the railing, until the moonlight falls on us. James makes a gasp. I know all his little sounds now. His face hides into my neck again.

'Don't look down,' I say.

'I won't.'

'James. Look up.'

He raises his head slowly, and the heavens kiss his cheeks. 'Oh, wow.'

'Yeah.'

'You can see the stars from here.'

'I know,' I say, and I smile.

ACKNOWLEDGEMENTS

First of all, a big gasp of relief – phew! We made it to the end!

This book was a struggle, and I'd first like to mention a few people who truly made it possible for me to go on and finish.

My partner, Geoff, worked hard to keep me on an even keel during the writing stage, and then propped me up while I was editing and stressed under deadline. Love you, darling (although that phrase never says enough).

Alisdair Daws (partner in crime) read the manuscript, critiqued, brainstormed, enlightened me about cryptography, coped with late-night phone calls about finale shoot-outs, and encouraged me every step of the way – Ali, respect, and love to your family.

Simmone Howell reminded me of a very salient fact – that I was finding this book difficult to write because I didn't want to say goodbye to the characters. So true! (Sob.)

Sophie Splatt at Allen & Unwin came right down to the wire with me on this one, and her chessmaster-like clarification of plot-lines is the main reason this book actually makes sense. Sophie – you are a righteous woman, I owe you more thanks than I can say.

Eva Mills is the best editor any writer could hope to have – Eva, all my gratitude and thanks.

But I should mention some other people too!

My boys – Ben, Alex, Will and Ned – have given hugs, taught me calm, and provided insight throughout this whole process (as well as inspiration for various thorny plot issues!). Huge hugs, and all my love, to each of you.

Catherine Drayton (Inkwell Management) is my agent, and my best advisor. Catherine, I'm incredibly grateful for your support, and for the way you go in to bat for me and for the *Every* series all over the world. (And you were right about Harris! He's awesome!)

Hilary Reynolds is always the woman I turn to when the final chips are down – Hilary, thank you so much for that last, special proofread that made this book (and all the others) as good as it could possibly be.

Where would Rachel and James and I be without the hardworking crew from Allen & Unwin (Melbourne & Sydney)? Probably languishing in a quarry somewhere. Massive thanks to Liz Bray, Clare Keighery, Theresa Bray, Lara Wallace, Lisa White and every person who has worked to make the *Every* series such a knockout. All you folks truly go above and beyond the call.

Huge thanks too, to Sylvia Chan and the lovely team from Tundra who have welcomed Rachel and James so beautifully, and made it possible for the series to reach readers far, far away.

Other people have kept me sane through this whole series-writing process – I've been sustained by the friendship and encouragement of the YA writing community in Australia and overseas. I'd particularly like to thank Rebecca James, Melissa Keil, Nicole Hayes, Brigid Kemmerer, Amie Kaufman and Fleur Ferris, who gave me gentle pushes and pats whenever I needed it. To all the writers who've inspired and supported me on this road, thank you for your care, your enthusiasm, and your amazing welcome.

Thank you to a very special organisation – Sisters in Crime (Melbourne). There aren't many groups that do what these ladies (and brothers-in-law) do: that is, truly support, encourage, celebrate and generally bang the drum for women writers at a grassroots level. I feel hugely honoured to be involved, and I love the camaraderie of being a Sister – if you're an Australian woman crime writer, go get on board! All my love to Carmel Shute, a giant hug for Angela Savage, and special thanks to Honey Brown, Leigh Redhead, Lindy Cameron, Jacqui Horwood, Liz Filleul, Maggie Baron, and all the gang.

Another organisation that deserves a mention just for awesomeness: the Centre for Youth Literature (State Library Vic). Thank you to Adele Walsh, Anna Burkey and Jordi Kerr for all your support. Thanks also to Children's Book Council of Australia (Vic), especially Deborah Marshall and the students of Ballarat High.

Every Move wouldn't be in your hands right now without the enormous generosity and expert advice of these people: Dr Lucy Marney, who proofed the medical details (if I've stuffed it up, Luce, it's not your fault!); Mick Walden and David Walker of Hanson quarries (Carisbrook); Fleur Ferris, former resident of Patchewollock; and the staff of the Victoria Hotel, Ouyen.

I also have to mention my local support network – which is basically everyone in Castlemaine! Heartfelt thanks to Jess Saunders and Marion Yates, and other staff of the Castlemaine

Library; staff of Stoneman's Bookroom; staff and students of Castlemaine Secondary College, especially Andrea McDonald and Jane Sanderson; staff and students of Kyneton Secondary College; and staff, students and parents of Castlemaine Steiner School and Kindergarten. Friends everywhere, if you've ever given me a pat on the back, or a word of encouragement, or a hug (when I've been shambling around in my pyjamas-slash-writer's-clothes, with pens in my hair and a dazed expression), please know that each of those small gestures adds up to something enormous – I'm truly grateful.

Another mention – and this is a big one: Rachel and James and the *Every* series would not have been the same without the amazing support of fans. Students, teachers, librarians, booksellers and readers of all stripes – I salute you. Thank you for making it this far, thank you for coming on the journey with me. *You all rock*. And book bloggers! My god, you folks are the best. If I could send you all Tim-Tams, I would (group hug!). Thank you for the huge groundswell of support for the series – for a writer, there's nothing better. Knowing that people out in the world are reading the books and loving them has buoyed me up during the writing, kept me focused, and made me feel incredibly happy. Thank you!

This book is dedicated to my mum and dad. For love and support, and for raising a daughter who found her voice at last – thank you forever.

Finally . . . I think I'd like to give a hug to Rachel Watts and James Mycroft. You are fictional, but you've become my best friends, and you've carried me along on this crazy adventure with you. Thanks guys – drop in for visits anytime ☺

Xx Ellie

ABOUT THE AUTHOR

Ellie Marney was born in Brisbane, and has lived in Indonesia, Singapore and India. Now she writes, teaches, and gardens when she can, while living in a country idyll (actually a very messy wooden house on ten acres with a dog and lots of chickens) near Castlemaine, in north-central Victoria. Her partner and four sons still love her, even though she often forgets things and lets the housework go.

Ellie's short stories for adults have won awards and been published in various anthologies. Ellie's debut novel, *Every Breath*, was shortlisted for the Davitt Awards Best Young Adult Novel, the Ned Kelly Awards Best First Crime Novel and the Centre for Youth Literature's Gold Inky. *Every Move* is her third novel for young adults and the follow-up to *Every Word* and *Every Breath*.

Drop in at www.elliemarney.com, send her a line on Facebook or follow her on Twitter @elliemarney.

What if Sherlock Holmes was the boy next door?

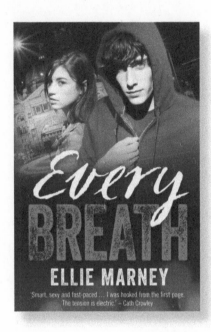

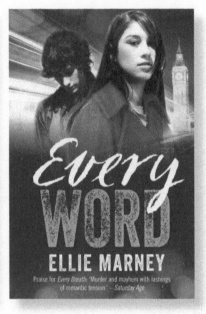

'Smart, sexy and fast-paced ... I was hooked from the first page. The tension is electric.' – Cath Crowley

'Murder and mayhem with lashings of romantic tension.' – *Saturday Age*